Available i...
from Mills...

DROP DEAD GORGEOUS

Dillon wasn't anywhere close to hauling her into his arms and kissing her senseless.

Not in the traditional sense, that is. Even more, there was nothing wild and uncontrollable about his actions. The hands that pressed against her thighs were too purposeful, the mouth nibbling at her too intent. As if he were in complete control with one objective in mind – to push her to the edge until she was the one who lost her wits.

Never.

That's what she told herself. What she fully intended to tell him. But it had been so long since a man had touched her like this – forever, in fact – and she couldn't seem to find her voice.

"I'm betting we don't make it to the sofa," Dino said.

Cat didn't reply because it was taking all her concentration to lower his zipper. Biting hard on her lower lip, she started to drag down the snug-fitting jeans.

"Wait."

Stilling her hands, she glanced up in time to see him dig into his back pocket and drop a few condoms onto the table.

"There are three," he said. "Since I go with my feelings, I like to be prepared."

Cat sank to her knees and refocused her attention on tugging his jeans down his legs. Beneath them, he wore a pair of black briefs, stretched almost sheer, which clearly revealed the size of his erection. Licking her suddenly dry lips, she said, "It's like a present."

Dino groaned as Cat traced a finger down the length of him. "Consider it yours. *Please.*"

First published in Great Britain 2009
Harlequin Mills & Boon Limited,
Eton House, 18-24 Paradise Road, Richmond, Surrey TW9 1SR

Drop Dead Gorgeous © Kimberly Raye Groff 2008
Come Toy with Me © Carolyn Hanlon 2008

ISBN: 978 0 263 87496 9

14-1109

Harlequin Mills & Boon policy is to use papers that are natural, renewable and recyclable products and made from wood grown in sustainable forests. The logging and manufacturing processes conform to the legal environmental regulations of the country of origin.

Printed and bound in Spain
by Litografia Rosés S.A., Barcelona

DROP DEAD GORGEOUS

BY
KIMBERLY RAYE

COME TOY WITH ME

BY
CARA SUMMERS

MILLS & BOON

DROP DEAD GORGEOUS

BY
KIMBERLY RAYE

Kimberly Raye has always been an incurable romantic. While she enjoys reading all types of fiction, her favourites, the books that touch her soul, are romance novels. From sexy to thrilling, sweet to humorous, she likes them all. But what she really loves is writing romance – the hotter the better! She started her first novel back in high school and has been writing ever since. Kim lives deep in the heart of the Texas Hill Country with her very own cowboy, Curt, and their young children. She's an avid reader (she reads *all* the Blaze® books) who loves Diet Dr Pepper, chocolate, Toby Keith, chocolate, alpha males – *especially* vampires – and chocolate. Kim also loves to hear from readers. You can visit her online at www.kimberlyraye.com or at www.myspace.com/kimberlyrayebooks.

For my caring, supportive, ultra-fabulous editor Brenda Chin, for NOT moving to England.

1

IT WAS THE BEST SEX she'd had in months.

The only sex.

Which wouldn't have been such a bad thing except that the elusive O came courtesy of a red fluorescent vibrator called the Big Tamale rather than some hot, buff cowboy with a slow hand and an intoxicating smile.

Margaret Evelyn Sweeney, aka Meg, hit the three different Off buttons—vibrate, swivel and *aye carumba*—and stashed Big in its matching red case. She drew a deep breath, swung her legs over the side of her bed and got to her feet.

Five minutes later, she stood in her kitchen and leaned over a hot-pink three-ring binder—her own personal Pleasure Manual—to document tonight's results. She flipped to page fifty-eight, which included a quick summation of last Tuesday's class entitled *Masturbation Mania* and a worksheet for homework. She scribbled in the date and tackled the questions.

Intense sensation? Check.

Spontaneous groaning (the good kind)? Check.

Uncontrollable moaning? Check.

A full-blown scream? Check.

Overall level of satisfaction?

She eyed the scale that ranged from one to ten, *zip* to *zowee*, and finally circled *seven* before moving on to the last question.

Did this sexual experience include a partner? She ignored the crazy urge to jot down a big fat *yes*. This wasn't about soothing her fragile ego and saving face with the other women in the painfully small town of Skull Creek, Texas.

The whole purpose of attending carnal classes with a certified carnal coach was to invest in her future. Sadly enough, she was thirty years old and she could count on one hand the number of romantic entanglements she'd had in her lifetime.

Actually, she could count them on two fingers. Three if she included her encounters with her good buddy and childhood friend, Dillon Cash. While Meg had been a mega tomboy, Dillon had been a major geek. Either way, they'd both never really fit in with the opposite sex—not romantically—and so they'd turned to each other back in the ninth grade when they'd realized that they were the only ones—with the exception of Connie Louise Davenport, Reverend Davenport's daughter—in the entire freshman class who hadn't known how to French kiss.

Okay, so they hadn't known how to kiss, period. No quick pecks. No slow, lingering smooches. No open mouths and plunging tongues. They'd been fifteen and very green, and so it had seemed like a good idea to work out the awkwardness with each other.

Several hours, a bootleg copy of a *Nine 1/2 Weeks* video, and a dozen clumsy attempts later, they hadn't been any more skilled than when they'd started.

In fact, the entire experience had solidified what she'd known from the get-go—Dillon was and would always be just a good friend. She hadn't liked him like *that*.

No heart stutters. No tummy tingles. No rip-off-your-panties-and-go-bonkers lust.

Which was why, despite the experimental kissing, she felt inclined to leave him out of the tally when it came to her sexual past.

That left Oren and Walter. She'd lost her virginity to Oren, aka the Orenator, at the ripe old age of eighteen. He'd been the best defensive end the Skull Creek Panthers had ever seen, and he'd taken them to the state championship during his senior year. *And* he'd actually liked her, enough to ask her out for Homecoming.

They'd gone to the school dance, and then they'd gone parking down by the river.

Ten minutes in the backseat of his daddy's Chevy listening to recaps of the Cowboys vs. Redskins game, and she'd had enough. She'd thrown her arms around him, pressed her body up against his and offered herself shamelessly. Other than a few initial moments of shock and a frantic "What are you doing?", he'd finally given in to her persistent lips. She'd lost her innocence along with one of her new hoop earrings and her undies.

Yes!

Not that the experience itself had been all that great. While he'd given in, he hadn't taken the initiative and swept her off her feet. Rather, she'd taken the lead, pushing and urging and giving a whole new meaning to her nickname Manhandler Meg.

Still, it had been the principle of the thing. It had been the beginning of a new chapter in her life. A chance to start over. To completely forget the tomboy she'd once been and embrace all that was feminine.

Change.

That's what it had all been about. Meg had grown up being a carbon copy of her father. He'd been a single parent—her mother, a diabetic, had died of renal failure shortly after Meg's birth—and an athletics coach at the local high school. Growing up, Meg had been determined to follow in his footsteps. She'd watched him, learned from him, idolized him, and then one day he'd been gone.

She'd been barely seventeen and it had been the start of the summer after her junior year. She'd gone home early to pack (they were going camping to celebrate the end of classes) and he'd stayed late to finish cleaning out his desk. He'd been in a hurry to get home, not wanting to lose their camping spot at a local state park. He'd failed to stop at a nearby intersection and had been hit by an approaching car. That had been the end of him.

And the end of Meg.

The old Meg.

She'd gone to live with her grandparents and, much to their

surprise, had packed away her soccer ball and kneepads. She'd ditched her favorite baseball bat and glove, her autographed Troy Aikman football and her lucky San Antonio Spurs basketball jersey. Even more, she'd packed away her all-time favorite sweats and the lucky Dallas Cowboy T-shirt her dad had bought her. She'd taken out a subscription to *Cosmo* and had learned all the latest fashion trends. She'd even forfeited helping her granddad on his tractor so that her grandmother could teach her how to sew.

In one summer, she'd traded in her love of sports for an infatuation with shoes and clothes and all things feminine, and had started her senior year as a different Meg. A woman determined to forget her past, to bury it right along with her father.

When Oren had chronicled their night on the wall of the boys' locker room, her undies hanging from one of the locker pegs as proof, she'd been thrilled. The male population of Skull Creek High would finally see her as more than just a competitive edge during game time. She'd been so good at sports that she'd become the best buddy of every male athlete in school. They'd asked her advice on everything from touchdowns to golf putts.

They'd never, however, asked her out.

She'd been convinced that that one wild night with Oren would be enough to change her image.

She'd been wrong.

This was Skull Creek. The classic small town where people left their doors unlocked and the sidewalks rolled up at six o'clock every evening. Forget crime. The most exciting news centered around the occasional boob job or cheating spouse. Strangers were scarce and everyone knew everyone.

And that meant that once she was Manhandler Meg, she'd always be Manhandler Meg.

While she'd managed to change who she actually was, she'd never been able to change everyone's perception of her.

Not way back when Oren had written about her and the entire football team had assumed it was a really great practical joke— she'd gotten so many high fives that her hand had been raw—and not now that she wore high heels and sexy clothes and ran her own dress boutique, It's All About You, a small, exclusive shop located on Main Street, smack dab between Dillon's computer repair shop and the town's one and only full-service spa, Pam's Pamper Park.

People still saw her as a chip-off-the-old-Sweeney-block. The women rarely felt threatened and the men…Well, they actually *respected* her.

While she knew that most females would kill to be valued for their minds rather than their bodies, once, just *once,* she would like to have a man actually see her as a sex object.

So make a real change, pack your bags and get out of Dodge.

She'd thought about it. But the notion of leaving her grand-parents—even though they now lived an hour away in a retire-ment community outside of Austin, and she only saw them a few times a month—was even less appealing than being known as Manhandler Meg for the rest of her life. They'd helped her through her father's death, loved her, raised her, and she intended to return the favor. They'd been there for her when she'd needed them the most, and she intended to be there for them when the time came and they eventually needed her. She couldn't do that if she was God knows where.

Which meant she was here and she was staying.

Walter had been her second romantic entanglement. One that had continued over the years, on during football season and off after the Super Bowl, which kicked off the start of tax season— he was an accountant. While she knew Walter found her attrac-tive, he also liked to pick her brain for betting advice (he spear-headed the weekly football pool at his office). When he won, he got *very* happy and the sex was pretty good—*if* she ini-tiated (Walter wasn't one for making the first move). When he wasn't making money betting on his favorite sport, he was so boring he made a wedge of cheese look exciting.

He was neck-deep in IRS forms and for the past three months, she'd been flying solo.

A good thing, she reminded herself. Walter wasn't the man for her and so she'd broken things off for good after the last Super Bowl. She didn't want a man who only wanted her some of the time. Even more, she didn't want a man who didn't want her enough to make the first move. She was through initiating sex.

Hence the classes.

They'd originally been given by Dillon's sister, Cheryl Anne, who'd been desperate to break out of her shell and do something wild and crazy with her own life. She'd succeeded for a few weeks before she'd realized that actually having sex was much more preferable than talking about it with a bunch of clueless women eager to spice up their relationships. She'd handed over her classes to Winona, the owner of the only motel in town, and had married her long-time boyfriend. Cheryl Anne was now living the American dream.

Not that Meg's goal was to get married. Maybe. Someday. If the right man came along. Right now, however, she simply wanted to have sex with a man who really and truly wanted to have sex with her. A man who couldn't keep his hands off her.

A man who wanted her badly enough to make the first move.

The classes would teach her how to increase her sex appeal to the point that she was irresistible. Hopefully.

Meg finished documenting her results, closed her Pleasure Manual and headed back upstairs to her bedroom closet. After careful consideration, she settled for a hot-pink shell, a frayed blue jean miniskirt with rhinestone trim and a pair of high-heeled sandals she'd picked up on her latest shopping trip to Austin. The outfit met all of her must-haves—feminine and sexy and uber-trendy—which was why it had made it into her closet in the first place. As owner of the one and only upscale boutique in town, she wanted her own personal wardrobe to reflect her business image. While she might be striking out when it came to changing everyone's perception of her personally, professionally she was batting one thousand.

Her shop had become the go-to place for every special

occasion—from proms to anniversary parties to the occasional hot date. Women sought her advice on clothes, shoes and accessories, and her shop had even been named *Business of the Year* three consecutive times in a row by the Skull Creek Chamber of Commerce.

But while her shop was making the news, Meg wasn't.

Meaning she'd yet to garner even a mention in Tilly Townsend's infamous Hot Chicks list. The list was published every six months and featured the ten hottest bachelorettes in town. Likewise, Tilly also did a Randiest Rooster list that named the ten hottest bachelors. The list was the ultimate when it came to popularity—a who's who of the most sought-after singles in town. The women were smart, successful, vivacious and irresistible to men. The newest version came out in exactly two weeks and Meg wanted to be on it.

Meg ignored an inkling of hopelessness and headed for the shower.

She spent the next half hour upstairs getting ready and the last fifteen minutes downstairs sucking down a Diet Coke and re-reading her notes on last week's lesson. She was seated at her table, about to get to the *Understanding Your Vibrator* section, when a tongue lapped at her bare thigh.

She glanced down at the black-and-gray Blue Heeler who'd pushed through the doggy door and now stood next to her. Tail wagging, tongue lolling, the animal stared up at her, a pleading look in her big brown eyes.

"Don't even think it." She wagged a finger at her. "You know what the vet said. Sugar isn't good for a dog your age." Babe, named for the infamous Babe Ruth, obviously disagreed. She wagged her way over to the pantry and stared hopefully at the closed door.

"You can't have any," Meg told the dog, pushing to her feet. She bypassed the pantry to retrieve a small box from a nearby cabinet. "Doc said you could have a veggie biscuit instead." She held out the foul-smelling treat. Babe approached, took one sniff and wagged her way back over to the pantry. She nuzzled the door.

"No," Meg said, but the dog kept pleading.

Five minutes and some serious whimpering later, Meg pulled out a box of golden cakes and fed one to the anxious dog. Babe was getting old. Sixteen to be exact, which meant she no longer had the energy to chase Frisbees or bark at Mrs. Calico's Chihuahua next door. She'd given up chasing balls, too, and carting in the newspaper. Other than watching re-runs of *Sex and the City* and eating the occasional Twinkie, she had zero pleasure in her old age.

Meg fed her a second and smiled as she wolfed it down.

The dog whimpered for a third, but Meg shook her head. "Discipline, girl. It's all about discipline." She stuffed the box back into the pantry and closed the door.

Babe licked at Meg's fingers for a few seconds before heading back to the den and her doggy bed, obviously satisfied for the moment.

If only Meg felt the same.

Despite the orgasm, she was still restless. Anxious. Unfulfilled.

Because she was still every bit as invisible as she'd been way back when. That's why she was taking carnal classes. She wanted men to notice her, to lust after her, to find her completely irresistible.

The way the women were now lusting after Dillon Cash.

She stared at the lifestyle section of the *Skull Creek Gazette* spread out on her kitchen table and her gaze snagged on Tilly's weekly column—What's Hot and What's Not.

A picture of Dillon taken at Joe Bob's Bar & Grill blazed back at her. He was boot scootin' his way across the sawdust floor with Amelia Louise Lauderfield. The infamous Amelia Louise Lauderfield. Number six on Tilly's Hot Chicks list.

Dillon and a bona fide Hot Chick.

Meg still couldn't believe it.

One minute he'd been spending his Saturday nights holed up in his computer repair shop, and the next—a few months ago to be exact—he'd shown up in a nearby town at a local honky tonk, of all places. He'd ditched his glasses and swapped his button-down shirt and slacks for well-worn jeans and a T-shirt. Even more, he'd traded his car, complete with seat belts and air bags, for a custom-made motorcycle and no helmet.

It hadn't been the news of his physical transformation that had startled her so much as everyone's response to it—every female in the Cherry Blossom Saloon had fallen all over themselves for a chance to go home with him.

Then again, word had it he'd shown up after happy hour, which meant that the liquor had been flowing. More than likely, the members of his instant fan club had been extremely drunk. On top of that, the place was out of town. The women who'd gone gaga over his new look couldn't have been privy to his reputation.

At least that's the conclusion she'd come to after one of her customers, Cornelia Wallace, had relayed the rumors circulating around town. She could still hear the old woman's words.

"He's having one of them middle-aged life crisis things. I saw a special about it on the Discovery Health Channel. Said the threat of aging makes a man do crazy things."

"Don't you have to be middle-aged to have a midlife crisis?" Meg had asked the old woman. "Dillon's only thirty."

"Maybe it's one of them there near-death experiences. They did a *20/20* special about them last week. Said folks do all sorts of bizarre things when they almost meet their maker. Or maybe he's having a coming-out-of-the-closet moment and he's fighting it by trying to prove his manhood. Saw just such a thing on one of them cable channels last month. It was all about how this fella actually slept with three dozen women and fathered twenty-two young 'uns just so's he could prove to himself that he wasn't buttering his bread on the wrong side. What do you think?"

"I think you spend too much time watching television. Maybe it wasn't even Dillon over at the saloon. Maybe it was just someone who looked like him."

"It was him, all right. Heard it straight from Evangeline

Dupree, who heard it from her granddaughter, who heard it from her boyfriend who was there having his bachelor party. He swore it was Dillon."

But Meg wasn't so sure. Dillon at a saloon? Getting comfy with a bunch of women?

Not the Dillon she knew.

While they didn't spend a lot of time together now—he was busy at his shop and she was busy with her customers, so they only managed the occasional lunch—she still saw enough of him to know that he was every bit as awkward around the opposite sex as he'd been back in high school.

Up until two months ago, that is.

That's when things had changed.

When *he'd* changed.

Not that she'd seen the transformation firsthand. No, he'd been avoiding her, canceling their lunches, dodging her phone calls. She'd stopped by his shop to see him and put an end to all the nonsense that was flying around—there had to be a logical explanation, right?—but the place had been locked up tight. Ditto for his house. She'd even called his parents, but they'd been as confused as she was, and even more determined to hunt him down and find out the truth.

They'd been camping out in his yard for the past two weeks, trying to corner him and save him from himself.

Meg wasn't one-hundred-percent convinced that the sex object running around town was really him and so she'd taken a less radical approach—she'd left tons of messages on his cell. But he hadn't called her back.

Because he really was busy with his new social life?

Or because he'd left town for yet another computer seminar?

Everyone had a twin somewhere. More than likely Dillon's had moved to the next town and his midlife crisis/near-death-experience/coming-out-of-the-closet was simply a case of mistaken identity. One which he couldn't disprove because he was off learning how to tweak motherboards or dissect USB switches or something.

And the picture staring back at her?

Dillon's twin.

Maybe. Probably.

Sure, it would be great if he really *had* managed such a change. Then he could give her some pointers on how to nail *irresistible* and make it onto Tilly's Hot Chicks list. But Meg wasn't getting her hopes up. She knew the hazards of living in a small town. Last year Diana Trucker had been spotted buying a pregnancy test at the local pharmacy. By the time Meg had heard the news from Corny, the woman had been six months pregnant with quintuplets.

People had a way of exaggerating everything.

Which meant, until she saw actual proof of Dillon's newfound sex appeal, she wasn't buying one word of Corny's gossip.

She had her own sex appeal—or lack of—to worry over.

She'd just finished an online *How to Sex Up Your Image* seminar in addition to several self-help classes at the local junior college—*Dressing for Sexcess* and *How to Lick Your Lips Like You Mean It*. If that wasn't enough, she was now taking carnal Classes being offered in the lobby of the Skull Creek Inn.

At least that's what she told herself as she showered and dressed. She didn't want to be late for tonight's class.

SHE HAD TO BE SEEING things.

Meg sat in the motel parking lot near the corner of the building and stared across the dimly lit walkway that ran the length of the first floor. She stared through the windshield of her Mustang and her gaze zeroed in on the profile of the man who stood in front of the doorway to room four.

He wore snug, faded jeans, a fitted black T-shirt and a pair of black cowboy boots. A black Resistol tipped low on his forehead and cast a shadow across the top half of his face. Dark blond hair curled from beneath the hat brim and brushed the collar of his shirt. He was tall and muscular and...*Dillon.*

She blinked, but he didn't disappear. And neither did the beautiful woman pressed up against his back, her arms locked around his waist as she waited for him to slide the key into the lock and open the door.

A heartbeat later, the door opened and he pried the woman loose long enough to step aside and motion her into the room. She slid by him, her hands brushing his crotch before she disappeared inside.

He quickly followed and Meg was left to wonder if Corny had been right and she'd just witnessed the transformation of a lifetime. That couldn't have been Dillon Cash.

Yes. No. *Hell,* no.

The next few minutes were spent debating between the three as she gathered up her purse and Pleasure Manual, climbed from the front seat and headed for the hotel lobby.

She didn't mean to slow down, but she couldn't help herself. She paused briefly at the door to room four, but the only sound she heard was the frantic beating of her own heart.

2

"LET'S DO IT RIGHT NOW," the soft, breathless voice slid into his ears and sent a burst of *yeah, right* straight to his brain. *"Please."*

Dillon Cash stared at the woman who'd preceded him into the motel room, her eyes gleaming with a mix of passion and desperation. He barely resisted the urge to pinch himself.

No way was this happening.

This was Susie Wilcox, a former Homecoming Queen and now the hottest divorcée in Skull Creek, according to the local paper and Tilly Townsend who'd given the sexy blonde the number one spot on last year's Hot Chicks list.

Rumor had it Susie was a shoe-in for this year's list, as well.

She had long, silky hair. Legs up to *here*. Breasts out to *there*. Her tiny waist begged for his hands and her heart-shaped ass made his mouth go dry. She'd been the star of his wettest dreams back in high school, and a few dozen erotic fantasies in the twelve-plus years since.

She was everything he'd ever wanted in a woman and she was here.

Now.

With *him*.

And she was getting naked.

She kicked off her high heels, grabbed the edge of her tank top and pulled the cotton up and over her head. Popping the buttons on her jeans, she shimmied the ultra-tight denim down her long legs and stepped free. Her fingers went to her bra clasp and just like that, her impressive DD's popped free. She stood before him then wearing a pink mesh thong that left little to the imagination and a rosy red flush that said she was as hot and bothered as a woman could get.

Surprise snaked through him, but he tamped it back down and focused on the hunger stirring deep inside of him.

"I can't stop thinking about you," she said. Her gaze, intense and unwavering, glittered with passion. "About us." She shook her head. "I don't know why, but the first moment I saw you tonight, I knew we would end up here." She smiled. "I feel like I can't keep my hands off of you." The smile faded into a look of raw, inexplicable need. "I feel like I'm going to explode right now if I don't get close to you." She moved toward him, eating up the distance between them with determined steps. "*Very* close."

Maybe she wasn't privy as to *why* she wanted him so badly. And Dillon wasn't about to tell her.

It had started two months ago when a stranger had ridden into town. Jake McCann had turned out to be more than the average drifter. He'd been a vampire determined to lay his past to rest, to slay his demons. Literally. And Dillon had gotten caught in the middle of the struggle.

One minute Dillon had been trying to protect an old friend and the next, he'd had a pair of bloodthirsty fangs—courtesy of Jake's nemesis—gnawing at his neck. He'd come *this close* to dying, his life spilling away on the pavement of the town's main square, but then Jake had stepped forward, shared his own blood, and changed Dillon forever.

Thankfully.

Sure, it wasn't the most practical lifestyle—no more lounging on the beach or scarfing chicken fried steak. But being bitten and turned into a vampire who thrived on blood *and* sex—especially sex—wasn't such a bad thing.

Not to a man whose parents had been a pair of obsessive-compulsives who'd worried about *everything*, particularly the health and well-being of their only two children. Dillon and his younger sister, Cheryl Anne, had been smothered and coddled to the point that they'd been isolated from their peers. Harold and Dora Cash had never taken their children on a trip to the beach—and risk the possibility of sun damage? Nor had they allowed them to eat chicken fried steak or anything with an overabundance of trans fat.

Dillon had grown up playing solitaire and chess while other kids went camping and joined Boy Scouts. He'd also been a computer whiz who'd spent his summers reading and taking online courses instead of catching fireflies and going on picnics or swimming down at Skull Creek river.

At thirty-one, he'd become his own boss—he owned the only computer store within a fifty mile radius that handled both new sales and repairs. He was independent, financially solvent, and still a major geek.

Up until two months ago, that is.

"Once a geek, always a geek."

Susie's words echoed in his head. That's what she'd told him back in high school when he'd worked up the nerve to ask her out. He'd gotten a new haircut and ordered a cool pair of jeans and an AC/DC T-shirt online. He'd even invested the money he'd made typing English papers on a pair of contact lenses. But it hadn't been enough. By then, the damage had already been done, his reputation established. His new look had failed. Even more, one of his contacts had popped out and Susie had ground it into the concrete as she'd spun on her heel, told him to get lost and walked away.

Her rejection had set the stage for many more to come. He'd gone on to have a measly three sexual encounters in his lifetime (not counting the experimental petting he'd done with his buddy Meg back in the ninth grade), and not one woman had ever come back for seconds.

In fact, he'd had a pretty hard time talking them into firsts.

All that had changed the night he'd been turned.

He'd changed.

A gleam of yellow pushed through the part in the drapes and sliced across the carpet at his feet, but it did little to illuminate the rest of the room. He blinked, his gaze piercing the darkness, drinking in every detail of the small hotel room—from the faint scars on the worn dresser to the tiny thread that unraveled at the corner of the bedspread, to the shimmering spiderweb that dangled in the far corner. His vision had improved and sharpened to the point that he had no need of the black coke-bottle glasses he'd worn since the age of five.

His dark blond hair was shinier and thicker, too, his body more muscular and defined. His acne had completely cleared up and his tongue no longer tied itself into knots when a pretty female looked his way.

Now he knew exactly how to talk to a woman.

How to look at her. To touch. To seduce.

He was now a vampire who craved sexual energy as much as he craved the sustenance of blood. More, in fact. And after thirty-one years of near celibacy, Dillon Cash had no qualms feeding the hunger that now lived and breathed inside of him.

His nostrils flared and the scent of warm, ripe woman filled his head. His body responded instantly. His hands itched to reach out. His muscles tightened in anticipation. The blood pounded through his veins. His dick stirred, growing hard, hot, *ready*.

Still. As great as he knew the sex would be, this encounter would just make him that much more anxious for the next.

Another woman.

Another rush of succulent, sweet, drenching energy.

He needed it. He thrived on it. He fed off of it.

Gladly.

Unlike the vampire who'd turned him, Dillon wasn't the least bit anxious to escape the hunger. Not when it came with so many perks. He knew he would inevitably miss his humanity. He would then get as serious as Jake about finding and destroying the Ancient One, and putting an end to the vampire curse once and for all.

After he'd broken Bobby McGuire's record for having slept with the most women in town.

Bobby was a legend in Skull Creek. He'd held the number one

spot on the town's Randiest Rooster list for a record twenty-eight years, right up until he'd turned forty-eight and had had his first heart attack. The doc had put him on a strict No Excitement diet, and he'd been booted off the list. Before however, he'd been a major gigolo rumored to have done the deed with over three hundred women, a count he'd recorded by carving notches into his pine headboard. That proof had sold for over two thousand dollars last year at a local charity auction when Bobby, now an old man, had donated a houseful of furniture and moved to a retirement community in Port Aransas.

Over the years, some had called Bobby a sex maniac. Others had called him a liar. A few had even said he was delusional.

But no one—not a single soul—had ever called him a geek.

Not that Dillon cared what other people thought. Nor did he have any desire to land himself on the notorious list.

This wasn't about proving something to the folks of Skull Creek. It was about proving something to himself. After so many years of having zero luck with the opposite sex, he'd started to think that maybe, just maybe, Susie had been right about him.

He'd never really thought so. He'd always walked the straight and narrow because of his parents. He didn't want to cause them any more grief. He'd caused enough as a child when he'd nearly gotten himself killed.

It had been his seventh birthday and he'd been determined to camp out down by the creek. His parents had said no, but he'd snuck out anyway. He'd been walking around without shoes near the water and had stepped on something sharp. In a matter of days, a small puncture wound had morphed into a full-blown staph infection.

A near fatal infection that had turned his parents from normal and easygoing people to smothering and obsessive caretakers in less than six months.

Cheryl Anne was too young to remember—she'd been four at the time—and too young to blame him for the stifled life she'd been forced to lead. But he remembered how things had been before the incident. His parents had been fun-loving and adventurous back then. And Dillon? He'd been outgoing. A risk taker with a zest for life.

He'd buckled under the guilt, suppressed that lust and obeyed his folks from then on. To everyone else, he'd seemed like a quiet, shy, timid kid, but deep inside he'd been just the opposite.

An act. That's all it had been, or so he'd always thought up until he'd graduated high school without even making it to second base with a girl. The doubts had set in then—the notion that maybe he wasn't really pretending. Maybe he really had morphed into a bona fide geek.

Even now that he was a vampire there were still moments—quick bursts of thought whenever he found himself in the most unreal situations—when he knew, he just *knew,* he had to be dreaming and it was just a matter of time before reality intruded and he morphed back to his old, boring self.

But he was going to change all of that and silence the doubts for good. He'd fantasized about breaking Bobby's record—what hormone-driven teenage boy hadn't?—but he'd never had the opportunity.

Until now.

Two months, an uncontrollable hunger and a nearly impossible number of women—he was now only two shy of his goal.

Training his gaze on the tall, voluptuous blonde, he sent a rush of mental images, leaving no doubt in her mind what he wanted to do to her.

She didn't walk away this time. She couldn't. She wanted him with a greedy desperation that she'd never felt for any other man.

He read that truth in her eyes—another vampire perk—along with the fact that, despite her beauty and the prestige of being number one on Tilly's Hottest Chicks list, she was the loneliest and most miserable of all her friends. Contrary to rumor, she hadn't left her second husband because he'd filed bankruptcy after some bad business investments. He'd been cheating on her with a giggling twenty-one-year-old barmaid and had spent their entire savings on hair plugs, liposuction and a penis enlargement.

"Touch me," she begged. "Please."

And because Dillon needed her as much as she needed him, he did.

"CAN ANYONE TELL ME THE key ingredient to a successful relationship?"

Meg wiggled in her seat, craned her neck and peered between two gigantic teased and sprayed hairdos. Her gaze went to the woman who stood center stage in the small lobby of the Skull Creek Inn.

Winona Atkins was well into her seventies. She wore a flower-print smock, white orthopedic shoes and a penis-shaped name tag that read Carnal Coach. Rolls of snow white curls covered her head and a pair of gold-rimmed cat's eye glasses hung from a chain around her neck.

The old woman arched a white eyebrow as she eyed her roomful of eager students. "Well, come on now." She waved a bony hand. "I ain't got all night. Somebody bite the bullet and take a stab at it."

"Honesty?" someone called out.

"Mutual respect?" asked another.

"Separate bank accounts?"

Winona smiled, her face breaking into a mass of wrinkles. "Those are some fine answers, ladies. Mighty fine." She shook her head. "But I'm afraid they ain't even close. See—" she retrieved the hat rack standing in the far corner and hauled it front and center "—every man, no matter how upstanding or uptight he might be, likes a little hooch ever once in a while."

"Hooch?" one woman asked. "Is that like a floozy?"

"Exactly. It's a woman who can cut loose and shed her inhibitions. A woman who's got confidence and isn't afraid to show it. A woman who'll strip buck naked and wrap herself around the nearest pole." Winona gripped the hat rack and did a little shake and shimmy. "I call this move "Circling the wagons", ladies." She went around the cedar rack once, twice. "I know it looks complicated now, but after tonight's lesson, you'll all be able to do it with your eyes closed. Which is a plus if you're like Sally, there, who's got cataracts." She indicated a seventy-something woman straining to see with her bifocals. "Not that you're s'posed to close your eyes. Eye contact is a powerful thing between a woman and a man."

Winona's words stirred a sudden vision of Dillon standing in the hotel doorway, his gaze hooked on Susie Wilcox, his eyes bright. Gleaming. Powerful.

A pang of envy shot through her. A crazy reaction because no way—repeat, no way—was she even remotely attracted to Dillon Cash.

Sure, she'd felt a few tummy tingles when they'd tried the kissing thing way back when, but what red-blooded, curious, hormonal teen girl wouldn't after watching Mickey Rourke seduce Kim Bassinger? It hadn't been Dillon. It had been the heat of the moment.

Luckily, the temperature had quickly fizzled after the first disappointing attempt at a kiss. She hadn't felt even an inkling of attraction to him since.

Not then and certainly not now.

Forget jealous. She was envious. He had a hot woman falling all over him, and she wanted the same. Not a hot woman, mind you, but a hot man.

Yep, she was envious. *If* it was really and truly him, that is.

She latched onto the doubts and turned her attention back to the front of the room.

"…start with Mary." Winona pointed to a woman seated on the front row. "I want you to get up and try circling the wagons. We'll keep going seat by seat until everyone gets a turn. While everyone's trying out the technique, I'll have a look at the homework assignment from the last class."

Pages fluttered as everyone pulled out their notebooks.

"I don't know if I can do this," Mary said as she pushed to her feet. "I'm not used to working with an audience."

"That's what these are for, dear." Winona retrieved a platter of petit fours from a nearby table. "I call 'em pleasure bites. These little buggers will have you stripping off your clothes and shedding your inhibitions quicker than Arlen Wilson can chow through an apple with those new titanium dentures of his."

"Are those made with that wacky tobacky Mildred Pierce always puts in her brownies?" Mary asked.

Winona frowned. "I run a reputable business here, ladies. This here's made with Everclear," Winona said. "Colorless, taste-less and completely legal."

"Well, then." Mary grabbed one and popped it into her mouth before helping herself to a second and then a third. She drew a deep breath and eyed the hat rack.

Meanwhile, Winona handed the platter to the next woman in line and the goodies started to circulate.

"Billy and I had such a good time last night," Mabel Avery told Winona as the old woman stepped toward her and confis-cated her journal. "He loved watching me with that pink vibrator I ordered off the Internet."

"My Hank liked watching me, too," another woman said, waving her spiral notebook. "But mine's purple instead of pink."

"My Melvin said it was his fantasy come true," said another.

As the comments continued, Meg made a show of search-ing around her seat before throwing up her hands. "What do you know? I think I left my notebook in the car," she said to the woman next to her. She pushed to her feet. "I'll just pop out and get it."

Five seconds later, she closed the lobby door behind her and breathed a sigh of relief.

Coward, a voice whispered. *The entire town knows you're unattached.*

But knowing it and hearing it, complete with written docu-mentation to back it up, was a totally different thing. It was bad enough she'd had to try out the vibrator alone. She wasn't going to admit it to a roomful of nosy women.

No, she'd take her time going to the car, then slip back inside once Winona went back to her pole dancing techniques.

She was halfway down the walkway when her gaze snagged on the door to room four.

It was shut solid. The curtains were drawn on the window just to the left. No light spilled past the two-inch gap in the drapes.

Make that a three inch gap.

Not that she was looking.

She was *not* going to look.

That's what she told herself as she started to walk past.

For one thing, it was rude and intrusive. Two, she could care less what was going on inside. Sex or scrabble. Neither were her business.

At the same time, if Dillon really was having sex with Susie Wilcox, it meant that not only had he changed, but the town had let him. Somehow, someway, he'd killed a lifetime of perception in a matter of months.

And she couldn't help but wonder how he'd done it.

If he'd done it.

Curiosity burned through her and her footsteps slowed. She'd take one quick little peek and no one would be the wiser. Cupping her hands over her brow, she leaned toward the window.

She blinked and the dimly lit room started to focus. A pair of jeans lay in a heap on the hardwood floor. A lacey bra dangled over the back of a nearby leather chair. One red high heel peeked out from under the corner of the bed. The covers bunched at the bottom of the mattress, the bedspread a tangled heap on the floor.

A very naked Susie Wilcox lay on her stomach, her cheek nuzzling a pillow, one arm slung over her head, the other resting on the empty spot next to her—

Wait a second. Empty?

Just as the thought struck, she heard the deep, familiar voice. "Nice view."

The words slid into her ears and her heart stalled. The hair on the back of her neck prickled. Awareness zipped up and down her spine, along with a rush of embarrassment.

She was *so* busted.

3

SHE KNEW IT WAS DILLON even before she turned around.

Before her gaze swept from the long bare feet peeking from beneath the frayed hem of a worn pair of jeans, up denim-clad legs, past a trim waist and an enticing funnel of whiskey-colored hair that bisected washboard abs, over a muscular chest, thick biceps encircled by slave-band tattoos, a corded neck, to the familiar face—

Wait a minute.

Tattoos?

Her attention swiveled to one sinewy arm. Sure enough, an intricate black design snaked around the bulging muscle, making it seem larger and more powerful. Her gaze swiveled to the other arm. *Ditto.*

"Nice view," he repeated.

The deep timbre of his voice drew her full attention and made her tummy quiver. Her thighs trembled and her nipples pebbled and—

Girlfriend, puleeeeease. We're talking *Dillon*. The guy who'd given her dry-cleaning coupons for her last birthday. Other than those few ridiculous moments in anticipation (thanks to Kim and Mickey) of their first kiss, she'd never felt anything for him other than friendship.

Certainly *not* the overwhelming need to get hot and sweaty and naked.

Then again, she'd never seen him wearing nothing but worn, faded jeans, the top button undone, a pair of dark and dangerous tattoos and a relaxed, confident, sexy-as-hell smile.

"Yeah," she blurted, eager to distract herself from the sudden trembling of her body. "She's, um, really pretty." Her throat tightened around the words as if it actually bothered her to admit as much.

As if.

"I wasn't talking about the view inside." His gaze slid from her eyes to her mouth and lingered for several seconds.

If she hadn't known better, she would have sworn she felt a distinct pressure on her bottom lip. Like an invisible finger tracing the plump fullness, testing it... *Crazy.*

She licked her lips, killing the strange sensation, and his gaze collided with hers.

"I'm talking about the view out here," he added. Something hot and sensual shimmered in the green depths of his eyes and her pulse jumped.

"I've left over a dozen messages," she blurted, eager to ignore the sudden butterflies that fluttered away in her stomach. She gathered her indignation and nailed him with a stare. "Did you forget how to use a phone, or have you been avoiding me on purpose?"

The corner of his mouth crooked into the faintest hint of a smile. "I've been a little busy."

She glanced at the window. "Too busy to call your folks?" She eyed him. "I saw your mom at the hardware store last week. She's worried about you."

He shrugged, his biceps flexing. The tattoos encircling his arms seemed to widen. "I haven't been able to call."

"You haven't been able to, or you haven't wanted to?"

"Things are different for me now. I'm different. I doubt they'd understand."

Meg doubted it, too. They'd freaked out when he'd stepped in an ant bed back in the fifth grade and had pulled Doc Wilmer away from a championship golf game just to apply Benadryl. Meg could only imagine what they would do if they knew Dillon was stepping into motel rooms, and every place else it seemed, with every available woman in town.

Correction—almost every available woman. He'd been avoiding her like the plague.

"What's going on with you? You never miss pepperoni day." She didn't mean to sound so accusing. So what if he'd blown off their monthly lunch at Uncle Buck's Pizza not once, but twice now? She would have skipped their infamous double-decker pepperoni in a heartbeat in favor of a date with a really hot guy. "You could have at least called."

"I meant to." The sexy confidence faded for a split second and she glimpsed a twinkle of true regret. "Don't be mad."

"Because you're going through some major life crisis and didn't have the decency to tell me? You really think I'd be mad at a little thing like that?"

"You're not mad, then."

"I meant that sarcastically." He grinned and she felt her indignation melt. "Okay, spill it. What's up?"

He gave another shrug. "What can I say? I'm finally coming out of my shell."

"At thirty-one?"

"Maybe I'm a late bloomer."

"And maybe I'm wearing polyester to the next VFW dance." She shook her head. "It's more than that. Something happened to you."

"You've found me out." He leaned one hand on the window near her head and leaned down, his lips brushing her ear as he murmured, "I'm not really Dillon. I just look like him."

The scent of him, so raw and masculine, slid into her nostrils and filled her head. For a split second, she had the urge to lean closer, to press her lips to the side of his neck, to taste him with her tongue, to—

She fought the urge and leaned back.

"I suppose you're really a pod person and we're about to be invaded by little green men."

"They're purple, but you get the idea."

"You're so full of it." She leveled a stare at him. "I was really worried."

A strange gleam lit his eyes, but then it faded into a vivid green that sparkled and glittered so bright she found herself staring for the next few heartbeats until reality zapped some common sense into her and she managed to shift her attention to his mouth.

He had really great lips. Full, but not too full. Just right for a man.

She'd always thought so. At least for those few moments before he'd given her some of *the* worst kisses of her life.

He stiffened. "I'm sorry you were worried, but I can take care of myself." His sudden frown faded into an easygoing grin. "And most anyone else who comes along." The words were ripe with innuendo and her tummy did a quick somersault before hollowing out.

Dillon, she reminded herself. *Dry-cleaning. Zero attraction.*

But while her brain received the crucial messages loud and clear, her body had tuned in to a different frequency.

Warmth zipped up and down her spine, sending out blasts of heat to every erogenous zone in her body, from the arches of her feet and the sensitive skin below her belly button, to the ripened tips of her breasts and the back of each ear.

She had the sudden urge to step forward, close the fraction of distance between them and press her body flush against his.

So do it.

The words, raw and sexy, rumbled through her head as if Dillon himself stood next to her and murmured the encouragement directly in her ear.

He didn't. He stood inches away, his mouth crooked in a sinful grin, his eyes gleaming with desire and a knowing light that said he read every lascivious thought that raced through her mind.

Yeah. Sure.

She'd obviously had one too many of Winona's pleasure bites. No way would she ever make the first move on a man again.

Been there. Done that. Uh, uh.

And she certainly wouldn't make the first move on *Dillon,* of all people. He wasn't her type. He never had been. She went for tall, sexy, aggressive.

Okay, so maybe he *was* her type. All except for the aggressive part.

There were no strong purposeful hands reaching for her, no seeking lips. Gone was the uncertainty that had always simmered so hot and bright in his greener-than-green eyes when it came to women. The fear. Rather, his gaze blazed with a newfound confidence that did crazy things to her heartbeat.

He stood there, ready and waiting, as if he expected her to be overcome by lust and fall all over him.

"You did it, didn't you?" she blurted as the truth crystallized.

He arched one blond eyebrow. "You're the one looking through the window. You tell me."

His meaning sank in and her cheeks started to burn. Or maybe it was the sudden knowing gleam in his eyes that made her face heat. Either way, her body temperature climbed degree by dangerous degree with each passing second. "Not *it* as in sex," she said, managing to find her voice. "Although you obviously did that, too. I'm talking about you. You've really changed." Somehow, someway, Dillon Cash had managed to accomplish in a matter of months what she'd spent half her life trying to do. "You're really and truly—" she swallowed "—*sexy*."

His mouth slanted into a grin. "You say that like it's a bad thing."

"Not at all. It's really good. Great, in fact." She shook her head. "I just can't figure out how you did it. I mean, obviously, you did the whole makeover thing—" she eyed his jeans "—with the exception of the clothes, but it's more than that." Her gaze met his. "I've read every self-help sex book known to man. I've taken tons of seminars at the junior college. I've completed several online courses. This is my eighth class with Winona since she took over for Cheryl Anne." She shook her head. "And I'm still trying to get onto Tilly's list." She glanced through the handspan of window space at the beauty draped across the bed.

He'd done it, all right. He'd finally uncovered the secret she'd been searching for all these years—he'd found a way to make himself ultra attractive to the opposite sex.

Women ogled him. Fantasized about him. Stripped off their clothes and hopped into bed without a thought.

Skull Creek's biggest geek had become a bona fide sex object.

To every other woman, that is, except Meg.

She knew firsthand that people couldn't just change. Not deep down inside. Not overnight. It had taken her years to complete the process. There was no way he'd managed it in a matter of months.

No, he was still the same Dillon beneath the silky hair and toned muscles. Still the same guy who'd thrown up after Darla Sue Alcott had turned him down for the Homecoming dance.

She knew that, even if it was getting more difficult with each passing second to remember it.

A strange look crossed his face, as if he'd peeked into her head and glimpsed her thoughts. But then the expression faded into an easy grin and her heart gave a double thump.

"Six months ago, you couldn't even talk to a girl," she pointed out, her own desperation getting the better of her. "And now you've got Susie Wilcox offering herself to you like some pagan sacrifice."

"Talking's overrated," he said, his deep voice rumbling through her. "There are much more interesting ways to communicate."

"And you learned this how? Book? Seminar? Gene therapy that replaces geek DNA with a hung-like-a-horse chromosome?" The last comment drew a full-blown smile from him. "Because whatever it is, I want some."

He arched an eyebrow. "You want to be hung like a horse?"

"You know what I mean." Her gaze locked with his. "I want the female equivalent. I want to know your secret." A secret that would surely land her on Tilly's newest Hot Chicks list. If Meg could make the list, she had no doubt that the men in town would view her differently.

Bye, bye Manhandler Meg, hello irresistible sex object.

"You owe me," she told Dillon, "so pay up." When he gave

her a questioning look, she added, "For your half of the pizza,
plus the tip. Add in pain and suffering because I had to sit there
alone, and punitive damages to my hips because of all the extra
calories I consumed since I don't believe in wasting, and I'd say
you owe me big-time."

His gaze dropped. "Your hips look pretty good to me."

The butterflies started again. An insane reaction because the
old Dillon had never acknowledged anything about her. Not her
hips. Or her trim waist. Or even the decent rack she'd been
showing off with a Wonderbra since senior year.

This Dillon seemed to notice everything.

And made her want to offer herself up as the second willing
sacrifice of the night.

She shook away the sudden visual—Dillon naked and panting
above her—that popped into her head and focused on her grum-
bling stomach. She hadn't eaten yet, so it was no wonder she was
feeling so deprived.

She wanted food, not Dillon. Not really.

She swallowed and did a mental recitation of the menu at her
favorite restaurant. "Good try, but you're not changing the
subject. Give," she persisted.

"Since when did you get so bossy?"

"Since birth. Seriously, I want to know." Desperation bubbled
inside of her, along with the deprivation niggling at her gut. "I
need to know."

He eyed her for a long, drawn-out moment and she had the
feeling that he faced some internal struggle.

"You're sure? You *really* want to know?" he finally asked.

Excitement rushed through her and she nodded. "Tell me
everything."

"I've got a better idea." His gaze gleamed with a hidden
knowledge. His fingers flexed on the glass next to her as he
leaned forward. His stubbled jaw rasped her cheekbone. His lips
grazed her ear. "Why don't I show you instead?"

4

WHAT THE HELL WAS HE thinking?

The thought pushed its way past the ferocious hunger that gripped Dillon's insides and sent a burst of reality straight to his brain.

This was Meg. His buddy. His pal. His friend.

Meg was the one woman he could actually talk to.

The only woman who'd ever cared what he had to say.

No way was he thinking about pushing her up against the nearest wall, sinking himself into her hot body and soaking up her delicious energy while he pumped in and out and drove her to a screaming climax.

And there was *no* way he was thinking about sinking his fangs into her sweet neck and drinking in her essence while he pumped in and out and drove her to a screaming climax.

While he fed off blood and sex, he never indulged in both at the same time. That was the first rule Garret, his other vampire mentor, had taught him. The big no-no because it forged a bond that was unbreakable. *Forever.*

The last thing Dillon wanted was to tie himself to one woman for the rest of eternity. Not when he was *this* close to breaking Bobby's record.

That's what he told himself, but with Meg's scent filling his nostrils and her frantic heartbeat echoing in his ears, forever didn't seem like such a long time. His muscles tightened and his gut ached and he had the sudden thought that he wanted her more than he wanted to break Bobby's record.

And she wanted a double pepperoni pizza with extra cheese.

The thought slid into his head and he pulled back. His gaze drilled into hers. Sure enough, he saw an image of Uncle Buck's Pizza Joint, a table, an extra large pie, and Meg scarfing it down to her heart's content.

She didn't want him.

Or at least, she didn't *want* to want him. She responded to him. All women did. But she wasn't falling all over him like every other woman he'd come into contact with in the past few months—with the exception of Nikki, the owner of the local beauty salon.

Nikki was totally enamored of Jake and so her lack of interest didn't bother Dillon.

But Meg… She was a single, red-blooded female. She should be out of her mind with lust.

Or at least a little overwhelmed.

He drank in the sight of her. No inviting smile. No come-and-get-me-now gaze. No pleading or begging.

"Please."

All right, so she was begging. A little. But not in the way he'd become accustomed to since stepping over to the vamp side. She wanted his help. His guidance. His advice.

What she didn't want was to jump into the sack with him.

Correction, she didn't want to want to jump into the sack with him. He stared into her bright gaze and read the truth as if it were spelled out in neon. She was determined to resist temptation, to wait for a man—any man—to make the first move when it came to sex. She was even more determined to resist Dillon. They had too much history. Even more, she knew for a fact—makeover aside—that he couldn't kiss worth a flip and she was in no hurry to try it again.

He fought down the urge to press his lips to hers and prove her wrong right then and there. He would have, if he hadn't been so determined to break Bobby's record.

Bobby hadn't put the moves on any woman. Rather, they'd come to him, eager and willing.

Ditto for every woman in Dillon's recent past. He was on a mission and he wasn't about to get distracted now.

"I've been trying to make Tilly's list forever," Meg continued. "If I can beef up my sex appeal, I'll be a shoe-in. You have to give me some pointers."

"And what will you give me?" He waited for a long list of seductive suggestions starting with "I'll strip naked and give you a lap dance."

"New clothes."

He blinked. "Excuse me?"

"While you've made a decent transformation physically and, obviously, mentally, what with overcoming your shyness and everything, you haven't come anywhere close to finding a sense of style." She eyed his jeans. "Designer?"

"Who cares?"

"The majority of women the world over, every homosexual on the face of the planet, and let's not forget the metrosexuals, bless their stylish little souls."

"When I look at a woman, I seriously doubt she cares what sort of jeans I'm wearing." He gave her an intense look and grinned at the way her pulse suddenly leapt at the base of her throat. But while the reaction was immediate and intense, it quickly faded and once again she was fantasizing about the pizza. "My jeans are irrelevant."

"Maybe. But if you're going to do something, you might as well do it right. Namely, if you want to make a complete transformation, it means looking the part right down to your skivvies." She arched an eyebrow. "You still doing the Spider-man boxers?"

"Not since the third grade." Her dad had gone out of town and she'd slept over at his house. She'd worn an oversize Green Bay Packers T-shirt that night, while he'd been in his webbed boxers and a plain white T-shirt. She'd brought her army men and a flashlight, and they'd snuck into his closet after bedtime and played until dawn. While she'd looked and acted like one of the boys back then, she'd smelled a hundred times better. He could still remember the scent of her strawberry shampoo.

His nostrils flared. Beneath the perfume and hair products, he caught a whiff of the familiar scent.

"Whites?" she persisted. "Solids?"

"Neither." He inhaled again and electricity spiraled straight to his groin. He fought against the hunger and focused on giving her another grin. "I'm in commando mode."

"Oh." Her gaze shifted nervously and he knew she was racing to think of something else to say to distract herself from the sudden mental image he'd stirred. She shrugged. "Okay, so you don't really need any advice when it comes to undergarments. But these jeans…" She shook her head and wrinkled her nose.

"There's nothing wrong with them."

"They're from last year's bargain bin at the Shop-'til-you-drop, aren't they?"

"So?"

"So you need a pair that are a little more updated, not to mention a shirt to go with them. An outfit that says cool, classy, sexy, which I can certainly provide." She leveled a blazing blue stare at him and made her proposition. "You educate me in the finer points of being a convincing sex object, and I'll help you find a look that does your new image some justice."

He seriously doubted she could come up with anything that could do more for his sex appeal than the vamp blood flowing through his veins, but the thought of letting her try definitely snagged his attention.

Resisting him during a brief run-in like this might be easy. But no way could she hold back if they spent more than five minutes together. The thought struck and suddenly he knew exactly what he needed to do—seduce Meg Sweeney to the point that she stopped holding back and offered herself to him like the countless other females in Skull Creek.

Not only would he break Bobby's record, but he would disprove beyond a doubt what he'd started to suspect—that he was, indeed, as geeky as everyone thought.

Tempting a woman determined not to be tempted would be

the ultimate proof, not to mention he'd spent a lot of years wishing he could go back and re-do that first horrific kiss.

His memory stirred and he saw the disappointment in her eyes, the reluctance to try it again.

The image fueled his determination and he gave her his most seductive smile. "You've got yourself a deal, darlin'."

DARLIN'? SINCE WHEN DID Dillon Cash use the term *darlin'*?

Since he's morphed into a megalicious stud-muffin who makes you want to rip off your panties and do the happy dance all over him.

Not that she would.

She was through taking the lead. She wanted a man to want her so badly that he couldn't keep his hands off of her. A man who would gladly rip off *his* boxers and do the happy dance all over *her*.

Holding tight to her resolve, she drew a deep breath and concentrated on putting one foot in front of the other as she walked back toward the motel lobby.

She could feel his gaze on her and awareness zipped through her. Her nipples pebbled and she became painfully aware of the way the lace cups of her bra rubbed back and forth with the slight swinging motion of her arms. Her blue jean skirt tugged and pulled and her thighs actually trembled.

Thanks to Dillon and his suddenly overwhelming sex appeal.

As tempting as he was, she couldn't deny her good fortune. She'd definitely found the key to her future success. Once they started lessons—

Her thoughts slammed to a halt. She'd been so anxious to escape her traitorous thoughts that she hadn't proposed a time and date for their first session.

"What about tomorrow morning—" she said, but the words died as she turned and found the walkway empty.

June bugs bumped against the single bulb that lit the concrete path. Her gaze traveled back to the spot where he'd stood and she eyed the closed door.

No rustle of denim as he'd turned. No creak of metal as he'd opened the door.... No thud as the door had shut behind him. Nothing.

One minute, she'd felt his gaze and the next...*poof*. He'd disappeared.

Right.

She ignored the strange tingling that worked its way up her spine. He wasn't actually *gone*. He was inside and she'd obviously been too wound up in her thoughts and her body's traitorous response to notice the details.

Grasping at the explanation, she fought down the notion that something wasn't quite right and turned back toward the lobby.

She would give him a call in the morning and set up a meeting. Maybe midmorning. While she didn't have any men's clothes in her shop, she could take his measurements and then do some online shopping later. He would tell her what books he'd been reading, give her some pointers, and then they could head over to Uncle Buck's for a makeup lunch.

Thanks to her lustful thoughts and her desperate attempt for a diversion, she had a sudden craving for double pepperoni that even a dozen pleasure bites couldn't touch.

A craving that haunted her for the next hour as she turned in her homework, finished her class and headed home. A craving that drove her straight to her kitchen in search of satisfaction, aka junk food.

In massive quantities if possible.

Since it was the end of the week and she hadn't yet made it to the grocery store, she quickly ruled out *massive* and settled for Babe's three remaining Twinkies. She also snatched up what was left of a bottle of wine she'd received from one of her customers the Christmas before last.

Bottle in one hand and sponge cake in the other, she headed upstairs and tried not to think about Dillon and whether or not he'd improved in the kissing department.

Obviously, he had. Otherwise, he wouldn't have every woman in town falling all over him.

Most of the women in town, that is.

They were just friends, she told herself as she peeled off her clothes and crawled into bed.

Just like she saw the real Dillon, he saw the real Meg. The one who hadn't managed to cancel her subscription to *Sports Illustrated*. The one who still tossed around a baseball in the back-yard every now and then when she was sure her neighbors weren't looking.

Which explained why he'd done little more than flirt with her tonight. Not that she'd wanted him to do more.

It was the principle that mattered.

Obviously, like everyone else in town, he just couldn't see the Hot Chick that Meg had become.

Not yet.

Not ever a voice whispered. One she quickly ignored as she devoured two of the three cakes, downed a long sip of wine and snuggled under the sheets.

If Dillon could convince an entire town full of people he'd known since birth, so could she. Even more, she could be convincing enough to get herself into Tilly's top ten.

All she had to do was buckle down, learn everything she could from Dillon, and *not* jump his bones in the process.

No problem. Manhandler Meg was ancient history.

At least that's what she told herself.

5

SHE NEEDED HIM TO SEX her up.

Even more, she *wanted* him to sex her up.

Dillon sat in the small office that housed the administrative portion—aka a desk, a file cabinet and a state-of-the-art computer system—of Skull Creek Choppers and tried to push Meg and her proposition completely out of his head.

The truth echoed through his head, tightening his groin and stirring the damned need that twisted his gut. He fought against the sensations and tried to focus. He had work to do. He was smack-dab in the middle of developing custom-design software for a new line of choppers being introduced in the Fall.

He'd spent the past hour since leaving the motel hard at work on the templates that would be the starter point for each bike. At the moment, Jake and Garret were working from a sketch only, crafting the cycles from the ground up and dealing with problems as they arose during the building process. The computer program Dillon was developing would simplify everything and allow them to foresee any structural and/or mechanical problems before they encountered them. They would be able to enter in the measurements and must-haves for each bike. The computer would process the information and put together a cyber model, pinpointing errors and "fixing" them before any actual fabrication. Dillon was just days away from putting the final touches on the program, which meant he didn't need a distraction right now.

He stared at a particular line of code, but instead of seeing the sequence of numbers and letters, he saw Meg, her lips so full and kissable, her blue eyes filled with determination.

A sliver of excitement went through him, followed by a wave of disbelief. He still couldn't grasp the fact that she'd asked for his help. Thanks to his ability to read minds, he now knew she never asked a man for anything.

Never demanded or pushed or manhandled.

Not anymore.

She'd sworn off any and all aggressive behavior when it came to sex. She wanted a man to lust after her. She wanted to feel desirable and sexy and confident that her own transformation—from pudgy tomboy to curvaceous woman—had been successful.

Deep down, she wasn't so sure.

He'd seen the truth in her gaze, the way he saw everything else about her—she was up to her neck in mortgage payments on her dream house, she had a dog addicted to Twinkies, she loved her job even if it did mean being cooped up most of the day and, thanks to the upcoming prom season, she was certain she would double her profits this year.

Yes, he saw it all. Her hopes. Her dreams. Her fears—the biggest being that she was doomed to a lifetime of being Man-handler Meg, regardless of how much she tried to change things.

Which was why she'd asked for help. She needed him.

Him, of all people.

The sudden burst of skepticism made him all the more confident in his own decision. He would help her, all right, and teach her his "secret."

Not that he was going to sink his fangs into her sweet neck and bring her over to the dark side, not when he had zero intention of staying there himself. He would never do that. He wasn't sure he even could. He was still learning the ropes from Garret and that wasn't something the older vampire had ever addressed.

But while he wouldn't turn her, he *would* teach her what he'd learned about seduction since his own turning.

One of the key factors that made vamps such sensual creatures was that they were fine-tuned to everything. They saw things more vividly, smelled them more intensely. They were aware of even the smallest sound, the briefest touch. While Meg's senses weren't supercharged like his, she still had them. If she learned to tap into them more, to use them, trust them, he had no doubt it would boost her sex appeal tenfold.

Enough to make her irresistible to every man in town.

The notion stirred a rush of jealousy. Understandable, of course. They were friends. It only made sense that he would feel protective of her. That, and he felt even more aroused than usual because she wasn't throwing herself at him like every other woman he met. She knew the real Dillon, which made her all the more determined *not* to sleep with him. Which made him all the more determined to sleep with her.

Thanks to free will, humans were much more powerful than they realized. While a vampire could, indeed, mesmerize and hypnotize, such supernatural persuasion meant a hill of beans if the subject wasn't willing.

Most women wanted to be swept away by passion. Deep down, they longed to experience wild, earth-shattering sex with a charismatic stranger, and so they were wide-open and vulnerable to his seduction.

Meg wasn't much different from every woman in that respect, and that was the problem in a nutshell. Dillon wasn't a stranger and so the last thing, the very last thing she wanted was wild, earth-shattering sex with him.

If he could seduce her to the point that she saw past the geek he used to be and embraced the hunk he'd become, he would know deep down inside that he truly had been acting all these years. That he wasn't a loser when it came to women.

That he wasn't a loser, period.

Seducing her would be the ultimate validation.

Excitement rippled through him. The scent of her strawberry shampoo spiraled through his head and hunger gnawed in his gut.

His mouth watered and his muscles tightened and it was all he could do to keep his ass in the chair.

He had to get a grip and take things slowly. One lesson at a time. Until she reached the point of no return. It might take a day. It might take a week. But eventually she would offer herself to him. Of that he felt certain.

In the meantime, it was business as usual.

He spent another fifteen minutes working on the code before closing the design screen and moving on to his second order of business—keeping his promise to Jake and Garret.

He stared through the wall of windows that separated the office from the fabrication shop. Jake McCann stood near a large metal table that held the skeleton of what would soon be the next custom chopper to roll through the doors of the motorcycle shop. Unlike most of the bikes they'd been doing, this one wasn't headed for a specific individual. Rather, it was a spec model being sent up north to advertise Skull Creek Choppers to the rest of the country. Jake took a few measurements before walking back over to another table that held a sheet of metal that would soon be the gas tank. He reached for a special tool and started tracing out the measurements.

Like most every other man in the small Texas town, Jake wore cowboy boots, jeans, a faded Resistol and an easygoing grin. But unlike most every other man in town, Jake was the real deal. A bona fide cowboy who'd been turned back in the eighteen hundreds. He'd spent his human life and a good chunk of his afterlife riding and working horses for a living. In the past decade or so, he'd traded in his horse for a hog. He was now one of the best cut-and-design guys in the chopper business. He was also deeply in love with Nikki Braxton, owner of the town's most popular beauty salon. Nikki was nice and beautiful and still very human. And she was staying that way as far as Jake was concerned.

As long as there was hope of finding and destroying Garret's sire.

Dillon's gaze shifted to the second man clad in jeans, a white T-shirt with a skull and cross bones on the front, and biker boots. He stood in the far corner near a large welding unit. He had a red, white and blue bandana tied around his head, a worn straw Resistol perched on top, and a pair of goggles secured over his eyes. Gloved hands reached for a long strip of metal. He powered on the ARC Unit and worked at the piece, firing and shaping until it started to resemble a rear fender.

Despite the hat, Garret wasn't anywhere close to a real cowboy. When he'd been turned back in the seventeen hundreds, he'd been a Texas patriot. A bona fide hero, and one of the founding fathers of Skull Creek. Not that anyone in town knew his identity. No, they thought he was just another leather-clad biker who'd invaded their small town to set up a manufacturing shop for his business. He liked fast motorcycles and even faster women, and he'd become somewhat of a role model for Dillon. The older vampire had been teaching him about his new vampness, showing him the ropes and outlining the vampire equivalent of the Ten Commandments.

Number one? No entering a home unless invited by the host. Public buildings were fair game, from the Piggly Wiggly to the local VFW Hall, but no personal dwellings unless specifically asked.

Number two—no direct sunlight.

Number three—no sharp objects, including knives, stakes and giant toothpicks like the ones used over at the Pig in the Poke Barbecue Joint.

Number four—no Italian restaurants. The old legend about garlic warding off vampires had turned out to be true. While it couldn't kill one of Dillon's kind, it could cause a lot of pain.

Number five—no solid food.

Number six—no changing eye colors. A vampire tended to reflect his emotions with his eyes and so they changed color frequently depending on his mood. Most vampires could control this. Since Dillon was young (in vamp years), he wasn't able to leash his feelings as easily as his older vamp buddies, but he was learning.

Number seven—no changing into a bat. Such a change took its toll and made the vampire weak and vulnerable. Which meant it was usually avoided.

Number eight—no indulging in blood and sex at the same time. Unless he wanted to tie himself to one woman for the rest of eternity. Talk about a snowball's chance in hell. Dillon had waited too long to unleash the wildness inside. He wasn't screwing things up by landing himself in a permanent relationship.

Number nine—no spending more than one night with any one woman. The more sex a vampire had with a woman, the more she wanted him. The last thing any vampire needed was a *Fatal Attraction* chasing him all over town.

Which led to number ten—keeping a low profile. A vampire's survival hinged on blending in with mainstream society, laying low and playing it cool.

Hence Garret's cowboy hat. The vamp was now living in a small Texas town, and *When in Rome*, as the saying went.

While Garret taught the importance of blending and urged Dillon to accept what he'd become, the vampire didn't seem all that content in his own skin.

Rather, he seemed restless.

Anxious.

Hungry.

But not for sex and blood. No, Garret wanted what Jake wanted—his humanity.

Dillon turned his attention back to the computer and clicked on his Internet Explorer. A few seconds later, he logged in at MeetVamps.com and scrolled down the screen to the first comment posted on his page yesterday.

Lovrgrlvamp: Hey, there, Skull Creek. I'm not wearing any panties and it's soooo hot. I'm here waiting for u, baby.

O-kay. It wasn't exactly what he had had in mind when he'd signed up and started blogging a few weeks ago—to get some sort of lead on the Ancient One—but at least he had visitors. Not that he really thought the father of all vamps would be chatting online, but it was all he'd been able to think of to track down the vampire who'd sired Garret.

The same vampire who held the key to humanity for all three of them.

Destroying the source would reverse the curse for Garret and anyone that he'd turned, which meant Jake and Dillon would be free, as well.

As much as Dillon liked being a vampire, he knew he couldn't stay that way. He'd caused his parents enough grief, which was why he'd yet to break the news about his new fanged status. He was hoping he wouldn't have to. The blogging had given him a few leads so far—a couple of names and locations that he was busy following up on. With any luck, he would gather even more information and, eventually, hit the jackpot. Once he located the Ancient One, Dillon would help the other two vamps destroy him. Then he would embrace his humanity once again and go back to playing the town geek.

The notion sent a wave of anxiety through him and made him all the more eager to break Bobby's record. Because he knew that this was it. His one chance to prove the truth to himself and build enough memories to last him through all the long, lonely human nights that lay ahead.

It was now or never.

He tensed, raking stiff fingers through his hair. His groin throbbed and he shifted in the leather seat. He was wound tight. Hungry. Starving even.

You should have gone for round two with Miss Hot Chick.

That's what he usually did. What he'd been doing since he'd come to understand what he'd become and learned the all-important fact that sex was as crucial a sustenance as blood. More so because feeding off sexual energy curbed the need for blood. Sure, he still had to feed in the traditional sense, but not nearly as often.

All the more reason he should have gone for an all-nighter.

He'd meant to, but when he'd walked back into the motel room after Meg and her proposition, he hadn't been able to push either out of his head. And while he'd turned into an oversexed, greedy vampire, he wasn't a two-timing, oversexed greedy vampire.

He hadn't been able to make himself get busy with one woman while thinking about another.

Which meant he wasn't anywhere close to being satisfied.

He raked another hand through his hair and took a long sip of the ice-cold beer sitting on the desk next to him. It did little to relieve the heat burning him up from the inside out.

He forced his attention back to the screen and read his own post. He'd been trying to spark somebody's memory.

SkullCreekVamp: I had the dream again. The details were so clear that I'm starting to think that it's not a dream at all, but the real deal. I'm remembering what happened to me. The pain. The hunger. The presence. Anybody else remember details? I want to remember a face, but I can't. Not yet.

Of course, that wasn't true. Dillon knew exactly who was responsible for his current state—Jake. The older vamp had turned him in a desperate attempt to give him back the life that had been ripped away when Garret had inadvertently attacked him. It had been the anniversary of Garret's turning and he'd been instinctively called back to the place of his death to relive those few moments when his humanity had slipped away. Like any vampire going through the turning, he'd been out of control. Mindless. Dillon had gotten in his way. He'd be six feet under right now if Jake hadn't intervened and turned him before it was too late.

Dillon would never forget that moment. The anguish at feeling his life slipping away, the excitement when he'd drank from Jake and new life had rushed back through him, strong and more potent than anything he'd ever felt before.

Likewise, Jake remembered his own sire—Garret.

Garret was the only member of the vamp trio who couldn't remember. Sure, he had a few images and impressions that had lingered in the two hundred years since he'd been turned in what was now the town square, but nothing clear when it came to the vamp responsible. One minute he'd been heading home after

Drop Dead Gorgeous

fighting for Texas independence, and the next he'd been attacked by a band of Mexican bandits. They'd robbed and killed him, or so the history books said. But someone—something—had happened along and changed all of that. One of the bandits? Maybe. Maybe not. He didn't know. There'd been no formal "Hi, I'm so-and-so, the ancient vampire who's going to turn you instead of leaving your dying carcass to rot." Rather, one minute he'd been following the light into the hereafter, and the next that light had been obliterated by a shadow looming over him. He remembered the pain ripping through his body, the smell—sweet, intense, intoxicating—that had filled his head, and a gold medallion.

Dillon glanced at the small sketch Garret had made of the piece of jewelry. He was hoping to gather a little info on some recent turnings to see if he could find a newly turned vampire who remembered the same gold pendant. If so, maybe the new vamp would remember even more—a physical description, maybe even a name.

He scrolled down the screen, his gaze drinking in the various posts.

Wannabevamp: Stop worrying about the f@#$%^& dream and just enjoy. I would give anything to turn. I tried the new enamel fangs and while they worked pretty well, they're nothing like the real thing.

Vamp4Life: Pain is a state of mind. A place you visit. If you choose not to go, then you're home free and you don't have anything to worry about. That, or you can try a Vicodin. Or even Xanax. Both work for me.

DarkAngel: So what if there was pain? The trick is not to fight it. Embrace the feeling, relish it, worship it. It's who you are. Who we are.

BradtheImpaler: Got 3 prs of fangs. This really rad dentist in Queens made them 4 me and they're sharp as hell. I get a discount on my next pair if I send him a referral. Wannabe, if ur up near Queens, want me to hook u up?

Fangtastic: I sell some high quality incisors if anyone's inter-

*ested. I'm even a preferred seller on eBay. I offer free shipping,
too, if you order more than one pair. I also have some really cool
vampire porn.*

Lovrgrlvamp*: I like pain. Spankings are my favorite. Maybe
we should get together and whip each other. I'm game if you're
ever out the Chicago way. Or maybe I could head down to Texas.
Whip me, cowboy. Whip me goooooooooo…*

He read the rest of the comments—most of which, with the
exception of Dark Angel, were ripe with sexual innuendo and tips
for going vamp—before posting his next entry where he mentioned the location of his turning (also Garret's) and the timing
(over two hundred years ago). He was just powering off his
computer when Jake opened the glass door and ducked his head
inside the office.

"Hey, bud, can you help me out for a second? I want to fit the
new tank in place and I need an extra pair of hands."

"Sure thing." Dillon followed Jake into the shop and helped
hold the tank in place so the vamp could take more measurements.

Then he spent the next few hours learning the finer art of tank
shaping. A good thing since he was desperate for a distraction
from the need gnawing at his belly and the sudden vision of
Meg—her naked body stretched out beneath him, her eyes glazed
with passion, her bottom lip full and swollen from his kisses, her
breasts flushed, her nipples hard and greedy, her body so warm
and wet—that stuck in his brain.

But the more he trailed his fingers over the warm, smooth
metal, kneading and shaping, the more the vision turned to a full-
blown fantasy.

He felt her warm skin beneath his hands. Her breasts, hot and
flushed, pressed against his chest. Her mouth ate at his. Her
body sucked at his cock…

Shit. He wanted her now.

Not tomorrow when they met for their first lesson.

Not a few days from now after he'd seduced her to the point
that she no longer resisted the attraction between them.

Not next week after they'd had a chance to spend more time together and she fell hook, line and sinker for his vamp charisma.

Now.

The need ate away inside of him as he finished the tank and finally called it a night. He had little more than an hour until daylight. Plenty of time to head out to Garret's place.

He'd been staying with the older vampire at a large ranch on the outskirts of town now that his own house was off-limits. While he had a pretty secluded place, he had far too many windows for comfort. There was also the fact that his parents were camped out in his front yard, hell-bent on deprogramming him from whatever cult he'd fallen in with.

Garret's ranch house had an old wine cellar that provided a dark, safe place to sleep during the day. The spread was also sizable, which afforded plenty of seclusion.

He climbed onto his motorcycle and kicked the bike to life. He sped out of the parking lot with every intention of turning east toward the ranch.

Only his hands seemed to have a mind of their own as they hung a sharp left and headed west. He opened up the engine. The bike screamed toward the center of town and the small two-story colonial that sat a few blocks over from Main Street.

He went left again, then right. His headlamp cast wicked shadows across the pavement as the motorcycle ate up the distance to the brick structure that sat several houses down from the corner.

Easing his bike over to the curb on the opposite side of the street, he killed the engine. The motor sizzled and hissed, the faint noise blending in with the buzz of crickets and a dozen other sounds that drifted on the cool April breeze. Sounds barely discernable to anyone but Dillon.

Since he'd been turned it was as if someone had upped the amp level in his brain. He heard *everything*—the snores of an old couple several houses down, the obnoxious voice of the host of some infomercial blazing from a nearby neighbor's television set, the rustling of cans and paper as a raccoon clawed through a trash can, the steady *shhhhhhhh* as someone took a whiz in their john.

He fixed his gaze on the house surrounded by a white picket fence and overflowing flower beds. A large wraparound porch spanned the bottom level. A swing sat at the far corner. The second level had a wraparound balcony filled with potted plants and white wicker patio furniture.

It was far from the small log cabin Meg had shared with her father before his death, but then Dillon knew that was the idea—to bury the past and forget. This place had lots of windows and French doors and bright yellow trim. It looked as feminine as the woman who now lived inside it. Her car sat in the driveway, the brand-new yellow Mustang convertible, a far cry from the old brown Chevy pickup she'd driven her junior year of high school. The car was flashy, sexy, exciting.

Just like Meg.

He'd always thought so, even way back when she'd driven the truck. He'd just never had the courage to tell her, particularly after those disastrous first kisses.

The house was one of the oldest in town, built sometime back in the 1800s before central air and heat. A portable air-conditioning unit sat in the window near a set of French doors on the second story. The engine purred steadily until Dillon narrowed his gaze. He felt the heat rush through his body as he sent the silent command. The motor coughed and sputtered. The *purrrrr* turned to a distinctive whine.

The minutes ticked off one by one, as he waited for Meg to appear in the doorway.

She was yards away, the room where she stood completely black, yet he saw every detail. She wore only a pink T-shirt and lace panties. Sweat dotted her brow and beaded on her skin as she threw the lock. Hauling open the doors, she stood there framed in the double doorway, the sheer curtains billowing behind her as she drank in the fresh night air. She took several deep breaths and her frustration mounted.

She needed more relief than the cool breeze whispering through the trees.

She'd been sleeping alone with the exception of a bright red vibrator she kept in her top nightstand drawer and she was desperate. She needed a real man, and she needed him soon.

The thought carried on the breeze, through the trees and across the pavement. It slid into his brain where he stood yards away.

Watching.

Waiting.

Wanting.

Hunger gripped him, a fierce ache that started in his gut and spread through his entire body, making him tremble and shake. And suddenly it didn't matter who came on to who. He wanted to touch her. He needed to.

He was going to.

Right. *Now*.

6

SHE NEEDED TO DITCH THE failing window unit, take a bite out of her savings and invest in central air-conditioning.

Meg came to that conclusion as she stood in the doorway and welcomed the faint rush of wind that whispered over her flushed skin. She'd been tapped out after paying the down payment on her dream home, and rather than replace the major appliances, she'd tried to get away with repairing and refurbishing.

In the five years since buying her place, she'd fixed the upstairs unit not once, but four times now.

The air conditioner grumbled and growled.

Make that five.

She made a mental note to call Mr. Abel, the air conditioning guy, first thing in the morning and moved on to the next window in the room. A few seconds later, she had all three of the room's windows wide-open. Air filtered through the space, relieving some of the stifling heat that had pulled her from sleep.

Then again, it hadn't been just the heat that had kept her from nodding off. She'd spent the better part of the past hour tossing and turning, trying to push Dillon Cash completely out of her head.

So what if he was sexy now? And handsome? And—with the exception of his clothes—had the whole hot-guy thing going? He was still just Dillon. Her buddy. Her pal. The guy who'd given her *the* worst kiss of her entire life.

Sure, he appeared convincing, but she knew better. She wasn't the least bit hot and bothered by his new image.

She *wasn't.*

Ignoring a sudden ripple of awareness that drifted down her spine, she walked back over to the bed. She cast a quick glance at the open doorway. Moonlight spilled onto the balcony, illuminating the potted azaleas, the small white wicker table and matching chairs, a swaying wind chime. The soft *ting ting* echoed in her ears. Everything looked and sounded the same, yet she couldn't escape the sudden inexplicable feeling that something was different.

That someone—or something—was there with her.

For a split second, she saw a tall, muscular figure standing near the rails, the broad shadow edged in moonlight.

Her heart kick-started and she blinked. Just like that, the image disappeared.

She ignored the sudden drumming in her chest, walked back over to her bed, stretched out on top of the covers and clamped her eyes shut. Her hormones were definitely getting the best of her. She was so wound up, so desperate for some male company that she was starting to imagine it.

A man on her balcony.

If only.

Forcing a deep breath, she focused on the steady rise and fall of her chest. *Up. Down. In. Out…* Soon, the tension in her body slipped away. Her muscles went lax and her mind grew fuzzy.

She was this close to dozing off when a sudden gust of wind rushed through the window and the curtains billowed and snapped.

Her eyes popped open and her skin prickled. Goose bumps danced along her arms. She reached for the lamp and a blaze of light chased away the shadows. Her gaze ping-ponged from one corner of the room to the next, but there was no one there. Just a dresser overflowing with cosmetics, a stand-up mirror, a pile of undies she hadn't had the time to fold and a stack of new fall fashion catalogs from various distributors.

She killed the light, wiggled her way under the sheet and clamped her eyes shut again. She forced aside the sudden image of Dillon that popped into her head—his bright gaze green and blazing, his mouth crooked into a killer smile—and concentrated on mentally reciting tomorrow's schedule.

She had the Weatherby twins for a prom fitting at ten. Elise Harwell and her youngest daughter at eleven. Melissa Sue Jones and her four bridesmaids at noon. Melissa Sue's mother at one. Old Mrs. Cromwell at two-thirty… While she had an idea what she was going to show the twins and Melissa Sue, she was at a loss for Elise. While she'd seen the woman's youngest daughter around town, she'd never actually met her face-to-face. She had no clue what colors the girl liked or what sort of styles she might be interested in. At the same time, she couldn't be all that different from her four older sisters who were the spitting image of their well-groomed, fashion-conscious mother. Elise lived for the latest trends and hottest colors.

By the time Meg had mentally rifled through her newest selections and narrowed them down to a handful of the most chic possibilities, her heart had slowed and her nerves had calmed. Peace seeped through her, pushing away consciousness and muffling the whine of the failing air conditioner, the *tick-tock* of her bedside clock, the occasional *snap* and *pop* of the window sheers.

She was *this close* to conking out completely when she felt the faint pull and tug on the cotton sheet.

She cracked open one eye in time to see the sheet slither south, down her legs, to puddle around her ankles. The wind whispered over her toes. The sensation crept higher, feathering over her calves, her knees, her thighs. The edge of her T-shirt lifted and the hem slid upward, baring a pair of silky pink panties, several inches of pale skin, her navel, more skin, the undersides of her breasts. Her nipples tightened. The material snagged and caught on the ripe tips.

Her breath caught, her chest rose and her breasts strained against the fabric. It was a highly unsettling sensation. Erotic. Forbidden. *Impossible!*

Her other eye opened and she watched in stunned amazement as the material lifted, easing over her nipples, exposing the throbbing peaks. The edge of the shirt bunched as if invisible fingers tugged at the thin covering—

She clamped her eyes shut as her heart started to pound.

The wine. It had to be the wine.

She'd never been much of a drinker, which was why the bottle had lasted her over a year. She'd used it primarily for cooking and had indulged in the occasional glass with dinner. But never right before bed. And with a Twinkie chaser.

Sugared and sloshed. That was the problem. No wonder she was imagining things. The sheet. The T-shirt. The man framed in the doorway—

Wait a second.

She blinked and for a split second, she saw the familiar green eyes and sensuous mouth, but then the image blurred and faded.

Uh, yeah. Because he's not real. No way is Dillon Cash standing on your balcony. You're sloshed and hallucinating, end of story.

No more wine, she vowed, tugging her shirt down and yanking the sheet back up. She clamped her eyes shut. A dream. That's all it had been. A crazy, bizarre dream brought on by too much sugar and alcohol.

A crazy, bizarre, semi-pleasant dream, she admitted several minutes later, her body still buzzing from the sensation of fabric gliding this way and that. She drew a deep breath. Her nipples rubbed against the cotton of her T-shirt and her breasts tingled.

Okay, so maybe there was something to be said for a good Chardonnay and a couple of Twinkies right before bed.

On that stirring thought, she drifted into a deep sleep, not the least bit alarmed when the sheet started to glide down and her T-shirt started to inch its way up.

Again.

HE COULDN'T ACTUALLY touch her.

The truth crystallized as he stood in the open doorway and tried to step over the threshold. An invisible wall barred his way and refused to give him access to the tempting woman stretched out on the bed. Her T-shirt was up under her arms, her luscious breasts full and flushed, the sheet bunched down at her feet. Her skin was pale and soft looking against the pastel green sheets. His gaze went to the skimpy panties she wore. Not even a wisp of hair pushed through the scant lace and he knew the skin beneath was as smooth and as bare as the rest of her.

His mouth watered and his hands trembled. He could feel the need vibrating from her lush body. It called to him, begging him forward, tempting him until he shook with the force of it.

Wake her up, a voice whispered. *She'll invite you in.*

If she were every other women in town.

She wasn't. She was the one woman, the only woman who'd managed to resist him. That was why tonight wasn't about sating his own hunger.

It was about stirring hers.

He held tight to the thought and stiffened against his own urges.

Focusing his attention on the nearly empty wine bottle, he narrowed his gaze and sent a mental command. The bottle lifted, floating from the nightstand until it hovered over her full breasts. He gave the slightest motion of his head and the bottle tilted. A trickle of wine splashed over one nipple and her eyes popped open.

Panic chased confusion across her expression as her gaze darted between the wine bottle and the open doorway where he stood. Her gaze collided with his.

Relax. He sent the mental command and hoped that she would be too exhausted, too half-asleep to refuse. Her eyes widened, her lips parted and he had the fleeting thought that she was going to scream.

It's just a dream. He sent the silent thought and she caught her bottom lip. Her eyes glazed with need. *A fantasy,* he added. *So sit back and enjoy yourself.*

Her eyelids fluttered closed and her body relaxed.

He shifted his attention back to the wine bottle and watched as the glass tilted again. Another trickle splashed over her nipple and dribbled down the side of her breast to dampen the sheet beneath her.

The tip pebbled, responding to the sensation, begging for more. Her body arched, seeming to strain for more of the sensation, but she didn't open her eyes this time.

Because it was just a fantasy to her.

A very vivid, very erotic figment of her imagination.

The realization sent a rush of relief through him—he wasn't in a hurry to blow his cover and dodge a lynch mob—followed by a wave of irritation. Because as much as he liked being the star of her erotic musings, he wanted her fully awake and conscious when she gave herself to him.

The thought plagued him a full second before she drank in a deep breath and her chest lifted. Her nipple quivered and his gaze went to the faint blue vein barely visible beneath the translucent skin near one areola. Pain splintered his head and he felt the sharpness of his teeth against his tongue. His cock throbbed.

From the corner of his eye, he caught his reflection and saw the deep purple glow of his gaze. He stiffened, fighting against the emotion whirling inside of him until his eyes brightened into a rich vivid green.

Easy.

The command whispered through his head and he held tight to his control. He shifted his attention back to the wine bottle. The glass dipped until the edge grazed one of her ripe nipples. She gasped. The sound sizzled across the open space between them and slid into his ears, stirring what lived and breathed inside of him. A rush of longing pulsed from her flushed body and suddenly he knew beyond a doubt that she hadn't been with a man in one hell of a long time.

The realization sent a strange rush of satisfaction through him and made him all the more determined to resist his own damned hunger and satisfy hers.

The bottle tilted, drip-dropping wine over her bare stomach.

The rosy liquid pooled in her navel, slid decadently toward her lace panties and turned the white edge a pale pink.

She moaned and he moved lower, dribbling a little more here, a little more there, until the bottle was completely empty and her panties were damp with wine and her own need.

He trailed the cool edge of the bottle down the outside of one bare leg, up the inside of her knee, her thigh, building the anticipation until he reached the lacy barrier between her legs. He rubbed the mouth of the container up and down against the already drenched material. She gasped and wiggled her hips for more.

He felt his own gaze burn as he willed the scrap of lace down her legs until it tugged free of her ankles and feet and collapsed on the bed beside her.

Her thighs fell open, giving him an unobstructed view of the slick, pouty folds that begged for his attention.

At the first touch of the cool glass against her soft, tender slit, her eyelids fluttered open again.

She gazed first at the bottle between her legs and then at him. There was an instant of confusion and panic, and then the feelings eased into a glaze of passion as she smiled and mumbled, "No wonder Babe likes Twinkies."

He rubbed her with the bottle as her heavy gaze drank in his face, burning a path over his shoulders, his chest, down to the prominent erection that threatened to bust out of his jeans. Her attention lingered and the urge to step inside the room, shove his zipper down, spread her legs and sink into her wet body nearly overwhelmed him.

He couldn't and so he stared at her, into her, willing her eyes shut again. Finally, she complied, leaning her head back into the softness of the pillow as she gave in to the rush of sensation.

He continued the stroking, up and down, side to side until a drop of warmth spilled from her slick folds and slid down the neck of the dark glass. Her back arched and she came up off the bed. A breathy moan sailed past her lips as a wave of ecstasy crashed over her.

Watching her body tighten and pulse was almost as satisfying as relishing it firsthand. He could practically feel the rush of warmth as she milked him.

His erection throbbed and he felt the bubbling warmth that pulsed along its length, along with something else. A prickling awareness at the base of his spine that told him his time was nearly up.

Gathering his last shred of control, he drank in one last look at her and forced himself away from the doorway. Without a sound, he scaled the waist-high rail and dropped to the ground. In the blink of an eye, he covered the distance to his bike.

A faint glow tinged the horizon as he straddled the seat and gunned the engine. A few minutes later, he sped through town and hit the county road that led to the ranch.

He reached his destination just as the first rays of sunlight topped the surrounding trees. His boots started to smoke as he strode toward the house. Heat sizzled through the soles of his feet and sent spurts of pain up his calves.

He hit the front porch and stumbled inside. While he was out of the direct sunlight, there was still light filtering in through the windows, sucking at his strength as he wobbled toward the back hallway and the door that led to the wine cellar. He fumbled for the handle, tugged open the door and fell down the first few steps. The wood creaked shut behind him and the darkness quickly swallowed him up. He found his footing and took the steps two at a time until he reached the bottom of the staircase and another hallway.

Garret had spent an entire month breaking the cellar down into two large living areas. A single hallway divided the two sections. The door to the left was shut solid. A powerful presence emanated from inside and Dillon knew Garret had been wise enough to get his ass in bed at a decent hour.

Dillon reached for the second doorknob. A few seconds later, he yanked off his smoldering boots, stretched out the king-size bed that sat in one corner of the massive room and tried to calm his rapidly beating heart.

In the two months since he'd turned, he'd never stayed out past daybreak. He knew better. He closed his eyes and tried to welcome the all-encompassing blackness, but he was too worked up.

Not because he'd nearly gotten himself roasted.

Rather than the sharp odor of melted rubber and blistered skin, he smelled the intoxicating aroma of sweet wine and warm, aroused woman.

His nostrils flared and the scent magnified, along with the image of Meg, her body flushed and panting and eager for more.

Bobby's record didn't stand a chance in hell.

IT HAD BEEN THE MOST incredible sex *ever*.

That is, it would have been the most incredible sex *if* it had been real.

That's what Meg told herself when she opened her eyes the next morning, her T-shirt still bunched up under her arms, her undies laying next to her feet. Sunlight streamed through the open French doors, illuminating the stained sheets and empty wine bottle.

Heat rushed to her cheeks as she forced herself upright. She set the bottle on the nightstand, tossed the leftover Twinkie wrappers into a nearby trash can and tried to ignore the telltale ache between her legs as she climbed from the bed. She had nothing to be embarrassed about. She'd masturbated dozens of times before.

But never with Dillon Cash watching her.

A *fantasy* Dillon, she reminded herself as she headed for the bathroom and a cold shower. While last night's orgasm had been very real, the circumstances surrounding it had been anything but.

Dillon had *not* been standing in her doorway.

The wine bottle had *not* moved on its own.

N-o-t.

Her mind made up, she spent the next half hour getting ready for work.

When she finally walked out her front door, coffee in hand,

she'd managed to dismiss all of her crazy thoughts and face the truth—she was horny. So much so, that she was cooking up hot, sizzling fantasies and trying to turn them into reality.

She tossed her briefcase onto the passenger's seat, set her mug in the cup holder and turned to retrieve the newspaper that sat near the curb.

She didn't have time to waste entertaining the impossible. She had a business to run. She had a new ad running today, complete with a coupon, and she hoped with all of her heart that Glenda, the owner of Skull Creek's one and only newspaper, had gotten it right. Last time Meg had wanted to run a twenty-percent-off coupon, Glenda—who was seventy-six and extremely hard of hearing—had printed it as sixty. Meg had felt obliged to honor the coupon rather than piss off any customers, and so she'd lost a ton of money.

Instead of calling in the ad this time, she'd typed it out and handed it to the old woman herself.

She leaned over and reached for the paper. Just an inch shy, her gaze snagged on the black marks near the curb.

Her memory stirred and suddenly she was back in her bed, her breathing ragged and her body convulsing. Through the pleasure beating at her temples and the pounding of her heart, she heard the grumble of an engine and the squeal of tires and—

She abandoned the crazy thought, ignored the strange tingling in her gut and grabbed her newspaper. Climbing into her car, she shoved the key into the ignition and backed out. Shifting into Drive, she hit the gas and didn't look back.

Not even a peek.

Because no way in hell, heaven or the in-between had Dillon Cash shown up at her house last night, climbed onto her balcony and watched her have the best orgasm of her entire life.

At least that's what Meg told herself.

The trouble was, deep down, she wasn't so sure she believed it.

7

"GET. *OUT*."

The incredulous voice slid into Meg's ears. She glanced from her computer screen to the young woman who sat at a small table in the far corner of the stockroom, a newspaper spread out in front of her.

Terry Lynn Hargrove was Meg's one and only full-time employee. Unlike Meg's three part-time employees, she wasn't a local. She'd been born and raised in nearby Junction. They'd met nearly ten years ago at a community college in San Antonio when they'd both been fashion merchandising majors. Meg had gone on to graduate from SACC while Terry had quit to marry the man of her dreams.

Said man was now her ex-husband and the star of her revenge fantasies—she'd caught him cheating. Terry now lived in Skull Creek, worked for Meg during the day and went to school via several online study courses at night.

She had long brown hair, a centerfold figure, perfect teeth and brown eyes so wide and innocent they would make Bambi envious. She could also spot a couture knockoff at fifty paces. She wore the latest wraparound skirt with rhinestone rocker tee and knee-high cowboy boots. Back in Junction, she'd been Junction High's Best-Dressed Senior, as well as head cheerleader and homecoming queen. Last year, she'd earned the honor of being the first out-of-towner to make Tilly's coveted list. A huge honor she'd celebrated by going an extra five miles on her treadmill.

Terry was also a serious health nut since she'd packed on a

whopping twenty pounds while married to The Loser. She'd lost the weight along with the man, and was now determined to steer clear of both.

She sipped a soy protein shake and held up the newspaper. "Did you see this?"

"What?"

"The picture on the front page of last week's Lifestyle section?" Terry waved several sheets of newsprint.

"I haven't had time." Meg turned her attention back to the computer and finished ordering the prom dresses for the Weatherby twins—they'd settled on floor-length, bubblegum colored taffeta with rhinestones. A fitting that had gone surprisingly fast since the girls had come prepared with a copy of teen *Vogue* and a clear idea of what they wanted. "Why are we reading last week's paper?" she asked Terry.

"To catch up on the soaps. I'm here all day, so I don't get a chance to watch my favorites anymore, and I had a lot of homework last week so I couldn't read Marge's Titillating TV column. Claire told Darius she was pregnant."

"And Darius is…?"

"Only the hottest hunk on daytime TV. Claire says it's his, but she's a skank. I bet it's Juan's."

"Why don't you just record the shows?"

"Because then I would have to buy a DVD player that's made in China. I refuse to support an industry that's neck-deep in child labor."

Terry was also a humanitarian, a member of PETA and just last year she'd participated in a walk to free the lobsters.

"You could always get Tivo."

"And contribute to corporate world domination?"

"You can record multiple shows."

She seemed to think about it. "I *could* write an explicit letter of disapproval when I sign up. Just to make my position clear. Then it wouldn't be as if I were compromising my principles."

"Just bending them a little."

"Exactly." Terry's attention shifted back to the newspaper and she shook her head. "Dillon Cash and Ava Laraby. Can you believe that?"

Meg's fingers stalled on the keyboard. Obviously she wasn't the only one who hadn't bought his startling transformation.

She remembered last night and awareness rippled through her. *You bought it, sister, and it's just a matter of time until you're falling all over him just like every other woman in town.*

She ignored the sudden zing of excitement that spiraled through her and summoned her initial disbelief. "It is pretty wild, isn't it?" Ava Laraby had been the dance captain for the Skull Creek Stars way back when. She'd been beautiful and outgoing and Dillon would have sold his soul to the devil for even a smile from her. "Not that people can't change," she heard herself add. "They most definitely can and we shouldn't be so judgmental."

"I'll try, but it just isn't that easy. I mean, *Dillon* and *Ava*. They don't blend. They're like water and oil. Fish and red wine. Gucci and Donna Karan."

"I wouldn't say they're so different. Dillon's not that far out of her league."

"Are you kidding?" She gave Meg a *get real* look. "*She's* way out of *his*. Her hotness has definitely fizzled even since I've known her. Look at that outfit? There's a reason they call them skinny jeans. They're for skinny people, otherwise they make your ass look like a billboard and I speak from experience." She took another drink of her shake. "And that shirt. Somebody needs to tell this girl that floral is over." She squinted. "And is that a spiral perm? Do they even do those anymore?"

"I happen to know for a fact that To Dye For does at least five spirals a month." When Terry arched an eyebrow, Meg shrugged. "Nikki mentioned it the last time I was in. She said it's still one of her hottest dos."

"Yeah, for the middle-aged mom's club." Terry shook her head. "They're opposite sides of the spectrum."

"You honestly think Dillon is too hot for Ava?"

Terry nailed her with a pointed stare. "You don't?" She tossed the paper.

Meg caught the newsprint and stared at the picture taken a few weeks ago at one of the local honky tonks. Even in worn Levi's and his *Computers Need Love Too* T-shirt, Dillon looked hot. Intense. Sexy. His hair was mussed, his jaw shadowed with stubble. His eyes glittered with a knowing sparkle that made her insides quiver.

"He looks even yummier in person," Terry continued. "I saw him over at Jimmy Jo's sports bar a few weeks back. I thought I was going to hyperventilate. But then I don't have to tell you that. You two are friends, right?"

"We don't see each other as often as we used to, but yes, we still talk."

Among other things, a tiny voice whispered. A voice Meg quickly stifled.

Terry grinned. "Maybe you could introduce us."

"I've already introduced you about a dozen times." But Terry had never given Dillon a second glance.

Until now.

Meg tossed the paper back and the girl grinned.

"My bad." She stared at the picture again. "I honestly don't remember him looking like this. He's definitely upped his hotness level. Has he been taking that Carnal class with you?"

"He's doing research online."

"On how to be a hottie?"

"Something like that."

"It's working."

Unfortunately.

Meg ignored the crazy thought. Dillon's newfound sex appeal was a good thing, even if it tested her control.

Because it tested her control.

If he could make her forget the man he'd been and inspire a megadose of lust for the man he'd become, then he could teach her how to do the same. Starting today. She'd already left two messages about lunch. Once he called her back, they would meet and the lessons would begin. Her next sexual encounter was sure to involve a man actually coming on to her, rather than the other way around.

That is, if she didn't backslide, forget her principles and hump Dillon first.

Her nipples tingled at the thought and she frowned. "Speaking of work—" she hit the Place Order button and pushed to her feet "—Elise and her daughter should be here any minute."

As if on cue, the bell on the front door tingled.

Terry sighed and set the paper aside. "Any ideas what you want me to set up in the dressing room?" she asked as she got to her feet.

"I don't think we need to get too complicated. All of Elise's girls went for the first Marc Jacobs I showed them."

"Marc Jacobs it is." Terry grinned. "The girl would have to be nuts to break that tradition."

Nuts, or just plain stubborn.

Meg came to that conclusion after a fruitless half hour with Elise's daughter, Honey Harwell.

She eyed the seventeen-year-old who stood on a platform in the monstrous dressing room. Honey had the same shade of blond hair as her mother and her four older sisters. But unlike the other Harwell women, Honey didn't wear her silky locks styled in the latest trend. Rather, she'd stuffed them under a baseball cap that read Lady Bulldogs in honor of the local girl's volleyball team. She wore blue jean overalls, a baseball jersey and tennis shoes.

"But your sister wore a dress just like this when she went to her prom," Elise Harwell told her youngest daughter. A former local beauty queen, the forty-something woman was now the mayor's wife and mother of five. As usual, her long blond hair was perfectly coiffed, her nails buffed and polished, and her face made-up with the latest Chanel lipstick and Christian Dior eye shadow. She wore a cream-colored silk blouse, matching skirt, a pair of gold sling-back stilettos and a determined look that said she wasn't leaving without a dress. "You simply *have* to go with this. It's too fabulous for words."

Honey eyed the dress her mother held up and shook her head. "No."

"But this is perfect," Elise insisted.

"It's *yellow*."

"Buttercup, dear—" the older woman waved a hand "—and it's the ideal shade for your skin tone. Just try it."

Honey shook her head and crossed her arms. "I'm not wearing anything named after a flower. Or anything that has flowers on it. Or anything that looks flouncy. I'm *so* not doing flouncy."

"But—"

"*No.*"

The woman looked ready to argue, but then her lips tightened. "All right, then. No flowers," she finally muttered. She let out an exasperated sigh as she handed the dress back to Meg. "And no flounce."

Bye-bye Marc.

"Of course." Meg slid the hanger onto a nearby peg and reached for a soft, shimmering pink number that hung on a nearby rack with several others Terry had brought in after Honey's first *"Not in this lifetime."* "I bet this would look great."

The girl took one look and pursed her lips. "If I wanted to look like a giant piece of bubble gum."

O-kay.

"If I didn't know better—" Elise forced a smile despite her pinched brow "—I'd say someone isn't even remotely excited about going to her one and only senior prom."

"I'm not excited about going. I don't want to go. You're making me."

"Nonsense." The woman waved red-tipped fingers. "Everyone goes to their senior prom. Why, every one of your sisters was either prom queen or a member of the royal court."

"I'm not my sisters, and I'm not going to be part of a royal anything. Talk about lame."

"There's nothing lame about being popular, dear," Elise said with tight lips, the flush creeping higher, all the way into her cheeks. "What about forest green? To match her eyes?" she asked Meg.

"Forget it," the girl said before Meg could reach for another selection. "I'm not going as a cucumber."

Elise's smile slipped. "Perhaps we could try something in red?"

"I'll look a Fruit Roll-Ups."

"How about salmon?"

The girl rolled her eyes. "That's just a fancy name for orange. I'm *so* not doing orange."

The woman's flushed cheeks turned splotchy. "How about navy blue?" she questioned.

"Too dark," Honey chimed in.

"How about bronze?"

"Too flashy."

"How about chartreuse?"

"Too Shrek-ey."

"How about a valium?"

Meg smiled. "I'm afraid I haven't restocked my supply of prescription sedatives, but I do have a nice Chardonnay chilling in the back."

"Thank God." Elise waved a hand. "I swear this child is going to send me to an early grave."

"We don't have to do this," Honey reminded her mother.

"Yes, we do. You can't miss your senior prom."

"Why not?"

"Because," Elise countered. "It's a once in a lifetime thing. A tradition. No daughter of mine is *not* going to her one and only senior prom. You'll regret it."

"I will not."

"Will, too."

Both Elise and her daughter stared at Meg. "Tell her," Elise said. "She'll regret it."

"Tell her I won't."

"I hate to say it, but you probably will."

Honey shrugged a stubborn shoulder. "You're just taking her side because you want to sell us a dress."

Meg opened her mouth to tell Honey that she didn't just want to sell a dress—she knew the regret firsthand—but Elise cut her off. "Honey Helen Harwell, that's a very unladylike thing to say. Just wait until I tell your father. You'll be lucky if he doesn't ground you."

Honey gave her first smile of the day. "Maybe he'll do it on prom night."

"Oh, no you don't. Don't think you're getting out of it that easy—"

"One glass of chilled Chardonnay coming right up," Meg cut in. "Why don't you two come up with a few must-haves—cut, color, style, etc—and when I get back I'll see what I can do to find something that makes everyone happy?" Elise nodded, Honey shrugged and Meg decided to get the hell out of Dodge before things turned physical between the former Miss Skull Creek and the captain of the Lady Bulldogs.

"Let's start over," Elise let out an exasperated sigh as she turned toward her daughter. "What color did *you* have in mind?"

"I don't know. Maybe camouflage."

"Forget the glass," Elise's voice caught up with Meg just before she disappeared through the curtained doorway. "Just bring me the whole damned bottle."

HE WAS THE HOTTEST GUY in the Piggly Wiggly.

Meg came to that conclusion later that afternoon as she stared at the tall dark haired stranger who stood in the meat section next to a life-size cutout of Roger the Rump Roast.

A white dress shirt, undone at the collar, framed his broad shoulders. Black trousers accented long legs, a trim waist and a really tight butt.

The guy, not Roger.

He leaned over to pick up a boneless shoulder roast. His trousers pulled and tugged in all the right places and Meg's mouth went dry. Her grip on the box of Twinkies she'd been holding loosened and thudded into her shopping cart. Last night's fantasy must still be affecting her.

She'd closed up shop over a half hour ago, after a long, endless day waiting for Dillon to return her phone calls.

Obviously he wasn't all that interested in her proposition, despite his claim otherwise.

And why would he be? He was already smoking hot. Wardrobe tips were just the icing on the already scrumptious cake.

Meanwhile she hadn't even made it into the oven.

If Dillon wasn't going to share his secret, then all hope of making Tilly's list was shot to hell and back. She was back at square one, still looking for that extra something that would give her an edge and force the men in town to see her in a different light.

A sexy light.

Sexually frustrated or not, she wasn't breaking her vow—no more first moves. No, if Dillon wasn't going to help her, she was doomed to wait until she found that extra something herself, which meant she was in store for more frustrating nights like the last one.

Which meant she needed Twinkies. Lots of Twinkies.

Hence her impromptu visit to the nearest grocery store.

She eyed the man again, doing a sweep once, twice, before shifting her attention to old man Darlington who stood near the frozen chickens, eyeing a package of chicken wings. Moving on, she spotted Hubert Humsucker stockpiling chocolate Ho Hos just a few feet away and Leonard Bunker who stood near an end cap checking out a Spam display.

Yes, he was definitely the hottest guy to make it past the open hoofs at the front entrance. Sure, he wasn't as super sexy as the star of last night's fantasy, but he was close.

An image stirred and she saw Dillon looking dark and delicious in faded jeans, a worn T-shirt and an expression that said he wanted to swallow her whole.

Okay, maybe hot guy wasn't *that* close. But he definitely beat out the handful of losers from her past. He was handsome enough. He was also new in town—the cousin of a cousin of a cousin of Shirley Waltrip who owned a local real estate firm. She had hired him straight out of broker school—which meant he had no preconceived notions about Meg. And, more importantly, he was smiling at her.

He was smiling at *her*.

She tamped down the urge to waltz over and introduce herself. Instead, she waited, maintaining eye contact, mentally urging him to come to her.

He abandoned the roast and stepped toward her. *Atta boy*. Her heart kicked up a notch, but it wasn't anywhere close to the breakneck stampede she'd felt last night.

Not that she was making comparisons. Last night had been so far out there. A wild and crazy dream.

This was the real thing.

He stepped closer, his strong, purposeful stride eating up the distance between them and she started to think that maybe she didn't need Dillon's secret, after all. Really, she'd been walking the walk and talking the talk for twelve years. It only made sense that some man would finally notice on his own.

She smiled and said, "Hi."

He smiled and said—

"Game three of the NBA finals. Spurs or the Heat?" she heard a voice say behind her.

Meg's head whipped around and she found herself staring at a short, squatty woman in her fifties. The lady wore a hair net, a white smock and a badge that read *Fiber is my Friend*.

Genevieve Crandall was one of the store's clerks. She worked the register and handled the incontinent section, which had grown to take up a complete aisle since the second retirement community had opened up on the outskirts of town just last month.

"The employees got a pool going with some of our steady customers," she told Meg. "Most everybody's putting their money on San Antonio, including Paul in cleaning products, on account of it's the closest thing we got to a home team. But Darlene in dairy likes the Heat because she has a sister down in Florida. Loretta and Lettie, the Bakersfield sisters who buy all the pork-'n-beans every time we run a special, put their money on Florida, too, 'cause they got a thing for that *CSI Miami* show. I like the show, but I ain't sure it's worth risking fifty bucks. I thought you could give me your pick."

"I'm sorry, Genevieve. I was talking to this nice gentleman." Meg shifted her attention back to hot guy. "I'm Meg. It's nice to meet you."

"Colt Grainger. I buy and sell ranch property."

"Shirley's cousin, right?"

"Twice removed, but yeah. I'm new around here and I could really use someone to show me around. I was wondering—"

"So was I," Genevieve persisted. "Come on, Meg. You gotta help an old lady out. I've got a new pair of orthopedic inserts riding on this. The Spurs have a better rebound record, but the Heat had multiple three-pointers last year. Both teams are neck and neck on blocked shots." She stared expectantly at Meg who stared expectantly at Colt.

A strange look came over his face as he eyed her. "You know basketball?"

"I—" Meg blurted, but it was Genevieve's crackly voice that chimed in, "Sure as shootin' she does. Why, this gal knows everything when it comes to sports. Girl was born to it. Daddy coached football over at the high school and took us to five con-secutive championships. Four for our basketball team. Six for soccer. Eight track-and-field state finals. There ain't nothing Meg, here, don't know when it comes to sports. The girl's a legend around here." Her gaze swiveled to Meg. "Come on, sugar, who's your favorite?" Genevieve persisted.

"I think this gentleman got here first." Meg's gaze met hot guy's. "I think you were about to ask me something…?"

He looked puzzled for a split second before a thought seemed to strike. "Actually, I did."

Her heart paused and the air lodged. This was it. This guy

wanted her. She knew it. From the first moment he'd abandoned his roast, up until now. She read the sudden determination that leapt into his expression. The eagerness that blazed in his gaze. The strange way he looked at her now, as if he'd found the woman of his most erotic dreams.

"Yes?" Meg prodded.

"Spurs or Heat?" he blurted.

Meg blinked. "Excuse me?"

He shrugged and glanced at Genevieve. "I'd like to get in on the action if it's not too late."

"No problem," the old woman told him. "Fifty bucks and you're in."

So much for flying solo.

Meg spent the next few minutes giving her opinion on the upcoming game—it wasn't like she couldn't *not* help Genevieve, particularly when the woman offered to throw in a case of Twinkies at cost—and then turned on her heel and went in search of Dillon Cash.

They didn't call her Manhandler Meg for nothing.

8

"THERE'S A WOMAN IN TOWN looking for you." Nikki, Jake's girl-friend, made the announcement that evening when she opened the door to the small office where Dillon sat taking notes on the computer screen that blazed in front of him. He'd been at his terminal for an hour now, since sunset to be exact, and he had no intention of powering off anytime soon.

He was finally onto something.

Even more, he was now sufficiently distracted from the damned hunger that had gnawed away at him all day. The more he'd tried to sleep, the more he'd thought about Meg. He'd been so worked up by the time he'd rolled out of bed, that he'd needed to kill some time and cool off before he saw her again. He'd needed something mundane and boring, and so he'd headed to work.

But when he'd logged on to his blog—after perfecting the last line of code for his new software program—he'd gotten a shock that had juiced him up almost as much as the thought of Meg's sweet, succulent body.

Listed among the *Do me, baby* and *Let's be butt buddy* comments were four posts that actually detailed turning experiences similar to Garret's—the same sweet scent and the same medallion. All four were recent experiences and one even listed an actual name—Joe—and a location, Bryan Street, south side of Chicago, approximately six months ago.

It seemed that Joe had taken a bite out of IttyBittyVamp while he'd been club-hopping down in Chi town. In between clubs, Itty had run out of gas and had elected to knock on some poor sap's door to ask to use the phone, since he'd had a cheap cell phone and zero service.

Joe had given Itty a helluva lot more than a call to Triple AAA.

The newbie vamp was still screwed up over the sudden change, still trying to figure things out and deal with what was happening to him, and so he couldn't remember Joe's actual address. He just remembered waking up a block or so from the last club he'd gone to. He'd been bloody and alone and clueless as to what had just happened to him.

But he knew now and he was frantically trying to find a way to reverse the situation.

Dillon had given him the basic lowdown—destroy the source in order to free himself—and then he'd spent the hours afterward cyber-searching Joes in and around the area where Itty had opened his eyes for the first time as a vamp.

He'd come up with four of them.

"She's been asking around for you all day today," Nikki persisted, pulling Dillon from his thoughts and the computer screen.

He glanced up at the attractive blonde who stood in the doorway and shrugged. "What can I say? When you've got it, you've got it."

"Obviously." She grinned. "Candy Morgan—that waitress from the Shade Tree—talked nonstop about you last week. I think she wants seconds. And so does Lorelie Hellman and Gina Berkowitz and Tammy Fitzpatrick."

He shook his head. "As much as I'd like to oblige them all, Garret would have my head." That, and he couldn't actually remember any of those women. While he knew they'd been good—warm and sweet and sustaining—the only woman who lingered in his thoughts was Meg.

She was his biggest challenge, after all. So it only made sense she would get under his skin and stick in his brain.

That, or he actually *liked* her.

He shook away the thought and focused on Nikki. "So who was this woman?"

"Nobody I knew." Her expression grew serious. "When she

came into To Dye For, I thought she wanted a haircut. She sure as hell needed one what with all the split ends. But before I could get her in the chair, she started drilling me about you. How did I know you? When was the last time I'd seen you? What time did you open up shop? I told her you were on vacation and the shop was closed, but she didn't look like she bought it. I didn't think she would. I heard from Mary Lou Winegarten that she was at Pam's Pamper Park asking all sorts of questions, too. Knowing Pam, the woman probably got an earful about you being the new town stud." She shook her head. "But I'm a little worried. She seemed *too* anxious." Just as Nikki said the words, Jake appeared in the doorway behind her.

"Sounds like a vampire hunter to me," Jake offered, sliding his arms around Nikki's waist.

"Maybe." Nikki eyeballed the computer. "Whoever she is, I get the feeling that she's connected with your blog somehow."

"Why's that?"

"Because she referred to you as BigTexasVamp. She tried to cover up the slip, but I wasn't the only one who heard it. Charlie was doing highlights next to me and he thought she was talking about that new topless joint over in Tarpley—the one that features those dancers with the beehive hairdos who call themselves Big Texas Vampers. That's your screen name, right?"

Dillon nodded, his mind racing to find a connection between one of the posts and someone actually seeking him out. Sure, he'd had half a dozen women want to hook up with him, but to travel hundreds of miles just for sex?

As outrageous as it seemed, Dillon had watched enough Dr. Phil back in his human days—he'd always had the TV on while doing repairs at his shop—to know that there were desperate individuals willing to do just about anything to get laid.

"She came in during the day," Jake remarked. "So that means she's definitely human. She's either a vampire hunter, someone desperate to be turned, or maybe a groupie from another town who's heard about you and wants to see for herself."

Or maybe, just maybe, she had something to do with the Ancient One.

Dillon wasn't sure where the thought came from, except that it seemed too coincidental that the very day he received a concrete lead, a strange woman showed up in town looking for him.

"Regardless, you should watch your back," Jake told him, concern evident on the older vampire's face. "Garret and I are going to look around and see what we can find out about her. In the meantime, do what you can to lay low and avoid a confrontation."

"I can take care of myself."

"I know that, but there's no reason to prove it. Just be careful." He gathered Nikki closer, his arms tightening as if he never meant to let her go.

He didn't. He was crazy about her and she was equally crazy about him, despite the fact that she was still human.

Because of it, a voice in his head whispered.

Jake was a vampire and so any woman he took a fancy to would want him more than her next breath.

At the same time, there was something about the way Nikki looked at Jake that went beyond wanting to rip his clothes off and have wild and crazy sex. She wanted *him,* the man he'd been and the vampire he'd become. The whole package.

A pang of envy shot through Dillon as he watched the couple disappear out into the fabrication shop where Garret was busy welding the handlebars for his latest creation.

Not because he wanted anyone—especially Meg—to feel the same unconditional love for him. To feel love, period.

Sure, he liked Meg. But the last thing—the very *last* thing—Dillon wanted was for any woman to fall in love with him, and vice versa. He didn't need a relationship right now. He had a record to break and if the sudden anxiety pumping through his veins was any indication—that and the gut feeling that he was really and truly on to something—his days as a vampire were numbered.

All the more reason to table his research for now and get the hell out of the shop. He stored his notes and powered off the computer. Pushing to his feet, he tapped on the glass, signaled goodbye to Garret, Jake and Nikki and headed out the back door.

He'd promised to give Meg a few sex lessons, and it was time to start her education.

WHEN MEG PULLED UP IN front of Dillon's house and killed the engine, the sun had already set and darkness blanketed the area. He lived on the outskirts of town, the nearest neighbor at least a half a block down the gravel road. Not a single light burned inside the sprawling one-story building.

She debated whether or not to get out of the car. He wasn't home. She already knew that. Just like he hadn't been at the computer shop. The place had been just as dark, a sign hanging in the front window that read Closed Temporarily for Renovations.

Right. And she had a dozen men falling all over themselves to be her personal sex slaves.

She'd peered through the window and, sure enough, there hadn't been a ladder or a nail gun in sight. She'd tried room four at the motel, too, but he'd already checked out.

Relief niggled at her. Not that she cared if he did the nasty with Miss Hot Chick again. It's just that she'd hoped—she'd prayed—that they could start their lessons right away. The fact that he wasn't shacked up at the inn for another night was definitely a sign that he might be free.

If she could find him.

Her brain told her to put the car in Reverse, back out and look elsewhere—Big Bubba's honky tonk, the Shade Tree bar and grill, the Dairy Freeze—anyplace, *every* place where members of the opposite sex met to mix and mingle in Skull Creek. They were all possibilities worthy of a quick look now that Dillon had turned into Mr. Hook Up. He sure as hell wouldn't be sitting at home all by his lonesome.

Still.

She killed the engine and climbed out of the front seat just to be sure.

Maybe he was taking a nap. After last night—correction, after the last two months—he had to be exhausted. She grasped at the hope, ignored the apprehension that wiggled down her spine and started for the door.

The gleam of her headlights sliced through the darkness, pushing back the shadows and giving her a blazing trail toward the wraparound porch. Awareness prickled the hairs on the back of her neck with each step.

She couldn't shake the sudden feeling that someone was watching her.

If only.

The sad truth? Dillon was most certainly out on yet another date. At that very moment he was probably smiling that sexy smile of his and whichever woman was the flavor of the night was undoubtedly ripping off her clothes.

Meanwhile, Meg was here. The soft ground sucking at her favorite stilettos. The darkness chasing goose bumps up and down her spine. A rope tightening around her ankles—

The thought slammed to a halt as she glanced down. Sure enough, she'd stepped into a roped circle spread out in the grass. The slack had tightened. The rope had hiked up around her ankles. Nylon cut into her tender flesh and—

"Now!"

The man's urgent voice cracked open the silence and before she could breathe, much less scream, her legs were jerked out from beneath her. One of her heels stuck in the ground and the ankle strap snapped. Her foot yanked free and she flipped. In the blink of an eye, she found herself dangling upside down from a massive oak tree in Dillon's front yard.

The blood rushed to her head and she blinked, her body flailing as a pair of shadows rushed at her. The next few moments seemed to pass in slow motion, the voices unreal yet oh, so familiar.

"You were supposed to wait for me," said shadow number one, the voice high-pitched and distinctly female.

"Sorry, dear." Shadow number two struggled with Meg's flailing arms.

"No sense crying now," came the female's voice. "Just get the handcuffs on him."

"Handcuffs? I don't have the handcuffs," said number two. "I gave you the handcuffs to wipe down with antibacterial wipes."

"And I wiped them and gave them back. I set them right on the table next to the LYSOL. Didn't you pick them up?"

"Uh, oh." Shadow number two released Meg, turned and high-tailed it around the house.

Number one plopped a hand on her hip and shook her head. "I swear that man would forget his name if it wasn't for me."

Meg blinked against the sudden pressure in her skull and forced her eyes to focus. She peered through the darkness at the upside down figure dressed in a black jogging suit. "Mrs. Cash?"

The shadow loomed closer and a familiar face came into view. "Meg? Dear, is that you?"

Relief rushed through Meg and washed away the fear that had gripped her. "Guilty."

"I got the handcuffs," came the winded voice of the man who trotted around the corner of the house. He was dressed in black also, but unlike Dora Cash, his face was obscured behind a ski mask. "I brought the stun gun, too." He waved the small hand-held device. "I figure we'll zap him and then do the handcuffs—"

"No!" Meg and Dora said in unison.

"But we'll never get the handcuffs on," the man protested.

"It's not Dillon," Dora told her husband. "It's Meg."

"Meg?" Harold Cash lifted his ski mask, pulled a pair of bifocals from his pants pocket and shoved them on. "Meg Sweeney?"

"Hey there, Mr. Cash." Meg wiggled her fingers. "I was just looking for Dillon."

"You and us both," Dora told her. "We've been camped out in his front yard for the past few weeks trying to catch him when he came home. But he never showed. So we decided to switch tactics and move our tent to the backyard, that way he might think we've given up and come back. I mean, he has to come home sometime, right?"

"You would think so."

"One of us has been here day in and day out—with the exception of those three ER visits—and we still haven't seen him," Harold said.

"Poor Harold, here, had this red boil come up on the back of his neck," Dora chimed in. "My aunt's husband's sister had that and it spread until his entire head was inflamed. It caused major brain damage. Luckily, Harold's wasn't that bad."

"It was just a mosquito bite," the man told his wife.

"There is no *just*. Mosquito bites are dangerous. People die from them all the time. That's why I bought the mosquito netting even though we invested in four bug lamps, a dozen citronella candles and a case of bug spray. You can't be too careful."

"The second visit was because of a paper cut I got opening the carton," Harold added.

"Staph is a serious thing," Dora said.

"And then I got indigestion from a can of chili."

"People mistake heart attacks for indigestion all the time. Besides, I told you not to eat that chili. Spicy food is bad for your intestines."

"So is Mace, but that didn't stop you from making me go after that group of ferocious Girl Scouts."

"How was I to know they were armed? They were Girl Scouts, for Pete's sake. Besides, I thought it was Dillon."

"There were four of them, dear."

"I thought it was Dillon and a few of his fellow cult members."

"They were all less than four feet tall."

"They could have amputated his legs to keep him from running away."

"They were pulling a wagon full of cookies."

"The wagon could have been for my poor legless baby." She shook her head. "It was an honest mistake that could have been prevented if you'd been wearing your glasses."

"I can't wear them with this mask."

"So leave the mask off."

"It goes with the suit. Besides, if it hadn't been for the mask, I would have gotten a face full of Mace. That would have been ER trip number four. Our insurance company would have dropped us on the spot."

"They can't do that. We have the ultra premium plus plan that even covers pre-existing—"

"Excuse me," Meg cut in. "I have the cheap value plan that doesn't pay for any ER visits, so can someone please cut me down before I start bleeding out of my eyeballs?"

"Why, yes. Of course, dear. Harold, where's your knife?"

"I don't have the knife. You borrowed the knife to open that mosquito netting."

"And then I gave it back."

"No, you didn't."

"I most certainly did—"

"Everything's getting blurry," Meg cut in.

The two scrambled around back.

A few minutes later, Dora Cash worked at the nylon with a large kitchen knife while Harold kept a steady hold on Meg to keep her from crashing to the ground. A few more seconds, a near death experience when Dora nicked her finger, and finally the rope snapped.

Harold helped Meg to her feet before turning to his wife who clutched her finger. "Should I call 911?"

"Don't be silly." She smiled. "It's not like I'm going to drop dead at any moment." Her expression faded into serious intent. "It takes at least a few hours for most bacterial infections to set in, which means we have more than enough time to make it to the E.R. over in Junction."

"Sorry about the misunderstanding," Dora told Meg as Harold went to get their car, which they'd parked down the street. "We didn't mean to ruin your shoe." She indicated the one high heel that was still stuck in the ground.

"It's okay." Meg pulled the shoe free, stared at the broken ankle strap and tried to tamp down a rush of disappointment.

A feeling that had nothing to do with her ruined footwear and everything to do with the hot, hunky man she couldn't get off her mind or out of her fantasies.

The house had been her last hope since she had no intention of barging into Big Bubba's and interrupting Dillon with another woman. Which meant she was heading home, to an empty house and a box of Twinkies. And maybe even her favorite sweatpants and her lucky Cowboys T-shirt, still packed away in a box in her upstairs closet.

Hey, if she was going to backslide, she might as well go all the way.

She shrugged. "I didn't have any special plans tonight anyway."

SHE MEANT TO GO HOME.

She even went so far as to pull into the driveway and open the car door. But then she spotted the telltale tread marks near the curb, and just like that, she slammed the door shut, gunned the engine and headed over to her shop.

The next two hours were spent getting a jump start on tomorrow's workload and trying not to think about Dillon and the fact that he'd obviously changed his mind about helping her.

Because she wasn't sexy enough.

The truth taunted her, eating away at her self-confidence as she re-arranged her front window displays and moved on to unpack the new shipment of merchandise stacked near the main counter. She sliced open the first box, pulled aside several layers of bubble wrap and unearthed the metallic dresses she'd ordered at the last trunk show in Austin.

Not that she cared. It wasn't about being sexy enough for Dillon. It was about appealing to the rest of the male population of Skull Creek. She could care less if Dillon would rather boink his way through the current Hot Chicks list than keep his word to his oldest and dearest friend.

She fought down a wave of self-pity and pulled a low-cut silver number from the box. She held the dress up against her and eye-balled her reflection in the mirrored wall behind the cash register.

Not bad, but somehow, it wasn't as great as she remembered.

A few seconds later, she peeled off her clothes in a nearby dressing room and let the material slither over her head. A few tugs and pulls and…there. She walked back out to the front and stared at her reflection.

That was more like it.

The hem hit her mid-thigh, the silver fabric molding to her legs and waist. The neckline was a plunging halter that accented her cleavage and outlined her full breasts. Everything about it screamed *Hello? Hot female here.*

Which was why she'd ordered it in the first place.

Why she ordered every item in her store.

It was all about embracing her womanhood. Reveling in it.

She eyed her reflection again. Mission accomplished. She couldn't look any more feminine.

Yet here she was. All alone.

"It's not about the dress."

At the sound of Dillon's deep voice, Meg's head snapped up. She saw him standing on the other side of the glass door.

He wore jeans and a plain white T-shirt. The soft cotton molded to his broad shoulders, the sleeves falling just shy of the slave band tattoos that encircled both biceps. His green eyes gleamed with an intensity that screamed *hold on to your panties.*

She had the fleeting thought that no way could she have heard his voice so clearly and distinctly with a wall of thick glass between them. But then he grinned and her heart kick-started, and all thought faded in a rush of desire so intense it made her legs tremble.

He motioned her to unlock the door.

She fought down the urge to strip naked, haul open the door and do a full body tackle. Drawing a deep, steadying breath, she took one step forward, then another. Calm. Controlled. Still, her heart beat a frantic rhythm. Just as her hands touched the key to throw the dead bolt, a wave of anxiety went through her, followed by a bolt of pure, unadulterated lust. Her breath caught. She hesitated and sent up a fervent prayer for divine intervention.

As hot and bothered as she was—and at nothing more than a glance—she knew she was going to need all the help she could get.

9

"WHAT ARE YOU DOING HERE?" Meg asked, pulling open the door.

"Our first lesson." Dillon's gaze collided with hers. "Don't tell me you forgot about it?"

"I thought you were the one who forgot. It's half past nine."

"I had a few things to do first." He indicated the brown grocery sacks that filled his muscular arms. "But I'm here now." He winked. "Armed and ready."

Her tummy fluttered with excitement. "You're really good."

"How's that?"

"You've got the flirting down perfect." She shook her head. "But you don't have to do it with me." *Please*. "I don't need an actual demonstration. I just need to know *how* you do it."

His teasing grin faded into a serious expression. His green gaze brightened. "Then let's get to it."

"What's all this?" she asked as he deposited both sacks onto the counter near her cash register.

"A few things—" he rummaged inside one of the bags and pulled out a small jar of cherries "—to whet your appetite."

"I'm not really hungry."

He grinned and gave her a smoldering look. "Not yet."

She fought down a wave of excitement as she watched him unpack. A can of whipped cream, a small box of chocolates, a six pack of individual pudding snacks, three different pints of ice cream, a can of diet soda, a bottle of sweet tea, some orange juice and a large slush. "You've been to the Quickie Mart out on the highway."

"The Piggly Wiggly had already closed and it was the only

place open this late." He set the bags behind the register and shoved a large, tanned hand into his pocket to unearth a red, white and blue bandana. His gaze collided with hers and his eyes gleamed a bright, vivid blue—

She blinked. Just like that, the color faded into a rich emerald green. Had she just imagined the strange color?

Duh. Of course you imagined it. He has green eyes, not blue. He's always had green eyes.

"School's in session," he said, his deep voice killing any more speculation as he circled and came up behind her. The hard wall of his chest kissed her shoulder blades. She caught a quick glimpse of them in the mirror behind the counter and her stomach hollowed out at the provocative picture they made. He looked so large and powerful and intense. And she looked so…*hungry*.

The realization struck as she noted her glittering eyes and parted lips, the way her body fairly trembled in anticipation.

Of course, she was trembling. She'd been waiting for this for a long, long time.

Since the ninth grade.

His heavily muscled arms grazed her bare shoulders, distracting her from the ridiculous thought. He settled the bandana over her eyes and blotted out the truth staring back at her. "I want you to forget everything else and focus on what I'm going to put into your mouth."

"And how is this going to help me convince the rest of the town that I'm sexy?"

"Being sexy isn't about what clothes you're wearing or what kind of sheets you have." His deep, husky voice reminded her of last night's dream and she felt her cheeks heat. "It's about being sensuous." Strong fingers brushed her temple, her cheekbone as he adjusted the bandana. "This little exercise is going to get you in touch with your sense of taste. After that, we'll move on to the other senses—touch, smell, sight, sound."

With her vision gone, her others senses became sharper in that next instant. Her nostrils flared with the aroma of warm, hunky male. Her skin prickled from the heat of his hands burning into her arms as he led her to the far edge of the rectangular counter-top. He turned her until her back was to the end of the counter and then his hands went to her upper thighs.

When the realization hit, panic bolted through her, followed by an avalanche of excitement. Her breathing quickened. Her pulse pounded.

"What are you doing?" she blurted as he gripped the back of her thighs and lifted her.

"Making things more convenient."

She quickly found herself perched on the end of the long, rec-tangular countertop, the groceries spread out the length behind her. She could feel the coldness of one of the ice cream cartons seep through the thin material covering her right buttock. A freezing contrast to the heat of the male hands that slid down the outside of her upper legs, over her knees to the tender skin inside. He urged her legs apart and wedged himself between them. Worn denim grazed her inner thighs and awareness rushed through her. Her ears tingled at the deep, husky murmur of his voice.

"There. Now we've got plenty of room. You can lie back if you want."

Yeah, baby.

The notion rushed through her head and she stiffened. He was too close, too overwhelming and with her eyes covered, she ex-perienced a rush of vulnerability she hadn't felt in a long, long time. Suddenly, she was back in high school, her insides tingling in anticipation of her first actual kiss.

A kiss that had been *the* worst of her entire life.

"I'd rather sit." She shifted, trying to find a comfortable position where they weren't actually touching. "You know, I really don't see why you can't just give me a copy of your online research," she said, eager to put some distance between them and kill the intimacy. She went for the blindfold. "I'm really better at studying than any actual hands-on training." Strong, warm hands caught hers before she could pull the material free.

"That's the point, isn't it? To get you out of your comfort zone? Obviously what you're doing isn't working. We need to try something new." He urged her hands back down to her sides. "Stop fighting and work with me, Meg. Otherwise, I'm going to think you like sitting home every Saturday night."

"I don't sit home *every* Saturday night. I go out once in a while." She swallowed. "Just not with hot guys."

His warm rumble of laughter slid into her eardrums. "This will change that. *If* you give it a chance." Before she could reply, she felt the press of something hard against her lips. "Now stop fighting and open up."

The scent of chocolate filled her nostrils and her stomach gave a traitorous grumble.

"The object of this exercise is for you to guess what I'm feeding you," he continued. "Focus on the flavor and texture." His voice, so rich and deep, stirred her even more than the sugary sweet decadence. "Take your time to savor every mouthful. Then tell me what you think."

And what you want.

The deep command echoed in her head, as if he'd whispered the words right into her ear.

He hadn't.

She hadn't felt the rush of his breath against her temple, the graze of his lips. Nothing. Just the crazy feeling that he'd somehow, someway, invaded her thoughts.

Wariness wiggled up her spine and she had the sudden urge to hop off the counter and make a run for it. But then her stomach grumbled again and her mouth seemed to open of its own accord.

She sank her teeth into the sweet confection he fed her and focused on the burst of flavor rather than the urge to drag her tongue across the tip of his finger and taste him instead.

"Let's see…" she said, savoring the delicious mouthful.

Chocolate melted on her tongue, stirring her nerves into a euphoric buzz. She chewed and did her best to ignore the massive man who loomed in front of her. So close she could touch him if she leaned forward just so...

If.

She balled her fists and tried to concentrate on the specific flavors overwhelming her taste buds. His large hands settled on the tops of her thighs as he waited and awareness prickled her skin. Her stomach quivered as she swallowed.

"It's, um—" she licked her lips and tried to differentiate the different flavors that lingered in her mouth and made it tingle "—milk chocolate with a darker, more rich chocolate inside. Fudge," she blurted, as the realization hit. "It's milk chocolate with a fudge center. I'd say...a truffle from that box of chocolates?"

"You might be a quick study, after all."

She smiled, but the expression died when she felt the cool pressure of something at the corner of her mouth. His fingers moved and the thing he was holding slid across her bottom lip, teasing and tantalizing, until she forgot all about talking and opened her mouth.

A few seconds later, she bit down on a ripe, succulent piece of fruit. Juice spurted, drenching the inside of her mouth and trickling from the corner. "Cherry," she said, as she tried to catch the drop with her tongue.

"Bingo." The word was deep and husky. If she hadn't known better, she would have sworn she felt the soft flutter of his lips at the corner of her mouth, the soft flick of his tongue—

The thought shattered as she snatched the blindfold down to find him looming in front of her, his face several inches away, his gaze hooked on her face.

He frowned. "What's wrong?"

"I just thought..." *That you were going to kiss me.* She shook her head. "Nothing. I just got a little claustrophobic."

"Since when are you claustrophobic?"

Since the hottest guy in town walked into her boutique, hiked her up onto the far end of the counter, stepped between her legs and started mucking up her common sense.

"Can we just get on with this?" She pulled the blindfold back into place. "Come on. Give me something else." She opened her mouth. Several seconds ticked by, but then she felt the edge of a foam cup. A mouthful of slushee slid past her lips and iced her tongue.

"Cherry," she murmured.

"This isn't part of the test." He chuckled. "It's just to wash everything down."

"I don't need a drink. I'm fine. Just get to the next thing."

"Be patient, sugar. We've got all night."

All night? No way could she make it fifteen more minutes without making a move, much less an entire night.

"I'm hungry," she blurted. "Famished. Starved. Hurry up." Her heart thundered in her ears as she sat, waiting for more.

Her ears prickled to the tear of cardboard, the soft *pop* as a lid pulled free. After what seemed like forever, she finally felt the press of plastic at her bottom lip. A heartbeat later, he spooned a mouthful of something soft and sweet and scrumptious into her mouth.

"Chocolate pudding," she murmured, concentrating on the sudden rush of *yummm* that spiraled through her, rather than the man responsible.

She felt the hard press of his thigh against the inside of her knee and her nipples pebbled. She licked her lips.

Another spoon and the flavor of cold cream cheese and graham crackers exploded on her tongue. "Cheesecake ice cream." Another mouthful and her insides tingled. "Mmm... strawberry this time."

"Maybe you don't need me."

"That, or you've lost the element of surprise. I saw you unpack the grocery sack, remember?"

"So you know what I'm going to feed you before you taste it?"

She nodded. "We've done everything except the whipped cream. So I know that's what I'll get to taste next."

"That, or maybe I'll do a little tasting of my own." She felt his body weight shift as he dropped to his knees.

"What's that supposed to—" The words faded into a sharp intake of breath as he touched his lips to the inside of her thigh.

"Mmm," he murmured against her bare skin. "Definitely sweet." The soft rumble stirred a tremor and she felt the sudden wetness between her legs.

"You really shouldn't be doing this." *Excuse me?* This was exactly what he should be doing. What she'd wanted him to do from the very beginning—to make the first move and ravish her.

He was ravishing, all right.

At the same time, when she'd pictured a man falling all over her, he'd usually started a little higher up.

Dillon wasn't anywhere close to hauling her into his arms and kissing her senseless. Not in the traditional sense, that is. Even more, there was nothing wild and uncontrollable about his actions. The hands that pressed against her thighs were too purposeful, the mouth nibbling at her too intent. As if he were in complete control with one objective in mind—to push her to the edge until she was the one who lost her wits.

Never.

That's what she told herself. What she fully intended to tell him.

But it had been so long since a man had touched her like this— forever, in fact—and she couldn't seem to find her voice.

Her few sexual encounters had always been brief and to the point, and she'd always been the one in the driver's seat. The one on her knees, pushing some man to the brink rather than the other way around.

Not this time.

Dillon nibbled and licked his way slowly—deliciously slow— toward the heart of her and anticipation bubbled. She tried to remember that they were in her boutique, in full view of anyone who happened by and looked through the glass storefront.

Rather than zapping some sense into her, the thought made her that much more excited.

Instead of resisting, she found herself opening her legs even wider, her body begging him closer, while her head was telling her to pull off the blindfold and put a stop to this before she sailed over the edge, straight into the land of *Give it to me baby, or else!*

She wouldn't. No matter how much he worked her up.

No way. No how. Uh, uh.

While she wasn't resisting, she wasn't going to take the lead and move a muscle.

Her mind made up, she braced herself as he trailed his tongue over the silk covering her wet heat and pushed the material into her slit until her flesh plumped on either side. He licked, stroking and stirring the sensitive flesh until she squirmed and shoved her fingers into his silky hair.

Okay, so she *had* to move.

But there was a big difference between holding on for the ride and jumping into the driver's seat.

At the same time, there seemed nothing wrong with being a little enthusiastic. It wasn't like she was begging for it. She was just giving him a little encouragement.

He gripped the edge of her panties and she lifted her hips to accommodate him. The lacey material slithered down her legs. He caught her ankles and urged her knees over his shoulders. Large hands slid beneath her buttocks as he drew her to the very edge of the counter. At his first long lick, the air bolted from her lungs.

His tongue parted her and he lapped at her sensitive clit. He tasted and savored, stroking, plunging, driving her mindless until her body wound so tight that she couldn't stand it anymore. A cry vibrated from her throat and shattered the stillness that surrounded them. Her orgasm gripped her and held tight for the next several seconds. Her body trembled and her insides convulsed. She barely resisted the urge to haul him to his feet and press her body against his.

Because as great as the feeling was, it just made her want to forget her inhibitions, peel his clothes off, push him down and climb on top.

And suddenly, with her own ragged breaths echoing in her

ears and her heart pumping furiously in her chest, that didn't seem like such a bad idea.

After all, he'd started it.

DILLON DRANK IN THE intoxicating taste of her. His hands kneaded her sweet ass, holding her close as her orgasm rippled through her. It wasn't the actual act of having sex with a woman that fed the beast that lived and breathed inside of him. It was her orgasm.

Her essence.

When a woman peaked, she pulsed with the sweetest, most potent, most sustaining energy.

Meg Sweeney was the sweetest yet.

The thought struck as he fit his lips more closely on her throbbing slit. Her body convulsed against his mouth and he drank from her, relishing the rush of heat. Her essence fed him all of five seconds. But instead of being satisfied, he felt even hungrier. Starving. The urge to push her back onto the counter and sink his cock into the decadent warmth gripped him and the beast took control.

He pushed to his feet, the tight bulge in his pants brushing against her sensitive flesh as he pushed closer, urging her legs wider, her back flat against the counter top. Candy bars sailed to the carpeted floor. The can of whipped cream upended, clattering on the counter and diving over the edge.

Tugging at his waistband, he unfastened the button and gripped the zipper. He was just about to shove the zipper down when her soft voice pushed past the roar in his ears.

"Wait. I want to see this."

Her hands went to the blindfold and his memory stirred. He remembered the excitement on her face when he'd leaned in for that first kiss so long ago. Followed by the disappointment when it was all said and done.

He stiffened as she pulled the bandana down and gazed up at him, a victorious light gleaming in her blue eyes. Her full lips curved into a smile and where he'd been about to pull away, suddenly he had half a mind to finish what he'd been fool enough to start.

He liked seeing her smile.

Things are different now.

You're different.

It was true. He wouldn't come anywhere close to disappointing her now the way he had back then. He *knew* it.

Still…

She was different. She had a strong will. Strong enough to resist him despite his vampire charisma. Which meant there was the smallest possibility that she might not think he was all that in the sack.

Not unless she was already out of her mind with lust.

So much that *she* reached out to *him*.

He stared down at her. She made an inviting picture, the metallic dress riding her waist, her legs spread wide, her ass bare on the glass countertop, her nipples hard, throbbing points beneath the skimpy material. Expectancy etched her beautiful features as she waited for him to free his cock and sink into her.

Hunger gripped him, twisting at his insides, shaking his already tentative control. He fought against the sensation and fixed his attention on her eyes. He could see the victory that pulsed through her.

The anticipation.

The *hell, yeah.*

"I think you're getting it, sugar," he said, his voice deep and raspy and raw. He slid his button back into place, planted a quick, rough kiss against her full lips, then turned on his heel and walked away.

Because no way was Dillon blowing his one chance to prove to himself that he wasn't the geek that everybody thought. He'd waited too long and battled too many doubts.

The next move was Meg's.

10

SHE COULDN'T MOVE A MUSCLE.

Meg came to that conclusion as she stared up at the ceiling, her body still tingling from Dillon's delicious mouth. Even more, she didn't want to move. She wanted to lie there, to remember the feeling of his hands and his lips on her body. To bask in the tiny convulsions still clenching and unclenching inside of her. To revel in the knowledge that her dry spell had ended.

Sort of.

Reality struck and she tried to summon her disappointment that they hadn't actually had sex.

She should be upset.

She wasn't. Rather, she felt content.

And relieved.

As worked up as she'd been, she hadn't reached for him or pulled him close. She'd resisted the temptation and let him make all the moves.

Including that first kiss.

She swept her tongue over her bottom lip and tasted the wild ripeness of his mouth. A hungry spurt of desire went through her, followed by a burst of excitement.

He'd kissed *her.* A quick press of his lips that had been brief and to-the-point, and a hundred—no, make that a million—times better than the first.

Because he was different now. Bold. Confident. Sensual. *Sexy.*

And she was one lesson closer to following in his footsteps.

A smile curved her lips as she slid from the counter, retrieved her undies, and turned to clean up the mess they'd made. More than once, she caught herself tasting the leftovers, savoring them before she bagged them back up.

Sweet chocolate melted on her tongue.

Light, frothy whipped cream filled her mouth.

Fruity slush slithered down her throat.

The different tastes were highly stirring. The various textures extremely erotic.

By the time she'd put away the last of the supplies, her entire body felt alive. Aroused.

She shoved the bags into a nearby trash can and turned. Her gaze snagged on her reflection in the mirror and her breath caught.

This time she didn't notice the sexy cut of the metallic dress, but the woman beneath it. Her eyes appeared heavy-lidded, her cheeks flushed, her lips slick and red from the slush. She looked as if she'd just rolled out of bed after a night of wild lovemaking.

She looked desirable. *Sexy.*

Even more, she felt that way.

It was a feeling that stayed with her as she closed up shop and headed home to bed.

She didn't stop off for a quick Twinkie fix. She didn't bother putting on a pink nightshirt or a slinky nightie or even a skimpy thong.

For the first time, Meg Sweeney peeled off her clothes and crawled between the sheets wearing nothing but her own skin.

DILLON STARED AT THE woman behind the bar and noted the sway of her hips as she walked the few steps to the cooler, the way she positioned herself so that she could give him a bird's-eye view of her ample cleavage when she leaned down and reached for a chilled beer mug.

Her breasts jiggled and swayed as she set the mug on the counter and gripped the draft handle. Gold liquid streamed into the frosted glass and she licked her lips. Her nipples pressed decadently against the thin cotton of her tank top, *Grady's Bar & Grill* emblazoned across the front.

Either she was extremely thirsty and close to bursting at the thought of sucking down a cold one, or she wanted to suck something altogether different. One glimpse into her eyes—her thoughts—settled the controversy.

Libby Sue Wentmore. Early twenties. Bartending was just a way to pay the rent until she got her big break at the *American Idol* auditions and made it to Hollywood. From there it was a straight shot to the big time—from making the actual show and the final two, to a recording contract and an appearance at MTV's VMA awards, to her very own quarterback boyfriend. But she had her sights set on the hunk running the ball for the Packers rather than the Cowboys. Puh-lease. *Everybody* knew Green Bay kicked royal ass.

And speaking of ass…

She was more than willing to hand hers over to him.

"Here you go." She set the ice-cold draft down in front of him and gave him her most provocative smile. "Good for what ails you."

"Thanks." He lifted the mug and touched it to his lips.

Her gaze riveted on the motion and she licked her own lips.

"Is this your first time at Grady's?" she asked after he'd taken a long pull on the beer. "I don't think I've seen you around here before."

"First time." Dillon had driven over to Oyster Creek, a small town about a half hour north, on purpose. He'd been too worked up to go back to the bike shop. And much too hungry. He'd needed a woman.

One who wouldn't remind him of Meg, or Skull Creek, or the all-important fact that he still hadn't managed to break Bobby's record.

"I'm not from around here," he added.

"A tall, hunky stranger." She smiled again. "I like." Her expression faded into a look of pure hunger. "I get off in fifteen minutes. I could show you around if you're interested."

He tipped his mug toward her and took a long swig. "I'll meet you out back."

He spent the next ten minutes finishing his beer before he tossed several bills onto the counter and pushed to his feet. He cast one quick, hungry glance at the bartender who looked ready to hop up on the counter and take him on right there. She winked and he could practically feel her pulse beating against his lips, her lifeblood gushing into his mouth.

His groin tightened and his stomach grumbled and he turned just as one of the waitresses approached him.

"Hold up, buddy. This is yours." She held out a fresh beer.

"Sorry, but I didn't order another."

"Someone did." She pointed to the far end of the bar at a now vacant barstool. "That's funny. She was there just a second ago. Oh, well." She shrugged. "Enjoy."

He might have if he hadn't had the distinct feeling that something wasn't right. He felt it in the tightening of his chest and the tensing of his muscles. He drank in the faces that surrounded him and a barrage of thoughts rushed at him. He picked through fact after fact, searching for…

He wasn't sure. Something out of the ordinary maybe.

Or someone.

Most likely a groupie. At the same time, he couldn't dismiss the possibility of a vampire hunter. By blogging, he'd opened himself up to both.

He stiffened as a wave of anxiety washed through him. Followed by a burst of sheer desperation. Because as much as he knew it had to be one of the two, he couldn't shake the gut feeling that it was neither.

That whoever—whatever—was after him had something to do with the Ancient One himself.

"Let's get out of here." The bartender came up beside him. "Maybe pick up a pizza and head back to my place." She winked. "I'm starving."

The music and chaos seemed to fade, along with his speculation. Her pulse echoed a steady *ka-thunk*, *ka-thunk* in his head. His gut tightened and his gaze fixed on the smooth column of her throat. "You just read my mind, sugar."

"IT'S ABOUT TIME YOU showed up." Garret Sawyer sat at the kitchen table, a laptop open in front of him. He looked like a classic biker tonight with a black bandana tied around his head, a black Harley Davidson T-shirt and worn jeans. His feet were bare, his boots discarded a few feet away. "You're pushing it, don't you think?" He glanced at his watch. His arms flexed and bulged, accenting the telltale tattoos that encircled his biceps. "It's fifteen minutes until sunup."

"Plenty of time." Dillon collapsed in the chair directly across from Garret's.

"If you've got a hankering to deep fry your ass." Garret's attention shifted back to the laptop. He hit a few more keys before closing the lid and eyeballing Dillon. "You look like hell."

Garret had just fed.

Dillon could tell by the fierce gleam in the vampire's eyes, the flush of his cheeks and the sweet, sharp scent of blood that still clung to him.

His own stomach grumbled. "Thanks for the compliment."

Silence stretched between them as Garret continued to stare. "Have you been feeding?" he finally asked.

"I fed tonight."

"I'm talking blood, not sex." His eyes gleamed with a knowing light. "You're young. You need both right now."

Dillon knew that, which was why he'd taken the bartender back to her place. He could still see the tempting picture she'd made standing in the small living room, her eyes bright and determined and hungry.

She pulled her tank top over her head and bared her breasts. "Give it to me, baby," she said as she stepped toward him.

"Why don't you give it to me?" he countered as she pressed her body against his.

Her gaze collided with his and just like that, she knew what he wanted. Not consciously. But deep down she knew what he really wanted from her. What he needed.

She swept her hair aside and tilted her neck, offering him the sustenance he so desperately sought.

His groin tightened and his stomach clenched and he leaned forward...

And then he'd stopped.

Shit.

"You have to feed." Garret pushed to his feet and walked over to the refrigerator. He hauled open the door and retrieved a dark red plastic bag. He tossed it on the table. "You can't live on this stuff." The "stuff" referred to a limited supply of bagged blood Garret had managed to get his hands on when he'd paid a visit to an ex-girlfriend who worked a local blood bank. "It serves a purpose in a pinch—when you're trying to lay low or curb the hunger when it threatens to rage out of control—but it isn't a permanent fix." He snagged a beer from the fridge and picked up his laptop. "You'd do well to get used to what you are for now and just do it."

Dillon nodded. Not that he had a problem embracing his need for blood. He had no problems sinking his fangs into a warm, willing woman. It was just that he didn't want to. Not unless the warm, willing woman happened to be Meg.

Double shit.

"Don't fall for anyone," Garret told him. "I know Jake is hooked on Nikki, but he's the exception to the rule. The only exception. For the rest of us, it just doesn't work."

"It's not about a woman." It wasn't. He wasn't hung up on Meg herself, but what she stood for. She was the ultimate challenge and bedding her meant blazing a new trail as the town's studliest guy. End of story.

"Nikki told me about the woman."

Dillon nodded. "Jake thinks it's a groupie or a vampire hunter."

"More than likely."

"And the not so likely?"

"It's not worth considering," Garret said, but his expression wasn't half as convincing as his voice. "Just feed." He motioned to the bag. "Either way, you're going to need your strength." He turned and started for the hallway leading to the cellar.

"You feel it, don't you?"

Garret stalled in the doorway and turned. His body hummed with tension. "Feel what?"

"I don't know." Dillon shrugged. "It's like an awareness. Like something's close. Watching." His gaze collided with Garret's. "Maybe the Ancient One isn't as far away as we think. Maybe my blog is working and instead of locating him, he's located us."

"We should be so lucky." Garret shook his head. "I would know if he was here. Vampires can sense other vampires. You sense me, don't you? And Jake?"

Dillon nodded. Their presence was a constant in his mind. He could feel their power as distinctly as he could feel his own.

"It's instinctive and fierce," Garret went on. "Not subtle." He shook his head. "I'm sure whatever's bugging you is nothing." Even as he said the words, Dillon could tell Garret didn't believe it half as much as he wanted to. "I'm installing a security system here at the house. If she's a vampire hunter, she'll come after us during the day when we're most vulnerable. I don't think she's clued in to our location yet, otherwise she wouldn't still be asking so many questions."

"And if she's not a vampire hunter?"

Garret winked. "Then we can both stop worrying and have a good time."

Easier said than done.

The notion stayed with Dillon as he downed the blood and headed for the cellar. He kicked off his boots and stretched out on the bed, his gaze fixed on the ceiling.

But he didn't see the cedar beams crisscrossing the Sheetrock. He saw Meg spread out on the countertop, her body lush and inviting and damn near irresistible.

He tasted her, too, the ripe taste of wild, forbidden fruit still potent on his lips.

He smelled her—the faint scent of strawberries and chocolate and warm woman.

He heard her—the frantic beat of her heart and the long moan when she'd come apart against his mouth.

He even felt her—her sweet, round ass warming his palms, her frantic fingers tugging at his hair.

Deep in his gut, he knew he couldn't begin to drink from any other woman until he finished what he'd started with Meg. Until he seduced her to the point of no return, shattered Bobby's record and proved himself once and for all.

The sooner, the better.

"LOOKS LIKE SOMEONE'S been having ultra hot sex," Terry said when she walked in the back door of the boutique the next morning.

Meg stood near a rack pulling dresses for her first appointment. When Terry smiled and gave her a knowing look, a rush of heat swept from her toes to the roots of her hair.

"Dillon and I did not do the nasty."

Not yet.

Meg ignored her body's traitorous whisper and pulled an orchid chiffon dress from the mix. "Last night was strictly business," she went on. "I'm still flying solo in the orgasm department."

"Not you." Terry tossed her purse on a nearby shelf and headed for the small fridge that sat in the far corner. "I'm talking about me." She pulled a bottled yogurt from inside and popped the top. "Hank dropped by last night. One minute we were arguing over who was supposed to get the Tim McGraw CDs and the next, we were doing it on my kitchen table."

Meg's hand stalled just shy of a navy blue sheath. "But you hate Hank."

Terry shrugged. "An ex is like a large order of French fries. You know it's bad for you, but sometimes you just have to have one." She looked doubtful as she took a sip of her yogurt. "But it was just a one-night stand. It's not like we're moving in together and I'm back to binge eating Ben & Jerry's. I *so* can't do refined sugar anymore. Besides, I think Hank's an asshole. And he still thinks I'm a bitch." She smiled. "Which I am." She shook her head. "No, it was just a one-time thing. It's still over between us."

"Let's hope Hank thinks so," Meg added.

A frown pinched between Terry's eyebrows. "He knows." Her expression eased. "I like it." She indicated the rose colored taffeta Meg had just pulled from the rack. "Honey will go nuts."

"You bet she will." Meg ignored her own doubts about the Hank issue and let the woman change the subject. Meg wasn't exactly the voice of experience when it came to men. "These are the dresses she picked out of the magazines I gave her. Narrowing it down from this bunch should be no problem."

"True." Terry nodded. "But I'll get the wine just in case."

HONEY HATED THE DRESSES.

Which meant that two hours later, Meg was ready to pull her hair out and Elise had consumed an entire bottle of Chardonnay. The woman was now paying homage to the porcelain god in Meg's backroom while Honey played Astroturf Warriors on her hand-held Sony PSP.

"We need something to settle her stomach," Terry announced after checking on Elise for the tenth time. "Maybe I should head over to the grocery store."

"And leave me here to deal with Honey?" As if on cue, Honey let out a long string of cuss words with a few *illegal tackles* and *slow running backs* thrown into the mix. A moan from the restroom punctuated the tirade.

"You're the boss," Terry told Meg, "which means you take the bulk of responsibility when it comes to this place. Meaning, you get to wash Miss Filth's mouth out with soap *and* you get to wash the puke out of her mother's hair."

"Being the boss means I get to delegate that responsibility as

I see fit. And I definitely see you staying here while I head to the Piggly Wiggly."

"Bitch."

"Happy washing." Meg grinned and grabbed her purse. "I'll get Honey to look through the latest magazines and pick out something else. That should keep her quiet while I'm gone. Try giving Elise some coffee in the meantime. I'll be back in fifteen minutes."

"I really don't feel comfortable feeding someone something that's so addictive."

"If you'd rather take her home with you and let her sleep it off, be my guest."

"A little coffee never hurt anyone."

Five minutes later, Meg walked into the nearby grocery store. She picked up three different types of antacids and had just handed everything over to the cashier when she heard the deep voice behind her.

"I owe you big-time."

She handed over a twenty before turning to find Colt Grainger standing behind her. He wore black slacks, a white button-up dress shirt, the sleeves rolled up to his forearms and a big smile.

"Really? How's that?"

"I went with your pick for the play-off game and won a hundred bucks." He set a pack of disposable razors on the counter and reached for his wallet.

"Good for you." Meg ignored a rush of disappointment as she took the change the clerk handed her and stuffed it into her purse.

"You've really got an eye for sports." He handed over his money for the razors.

"Thanks." She grabbed her bag and started for the door.

"No, I mean it." He waved for the cashier to keep the change, snatched up his purchase and hurried after her. "Wait." He caught her hand just as she reached the sliding double doors. "I want to talk to you."

"The Spurs," she blurted, noting the curious stares of several cashiers and old Mr. Wickerby who was busy paying for a gallon of buttermilk. "The Spurs have the strongest turnover record and they throw more three-pointers than anyone else in the NBA. Both of those factors are weak for the other team."

"That's not what I wanted to talk to you about."

"It's not?"

"No. I mean, I guess it was, but then I saw you and you look…" His voice trailed off as he gave her a once-over. "Did you change your hair?"

She touched the blond locks, which she'd been wearing loose and long since senior year. "I washed it, but I do that every morning."

Another once-over. "You must be wearing different make-up."

"Just my usual pink passion lip gloss and sunrise blush."

"A new outfit?"

"They're all new to you," she reminded him. "We just met a few days ago."

He grinned, the expression fading as he studied her again. "I can't put my finger on it, but there's something different from the last time I saw you. You look…I don't know." He shook his head. "You just look really good, that's all."

Really *sexy*.

The truth whispered through her head and her heart gave a tiny kick. "Thanks."

"What do you say you and I go out Saturday night? I'd really like to take you to dinner. Maybe dancing."

"Really? Like a date?"

"That's what I was thinking."

A rush of happiness went through her. It was far from *"I have to lay you down and make made passionate love to you right now, or I'll go berserk,"* but it was a start.

She reveled in the feeling for a few seconds before she shook her head. "Actually, I already have plans." Dillon was basing his lessons on the five senses. One down, which meant she still had four to go before she would be ready to put her newly learned sensuality to the test. It was already Thursday and even if she and

Dillon met every night, they still wouldn't be finished in time. "What about next Friday?"

Hope flared in his gaze and he grinned. "That would work." He gave her another thorough once-over. "Are you sure you didn't so something different?"

She shook her head. "Just the same old, same old."

On the outside, but the inside…

Her mind rushed back to last night. She felt the slick glide of the cherry along her lips, tasted the burst of flavor, and her stomach hollowed out.

"It's really good seeing you again," he said, his voice deeper and his eyes brighter, as if he read the thoughts racing through her mind.

He didn't. At the same time, he saw the way such thoughts made her feel. He saw the woman she'd become rather than the tomboy she'd once been.

Thanks to Dillon.

"Next Friday," she said.

"Next Friday it is." He winked.

Meg waited for her stomach to pitch the way it did when Dillon winked at her.

The only thing she felt was a burst of satisfaction. The lessons were working! And she had the date to prove it.

Now if she could just hold it together and control herself for the last four lessons, she would be home free. Forget just asking her out. Colt Grainger, as well as every other available man in Skull Creek, would be falling all over her. She would be a shoe-in for Tilly's new list.

In the meantime…

Dillon's image pushed into her head and she remembered the way he'd looked the moment before he'd kissed her—his body taut, his face dark with passion, his eyes so deep and green and mesmerizing.

Not that she'd been the least bit mesmerized. She'd held her own last night and resisted temptation, and she would do the same tonight.

She was *not* jumping his bones and begging him to have sex with her.

No matter how much she suddenly wanted to.

SHE WOULD BE ALL OVER him tonight.

Guaranteed.

That's what Dillon told himself when he arrived at the boutique an hour after sunset. He'd hadn't even bothered to stop off at Skull Creek Choppers. Rather, he'd rolled out of bed, taken a shower, spent a half hour learning the ins and outs of Garret's new security system—complete with video surveillance and several different alarm codes—and then he'd headed straight here.

"Get your purse and let's go." He grabbed her hand and led her around the counter.

"But I've got some outfits to show you." She motioned to several boxes that sat stacked near the counter. "I had a few things overnighted—some shirts and jeans, a sports coat. Stuff you might look good in."

"Later. I want to show you something."

"I've seen it," she said when he pulled out the blindfold.

He grinned. "Not this." He folded the material and came up behind her to tie it into place.

"How can I see anything when my eyes are covered?"

"Sugar, you can see everything. Your mind will paint a clear picture based on the information it receives from your other senses."

"So sayeth the man without the blindfold."

"Just trust your instincts," he murmured.

Hair as soft as silk brushed his fingertips as he secured it at the back of her head. Before he could stop, he threaded his fingers through her hair and let the strands tease his palms. He leaned down and took a deep breath. The scent of strawberries filled his head and sent an echoing throb to his groin. His hand grazed the skin at the nape of her neck and her breath caught.

The sound, so soft and nearly discernable, vibrated in his eardrums and mesmerized him for a long moment. He tamped down on the lustful thoughts that swamped his senses and drew a deep, steadying breath. Not that he actually needed it, but he was still a new vampire and it was a habit he'd yet to break.

"Where are we going?" she asked as he took her hand and led her out to the curb where his bike was parked.

"You tell me." He helped her straddle the powerful machine, then turned to retrieve an extra helmet. "That's tonight's test. Based on what you hear and smell and feel, I want you to tell me where we're at."

She smiled. "We're standing in front of my shop."

"Not now, smart ass." He barely ignored the urge to capture her full lips and kiss her like he'd done last night. But slow this time. And thorough. "Once we get there." His fingertips brushed the underside of her chin and he felt the frantic thump of her pulse. A shudder ripped through him and his hands actually trembled.

Crazy. He was a vampire in complete and total control.

A hungry vampire who'd yet to feed on anything other than the bagged blood back at Garret's place.

He needed a real woman.

A warm woman.

This woman.

"Let's go." He straddled the bike in front of her in the hope that having her out of eyesight would ease the throbbing inside of him. It didn't. Her arms snaked around his waist. Her full breasts pressed against his shoulder blades. Her pelvis cradled his ass and her slender thighs framed his, and it was all he could do to turn the key on the bike and crank the friggin' engine.

As for driving… Thankfully, he didn't have to have steady hands for that.

He could let his mind take control and guide them.

Once they hit the back roads and headed outside of town, he did just that. He fixed his gaze on the moonlit road ahead and sent out the silent commands to the mass of metal beneath him.

Pick up the pace and get there already.

The engine roared and the bike gained speed. The tires ate up the dirt road at a furious pace, leaving a cloud of dust in their wake. While he still rested his hands on the handlebars, he wasn't the least bit concerned with steering.

No, the hands he kept in place to keep from touching her.

There would be plenty of time for that once they reached their destination.

11

"I'M REALLY NOT DRESSED for this," she yelled above the rush of wind.

Meg's skirt slid higher up her thighs, her crotch nestled firmly against Dillon's butt. The only thing between them was the thin cotton of her thong and his jeans, and it wasn't nearly enough at the frantic pace they were moving.

Not with the bumps and lurches and *ahhhhhh…*

His denim-clad butt rubbed deliciously between her legs and the sudden friction caused an avalanche of heat that doused her and cut off her oxygen supply for several long seconds. Pleasure speared her and she barely caught a moan before it sailed past her lips.

"What was that, sugar?"

"Nothing." It was bad enough she was getting turned on with little effort on his part. He was driving, for Pete's sake. Not paying her the least bit of attention. No flirty comments or smoldering looks or purposeful touches.

She blew out a deep breath. Jesus, she might as well just jump him right now.

Squelching the notion, she scooted as far back as she could on the seat and concentrated on keeping a scant inch between them. There. That was much better.

Except when they swayed, she slid from one side to the other. The leather rubbed against the backs of her thighs and she couldn't help but remember Dillon's hands gliding along her bare skin, cupping her bottom and pulling her closer—

Stop, already.

She stiffened and let the stinging wind whip some sense into her.

You don't want to have sex. You don't want to have sex. You don't want to have sex.

She recited the silent mantra and managed to distract herself all of five seconds before they veered to the right. The motorcycle hit a rut and jumped. She jerked on the seat, slid forward and just like that, she raced right back into the land of temptation.

She caught her bottom lip against a fierce burst of pleasure. She tangled her fingers in the soft cotton of his T-shirt, eager to keep her hands anchored in place at his waist. The last thing she needed was for him to know exactly how turned on she was.

While he'd made a few moves, he hadn't made *the* move— no whipping off his clothes and having sex with her. Which meant he didn't find her completely and totally irresistible.

Still, he had to be a little turned on, right?

She couldn't help but wonder. A curiosity that could be easily satisfied with a little southward gravitation of her hands. A few inches lower. A few strokes here. A few strokes there.

You don't want to have sex, remember? You don't want to have sex. You don't want to have sex. You don't.

Another bump and her body jumped. Her hands slipped. Her fingers grazed his crotch—accidentally, of course—and his spine went ramrod straight.

He was turned on, all right, and there was nothing little about it.

The knowledge stirred a burst of satisfaction that she wasn't alone in her desperation. At the same time, it made her that much more aware that she *wasn't alone in her desperation.*

Dillon wanted her, all right.

But enough to make the first move?

She felt the tautness of his muscled abs through the thin cotton of his shirt. Her nostrils flared and the scent of him—denim and fresh air and a wildness that stirred something deep and primal inside of her—slid into her head and skimmed across her senses. Stirring and rousing.

Another bump and she rubbed deliciously against him. Once. Twice.

By the time they skidded to a stop, Meg's entire body buzzed with awareness.

She hoped Dillon felt the same, but then he climbed from the bike and killed their connection, and she wasn't so sure. Even more, his voice was as smooth, as controlled as always and her hopes plummeted.

"We're here." He took both her hands, his fingers burning into her as he helped her get her footing. "Any ideas where we're at?"

She had ideas, all right.

Unfortunately, none involved their location.

She tried to ignore the way her nipples rubbed against her bra with each breath she took. Her legs trembled and her thighs ached, and none of it had to do with the ride they'd just taken. No, she couldn't help but anticipate the ride ahead.

Dillon over her, between her legs, his hands trailing over her body—

"Are you okay?" His deep voice shattered the image, pulling her back to the present, to the man standing in front of her and the distinct possibility that he didn't find her half as exciting as she found him.

Duh. You already know that. Last night was proof. Just give it up and focus on learning as much as possible. This isn't about Dillon. It's about wowing Colt Grainger, and every other available man in town.

It *was*, she told herself, ignoring a ripple of disappointment.

"Meg?" Dillon's voice pushed into her thoughts.

"Fine," she finally managed. "I'm great."

"Good. Come on." He led her several feet, the deep, husky timber of his voice guiding and coaxing, until they finally stopped and he let go of her.

"Any ideas?" he asked after several long moments.

"None that are G-rated." The words were out before she could think better of them.

A warm chuckle sizzled along her nerve endings and she felt the powerful presence in front of her. "X-rated thoughts mean you're in tune with your body, which is definitely good." The presence shifted, and suddenly she felt him next to her. "Listen to your surroundings." He continued to circle, his voice suddenly behind her. "Drink in the different scents." She heard him on her left this time. *"Feel."* He'd made a complete circle to stand in front of her again. "And tell me where you're at."

"I guess this means we're doing three lessons all at once. Which is good," she rushed on, dodging another niggle of disappointment. "Tilly announces her new list in a little over a week, which doesn't give me much time. So the quicker we get this over with, the better." *Really*. She drew a deep breath and braced herself.

She ignored the urge to reach out and set her mind to the task at hand. Her ears prickled and her nostrils flared and she concentrated on tuning in to her surroundings rather than the man who stood so close.

Too close.

The seconds ticked by. "Let's talk sounds," he finally said. "What do you hear?"

"Nothing, really." Just the steady thud of his boots on the soft earth as he circled her, the brush of denim against denim with each step, the soft in and out of his breaths.

"What about smell? You have to smell something."

"I can't actually distinguish anything." Except the detergent from his freshly laundered T-shirt, the faint whiff of aftershave. The sharp scent of desire carried on the breeze, circling her, surrounding her, along with the man himself.

"What do you feel?"

You.

The truth vibrated through her, pushing and pulling at her already tentative control. The sensations assaulted her again—the deep timbre of his voice, the raw, stirring scent of his body, the awareness that he stood right next to her, in front of her, surrounding her.

Her fingers itched and her nipples ached and she wanted to reach out more than she wanted her next breath.

"Come on, sugar," Dillon pressed. "Tell me."

"I…" She licked her lips. "I—I don't have a clue." She shook her head. "This just isn't working." She reached for the blindfold, but he stepped up behind her and caught her hands before she could pull the material from her eyes.

"Easy." The word rumbled in her ears as he checked the blindfold, his fingertips lingering at her temples, feathering over her cheeks, down the smooth column of her throat. "You're too wound up." The pad of one finger lingered at her pulse beat. "You need to relax." He drew a lazy circle against the area. "Think about something else."

His touch, so soft and rousing, played over her neck, her collarbone, and she felt some of her tension slip away. He seemed to feel it, too, and he kept going, trailing his fingertips over her shoulders. He massaged and stroked, working his way down her arms.

She barely kept from groaning. "You've got really good hands."

"You haven't seen anything yet." He kneaded her palms for several long moments before his touch drifted back up, softer this time, mesmerizing as he teased the insides of her wrists, her elbows, her biceps. Finally, his hands circled her waist. "Tell me about your first sexual encounter."

She became acutely aware of the fingers that splayed against her rib cage. A burst of panic went through her, a bubble that quickly popped and fizzled, the steady touch lulling her as much as the hypnotic stroking a moment ago. "Do I have to?"

A warm chuckle vibrated the air around them. "That bad, huh?"

"Aren't all first times?"

He stiffened. "Our first kiss *was* pretty awful."

"Awful doesn't even begin to describe it. Try rotten. Horrible. Disastrous."

"Don't be shy, sugar. Tell me what you really think." He said the words jokingly, but they were laced with a hurt that reached out and tugged at something inside of her.

"The second kiss was much better," she heard herself say. "You've definitely mastered the art."

"So have you. You have great lips. Soft. Full." *Kissable*.

The last comment slid into her ears and whispered through her head. Warmth crept through her and she felt herself relax even more.

"So," he went on. "On a scale of one to ten—" he sounded only mildly interested, but she could feel the expectancy that gripped his body "—how would you rate last night?"

"I don't know…maybe a seven."

"*Seven*?" He stiffened. "It was at least an eight."

"If it hadn't been so quick. But the short duration kicked it down a notch. If you want eight, you'll have to take your time."

"I just might do that."

The implication of his words stirred a flood of anticipation. Her tummy tingled and her heart gave a traitorous double thump.

"Forget your first time," he went on, his lips grazing her ear. "Tell me about your most memorable sexual encounter."

No. That's what she should have said. Followed by a *"Please, let's keep this arrangement as impersonal as possible. That way I won't jump you, I won't be tempted to jump you, and I won't morph into Manhandler Meg."*

Maybe it was the blindfold that made the moment seem almost surreal and, therefore, not as threatening. Or maybe she'd proved to herself last night that she could stand strong and resist making the first move. Maybe a little of both. Either way, she heard herself murmur, "Okay."

Besides, Dillon was her friend. He always had been. He'd been there before her father had died, standing on the sidelines cheering her on when she'd tried out for the soccer team and then the baseball team, and even kicker on the boys' football team. He'd been there to console her when disaster had struck and her father had been killed. He'd gone with her to the funeral home and helped her pick out the casket and held her hand while she'd cried until she couldn't cry anymore. And he'd been there every day since, listening when she wanted to talk, reassuring her whenever she got discouraged at work.

She could tell him anything. Everything. And suddenly she wanted to.

"Set the scene. Where were you?" His deep voice filled her ears and she became instantly aware of the strong, warm hands that slid up to cup her breasts.

She had the fleeting thought that this went far beyond the usual conversation between even the best of friends, but she couldn't stop the answer that bubbled on her lips. "In my boutique."

"What did you smell?"

She took a deep breath. The sweet, intoxicating fragrance of cherries spiraled through her head, along with a dozen other distinct scents. Her nostrils flared and her chest heaved. "Fruit and chocolate and something else…a wildness, like the air when the sky's about to open up just before a big storm."

Like now.

It was *him*—his raw sexuality and insatiable hunger—that drifted through her head and teased her senses.

"What did you feel?"

"The hard counter at my back," she murmured. "Strong, purposeful hands trailing over my body." She trembled as heat swept through her.

"What else?" he prompted.

"A wetness between my legs…" Her breath caught and her legs threatened to buckle as she relived the memory for the next few moments. His lips and tongue caressing and devouring and—

"Here?" The word drew her away from the memory, back to the present and the fingertip that brushed across her crotch. A sharp bolt of desire shot from her head to the tips of her toes. She caught a gasp and bit down on her bottom lip.

"I'll take that as a *yes*."

She nodded as he circled the sensitive area with his fingertips. "Remembering a sexy encounter gets your juices flowing. It stirs you up and makes your body yearn for more." His touch drifted a delicious inch lower and his fingertips caught her hem. And then she felt him through the thin satin of her thong. He circled her before his touch drifted an inch lower and he stroked the slit between her legs. "Do you want more, Meg?"

She fought for her voice, but the soft, whispering strokes made it difficult. "I…"

"I didn't hear you, sugar." His finger went back and forth and her knees trembled. "Come on. *Tell me.*"

Her mouth opened and the frantic *yes* rushed to her lips at the same time that her brain issued a firm *don't do it!*

"You know you want me."

She did, and if she said it out loud, so would he.

She wouldn't be able to stop herself then. She would act on her want without ever knowing if the feeling was mutual. Without ever knowing if he wasn't just going along with the situation because he was horny and she was handy.

Without ever really knowing that he wanted *her*.

"I want to make the next *Hot Chicks* list," the words rushed out.

She snatched off the blindfold and found herself staring out over a blaze of twinkling lights, her toes flush with a sharp ledge high above the small town.

"Crazy Cooter's Ridge," she gasped as realization struck.

She was standing at the drop-off point where, ages ago, Cooter McWilliams had taken a nosedive to his death after his prize-winning hog, Gracie, had run away from home—hence the *crazy* tagged on to his name. Gracie had turned up a few days later, but Cooter had already taken the plunge and so the pig had inherited a shitload of money and had lived the high life at a local pet resort for several years before dying of old age. The huge cliff that overlooked the town had since become a ripe make-out spot for the local kids on the weekends.

Tonight was a school night, and so the area was deserted.

The wind licked at the tips of her bare toes peeking from her high-heeled sandals. Panic rushed through her as her mind rifled back through the past few moments. The wind whispering around her, the hands teasing her, Dillon circling her, his voice coming from one side then the other. The back and then the front—

Impossible!

She'd been in this exact spot *before* he'd started talking. Standing at the edge. There'd been no ground in front of her. No place for him to stand. To walk. To tease. Unless...

She remembered dreaming of him standing on her balcony. The way his eyes had blazed first one color and then the other. The way he seemed to always know what she was thinking, as if he could see into her thoughts and read her mind.

Yeah, sure.

Denial rushed through her. She was making something out of nothing. Maybe she was hard of hearing. Or maybe the wind had thrown her off. Or the high altitude. Or maybe she was just plain nuts.

The last one would certainly explain why no man wanted to jump her bones. Men thought women were complicated enough. Throw insane into the mix and, well, it didn't make for the most attractive package.

"I guess I get a great big zero for this lesson, don't I?" She started to turn, but he stopped her, his arms on either side of her, anchoring her in front of him.

"Not if you learned something from it."

"Such as?"

"Trust your instincts. That's the real key to being irresistible. A woman who trusts herself, who listens to her body and lets it guide her, is the ultimate in sexy. If you're feeling sexy, you act it."

"And if I don't feel sexy?" she managed to ask, despite every nerve in her body which screamed otherwise.

She needed to put some distance between them. He was too close, his chest cushioning her back, his hands anchored around her waist, fingertips burning through the thin material of her shirt. And damned if she didn't want him even closer, his hands under her shirt, between her legs.

"Don't be afraid," he said as if reading her thoughts.

"Easy for you to say," she said, her voice shaking. "If we plunge to our death, I'm going over the edge first. At least you'll have a cushion to land on. I'll be flat on the ground."

"You underneath me," he mused. "I could think of worse ways to go."

"Seriously." Her heart pounded in her chest. "I know the view is great and everything, but I really don't like this." She didn't want to like it.

To like him.

He tightened his arms around her waist. "I won't let you fall."

No, he wouldn't *let* her fall. He would push her right over the edge, and suddenly that scared her more than anything else—the notion of falling, helplessly, hopelessly, for Dillon Cash.

"I—I'm afraid of heights," she blurted. *Liar.*

He didn't move for several moments. He just stood there, his hands touching her, his body surrounding her, as if he didn't buy her explanation. As if the more he touched her, the more he could shake her control. He knew it. And so did she.

"Please," she added. *Please.*

Just like that, he let go. By the time she turned, he was already several yards away.

A strange sensation swept up her spine, but then he turned and his gaze collided with hers. Moonlight spilled down around them, outlining his powerful frame, making him seem taller, more imposing. His eyes seemed to glitter with an intensity that sucked the air from her lungs and made her heart beat even faster. "Let's go."

A trick of the light, she told herself as she forced her wobbly legs to move. She climbed on behind him, careful to keep her back straight and her hold loose as she slid her arms around his waist.

With her eyes wide-open this time, the ride back to town was even more stirring than the ride to Cooter's Ridge. Not only could she hear and smell and feel, but she could see him, as well—the wide expanse of his back, his broad shoulders, his muscular, tattooed arms. His powerful hands gripped the handlebars, his fingers flexing as he guided the bike with the controlled ease of someone who'd been riding his entire life.

He hadn't, she reminded herself. Months ago, he'd been as awkward, as uncertain, as *un*sexy as she was.

And just as desperate for a change.

She clung to the thought and tried to ignore the desire bubbling through her. A useless effort with most of her senses in major overload. One sweet, succulent taste of him and she would surely go over the edge.

The realization stuck in her head and urged her to lean forward, to trail the tip of her tongue down the side of his neck and relish the salty-sweetness of his skin…

She eased forward just an inch, her lips so close to his tempting skin.

Close, but not quite there.

Not yet.

Not ever.

Temptation pushed and pulled inside of her, threatening her fragile control. By the time he pulled up in front of her boutique, it was all she could do to pull away from him, climb off the bike and walk to the door. She could feel his gaze burning into her, but she didn't look back, not even to ask about another lesson.

Especially not to ask about another lesson.

She'd barely survived tonight with her dignity intact. The last thing she wanted to think about was facing the temptation all over again. No, she would have to come up with a different plan. The carnal classes would eventually pay off and she would have men crawling all over her. *And* she would make Tilly's list. She would just have to be patient until then and make due with her Twinkies and her fantasies.

"Tomorrow night," she heard his voice behind her as she slid her key into the lock. "I'll pick you up here."

She shook her head. "I don't think—" she started to respond, but then the engine growled, drowning out the rest of her refusal. She turned in time to see him take off down the street.

A few minutes later, Meg climbed into her own car, headed home and tried to come up with several convincing reasons to cancel.

No way was she meeting Dillon Cash tomorrow night.

She would play sick, she decided as she pulled into her driveway, climbed out of her car and headed inside the house. Maybe a rash. A fever. Maybe even some heavy-duty vomiting. Something really icky and contagious. Something that would have her lying on the floor, limp and lifeless—

Her thoughts skidded to a halt, along with her feet when she reached the kitchen doorway and spied the pile of fur that lay on the floor amid the remains of the three boxes of snack cakes Meg had picked up at the store earlier that day.

Babe was on her side, pieces of cardboard and cellophane littering the floor near her head. Crumbs clung to her whiskers, along with the scent of sugar and vanilla.

"Don't tell me you ate them all?"

The animal lifted her head and whimpered.

She'd eaten them all.

"Glutton." Meg dropped to her knees and stroked the animal's head. "I know it hurts, but I promise you'll live." But a few more whimpers and she wasn't so sure. She knew Twinkies couldn't hurt the dog.

One Twinkie.

Maybe even two.

But three dozen? Along with shreds of the plastic wrappers?

"It's okay," she murmured, gathering the large dog close.

The memories stirred and she found herself back home in the cabin where she'd grown up. She sat in the middle of the kitchen floor, a small puppy in her arms, the police officer who'd delivered the news of her father's accident standing awkwardly by as he waited for her grandparents to arrive.

Meg shook away the images and fought the sudden fear that gripped her.

A few minutes later, she loaded Babe into the backseat of her car, climbed behind the wheel and headed for the nearest twenty-four-hour animal clinic.

12

SHIT. SHIT. *SHIT*.

Dillon skidded to a stop in the parking lot of Skull Creek Choppers and killed the engine. Climbing off the bike, he stomped to the back door, his body stiff and tight. His gut clenched and unclenched as he shoved the key into the lock and threw open the door.

Inside, he bypassed the office and strode into the manufacturing shop. It was still early in the evening—barely 10:00 p.m.—and so the place was empty. Garret was out with whatever woman he'd taken a fancy to and Jake was with Nikki. Both vampires were no doubt drinking their fill in more ways than one.

A pang of hunger gripped him. His hands trembled, his muscles flexed and his jaw clenched. As worked up as he was, he wasn't about to try to park himself behind a desk and worry about his blog or his leads or even the Ancient One himself.

He needed to *do* something.

Hitting the power button, he fired up the high-tech computer terminal that he'd set up near the main tool table. The screen flickered to life and a 3-D image of a custom-made chopper appeared.

Dillon had entered the specifics for Garret's next order and the end result was the beauty on the monitor. His gaze shifted to the worktable and the simple frame that would eventually transform into the chopper.

Punching up several measurements, he surveyed the spreadsheet that scrolled across the screen. Following the details, he powered on the ARC welder and turned his attention to the hulk of metal that would soon be the custom-made fuel tank.

He spent the next few minutes working on the piece and trying not to think about Meg.

She was scared, all right. But it wasn't of heights.

She was scared of falling in love, of being in love.

With him.

And the problem is?

He had her right where he wanted her. If he tempted and teased her just a little more, he had no doubt she would make the first move. And the second. And the third.

She would offer herself up to him completely and he would get what he wanted—the chance to break Bobby's record and be remembered, not as the ultimate geek, but as the most legendary lover in town.

If.

Wait a second, there was no *if*. It was all about *when*.

Tomorrow night.

As for her fear of falling in love with him… He simply had to be reading her wrong. When she looked at him, she felt lust. Because of her past, she was afraid to act on that lust, afraid to perpetuate her own reputation.

Lust.

That's all she felt for him and all he felt for her. So he'd obviously been hallucinating. Since turning, he hadn't gone a full twenty-four hours without sex. He was going on seventy-two and lack of sustenance was making him punchy.

He needed to feed.

Tonight.

Now.

The thought struck as he saw a flash of lights through the window. He glanced up in time to see Meg's car haul ass past the shop.

Urgency spiraled through him, a feeling that had nothing to do with his own damned hunger and everything to do with the woman he'd just glimpsed. Her tear-streaked face. Her fear-filled eyes.

Something was wrong.

So? It doesn't matter. All you feel is lust, remember?

But it wasn't. They were friends, too.

Friends first.

And so Dillon did what any friend would do. He climbed on his motorcycle and hauled ass after her.

MEG FORCED HERSELF TO let go and handed Babe over to the night staff at Junction Animal Hospital. Her heart pounded painfully in her chest and her throat tightened as she watched her dog disappear through the double doors leading to the emergency exam room.

"You can have a seat." The woman behind the desk motioned Meg over to a small cluster of chairs, most of the seats already overflowing with worried pet owners. "It's a full moon, so we've had a busy night. Mr. McKinley's Jack Russell's got into a fight with a porcupine. Stu Morehead's rabbit, Fluffy, got her paw caught in some chicken wire. Jimmy Carmichael's prize-winning Arabian broke his leg near a gulley out by Old Sam's Creek and Agnes Carmichael's Great Dane ate one of her slippers." The woman smiled. "Just relax and help yourself to some complimentary coffee. This might take awhile."

Meg walked over to an empty chair, but a full thirty seconds later she was on her feet again. She paced a small area off to the side, in front of the coffee machine, and tried to fight the worry mounting inside of her. The scent of disinfectant filled her nostrils and dread settled in the pit of her stomach.

She had to be okay.

"She will be." Dillon's deep voice slid into Meg's ears a split second before she felt his strong, warm hand on her shoulder.

His presence seemed to wrap around her. The scent of warm male tinged her nostrils and an inexplicable wildness filled her head, chasing away the sharp odor of Lysol and animal fur that hung heavy in the air. She glanced up and her gaze met his. His green eyes gleamed with a certainty that eased her frantic heart beat. A strange sense of peace stole through her, pushing aside her worry and fear.

"She'll be okay," he said again as if he knew she needed his reassurance more than she needed her next breath.

And for the first time since leaving the house, Meg started to think that he just might be right.

"BASICALLY, SHE JUST ATE too much," Doc Jamison told Meg an hour later.

They stood in the doorway of one of the exam rooms. Inside, Babe lay on a large steel table. Dillon stood next to the animal and stroked her soft fur. Babe's leg gave an excited shake and relief swamped Meg.

"She has a bad case of indigestion," the vet went on. "A very bad case what with all the plastic she ingested on top of the sugar."

"But she's going to be okay, right? You'll give her some Tums and send her home."

"More than settling her stomach, we want to get her to pass everything, so she has a busy night ahead. You'll have to watch her, too, and keep her out of the pantry tonight. Otherwise, I might have to pump her stomach. That's as painful for dogs as it is for humans."

Meg nodded. "No more Twinkies."

"Or anything that isn't on this list." He handed over a neatly typed list of appropriate foods, along with at-home care instructions. "Don't give her anything tonight, but once she passes everything, she'll need nourishment. Namely, plenty of protein. I'm also going to give her a little something to ease the cramps. If you follow Shirley, there—" the vet motioned to the woman next to him who'd been sitting at the front desk "—she'll get you all taken care of."

Meg left Babe with Dillon and followed Shirley back through the double doors and out to the front desk. Five minutes later, she had a full bottle of pain pills along with a bottle of powdered fiber that she was supposed to mix and feed to Babe once they got home.

Meg took a deep breath as the news sank in. *Indigestion*. Not a heart attack or a stroke or any of the other horrible things she'd imagined might result from sponge cake overload.

"She's going to be okay."

Dillon's deep, reassuring words echoed in her head a split second before he appeared next to her, Babe cradled in his arms.

"I think she's starting to feel better," he murmured, nuzzling the dog.

Babe rewarded him with a lick on the cheek and Meg realized that Babe was just as susceptible to him as every other female in Skull Creek.

Every female, that is, except Meg herself.

The knowledge should have been comforting—she was standing strong, holding her own, waiting to be ravished rather than making a fool of herself and acting on her own one-sided lust. Instead, she couldn't help but feel as if she was missing out on the chance of a lifetime.

His deep voice pushed into her thoughts. "Ready?"

In more ways than one, she realized as she followed him out to her car and watched him load Babe into the backseat. He gave the animal another affectionate scrub behind her ears and Babe's tail twitched. She liked Dillon, and so did Meg. And she was *ready,* all right, to head home, to give in, to let go.

The notion stuck in her head and warred with her determination as she made the drive back to her place, Dillon following on his motorcycle. Once they pulled up in her driveway, he gathered Babe from the car and toted her inside.

A few minutes later, Meg watched him lay the animal on a batch of fluffy quilts that she'd pulled from the closet, and suddenly she wasn't half as scared to make the first move with him as she was *not* to make the first move.

To feel his arms around her and his lips eating at hers and his body so deep she didn't know where he ended and she began.

To lose herself in the sweet heat she'd been fighting since

she'd come face-to-face with the new and improved Dillon Cash just a few days ago.

And backslide into Manhandler Meg?

The question struck, reminding her of the past and her own reputation, and the all-important fact that she was still desperate to erase both.

Throwing herself at Dillon Cash would accomplish nothing.

At the same time, it was the one thing she wanted most at the moment. The only thing.

She busied herself for the next few minutes giving Babe her medication and getting her settled for the night. With each movement, she felt Dillon's gaze and while the tension between them was thick, there was something oddly comforting about having him there. She didn't feel so alone.

He'd been her friend back when she'd needed one most. And he'd been her friend tonight when she'd needed one most.

All the more reason to resist the crazy thoughts racing through her head.

"I should be going," he said.

Let him, her conscience urged. *Otherwise you'll regret it tomorrow.*

"Thanks for showing up at the animal hospital." She started for the front door.

"That's what friends are for." He followed behind her, so close she could feel the warmth of his body, the tightness of his muscles, the rush of his breath ruffling the hair on her head. Her skin prickled and her nipples throbbed and she felt the moisture between her legs. Her memory stirred and his voice echoed, so clear and distinct, it seemed he whispered them at that particular moment.

A woman who trusts herself, who listens to her body and lets it guide her, is the ultimate in sexy.

She turned on him. Their gazes collided. Surprise registered on his face as her hands went to the bottom of her blouse. Before she could breathe, let alone give in to the insecurity whirling inside of her, she whisked the material up and over her head.

By the time her gaze met his again, his eyes had fired to a fierce, glittering green. She felt a niggle of apprehension because as right as everything was, it wasn't. There was something different about him. Something that went beyond his sexy appearance and newfound confidence. Something dark and dangerous.

The notion struck as he stared at her, into her, but then his gaze dropped to her breasts and she forgot everything except the desire swamping her.

Lifting her hands, she worked at the bra clasp until it snapped and popped. The cups fell away and the scrap of lingerie landed at her feet. Her skirt soon slouched in a heap around her ankles and she stood before him wearing nothing but a pink thong. She hooked her thumbs at the waistband, slid the satin down her legs and stepped free. Just like that she was completely naked.

She felt a moment's hesitation as she stood there, but then he murmured, "You're so damned beautiful," and it was all the encouragement she needed.

Closing the distance between them, she reached for the hem of his T-shirt. He lifted his arms, letting her pull the cotton up and over his head. Where she'd seen him bare-chested back at the motel a few days ago, the sight of him now was a hundred times better.

Muscles carved his torso, from his bulging biceps and shoulders to the rippled plane of his abdomen. Gold, silky hair sprinkled his chest, narrowing to a tiny whorl of silk that disappeared beneath the waistband of his jeans.

She meant to slow down, to at least let him do something, but she couldn't help herself. She reached out and pressed her palm against his chest, feeling the hair tickle her skin. She followed the golden path lower until it stopped at his waistband.

He balled his hands into fists at his sides, as if it took everything he had not to cover her hand with his and urge her lower, wanting her to take the lead.

And where she would have stood her ground and tried to hold back a few moments ago, she'd already waved the white flag and given up.

She'd lost the battle with her own damned lust.

Oddly enough, she felt more like a winner than a loser as she dropped to her knees in front of him and reached for the waistband of his pants. The zipper hissed and he sprang hot and eager into her hands. She trailed her fingers over him, tracing the bulging veins until she reached the ripe, plump head of his penis. He stiffened and a drop of pearly liquid beaded at the tip. She leaned forward, closed her lips around the smooth ridge and lapped at his essence with her tongue for a long sweet moment before she felt his hands on her shoulders.

"Don't."

Her gaze met his and where she expected him to look victorious, instead he looked more startled.

"What's wrong?"

"Nothing." The word was raw and thick. He shook his head and the strange look faded into one of hungry determination. He pulled her to her feet and his mouth claimed hers in a deep, thorough kiss that took her breath away.

Dillon plunged his tongue deep, tangling with hers as he tried to understand what the hell had just happened to him.

Or rather, what had *almost* happened.

One draw of her sweet mouth on his cock and he'd been ready to explode. *Just like that.* Like some wet-behind-the-ears virgin. Like the town geek experiencing his first blow job.

The thing was, it wasn't his first and he certainly wasn't a virgin. And he sure as hell wasn't a geek, no matter how much a tiny voice inside of him screamed otherwise.

He was a vampire who thrived on sex.

He didn't get off until the woman got off. It was her climax—the sweet, dizzying energy—that seeped into him, stirred his hunger and sent him over the edge.

Not this time.

Not with Meg.

Because she's the ultimate challenge.

The explanation whispered through his head, easing the

anxiety that rushed through him. This was his moment of truth, and so it made sense that he would be a little out of sorts. On top of that, he was hungry.

So damned hungry.

He fought against the urge to push her up against the nearest wall and bury himself inside of her. Instead, he eased the pressure of his mouth and shifted the kiss from fast and furious to slow and wicked and thorough.

His tongue tangled with hers and he ate at her mouth. She stiffened at first, as if unsure as to the sudden change, but then she relaxed, sucking on his tongue, giving as good as she got.

It was the most passionate kiss of her life.

The most stirring.

The most unnerving.

He felt it as his hands slid down her trembling body, tracing the curve of her spine, kneading her sweet ass for several long moments until she clutched at his shoulders and slumped against him.

Sweeping her into his arms, he headed upstairs, down the hall, into her bedroom. Moonlight pushed through the French doors, filling the room with an ethereal light that bathed her flawless skin as he stretched her out on her cotton candy-pink sheets.

He didn't bother taking his jeans off or sinking to the bed beside her. As determined as he was, he didn't trust himself. His gut clenched too tightly, the hunger too fierce. The sharpness of his fangs grazed his tongue and electricity sizzled through him.

Easy.

"Dillon?" Her soft voice drew his attention.

She stared up at him, her lips full and slick from his mouth, her nipples ripe, her breasts flushed, her legs open. Her cleft was wet and swollen and desire knifed through him, along with a pang of hunger so fierce it stalled his heart for several fast, furious seconds.

"I want you," she murmured, as if she thought he waited just to hear the words.

That was exactly what she thought, he realized as he stared

deep into her eyes and saw the rush of uncertainty, the flash of defeat. His chest tightened and something shifted inside of him. Suddenly it wasn't about his own damned hunger, but hers.

"No." He leaned over her and slid a finger into her pulsing heat. "I want you." And then he captured her mouth with his.

Over the next few minutes, he stroked and tasted and drove her to the brink of orgasm. He plunged his tongue deep, mimicking the action with his fingers, in and out, deeper and deeper, until she whimpered and tugged at his jeans.

But he was a man on a mission and so he caught her hands and pushed them up over her head. He placed a long, lingering kiss on her lips before trailing his mouth over her jaw and down the side of her neck. Her pulse beat against his lips and his groin tightened. Heat swept through him and he trembled. He felt the sharp edge of his teeth graze her fragrant flesh. Once. Twice.

She gasped, the sound like a loud *pop* in his head that yanked him back to reality. He licked the tiny scrape he'd made on her skin and moved on, kissing and nibbling until he reached her breasts. He lapped at her ripe nipple before blowing on the tip and making her moan.

Her fingers threaded through his hair and held him to her as he drew her deep and sucked her long and hard. He heard her pulse beat in his head, throbbing against his mouth, and it took everything he had not to sink his fangs deep and feel the warmth flowing into his mouth at the same time he felt her tight, hot body close around his cock.

His mouth closed over hers again as he trailed a hand down, over her breast, her abdomen, until he reached her slick folds. He touched her again and she gasped. A drop of warmth spurted over his knuckle and trailed across his palm. His gut tightened and he grew harder, hotter, hungrier.

He slid a finger deep, relishing the incredible heat that sucked at him. With each thrust, the pressure built, pushing her higher until her eyes glazed over and her cheeks flushed. Another deep, dizzying thrust and suddenly she was there.

Her nails dug into his shoulders and she arched off the bed. A moan burst from her lips and he caught it, absorbing the sound the way he absorbed the delicious energy that rushed through him, quieting the roaring in his ears.

But there was none of the usual satisfaction that he usually felt at this point.

Just the fierce need for more.

For her.

He stood and kicked off his boots. Shoving his jeans and underwear down, he kicked them aside then joined her on the bed. He pushed her legs even wider, pulling them up at the knees to give himself better access. The head of his penis pushed a delicious inch into her sweet heat and pleasure spiked through him—

"Wait!" Her soft plea pushed past the sudden roaring in his ears and his gaze collided with hers. "A condom," she gasped. "We need a condom."

He hadn't had much need for protection during the past few months. Vampires couldn't catch anything—not with the mother of all viruses already flowing through their veins. Nor could they give anything. Passing on his vampness involved sharing his blood, not his body. As for making little vamp babies, that was pretty much impossible according to Garret.

But Meg didn't know any of that, and Dillon had no intention of letting her know he wasn't really half as sexy as she thought. It was his vamp charisma.

Here today, gone tomorrow.

A pang of regret washed through him, followed by a rush of *so?* Who cared why she wanted him so badly. The fact was, she did want him.

Badly.

He focused on the thought and reached for his jeans and the ancient condom that had been in his wallet since junior high. Tearing at the foil packet, he rolled the latex on in one swift motion, he pressed her down into the mattress and settled between her legs. The head of his erection slid along her damp flesh and she shuddered. Her soft, wet folds sucked at the very tip of his head and he groaned.

"Wrap your legs around me," he finally managed to whisper, his voice husky and raw.

Her legs snaked around his waist. The motion lifted her and he slid deep. Usually he paused at this point, relishing the heat, building the anticipation because he drew the most energy when a woman came apart in his arms.

But then he felt the same rush of desperation he'd felt when she'd taken him into her mouth, and he couldn't control himself.

He started to move, penetrating deeply with each plunge of his cock. His hands played over her body, feeling every curve and indentation. The feel of her roused him as much as the sight of her spread beneath him, her head flung back, her eyes closed, her lips parted, her body lifting to meet the thrust of his hips.

Catching the tip of one nipple between his lips, he sucked her in, drawing on her, feeling her soft flesh graze his fangs as he moved in and out. Her muscles tightened around him and her body went tense as he slid free. Another deep thrust and she exploded. She milked him as the ecstasy gripped her. Heat rippled through him, sating his hunger and feeding his own energy. He forced his mouth from her breast and stared down at her, drinking in the picture that she made lost in the throes of orgasm.

Her face and neck were flushed, her lips parted and trembling, her eyes glittering.

His hunger roared to life and suddenly, he couldn't plunge fast enough, deep enough. He tried, pushing and withdrawing and…there. Yes, *there!*

Pleasure splintered his brain and his body convulsed. He felt his gaze brighten and blaze.

"What the—"

Her soft voice pushed past the beating in his skull and lifted the haze of pleasure long enough for him to see the shock on her face as she stared up at him, into him.

He clamped his eyes shut and gave her a plundering, consuming kiss meant to distract her from what she'd just seen.

Or what she'd thought she'd seen.

No way could it have been real.

At least that's what she told herself. Denial rushed through her, easing her panic until she forgot everything save kissing him back.

Thankfully.

Otherwise, Garret would have his ass.

At least that's what Dillon told himself as he rolled onto his back and stared up at the ceiling, his heart pounding, his blood rushing. No way did he want to consider the possibility that he didn't want her to know because he actually liked her and wanted her to like him. *Now and tomorrow.* And if she knew the truth, she would surely write off her attraction as a result of his vamp charisma.

And she'd be right.

He ignored a pang of regret and tried to focus on the sweet rush of victory that spiraled through him.

He'd broken Bobby's record.

Instead of being the town's biggest geek, he would now go down in the history books as Skull Creek's most legendary lover.

Unfortunately, the truth didn't make him feel half as good as Meg did when she snuggled into his embrace, closed her eyes and fell asleep.

A realization that pushed him to his feet and had him reaching for his pants and boots. A few minutes later, he hit the front door, climbed onto his motorcycle and got the hell out of there.

Because no way was Dillon falling in love with her.

His life—or lack of—was way too complicated as it was. The last thing he needed was to muck it up with a relationship that didn't stand a chance in hell, heaven or the in-between.

13

MEG LISTENED AS THE rumble of Dillon's motorcycle faded in the distance. She barely resisted the urge to rush to the French doors and catch one last glimpse of him.

Instead, she slid her hand to the indentation he'd made next to her. The warmth seeped into her fingers and his lingering scent teased her nostrils.

"I want you."

His admission echoed in her head, but it did little to curb the disappointment creeping through her.

Because she'd given in first.

That's what she told herself. No way would she even consider the alternative—that she missed Dillon. That she felt more for him than mutual respect or friendship or simple like.

Ditto for all three, but nothing more. She certainly hadn't *fallen* for him.

Not even a little.

She'd been tired and upset and horny, and the three had made for a dangerous combination. Of course, she'd gone a little nuts. The guy was hot, sexy, irresistible, and so she'd caved.

But no more. She'd had enough sex to last her another six months and she was no longer terrified that she might lose Babe. A little sleep, and she would have her wits about her.

Tomorrow morning, she would wake up and get back in the game. Back to searching for a way to beef up her sex appeal and make Tilly's coveted list.

Without Dillon Cash.

She couldn't continue their lessons even if he wanted to—and she had her doubts considering the fact that he'd left without so much as a see ya. While she hadn't fallen for him yet, she wasn't going to take any chances.

It would be too easy.

And too heartbreaking.

Despite his admission, she knew he didn't feel the same I-have-to-have-you-right-now-or-I'll-die passion that she felt for him. Otherwise, he wouldn't have been able to hold back for so long. No, he'd teased and taunted the past few days and she had no doubt that, had she not made the first move, tonight would have ended like all the others—sexless and frustrating.

Regret washed through her and she stiffened. She pushed to her feet. A delicious ache spiraled through her along with several vivid, very graphic memories of the past hour. Her hands trembled and her legs shook and heat chased up and down her skin.

Yep, tomorrow she was back on the wagon.

As for tonight...

She headed for the bathroom and an ice-cold shower.

"Looks like someone didn't get much sleep last night," Terry remarked when Meg walked into work fifteen minutes late the next morning.

It was the same comment she'd heard from Doris Milligan when she'd stopped at the coffee shop for a double cappuccino with a shot of espresso. And from old Mr. Parker when she'd stopped at the Quick Stop for a copy of the latest *In Style*.

It was as if the entire world could tell with one glance that she'd had wild and crazy sex last night with Mr. Wild & Crazy himself.

"It wasn't anything serious," she blurted, telling Terry the same thing she'd been telling herself since Dillon had walked away last night. "We're just friends."

"I wasn't talking about you. I'm talking about me again." The woman hefted an armload of dresses to a nearby rack. "I swear I didn't get so much as a solid ten minutes." She reached for the protein drink sitting on a nearby table and took a long swig. "And I'm definitely feeling it this morning."

Meg set her purse on the shelf near a stack of Brighton leather belts and headed for the cluster of boxes to help Terry unpack. "Anyone I know?"

The woman shook her head. "Hank."

"Don't tell me you slept with him *again?*"

"I didn't sleep with him." She shook her head. "But he wants me to. He called all night long, first while I was trying to work out on my elliptical trainer. Then while I was on the treadmill. Then during my favorite *Move Those Buns* DVD. Then while I was scarfing down a double cheese and sausage pizza."

"You don't scarf pizza. You don't scarf anything."

"I do after eighteen phone calls from Hank."

"Eighteen?" Meg noted the worried glimmer in Terry's brown eyes and suddenly her own troubles didn't seem all that terrible. "Maybe you should call Sheriff Matthews."

"And tell him what? That I slept with my ex and now he wants a repeat?" She shook her head. "Hank's just lonely, that's all. Since we broke up, he hasn't had a relationship that's lasted over two months."

"Because he's a jerk."

"True."

"A jerk who's harassing you." Meg reached for a box cutter. "You should call the sheriff."

"He just wants to talk. He hasn't threatened or yelled, or *done* anything."

Yet.

The silent word hung between them for several long moments before Terry finally shook her head.

"I know Hank. He'll give it up eventually. He always does." She summoned a smile. "I swear the man couldn't stay focused long enough to hold a job or give me a decent orgasm. He'll move on to something else." She waved a hand. "In the meantime, I just have to hold tight and keep from encouraging him."

"And try not to gain thirty pounds in the process."

"You aren't kidding." She pinched at her waist before turning her attention to the boxes. She sliced open one box while Meg tackled another. A few seconds later, she unearthed a black sports jacket and let loose a low whistle. "Since when do we carry anything like this?"

"I've had a few requests for men's clothes, so I thought I'd have a some samples on hand just in case anyone is interested." Meg shrugged and ignored the sudden ache between her legs. "It's all in the name of good business."

"And here I thought it was all in the name of Dillon Cash."

Meg's head snapped up. "What are you talking about?"

"Come on, Meg. The entire town knows that you and Dillon are seeing each other. Margie Culpepper's daughter Dana saw you two out riding around last night. And Camille Harlingen's grandmother was out walking her dog and saw you two here at the boutique the night before that." Terry gave her a knowing look. "Either you guys are seeing each other, or Grandma Harlingen's doing more with that cooking sherry than making pot roast."

Meg's mind rifled back through the past hour. She'd had a ton of knowing looks while she'd been in line for her coffee. And even more at the Quick Stop.

Because they know.

Her hands trembled as she searched for her most nonchalant voice. "What, um, exactly did she see?"

"Enough to have you halfway down the aisle because you're carrying his baby."

"You're kidding, right?"

Terry shrugged. "You're a woman and he's a man. You were in the same room together and, if Grandma Harlingen's bifocals are still the right prescription, you were minus your undies."

"That still doesn't mean we had sex." *Not here.*

"Maybe not, though I can't for the life of me imagine that you would go undie-less and not jump Dillon Cash." She waved a hand. "But even if you didn't, Mabel's told everyone you're the reincarnation of Jezebel, so you might as well have."

"Who exactly did she tell?"

"Her Bunko group at the senior center. And you know that's as good as telling every person in this town." Terry grinned. "Looks like I might have some competition for next week's list."

Hope fired inside of Meg, dispelling her sudden embarrassment. "You really think so?"

"One more date with Dillon and I'm old news."

Terry's words were like a rush of wind and just like that, the hope died. "I wouldn't write a goodbye speech just yet." At the woman's questioning look, Meg added, "I'm not seeing him again."

Terry arched an eyebrow. "That bad, huh?"

That good.

Meg could still remember the feel of his skin beneath hers, his hands roaming her body, his hips pumping furiously, his penis plunging deep. Her cheeks heated. "I wouldn't exactly say he was *bad*. It just wasn't what I expected." It was more, which meant she couldn't—wouldn't—go out with Dillon again, not even for the sake of Tilly's list.

She tamped down a rush of disappointment and tried to focus on the positive. The lessons, however few, had obviously worked. She'd finally reached Jezebel status.

The trick now was to figure out a way to keep it, at least for the next week until Tilly announced her new list.

Her mind raced and rifled through dozens of possibilities as she turned her attention to unpacking merchandise. She'd just pulled a pair of Gucci silver slingbacks from a mound of tissue paper when genius seemed to strike.

If being seen with the town's hottest guy had upped her sex factor that much, then being seen with another guy—not as *yowza* as Dillon when it came to sex appeal, but still a respectable *wow*—might solidify it.

The notion struck and she almost pushed it back out. The

sudden thought of being with a good-looking man, touching him, kissing him, didn't stir the same excitement that it usually did.

Because of Dillon.

He wasn't just a hot guy. He was a double whammy—a hot guy and her friend, and last night she'd realized just how dangerous to her control such a combination could be.

Still, she'd come too far to give up now.

She reached for the phone and dialed the local real estate office. "Colt Grainger, please," she said when the receptionist picked up.

"This is Meg," she said when she heard his deep *"Yes?"* "I'd rather not wait until next Saturday. Why don't we see each other tonight?"

FOR THE FIRST TIME IN two months, Dillon Cash was alone on a Friday night.

He sat at the bar, a bottle of beer in front of him, a lively two-step number bouncing off the walls around him. The Roundup was one of about a half-dozen honky tonks that lined the interstate between Skull Creek and Junction.

The perfect place to pick up a warm, willing woman.

All he had to do was scope out the sea of hot bodies that filled the dance floor and pick whichever one caught his fancy. A blond bombshell with a nice ass or a brunette with big breasts or a redhead with long legs.

The trouble was, he'd already slept with most everyone in the place, and so he'd settled for a beer.

He took a deep swig of Coors, but the liquid didn't ease the tightening in his gut or sate the thirst that clawed at his throat. He needed to feed, to drink in enough sweet, rich blood to fortify him on top of the heavy dose of sex he'd had last night.

Then he could think again.

Concentrate.

He had a ton of things on his plate right now—the handlebars he'd started last night on the new chopper, his blog, the background checks on his list of possible Joes. Which meant he should give it up, head for a spot farther down the interstate where there were sure to be a few new faces, and get busy.

He knew it, but damned if he could make himself move. Instead, he downed another swig of beer and wished with all his heart that he could punch something.

His gaze fixed on the woman currently two-stepping her way across the dance floor with another man.

His woman.

She wore a brown leather vest that didn't have anything underneath it except skin, and a pair of tight, stonewashed jeans. Add a pair of high heeled cowboy boots, her jeans stuffed inside, and Meg Sweeney was definitely the hottest thing on two legs.

But her appeal went deeper than the clothes. Her long, blond hair was slightly mussed and flowed down around her shoulders. Her eyes sparkled. Her skin glowed. She looked as if she'd just rolled out of bed after a night of incredible sex.

Which wouldn't have been a problem if she'd been with the man responsible for said night.

Dillon downed another gulp and barely resisted the urge to haul ass across the room and inform her that she was making a fool of herself.

Why, she was hanging all over the guy.

Her arms looped around his neck. A smile tilted her full lips as she drank in his every word. She slid this way and that, her boots kicking up sawdust as she danced and had the time of her life.

She looked happy, vibrant, and completely oblivious to Dillon.

Not that he cared. Hell, no. Last night had been his final challenge and he'd proved himself. She'd been all over him, and she was now history.

End of story.

Bye-bye.

Sexually, that is. They were still friends. Hell, he'd sat at the vet half the friggin' night for her and he'd even dropped by her place on the way to The Roundup just to see if Babe was feeling better. Meg hadn't been home, of course, and so she hadn't known he'd sat for a full fifteen minutes, talking and petting the animal who'd toddled out her doggie door to see him until he'd felt certain the dog was on her way to a full recovery. Still. He was thoughtful and considerate and, basically, a great friend. The least she could do was look at him.

And if she doesn't know you're here?

That thought bothered him even more than the notion that she just didn't want to acknowledge him.

They'd slept together, for Christ's sake. He could still feel her hot, tight body pulsing around him. He could hear the soft breaths that sawed past her lips and the excited beat of her heart. He could smell the intoxicating aroma of warm, sweet woman. Her memory haunted him.

She, on the other hand, wasn't sparing him a second thought. Otherwise she would have looked as bad as he felt.

So much for leaving a lasting impression.

No, he was the one left with the impressions and damned if he'd had a moment's peace since he'd walked away from her. There'd been no consuming sleep that day. No smothering blackness to rejuvenate him. Instead, he'd tossed and turned and mentally kicked his own ass for leaving so abruptly.

He should have written a note or said goodbye or something.

But the *something* he'd had in mind had involved a lot more kissing and touching and so he'd gotten the hell out of there.

No seconds.

Garret had warned him and Dillon knew what would happen should he violate the rules. He'd barely made it out without biting her last night. He wouldn't be able to stop himself the next time. He would sink his fangs in as easily as he sank his cock deep, and the damage would be done.

They would be forever linked.

Like Jake and Nikki.

A pang of envy shot through him. One he quickly ignored by

downing the rest of his beer. He wasn't Jake. When the cowboy reclaimed his humanity, he would still be the ultra-cool guy he was now and Nikki would still be in love with him.

But Dillon...

He would go back to his life before and he already knew that Meg didn't find that guy the least bit attractive. As for her falling in love with him... That was an even bigger long shot than Roxy Thompson agreeing to dance with Herman Tremaine.

Dillon's gaze shifted to the short man picking his way through a maze of tables toward a tall, leggy brunette wearing a miniskirt and tube top.

Herman was six years younger and while Dillon didn't know the man personally, he knew he'd been president of the chess club and the captain of the chemistry team, and he'd gone to the state spelling bee championships both his junior and senior year, an accomplishment that no one other than Dillon, himself, could claim. Meanwhile, Roxy had been homecoming queen and dance squad commander. She'd since gone on to pose in three different Hooters calendars and had done a recent commercial for the local Piggly Wiggly. She'd also made eight out of the last ten Hot Chicks list.

Dillon's ears prickled. The music and laughter faded as he tuned into Herman's trembling voice.

"Hi, Roxy."

"Hey," she murmured. Her forehead wrinkled. *"Do I know you?"*

"I'm Herman. We went to grade school together. And junior high. And high school. We work together." When she didn't look anymore clued in, he added, *"At the bank."*

"You're a teller, too?"

"A loan officer."

"Oh."

"I, um, was thinking maybe we could, you know, dance or something. If you want," he rushed on. *"We don't have to. It's just a thought. But since the music's pretty good and you're not*

dancing with anyone and I'm not dancing with anyone, I figure we could dance with each other. That is, if you want."

"Sorry, Harry. My feet are really hurting."

"It's Herman."

"That's what I meant." She touched her temples. "And I've got this splitting headache, too," she added before turning to her friends and putting her back to him.

"Okay." He shifted nervously. "Um, well, I guess I'll see you at work tomorrow then." He turned and her soft voice followed, "Not if I see you first."

Talk about a crash and burn. One that hit much too close to home. Dillon had dealt with the same rejection for most of his life, and he had no doubt he would deal with it again.

It was just a matter of time.

All the more reason to push last night completely out of his head and get his ass out of here.

His gut tightened and his stomach grumbled.

He was hungry.

That was the only reason he was thinking such crazy thoughts, like how Jake and Nikki seemed so happy and how he might—if he tried really hard—be able to explain things to his parents in a way that wouldn't send his mother to an early grave. And how maybe, just maybe, he might forget all about finding the Ancient One, and he and Meg might forge their own bond.

Too late, a voice whispered. That same voice that had played at the back of his head all evening, reminding him of the strange woman who'd been asking around town about him.

She'd been at it again today. Nikki had left a message on his cell while he'd been in the shower.

"She's still here."

But even if she hadn't warned him, Dillon would have known.

He couldn't shake the awareness that rippled up and down his spine, the certainty that someone was there. Watching. Waiting. And while Dillon had meant to hunt down the Ancient One, he couldn't shake the feeling that, instead, he'd somehow drawn him out.

That he'd drawn him *here*.

Uneasiness rushed down his spine and he felt a tap on his shoulder. He put on his most charming grin and gave a polite "Thanks, but not right now" to the woman who'd come up behind him. She was the cousin of a cousin of a cousin visiting for the weekend and the only woman in the entire place—with the exception of Bobby Sue Montgomery who was here with her husband, Walt, celebrating their twenty-fifth anniversary—that Dillon hadn't slept with.

She was sex trophy, pretty with pouty lips and long, dark hair and a curvy figure and he forced himself to take a second look. Other than the slow, steady rumble gnawing at his gut, he didn't feel even a ripple of desire for her.

Nothing intense.

Nothing like what he'd felt last night.

He signaled the bartender to bring him a second round before shifting his gaze back to Meg.

The minute his attention fixed on her, she stiffened and missed a step. She teetered and the man caught her. His hands slithered around her waist and he pulled her close and—

No.

Hell, no.

He pushed to his feet and, just like that, Dillon forgot the hunger raging inside of him and gave in to a fierce swell of possessiveness.

Regardless of what happened tomorrow, right now, at this moment, Meg Sweeney was his.

He knew it.

She knew it.

And it was high time everyone else knew, as well.

14

DON'T LOOK.

Meg told herself that for the countless time since Dillon Cash had walked into The Roundup and turned what should have been the most exciting night of her life—Tilly was here, cloistered at a table in the far corner with a group from the *Skull Creek Gazette* and Colt Grainger was practically drooling all over her—into an agonizing exercise in self-control.

Don't even think about looking.

She ignored the urge to turn toward the bar and the man who'd been warming the stool for the last half hour, tightened her hold on Colt's neck, stared up into his eyes and kept swaying. And smiling.

The trouble was, she didn't have to look to know that Dillon was headed straight for her. She saw him out of the corner of her eye, a black shadow that pushed up from the barstool, bisected the dance floor and closed the distance between them. Even more, she could *feel* him.

Her skin prickled and heat skittered up and down her spine. It was all she could do not to turn when she he stepped up behind her.

"We need to talk," his deep voice slid into her ears, pushing aside the music and laughter and the frantic beat of her heart.

She stiffened against the urge to turn, wrap her arms around his neck and see if he tasted half as delicious as she remembered. But she was with Colt, she reminded herself, twining her fingers around the man's neck and giving him an apologetic smile. "I'm really busy," she told Dillon.

But Dillon wasn't giving up so easily. "It'll only take a few minutes."

"I'm on a date."

"I can see that." He sounded none too pleased and a traitorous slither of hope went through her. Ridiculous because regardless of what he had to say, she knew what her answer would be—a great big no. No more lessons. No more sex.

She wasn't blowing a friendship over a few hours of mindless pleasure.

Even phenomenal mindless pleasure.

She wasn't losing Dillon, too.

"Give me five minutes."

"And miss my favorite song?" She gave Colt another *Sorry about this* smile. "I love George Strait."

"This is Tim McGraw."

"Close enough."

"Look, buddy. The lady doesn't want to talk to you," Colt cut in. "So get lost."

"Mind your own business."

"This is my…" Colt stared past her and his words faded, along with his expression. A strange light glimmered in his eyes and then they became empty. It was as if he'd spaced out. His hands loosened on her waist and fell away.

"Colt?" She stared into his blank expression. "Are you okay?"

"He's fine. Let's go."

"No." She snapped her fingers in front of Colt and waved a hand. *Nothing.* "Colt?"

"I mean it, Meg. You've got five seconds to move."

"Or what?"

"Or I'm carrying you out of here."

Before she could draw her next breath, Dillon caught her arm and whirled her around. "Time's up." He hooked her knees and folded her over his shoulder, and in the blink of an eye she found herself dangling upside down.

Meg squealed and dozens of curious stares swiveled their way.

But Dillon didn't care. He strode toward the nearest Exit. He hit the bar on the door, carried her out behind the building to the gravel lot where the employees parked and dropped her to her feet.

She blinked away a sudden rush of dizziness as he pulled off his cowboy hat and ran a frustrated hand through his dark blond hair.

Where she'd avoided taking a good look at him inside, she couldn't help but look now.

He wore a black T-shirt, faded jeans and a look that said he was royally pissed. Tension rolled off his body and his jaw clenched. A muscle ticked wildly near his left cheek. His eyes glittered dark green, so dark that they seemed almost black in the dim lighting.

Almost purple.

She blinked and the color faded.

Obviously a trick of the light or her own frantic mind. She was dizzy, not to mention pretty well pissed herself.

Planting her hands on her hips, she glared. "Just what do you think you're doing?"

He set the hat back on his head and inched closer, making her crane her neck to look at him. "You wanted a man to make the first move. Well I just made it."

"That's not what I was talking about."

His voice lowered a notch. "Wasn't it? You wanted a man to act on his feelings, to take the lead, to be so insane with lust that he can't keep his hands off you. Well, here you go."

Excitement bolted through her, followed by a rush of doubt because no way—no way in *hell*—was Dillon Cash really and truly coming on to her.

Sure, she looked really hot in a new outfit she'd picked up at the boutique, but she had a closet full of hot clothes and they'd never made a difference.

Deep down, she knew she was a fake. A fraud. The entire town knew it and he was no exception. She wasn't sexy enough for him to make the first move.

Not in the past few days when they'd been smack-dab in

the middle of the most provocative lessons. Not last night when she'd stripped off her clothes and dropped to her knees in front of him.

And not now while they were standing in the middle of a parking lot, the air stagnant with the smell of French fries and stale beer from a nearby Dumpster, the stark light from a bare bulb gleaming overhead.

It was her imagination. Wishful thinking. Desperate hormones.

She'd gotten a taste of the richest, most decadent sex of her life, and she couldn't help but want another.

She *knew* it.

At the same time, there was no denying the fierce gleam in his eyes or the fact that he'd physically picked her up in the middle of a crowded honky tonk, in front of God and half the town, or the fact that he was staring down at her now, his eyes blazing with jealousy and a hunger that kicked her in the chest and sent the air whooshing from her lungs.

She swallowed past a sudden lump in her throat. "What exactly are you trying to say?"

"This." And then his mouth swooped down and captured hers.

Meg's heart beat double-time, the sound thundering in her ears, drowning out her conscience and every reason why this couldn't be happening. Even more, why it shouldn't—they were friends and she could fall for him too easily. He would inevitably break her heart because he wasn't the least bit interested in anything more than sex, and she would wind up alone and broken.

Again.

She slid her arms around his neck, stopped thinking altogether and just *felt*. The purposeful slant of his lips. The tantalizing dance of his tongue. The strong splay of his hands at the base of her spine. The muscular wall of his chest crushing her breasts. The hardness of his thighs pressed flush against hers.

Yum.

The kiss was hot and wet and mesmerizing, and much too brief. The last thought struck as she felt every muscle in his body go rigid. She opened her eyes just as he tore his mouth from hers. His head jerked around, his gaze fierce and searching and—

Nuh, uh.

She blinked once, twice, but his gaze didn't cool. Rather, his eyes gleamed like hot twin coals. Bright and intense and bloodred.

Her heart pounded, echoing in her head, drowning out the *whoosh* of cars from the nearby interstate, the crack of pool balls from inside, the crunch of gravel from behind a nearby Buick.

Her mind stalled on the thought and her gaze swiveled in time to see a shadow scramble away from the car.

A growl vibrated the air and her attention shifted back to Dillon in time to see his lips draw back. His fangs glittered as he whirled—

No.

Shock hit her like a thunderbolt and she clamped her eyes shut. The air rushed from her lungs and every muscle in her body froze.

Wait a second, *wait a second*.

She'd either had too much to drink or not enough, because there was no way she'd just seen…that he actually had…that he was actually a…. *No.*

Denial rushed through her, followed by a wave of panic when she opened her eyes to see Dillon, fangs still bared, eyes flashing. He took one step toward the Buick and collapsed.

Her gaze shifted to the small dart that protruded between his shoulder blades. Her heart hit the brakes and skidded to a stop. Fear rushed through her, cold and biting, dousing the anxiety and disbelief, and galvanizing her into action.

Not fear for herself that told her to get the hell out of there while she still could. No, she felt fear for him, spurring her to drop to her knees and reach out to him.

Because vampire or not, Dillon Cash was still her friend.

And he'd just been shot.

MEG CALLED JAKE MCCANN instead of the paramedics.

While she wanted to believe that her mind had been playing

tricks on her, deep in her heart, she knew that what she'd seen had been all too real.

Something had happened to Dillon two months ago. Something that went beyond a little Internet research on sex appeal. He'd really and truly changed. Physically. Mentally. Emotionally.

A *vampire*.

As much as she wanted to dismiss the insane notion, she couldn't.

Because it didn't just stir a rush of seemingly impossible questions. Instead it answered the biggest one of all—namely, how Dillon Cash had gone from geek to god virtually overnight.

One day he'd been the most clueless computer nerd in town and the next he'd morphed into Mr. Sex Appeal. He'd turned his back on Meg, pulled away from his family and embraced a new set of friends—the owners of the town's one and only custom motorcycle shop.

Jake McCann and Garret Sawyer had moved to Skull Creek around the time Dillon had changed. The men hadn't been friends of a friend or cousins of a cousin. They'd simply shown up one day, leased and renovated a local gas station, and Skull Creek Choppers had been born. While they kept up the pretense of being run-of-the-mill entrepreneurs—they sponsored a local little league team and paid their monthly dues to the local chamber of commerce—they didn't blend in with the other townspeople. No Sunday picnics at the park, no frequenting the one and only grocery store in town, no occasional lunches at the local diner. Rather, they kept to themselves and burned the midnight oil at their shop.

They were strangers for the most part. Tall, dark, hunky strangers who shared the same telltale tattoos on their biceps.

If Meg had had any doubts that Jake McCann had something to do with Dillon's transformation, they disappeared when he arrived in record time, picked up Dillon as if he weighed little to nothing, loaded him in the back seat of a black SUV, motioned Meg in after him and headed in the opposite direction of the nearest hospital.

She lifted her gaze from the man whose head she cradled in her lap and caught Jake's stare in the rearview mirror. His eyes gleamed bright and knowing and the words were out before she could stop them. "You're a vampire, too, aren't you?"

He didn't answer her.

He didn't have to.

For a split second, reality struck and the incredulity of what she'd just said hit her.

A bona fide, Bella Lugosi, *Dark Shadows,* Anne Rice, blood-sucking *vampire*.

Her brain railed against the notion, but then her memory stirred and she saw Dillon looming over her, his mouth hinting at the sexiest grin she'd ever seen, his eyes a bright, vivid blue. She remembered his pissed off look in the parking lot and the deep purple hue of his gaze.

A dozen other images rushed at her, pounding out the truth and fortifying it until it stared her in the face like a brick wall. Dillon showing up after sunset. Dillon appearing on her balcony. Dillon standing in front of her on the ledge at Cooter's Ridge. Dillon teasing and taunting and stirring her more than any other man in her past.

He'd done all of those things because he was more than a man.

"I know it's a little hard to believe," Jake said as if reading her thoughts. "I can't read them if you don't want me to," he added, sending a jolt of realization through Meg. "It's like closing the blind on a window. Nikki does it all the time."

Because Nikki knew the truth. And accepted it.

"She didn't at first. She didn't want to believe any more than you do. At the same time, she couldn't deny what was right in front of her." His gaze caught and held hers in the mirror. His eyes blazed as bright as the sun on a hot Texas day before cooling to a deep, fathomless blue. "Any more than you can."

"Maybe I'm hallucinating," she blurted, grasping for some plausible explanation.

"Does he feel like a hallucination?"

Her gaze dropped to the man stretched out on the seat next to her. She reached out, touching the tattoo that encircled one massive bicep. Warm skin met her fingertips as she traced the intricate pattern. Slowly. Carefully. Before easing to his chest. His heart beat a steady rhythm against her palm, answering one question but stirring a dozen more.

"We're susceptible to sunlight and garlic, a stake through the heart—the usual. We can't eat anything, but we can drink as much as we like. Though I don't usually advise it because we're very sensitive. We feel everything more strongly, more deeply than most, which makes us really cheap drunks. We have a reflection just like anyone else. We—"

"Could you just stop?" she blurted, her mind going into overload. Her temples throbbed and her forehead ached. It was all too much to grasp. "Please."

This was *not* happening. Not the bloodred eyes or the fangs or Dillon so limp and lifeless in her arms.

None of it.

Nada.

Zip.

It was all a bad dream brought on by too much stress and way too many Twinkies. Soon she would open her eyes, the sun would be shining and Dillon would be awake, his green eyes twinkling, his mouth crooked into a sexy grin.

"Don't worry," Jake's voice pushed past the frantic thoughts and she glanced up again. Her gaze locked with his and she saw the same flickering light she'd seen in Dillon's gaze so many times. "He isn't dead. Despite what most people believe, vampires are living and breathing creatures just like humans. We *are* humans." His gaze clouded. "Or we once were. Dillon is as alive as the next guy. More so now thanks to the blood flowing through his veins. My blood." An anguished light touched his gaze, dispelling yet another myth—that vampires were cold, ruthless creatures. "I had no choice. It was either turn him or let him die and I couldn't do that. He helped Nikki. He saved her. I had to return the favor."

As far out as it all seemed, her gut kept insisting otherwise and the words seemed to come despite her better judgment. "What exactly happened?"

"I…" He shook his head. "It's not my place to tell you." He shifted his attention back to the road. His hands tightened on the steering wheel as if he'd already said more than he meant to.

The rest would have to come from Dillon once he woke up.

If he woke up.

She forced aside the thought and the dozens of unanswered questions that raced through her mind. Resting her palm over the steady thud of his heart, she did the only thing she could think of at that moment—she prayed.

15

"DRINK."

The deep, familiar voice pushed into Dillon's head and peeled back the layers of darkness that smothered him.

He forced his eyes open. His head throbbed and the light hurt, seeming as if the drummer for Linkin' Park was playing a fast, furious solo in his skull. Pain gripped him like a vise, clamping tighter, building the pressure and urging him back toward oblivion.

The peace.

"Don't pass out on me now, buddy." A hand slid under Dillon's aching head and the hard edge of a glass pressed against his bone-dry lips.

The first few drops of intoxicating blood touched his tongue and his gut twisted. Then hunger took control. Where he hadn't been able to move a muscle just a moment ago, an instinct as primal as it was dangerous took over and he reached out. His mouth opened. His hands grasped the glass and he held on, gulping at the contents, eager for the life sliding down his throat.

"Easy, buddy. You'll make yourself sick drinking the bottled stuff so fast."

"More," Dillon groaned when he finished the last of the sweet, fortifying liquid.

His head dropped back to the pillow as he waited for Garret to refill the glass. He closed his eyes and relished the energy that pulsed from his stomach and spread through his limbs, firing his nerves and dispelling the last paralyzing shreds.

His heart sped, beating a fast, furious rhythm as he started to think.

To remember.

The images started at the club. He heard the music and smelled the cigarette smoke and he saw the woman standing across the room—

"Shit." The word burst past his lips as he bolted upright. His gaze skittered around the familiar room where he'd spent each day for the past few months. The recliner in the corner. The big-screen TV. The infamous bed with it's carved notches in the headboard.

There was no one sitting at the table or perched in the recliner or pacing a hole in the rug near his bed.

No one except Garret who sat on the edge of the mattress, an expectant look on his face, as he waited for Dillon to say something.

He couldn't. He couldn't think past the kiss and the pain and Meg staring at him as if he'd grown two heads. Or a very lethal looking pair of fangs.

Shit.

His gut twisted, a feeling that had nothing to do with the hunger and everything to do with the fact that she knew.

She knew.

Panic crashed over him, followed by a douse of anxiety and the desperate need to talk to her. *Now*. He started to move and a white-hot pain knifed between his shoulders blades. A groan ripped from his throat as he fell back to the bed.

"Take it easy. It's only been a few hours. You haven't had a chance to heal."

"What happened?" he finally managed to ask once the fire had died enough for him to think again. He took the refill Garret handed him and downed a huge gulp. "I was shot, wasn't I?"

Garret nodded. "But not with a bullet. Someone took you out with this." He held up a small dart. "It's a tranquilizer dart. The kind they use on animals. One shot and you can't move a lick. You've been sedated for the past three hours, your muscles paralyzed. It's starting to wear off, but it's going to take more time.

More sleep. And more blood." Garret held up the glass. "You can rely on this stuff, but it'll take longer to recover. If you want to heal quickly, you need the real thing."

He needed her.

The thought struck. A crazy, insane thought because Meg Sweeney was probably barricading her door at that very moment, hanging strands of garlic around the house and crossing herself sixty ways to Sunday.

She'd seen the truth for herself. He hadn't gone from the town geek to one of the hottest guys around. No, he'd gone from a town geek to a hot vampire, a round-trip ticket that would eventually bring him right back to where he'd started.

To being clueless and geeky and completely in love.

Love?

He wasn't in love with Meg. He liked her, of course. A helluva lot. She was his buddy. His pal. His *friend.*

The words were meant to reassure, but damned if they didn't make him that much more miserable.

"How did I get here?" he blurted, eager to ignore the rush of feelings that pushed and pulled inside of him.

"Meg called Jake and he picked you up. He called me on my cell—I was out—and I met you guys here. He went to pick up Nikki and the two of them waited around awhile before I finally convinced them that you were going to be okay. Actually, Jake knew it from the get-go, but Nikki wasn't buying it. She really cares about you." He shook his head as if the very thought puzzled the hell out of him.

As if Garret had seen far too much fear and revulsion in his two-hundred-plus years and couldn't grasp the concept of love and acceptance.

He couldn't and Dillon didn't blame him. Nikki was obviously the exception to the rule.

"Who shot me?" Dillon asked, his throat suddenly tight.

"You tell me." Garret leveled a stare at him. "Didn't you see someone? *Sense* them?"

"I…" The kiss rushed at him, the warm, sensuous lips eating at his, the lush body pressed to his, the sweet scent of strawberries and warm woman filling his nostrils, the soft, familiar gasps echoing in his head.

He'd sensed someone, all right.

"You went back for seconds, didn't you?" Garret asked.

"No." *Not yet.*

Not ever.

Because Meg was surely too scared to want him now. Unless Jake had mesmerized her. Vampires could look into a human's eyes and entrance them. It was a survival skill that helped them keep such a low profile. If someone saw too much, a vampire could easily erase their short-term memory. Like turning back the hands of a clock, Jake could have made Meg forget all that had happened in the past few days—Dillon's transformation in the parking lot, the kiss right before it, the sex the night before that.

That notion bothered him almost as much as the possibility that she feared him.

His body tensed and suddenly he needed to move. He forced himself upright, pushing his back up against the headboard. The movement brought with it a sharp pain between his shoulder blades and he winced.

Garret didn't say a word. He simply stared at Dillon, as if he could see the turmoil coiling inside of him.

As if Garret knew what haunted him—the fear of the past, of the future—because he dealt with similar demons.

The older vampire opened his mouth to say something, but then he seemed to think better of it. "You haven't been feeding properly," he finally murmured, killing the notion and shifting the subject away from Meg. "You're weak. It's no wonder whoever it was got the jump on you. You're lucky they didn't kill you."

"Why didn't they?"

"I haven't figured that one out. Obviously, we're not looking at a groupie. I've had women come after me before—" he winked

"—but they're usually tossing panties my way, not darts. A groupie wants to nail you, sure enough, but not like that."

"A vampire hunter?"

"I suppose it's possible." Garret shrugged. "But if it was, why didn't they stake you when they had the chance."

Because of Meg.

That's what he wanted to believe.

But Dillon knew enough about hunters to know that they were thorough. They saw vampires as the enemy and didn't mind killing a few innocents to further their cause. Meg's presence wouldn't have swayed them. They would have simply killed her, too.

"It's the Ancient One." Dillon voiced the one thought that niggled at him. "He knows we're out to get him, so he came to get us first."

"That still brings us back to the same question—why didn't he destroy you when he had the chance?"

"Maybe it was a warning. To let us know that he's on to us, that we'd better back off."

"Why not cut your head off and be done with it?"

"Because…" Dillon's mind raced. "I don't know. Maybe he likes playing games. Maybe that's what this is."

"Maybe." Garret seemed to think before shaking his head. "Go back to the blog tomorrow. Post again and then follow up on those leads. Get addresses to go with the names and then we'll take a little trip."

But they wouldn't have to. Dillon knew it, even if Garret wasn't half as convinced.

"If he was trying to warn us," Garret continued, "and we keep pushing, he'll be back. In the meantime—" he set the dart on the nightstand and pushed to his feet "—you need to sleep. I'll switch on the alarm system on my way out."

"So we just sit and wait for him to come after us? Shouldn't we do something?"

"You are doing something. You're healing."

Dillon rested a hand over his eyes to block out the faint glare. The movement sliced through him and he gasped.

"You're not in any shape to go searching for an ancient vampire who'll surely kick your ass before you can blink. Pain is a distraction."

One he desperately needed. He forced his legs over the edge of the bed and pushed to his feet. The pressure cut through him, ripping as he staggered to his feet. He focused on the sensation, letting the pain clear his head and force aside the worry and regret eating away at him.

"You really should stay in bed."

"I want to go to the shop." He paced toward the TV, his steps picking up the more he moved. He turned and walked back toward Garret. "I'm fine."

"You're not fine. You're hungry and unless you're going to go out and find a nice young redhead to sink your teeth into, then you might as well settle your ass back down and wait for the bottled stuff to kick in." When Dillon didn't immediately head for the door, Garret gave him a knowing look. "I'll bring your files back here." He motioned to the laptop sitting on a desk in the far corner. "You can work tomorrow."

"I can't just sit here and wait." Dillon turned and limped toward the TV again. *And think.*

"There are other options to pass the time."

"Yeah," he muttered, casting a sullen glance at the computer. "There's always solitaire."

"I actually prefer poker myself." The soft voice slid into his ears and Dillon's heart lurched.

It couldn't be.

That's what he told himself, but there was no denying the sweet scent of strawberries that filled his head and the frantic heartbeat that echoed in his ears.

His chest hitched and every nerve in his body tensed. He turned. And sure enough, there stood Meg.

16

"SO THIS IS WHERE YOU'VE been hiding out for the past few months." Meg swept a glance around the large, sprawling room, from a small sitting area complete with black leather recliner, chrome-and-glass coffee table and a big-screen TV, to a small oak table and chairs. An antique four-poster bed covered with lots of pillows and a down comforter dominated half the space. Soft rugs accented the hardwood floor and softened the otherwise masculine room. It looked like the typical man's apartment.

But Dillon Cash was far from typical.

Her gaze riveted on the nightstand and the small glass that held a quarter inch of dark red liquid. "So, you got all your sexy new moves from Internet research?" She shook her head and shifted her attention to the man who stood a few feet away. "I should have known there was more to it."

He still wore the same jeans he'd had on earlier, but he'd shed his shirt and boots. His chest was broad and bare. Gold hair sprinkled from nipple to nipple before narrowing into a thin line that bisected his six-pack abs. The soft silk circled his belly button before disappearing beneath the button fly of his jeans.

Her mouth went suddenly dry and she swallowed.

"You can find out anything online these days." He shrugged and the tattoos that circled his biceps flexed. "Why not sex appeal?"

"Because if it were that simple, I would have done it myself." Her gaze collided with his. "Why didn't you tell me the truth?"

"You wouldn't have believed me." He turned and walked a

few steps, pacing back and forth like a caged animal. "I had a hard enough time believing it myself."

"Actually, it's the one thing I would have believed. I've tried everything to change this town's perception, and you come along and do it just like that. The people here are set in their ways. It would take something phenomenal to open their eyes." A rip in the upper left thigh of his jeans played peekaboo with each step and gave her a glimpse of one hair-roughened thigh.

"So," she continued, her voice suddenly tight. "You really feed off of blood *and* sex?"

He nodded. "Sex more than the blood."

In her mind's eye, she saw him. He stood half-naked, towering over her. His penis, thick and ripe and proud, filled her hands.

"When a woman has an orgasm, it stirs the most delicious energy. I soak it up and it sates the bloodlust. For a little while, anyway."

"What about your own orgasm? Don't you have to…" She licked her lips, trying to force the image aside and quell the sudden butterflies in her stomach. "Don't you need to…" *He-llo? You're a grown woman. Just say the word.*

"Ejaculate?" His green eyes glittered with a knowing light. "It's not about my pleasure. It's about pleasuring someone else. If they get off, then I get off." His gaze drilled into hers, so deep and probing.

She shifted her attention to the massive headboard and the telltale notches. Curiosity washed through her, followed by a stab of jealousy. The words were out before she could stop them. "How many women have you actually slept with since the change?"

"The bed used to belong to Bobby McGuire. I bought it when they auctioned it off a few years back. Those notches are his. Impressive, huh?"

"If you're a fourteen-year-old boy who's just hit puberty." Her gaze shifted back to him. "So you haven't been keeping track the past few months?"

His green eyes twinkled. "I didn't say that."

"Then how many?" she pressed.

"Enough." He eyed her for a long moment, as if trying to decide what to tell her. Or what *not* to tell her. "But not here." His gaze darkened. "You're the first woman who's been here."

She ignored a sudden rush of joy and focused on the one question still burning inside of her.

He arched an eyebrow at her. "Only one?" he asked as if reading her thoughts.

He *was* reading them, she reminded herself.

He was a *vampire*.

He saw everything she saw, felt everything she felt. More so now that they'd had sex.

"Jake and Nikki filled me in on almost everything," she said, eager to ignore the sudden alarm bells that sounded and the small voice that whispered for her to turn and leave now. Before the bond grew even stronger. *Unbreakable*. "I know all the basics—no sunlight or garlic or wooden stakes. I also know that you can move faster than Margie Pinkerton at an all-you-can-eat buffet, and levitate and read minds. Your eyes change color depending on what mood you're in. You can even mesmerize someone and make them forget certain things if you want to."

"If they want to," he added. "While I can be persuasive, I can't override free will. Not if it's strong enough."

"I also know about the Ancient One, and how killing him will reverse the curse for all three of you." She licked her lips. "I know *how* you've changed, but I don't know about the change itself. The turning. What happened?"

"All vampires have a homing instinct that calls them back to the exact spot they were turned on the yearly anniversary of their turning. Once there, they relive those few moments where life and death collided. They feel the same pain and anguish. The same hunger. It can be overwhelming." He raked a hand through his hair. "You go a little crazy. Garret was in the middle of reliving his turning when I arrived on the scene. To make a long story short, I thought Nikki was in danger and I stepped in to protect her. Jake and I were facing off when Garret lost it. He went for my throat. I was dying, but then Jake offered me his blood." He shrugged again. "And here I am."

"You really tried to save Nikki?"

A grin crooked his lips. "Me and my Phillips screwdriver."

"That itty bitty thing you used to carry in your pocket?"

"The one and only."

She couldn't help but smile and for a few heartbeats, the tension between them seemed to ease.

"That was really brave," she said after a long moment.

A gleam lit his eyes and she had the inexplicable feeling that her opinion mattered a lot more to him than he wanted to admit. "I did what I had to do. What any friend would have done." His gaze caught and held hers. "By the way, thanks for calling Jake tonight."

She shrugged. "I did what any friend would have done."

The silence ticked by before his deep voice slid into her ears. "Is that why you're still here now?"

Her mind raced and she remembered the fear that had gripped her on the long ride to the ranch. She'd cradled his head and prayed for his safety. And she'd faced the truth—that she might never hear his voice again, or feel his touch or see his smile.

Tonight he'd been lucky.

But what about next time?

Someone was out there. A vampire hunter would surely come after Dillon again. And if it was the Ancient One himself? Then Dillon would go after him.

Either way, a confrontation was inevitable.

Meg had already lost one important person in her life. She wasn't adding her oldest and dearest friend to the list, not if she could do anything to help it.

It certainly wasn't because she wanted one more night with him. This wasn't about sex. It was about being a friend.

It *was*.

She held tight to the thought and reached for the buttons on her vest.

"I'm here for this." She opened the garment and freed her

breasts. She wasn't wearing a bra tonight and the first whisper of air against her nipples brought them to throbbing awareness. The material slid off her shoulders and fell to the floor. "And this." She kicked off her boots and shed her socks. "And this." She hooked her fingers in the waistband of her jeans. She wiggled the denim down her hips and legs until the material pooled around her ankles and she stepped free. "And this," she said, finally shedding her lace thong.

Dillon fought the urge to pinch himself.

A dream, he told himself. This had to be a dream. No way would Meg willingly offer herself to him now that she knew the truth.

Yet here she was. Completely naked. Her full lips trembled and her eyes blazed with desire.

Because she knew the truth.

Because Meg Sweeney was all about the big S. She'd built her life trying to be perceived as sexy. She longed for it. And, thanks to the turning, Dillon now represented everything that she wanted. He oozed sensuality and stirred the same in every woman he came into contact with.

Where she'd once been the ultimate challenge for him, he was now the ultimate challenge for her.

That's what his head told him.

But his heart… He couldn't shake the crazy notion that maybe she wanted more than his cock between her legs and his tongue down her throat.

That she wanted to give, as well as take.

He stared deep into her eyes, searching for the truth, and saw…

What the hell?

"Nikki told me how to protect my thoughts." Her gaze locked with his and sure enough, he saw nothing except his own lust glittering back at him. "A woman's entitled to her privacy." She gave him a small smile before the expression faded. "Nikki also said that the reason you got shot tonight was because you haven't been feeding properly. Your senses aren't as sharp as they should be." She stepped toward him, her breasts quivering with each step until she reached a point midway between them. He knew then that while she was offering herself to him in the most blatant way, she wanted him to make the same effort and meet her halfway. "Maybe we can do something about that."

He stiffened. "Get out of here," he said, his voice gruff. "Before you do something you'll regret."

Uncertainty creased her beautiful features before her mouth drew into a firm line. Her eyes narrowed and her look morphed into one of pure determination.

She drew a deep breath that flared her nostrils and lifted her luscious breasts. "You could go for the usual spot." Her fingers fluttered down the side of her creamy neck. "Or maybe you'd rather do it here." She touched the underside of one breast and traced her ripe nipple. "Then again, maybe you'd rather taste me here." A few tantalizing touches and she slid her palm down, over the soft skin of her abdomen, to the inside of one thigh. "Or—" her breath caught as she dipped a finger between her legs "—even here." A gasp bubbled past her full lips and his gut twisted.

"You don't know what you're asking for."

"I'm not asking for anything. I'm giving." The last word hitched as she slid another finger into her steamy heat.

In the blink of an eye, he pinned her to the nearest wall.

"What—" she gasped, but her startled expression quickly faded into one of pure excitement as she stared up into his eyes.

She wanted the vampire, all right. She wanted to walk on the wild side, to unleash the beast inside of him, and suddenly that didn't seem like such a bad idea.

For all her boldness, she'd yet to see what he'd really and truly become. A glimpse would surely send her running even faster than that first horrible kiss back in the ninth grade.

"Or maybe I'll just try each spot until I find the one I like best," he growled, pulling back his lips. A hiss worked its way up his throat as he bared his fangs. His body trembled and he touched his mouth to her ripe throat.

She didn't stiffen when he rasped her soft flesh with the sharp edge of his incisors.

Rather, she arched her neck, the movement pushing her soft flesh against his fangs and pricking her skin. Her gasp sizzled in the air as a sweet drop of blood bubbled and slid down her neck.

Dillon caught it with his tongue, licking to the source and drawing another few sweet drops before lifting her. Her feet left the ground as he pushed her higher up the wall until her nipple brushed his lips.

Her breath caught as he latched onto the ripe tip and drew it deep. His fangs grazed the tender flesh around her areola and his groin tightened. Her nipple throbbed against his tongue as he sank into her just a hair and drew a few more drops of her delicious heat. The salty sweetness sent a dizzying rush to his head. His insides clenched.

More, more, more.

The chant echoed in his head and he pushed her higher, pinning her in place with his mind rather than his hands because he needed them now. He slid his palms around to cup her ass as he tilted her forward just a fraction and touched his lips to the slick flesh between her legs. He licked her then, tracing the seam with the very tip of his tongue before parting her.

She closed her eyes, her hands braced on his shoulders, her fingers digging into his flesh. Holding on.

Urging him on.

The thought pushed past the thunder of his own heart, making him all the more determined to give her what she thought she wanted and frighten her off for good. He drew her clit into his mouth and she jumped. He suckled her for a long moment before replacing his lips with his fingers, and shifting his mouth an inch to the side, to the tender flesh of her upper thigh. The smell of sex filled his nostrils and fanned his hunger into a living and breathing thing that overwhelmed him. A growl rumbled past his lips and he sank his fangs deep.

So deliciously *deep*.

Convulsions gripped her and she clutched at him.

A shudder ripped through him as he started to draw on her. Her delicious essence filled his mouth and the energy from her climax seeped into him at every point where flesh met flesh.

It was the ultimate in fulfillment for a vampire, and it wasn't nearly enough.

Not the warm, succulent body grasping at him, or the sweet essence pulsing in his mouth.

Dillon wanted more than just Meg's body and her blood.

He wanted her heart.

The realization sent a rush of determination through him and he stiffened. He fought the beast inside of him, urging it back down until he managed to draw back. Blood trickled from the spot and he lapped at it, licking at her wounds until they stopped bleeding.

And then he forgot all about driving her away, and decided to do his damnedest to get her to stay.

17

MEG WAS STILL REELING from the most mind-blowing orgasm of her life when she felt the soft mattress against her back. The bedsprings protested as Dillon pressed her down. Her eyelids fluttered open and she stared up at the man who loomed over her.

Straddling her, his knees trapping her thighs, he leaned back to gaze down at her. The single lamp that burned in the room was at his back, making him more shadow than man.

All except for his eyes.

She saw them clearly, glowing green fire that skimmed over her, setting her nerves ablaze and making her forget all about the exquisite pleasure they'd just shared. Hunger yawned and anxiety skimmed up and down her arms. She wanted more.

She wanted him.

And he wanted to put the brakes on. She felt the sudden shift in his mood even before he reached for her. It was there in the way he simply towered over and drank her in with his eyes. His hands clenched at his sides for several long seconds as he seemed to fight for control. After several heartbeats, he seemed to find it. Where they'd been fast and furious a moment before, the hands that reached for her now were slow and purposeful and oh so steady.

"I've pictured you like this so many times," he murmured, his voice thick and raw. "Beneath me, open for me, wet for me…" He skimmed her body, his fingertips brushing her neck, her collarbone, the slope of her breasts, the indentation of her ribs. "When I saw you that night from the balcony, I could hardly stand it. I wanted to rush in, throw the damned bottle to the wall and pleasure you myself."

But he hadn't. Because he couldn't. She hadn't invited him into her house at that point and, therefore, he'd been stuck in her doorway, waiting, watching. *Wanting*. The truth burned in the brightness of his eyes as they deepened and shifted until they burned a rich, vibrant purple. She wondered at the change in color.

"It's because I'm turned on," he murmured and she realized her thoughts were wide-open to him again.

She tried to block him, to focus her attention on shutting herself off mentally just as Nikki had said. But then he leaned down and flicked the tip of her nipple with his tongue and she forgot everything except the sharp sensation that knifed through her.

The ripe nub responded, hardening and throbbing, begging for more than the one decadent lick.

More.

She wanted him naked and hard and inside of her. Now.

Forever.

Hardly. This wasn't about tomorrow. It was about right now. About being a friend and helping him when he needed her most. It was about now. Anxiety rushed through her and she reached for him.

He caught her hands with one of his own and forced them up above her head to the headboard.

"Easy," he murmured, his other hand going to her abdomen. "We've got all night." He traced lazy circles, touching, relishing as if he'd never felt anything as soft as her skin.

Then he lowered his head and drew her nipple fully into the moist heat of his mouth.

Meg clenched her fingers, pushing against the hand that constrained her. She wanted to touch him. To feel him. To push things back up to the frenzied pace of a moment before so she didn't have to think about what he was doing to her. And *why*.

Why the slower pace and the forbidden words and the sudden determination that coiled his body tight and held every muscle in check.

The questions pushed and pulled, warring with the delicious heat that simmered through her as he licked a path across her skin to coax the other breast in the same torturous manner.

She rotated her pelvis, rubbing against his chest. She wanted him, surrounding her, consuming her, filling up the emptiness inside her once and for all.

Forever.

The thought struck again and she fought hard, her legs parting and her body bucking, but she was little match for his strength.

He suckled her again, so long and deep and *ahhh…*

One rough fingertip traced the soft folds between her legs, pushing inside just a delicious fraction that made her quiver and gasp. He lingered, suckling her breasts, first one then the other. Back and forth. Over and over.

She clenched and unclenched around the tip of his finger, trying to draw him deeper, but he didn't budge. Not until she was panting and whimpering and so desperate that she thought—no, she *knew*—she would surely die if he didn't do something.

Dillon smiled, his teeth a startling break in the black shadow of his face. Then the expression faded as he gazed down at her. His attention shifted, traveling from her face, down the column of her neck to her breasts, to the spread of her thighs and his finger, which poised at her pulsing cleft.

He pushed all the way in and she moaned, coming up off the bed as pure pleasure pierced her brain. The feeling, so consuming and exquisite, sucked the air from her lungs and she stopped breathing for a long moment. He didn't move, just held himself deep inside as her body settled around him and clamped tighter.

"I want you more than I've ever wanted any woman before," his voice was gruff. *Or after.*

The words sounded so clear and distinct in her head, as if he spoke them directly into her ear. He didn't. He didn't have to. He'd invaded her mind as well as her body, and they were telepathically linked now.

An unbreakable bond.

A spurt of excitement went through her, followed by a wave of anxiety that gripped her and refused to let go. She lifted her pelvis, focusing on the pleasure that gripped her as she worked her body around his decadent finger. She leaned into him only to pull away. She swayed from side to side, her movements frantic, desperate, as she pushed herself higher and higher, desperate to feel rather than think.

"You're so beautiful." The words pierced the humming in her ears and she went still. Her eyes opened to find him staring down at her. "The most beautiful woman I've ever seen." He kissed her softly on her swollen lips. "Or touched." He kissed her again. "Or loved."

Before the words could register, his mouth swooped down and captured hers in a deep kiss that went way beyond the sweet press of his lips. He coaxed her open and slid his tongue inside and drew on her sweetly, tenderly for several long moments. Until her frantic heartbeat eased and she forgot all about sucking him deeper into her greedy body. Instead, she wanted to wrap her arms around him, pull him even closer and feel his heartbeat against her own.

A second later, she found herself free to do just that.

Her hands slid over his shoulders and held tight. She relished the feel of his body as it pressed against hers, his heartbeat so steady and sure against her breasts. She'd never felt closer to a man at that moment.

A vampire.

She tried to remember that all-important fact. It explained the sudden about-face and the fact that he couldn't keep his hands off of her and that they were having the hottest, most passionate sex of her entire life.

Because he was a vampire.

She could have been any woman, she knew. But damned if he didn't make her feel like the only woman.

His woman.

A trick of the trade, she told herself. Vampires could mesmerize. She'd learned that tonight. Dillon was just playing mind games.

And doing it quite well.

He canted his head to the side and deepened the kiss. He plundered her mouth with his, exploring and savoring. The air stalled in her lungs and her heart sped faster. A few more seconds and he tore his mouth from hers.

He slid down her body, now slick from the fever that raged inside of her, and left a blazing path with the velvet tip of his tongue. With a gentle pressure, he parted her thighs. Almost reverently, he stroked the soft, slick folds between her legs.

She was wet and throbbing and he swore softly. Tremors seized her when she felt his warm breath blowing softly on the inside of her thigh, directly on the tiny prick points where he'd drunk from her. His tongue darted out, flicking first one then the other, and it was like being zapped by white lightning. Pleasure sliced through her, cracking her open from head to toe. She gasped and dug her nails into his shoulders as wave after wave of ecstasy washed through her.

She wasn't sure what happened after that. She was too busy floating, her body weightless, her mind buzzing with sensation. She only knew that one minute he had his jeans on and the next, he was settling his naked body between her damp thighs.

A condom.

The warning sounded in her head when she felt his hard, hot length rub her pulsing clit. She tried to clamp her legs shut, but he was too close, his thighs wedging her open. His deep voice whispered through her head.

I can't hurt you. I wouldn't hurt you.

The seconds ticked by as he waited for her. She finally nodded and it was all the encouragement he needed.

With a swift thrust of his hips, he impaled her on his rigid length and all worry faded as heat drenched her. Sensation overwhelmed her at first. The feel of him so hot and thick pulsing inside her nearly made her come without any warning.

She anchored her arms around his neck and her muscles clamped down around his erection. She didn't want to let him go, but he had other ideas.

He withdrew and slid back in for the second time. His hard length rasped her tender insides, creating a delicious friction that sent a dizzying rush straight to her brain. He pulled out again, and went back for a third time. A fourth.

His body pumped into hers over and over, pushing her higher with each delicious plunge. She lifted her hips, meeting him thrust for thrust, eager to feel more of him. Harder. Deeper. Faster.

Look at me.

She opened her eyes and stared up at him as he poised over her. He pushed into her, his penis hot and twitching, and she knew it was his last and final time. He was going over the edge before her.

It's not about my own pleasure. It's about pleasuring someone else.

Yet here he was, mindless with pleasure, lost in his own orgasm.

His arms braced on either side of her, his muscles bulging and tight as he held himself. The tendons in his neck stood out. His eyes blazed a bright, vivid purple. His jaw clenched and his lips parted. His fangs gleamed as he let loose a loud hiss that faded into a long moan as Meg arched her pelvis.

His penis twitched and throbbed, and she felt a spurt of warmth. He bucked once, twice and she followed him over the edge. Convulsions gripped her body and suddenly she was floating again on a cloud of pure satisfaction.

Several breathless moments passed as she lay there, trying to come to grips with what had just happened.

He'd climaxed first.

This time, she reminded herself. But she'd come plenty of times before, when he'd had her pinned against the wall. He'd already drank his fill. Of her blood and her energy.

That's what she told herself because she certainly wasn't going to consider the alternative—that he might feel something more for her. Something that had nothing to do with being a vampire and everything to do with being a man.

A man in love.

Right.

Dillon Cash didn't love her. He couldn't love her. Because regardless of what had just happened—a fluke, of course—he *was* a vampire.

One who'd slept with a ridiculous number of women.

One who would sleep with even more.

He had to in order to survive. She wanted him to. That's why she'd offered herself to him tonight. Because he needed her.

Friends, she reminded herself.

But when Dillon rolled onto his back and pulled her flush on top of him, she felt like anything but his friend. His hands stroked her back, her buttocks, holding her close, touching her intimately. A lover's touch rather than a friend's.

The notion sent her scrambling from the bed.

"Meg?" His voice followed her as she snatched up her clothes. "What's wrong?"

"It's late," she blurted the first thing that popped into her head. "I need to get home." Dread welled inside of her and panic beat at her temples as she jerked on her vest and pants, her movements frantic and hurried. She needed to get out of here. *Now.* Before she did something she would surely regret.

Like climb back into bed with him and stay there forever.

"Wait!" His frantic voice followed her, his footsteps dogging her up the stairs to the ground floor. "Would you just wait a second?"

She rushed through the house, snatching up her purse as she headed for the front door.

"Dammit, woman!" He caught one hand while the other reached for the doorknob.

His fingers burned into hers and she yanked open the door. Early-morning light spilled through the open doorway. His hand fell away and a loud hiss sizzled in her ears. He murmured a fierce *shit* as he stumbled backward.

She barely resisted the urge to turn and reassure herself that he was okay.

He would be. She'd made sure of that tonight. She'd given him what he needed—her body and her blood—and that was more than enough to strengthen him against whatever he might face.

A vampire hunter. The Ancient One. A few rays of sunlight.

They were friends, she reminded herself, and then she stepped out into the morning sunlight, pulled out her cell phone and called Nikki for a ride home.

HE'D BEEN WRONG ABOUT her.

Dillon paced the floor in his room and ignored the exhaustion that tugged at his muscles. It was daylight and he needed to sleep. To rejuvenate.

Christ, he'd been wrong. So fucking *wrong*.

The truth crystallized as he stared at the tell-tale stain on his sheets from where he'd bitten her. His nostrils flared and his mouth watered. He could still taste her. Even more, he could feel her. The anguish that ate away at her. The uncertainty as she paced the front porch upstairs and waited for Nikki. The fear as she thought about going back inside to see him just one more time.

They were linked now and as much as that should have bothered him, it didn't.

He loved her. He always had, even way back when he'd been too young and naive to know it. And later when he'd been too damned uncertain to act on it.

And she loved him.

Man or vampire or both?

He didn't know, and he never would because he refused to take a chance.

That's why he'd convinced himself that her attraction wasn't to him, but to the sexy beast he'd become. Because deep down, beneath the confidence and charisma that came with being a vampire, he was still the same man. The same boy who'd acted on a whim so long ago and had ended up in the hospital.

He'd been scared to death ever since.

He'd blamed his parents for being overprotective and paranoid. But in reality, he'd been just as bad. Afraid to take chances, to live for the moment, to *live*, period.

Sure, he'd been burning the candle at both ends for the past two months, enough to break Bobby's record and go down in the history books, but that was different. Being a vampire reduced the risk. He knew no man could best him physically. And no woman could refuse him sexually.

No woman, that is, until Meg.

She'd held out at first and surprised the hell out of him.

He realized then that she wasn't just any woman.

She was every woman.

And she loved him even if she didn't want to admit it.

Right now, a voice whispered, taunting him as he collapsed on the bed and gave in to the darkness tugging and pulling at his senses. *At this moment. But later when things go back to normal?*

Maybe. Maybe not.

He didn't know. He only knew that it was a chance he was suddenly willing to take rather than face the thought of losing her completely.

For a lifetime.

Forever.

"LOOKS LIKE SOMEBODY HAD a busy night," Terry remarked when Meg walked into the boutique several hours later, after a half-hour ride back to town with Nikki and more than one knowing glance.

The woman hadn't said much when she'd dropped Meg off at home to check on Babe except "Don't worry. Everything will be okay."

The only trouble was, Meg couldn't shake the feeling that from this moment on, nothing would be okay. Her life had changed tonight. He'd changed.

And there would be no going back to the way things had been.

She ignored the crazy thought. Everything would be okay. Dillon was stronger now. Together, he and Jake and Garret would find and defeat the Ancient One. He would reclaim his humanity, go back to being her good buddy, and all would be right with the world.

All she had to do was keep her distance from now on until he was back to his old self—and not nearly as tempting—and everything *would* be okay.

She clung to the notion and focused on Terry. "Don't tell me—you hooked up with some hot and hunky cowboy and had wild and uncontrollable sex last night."

"Not me," the woman blurted. "You." Terry handed over the Lifestyle section from the morning's issue of the *Skull Creek Gazette*. "You made Tilly's *Around the Town* column!"

Meg unfolded the paper and stared at a picture that had been taken at The Roundup last night. She and Colt stood wrapped in a heated embrace, right above the caption *There's a new sheriff in town!*

She skimmed the three paragraphs about the town's hottest new real estate agent who seemed a shoe-in to unseat one of the regulars and make next week's Randiest Roosters list.

Oddly enough, Meg didn't feel half as disappointed as she should have over the fact that she didn't get so much as a mention. Instead, she skimmed the background faces, searching for one in particular.

She caught a glimpse of Dillon near the bar, his gaze trained on her. A very vivid image of last night rushed at her and she remembered his blond head between her legs, his mouth drawing on her tender flesh, and the rush of pleasure she'd felt.

He hadn't just taken from her. Rather, as her essence had flowed into his mouth, she'd felt something flow back—a fierce current that had pulsed from his body into hers, pulling them closer, winding them tighter, *connecting* them.

No.

He'd fed and she'd eased her conscience knowing that she'd done everything possible to help him in the battle that awaited him. Now it was back to work.

To life.

Bye-bye Jezebel.

Her gaze dropped to the article again. Not one mention of her. Or her sexy outfit or the fact that Colt hadn't been able to keep his hands off her.

Nothing.

She waited for the rush of disappointment, the clenching in her gut, the dread in her stomach and the certainty that her tombstone would one day read:

Here lies tough and rough Manhandler Meg,
Who loved sports and kicked ass and could drain a keg,
She tried shedding her image, but was still a bruiser,
Now she's six feet under and a perpetual loser.

But when she drank in the page, the only thing she felt was a strange tightening in her chest. Her gaze kept going back to Dillon and the dark look on his face.

As if he felt more for her than just a vampire's lust.

She remembered last night and the soft mattress at her back, the strong, purposeful lover leaning over her, the strange gleam in his eyes as he'd stared down at her.

A look that had had nothing to do with the fact that he wanted her and everything to do with the fact that *he* wanted *her*.

"Are you okay?" Terry's voice drew her back to reality.

"Fine." Meg shook away the haunting images. She drew a deep breath and swallowed past the sudden lump in her throat. "Why?"

"For a second there, you looked like you were going to cry."

"Cry?" She forced a laugh. "Why would I do something ridiculous like that?"

Because you love him, stupid. You. Love. Him.

Hardly. She liked him. A lot. They were the best of friends. But honeymoon-in-Jamaica, house-in-the-suburbs, kids-and-a-minivan, 'til-death-do-us-part *love?*

Love was the culmination of everything—admiration, respect,

comfort, protection, rip-off-your-clothes-and-get-naked-now-desperation, trust—the entire cake so to speak, complete with a layer of filling and sprinkles on top.

Meg was only interested in the butter-cream icing. The rich, decadent, addictive lust. She wanted to feel desired, sought after, *wanted*.

All the things Dillon had made her feel last night, and then some.

"Good," Terry said, drawing Meg's attention before she could dwell on the last thought. "Because one depressed woman around here is enough."

Meg took a good look at her assistant and noted the dark circles under the woman's eyes. "You look terrible."

"The end result of zero sleep and a gallon of Rocky Road ice cream."

"You ate an entire *gallon?*"

"Hank called. And called. And a little after midnight, he showed up."

"Don't tell me you slept with him again?"

"If I had, I wouldn't have needed the ice cream." She stiffened. "I stood strong, told him to get lost and then slammed the door in his face. And then I headed for the fridge."

"What did he do?"

"Nothing. He sat on my front steps for a little while and then he left. Then he came back and sat a while longer. Then he left. Then he came back. It was that way all night. I snuck out this morning as soon as he left for the eighth time."

"You should have called the police."

"Maybe." She shrugged. "But I feel responsible. I'm the one who let him back into my life." She shook her head. "I can't believe I slept with him. I mean, I know why I did it. The sex was always really great between us and I haven't actually had sex in a really long time, and so when I saw him, I couldn't help myself. But I knew it was the wrong thing and I did it anyway. What was I thinking?"

The same thing Meg had been thinking when she'd offered

her body and her blood to Dillon Cash—that she could handle it. That she could give herself to him and then walk away.

Forget.

If only she could.

"I'm so stupid."

"Aren't we all?" Meg ignored Terry's questioning look. "There's no use beating yourself up. Get over it. Move on. Have your phone number changed and if he shows up again, call the police."

Terry looked hesitant, but then she seemed to gather her courage. "Okay." She nodded and her determination seemed to deflate just a little. "I wish I knew what it is about this guy that makes me stop thinking like a sane rational adult."

"He's good in bed."

That was it. That was the only reason Meg Sweeney was thinking such crazy thoughts about love and marriage and happily-ever-after with a man like Dillon Cash. A *vampire*. He was the first to make her feel like a vibrant, sexy woman. Of course, she would feel more than friendship for him.

More, as in gratitude. Concern. And, of course, lust. He was hot and sexy. It only made sense that she would want him more than her next breath.

And fear. Not of him, but for him. She still couldn't shake the tightening in her chest when she'd seen him hit the ground last night or the all-important fact that he was still in danger.

Someone was still out there and it was just a matter of time before something happened.

A strange melancholy wrapped around her. She set aside the newspaper. "We should get going. We've got a busy Saturday ahead of us."

Terry nodded, gathered her composure and headed into the front part of the store to unlock the front door. Meanwhile, Meg sat down at her computer, determined to get a stack of orders finished before her first fitting.

She did her best to ignore the doom that settled in her gut and told her today was going to be the worst day of her life.

Impossible.

That day had already come and gone a long time ago and Meg wasn't ready for a repeat.

Not now. Not ever.

18

IT WASN'T THE WORST DAY of her life, but it was close.

Meg came to that realization as the hours passed and things seemed to go from bad to *really* bad.

First she discovered that the new seamstress she'd hired had eloped to Las Vegas. The woman had taken Chantal Mortimer's twenty-fifth anniversary dress for a simple hem three days ago. That morning, she'd appeared in the wedding announcements section of the *Skull Creek Gazette* wearing said dress and a wedding ring the size of a small third world country. Chantal had been furious—and jealous because her own ring weighed in at a whopping half carat less—and had demanded her money back. Meg had given her a prompt refund, only to have the woman rant for a full hour before she'd headed over to the diner for a complimentary lunch courtesy of the boutique.

Then Margie Westbury arrived. Margie had ripped her dress for tonight's banquet at the Elks lodge and now needed a new one, which wouldn't have been a problem had she not been a size twenty-eight special order. Tammy Greenburg wanted a one-of-a-kind sequined number she'd seen on CMT and couldn't understand why Meg didn't stock oodles of them (ahem—they call them one-of-a-kind for a reason). Sue Carrigan had gained twenty pounds and couldn't fit into the wedding dress she was scheduled to wear in exactly one week. And Honey Harwell nixed all ten of the special order dresses Meg had had overnighted for her Saturday afternoon fitting.

Then Terry's ex showed up. Not once, but five times.

And to make matters as bad as they could be, Meg couldn't stop thinking about Dillon.

Images played over and over in her mind. Memories. From when they'd been kids and he'd taught her to play chess and boot up her computer. Last Christmas when he'd handed over a new collar for Babe and a matching leash. The night at the motel when she'd seen him up close and personal for the first time since the turning. She'd gotten her first dose of pure, unadulterated lust then and she'd been craving it ever since.

Add a wonderful friendship to the overwhelming emotion, and it was no wonder she felt so mixed up inside. So drawn to him. That, and the fact that they were truly linked now that he'd drunk from her.

She could feel him, smell him, sense him.

Sensations that grew stronger once the sun dipped below the horizon and dusk settled over the town.

She knew the moment he opened his eyes. She felt the steady beat of his heart, the jump of his pulse and the power that lived and breathed inside of him. She even felt his determination.

Dillon Cash was coming for her.

Her pulse leapt and for a split second, she felt a rush of excitement. He was the first man to really and truly sweep her off her feet. The first to go nuts and ravish her. Her fantasy come to life.

It wasn't the man himself that made her heart beat faster.

No, it was the idea of him.

That's the conclusion Meg finally came to as the day faded into evening. She fought down a wave of nerves and picked her way through the front of the store, snatching up anything even close to Honey's size. The girl was still there, planted in a chair in the main dressing room, her iPod blaring as she waited for Meg to return with more choices.

Meg added a crimson-colored shift to her already overflowing arms and then turned to yet another rack. Her thighs touched and rubbed. Flesh grazed the twin prickpoints and desire knifed through her, sharp and fierce. Her legs trembled and her breath caught, and the dread churned deep inside of her.

Because the more turned on she was, the harder it would be to resist him.

She would resist. She didn't want to lose him as a friend.

That's what would happen. Romantic entanglements were fleeting. She knew that firsthand.

If she acted on the crazy lust burning her up from the inside out, she would enjoy herself for a little while. Maybe even a long while. But eventually Dillon would move on to another woman, or morph back into his old self and lose the desire for her that he felt right now. Either way, the fire would die, and so would their friendship.

She wasn't going to let that happen.

He'd been the one constant in her life over the past few years. The one person she'd always been able to count on. She didn't want to lose that.

She wouldn't.

Which was why when he showed up, *if* he showed up, she would simply set him straight and tell him the truth—while she really enjoyed the sex, she didn't have any romantic feelings for him and so it was best that they stop pretending and go back to being friends.

Her skin prickled as she retrieved the last dress and turned toward the dressing room. Awareness skittered up and down her spine.

He was coming, all right.

Good. The sooner she set the record straight, the sooner she could salvage their friendship.

If only she didn't get the sinking feeling that it was already too late.

TONIGHT WAS THE NIGHT.

Dillon stepped out of the shower and reached for a towel.

He was going to put it all on the line and pour out his heart.

Meg would listen, throw her arms around him and everything would be okay.

Or not.

He ignored the doubt, pulled on his clothes and snatched up his keys. It was early in the evening and Garret was still downstairs in his own apartment. Probably getting ready to go out and feed.

His own stomach grumbled as he bypassed the fridge—and the blood. But he'd had enough last night to last him awhile. He felt strong, his senses alert, his nerves alive. No, what he wanted now had nothing to do with the crimson heat flowing through her veins. He wanted more this time. *Everything*.

He spent the next ten minutes punching his way through security codes. Meg hadn't dealt with the same when she'd fled that morning because the alarm had been on a timer that hadn't kicked on until 9:00 a.m. Otherwise, she would have set off a world of noise when she'd hightailed it and ran.

She was still running, but not for long. Dillon intended to catch her and talk some sense into her. They could make it. Jake and Nikki were proof.

But Nikki loves Jake.

Meg loved Dillon, too. He knew it. He felt it. She was just too stubborn to admit it. But now was not the time to be ornery. Not with the rest of their lives at stake.

Fifty or so years if his instincts were correct and the Ancient One was close.

Forever if not.

He didn't know, he just knew that however long he had, he wanted to spend it with Meg Sweeney. Starting tonight.

He climbed onto his motorcycle and gunned the engine.

But first, he had something to take care of.

"DROP THE MACE, MOM," Dillon said a half-hour later as he stood in the front yard of his house and felt the woman who'd come up behind him.

In the blink of an eye, he whirled and faced her. She wore a black bodysuit, a determined expression and enough bug spray to kill every mosquito in Texas. And in her hand, she was holding the biggest can of Mace he'd ever seen. His gaze shifted to the second figure. His dad reeked of bug spray, as well. He also wore the same black bodysuit, as well as a mask. Thick bifocals perched on his nose and covered the eyeholes of the black knit. He clasped a stun gun in one hand and a net in the other.

But the older man wasn't the threat right now.

No, the tension washed off his mother in huge waves. She was worried and scared and she wasn't backing down until she had Dillon hog-tied in her tent.

"It's for your own good, baby," she told him, taking a tentative step forward. "They've brainwashed you and it's up to us to rewire you."

"I promise. I'm not brainwashed."

"Of course you don't think so. No one who's brainwashed ever thinks that they are. That's what makes it so obvious that you're under their spell. Who is it? Those Moonies? A satanic cult? That group I saw on *CNN* that worships Krispy Kreme donuts? I knew I should have let you have donuts as a child. Then you wouldn't have been so anxious to run out and get your sugar high somewhere else." Anguish fueled her voice. "But I was trying to protect you. Really I was."

"I know." His own voice was smooth and calm, a direct contrast to the nervousness raging inside him. He felt as if he were a child all over again, showing his mother his infected cut, disappointing her. "You didn't do anything wrong. You did a good job raising me."

"I failed. Not once, but twice. No more." She stiffened, taking another step toward him. "I'm doing my duty now. I'm saving my baby." Another step and her finger went to the spray trigger.

"Drop. The. Mace." He stared deep into her eyes and said it once more. He didn't want to push her too hard. He wanted her conscious for this.

At the same time, if he didn't resort to a little mind over matter, he was going to find himself hog-tied, hanging upside down in a nearby tent, his mom stuffing Krispy Kreme's donuts down his throat before he could get a word in edgewise.

Her mouth dropped open and her hand went slack. A glazed look came over her and the can clattered to the ground.

He turned to his father, but the man wasn't staring at him as if he'd grown two heads. No, he was staring at his wife's catatonic body.

"Just put the stun gun away," Dillon told his father, but the older man had already stuffed it into his pocket.

"I've been trying for years to get your mother to shut up like that." His father peeled off the mask he'd been wearing and eyeballed his son. "How'd you do that?"

"You really want to know?"

"Are you kidding?" A grin tugged at his father's mouth and genuine interest gleamed in his gaze.

The tension coiling in Dillon's gut eased just a little. Maybe telling them wasn't going to be as bad as he'd thought.

He spent the next half hour sitting on the front porch, filling his dad in on the specifics of what had happened to him while his mother sat in a small lounge chair, a passive look on her face.

Other than an initial rush of disbelief, his father didn't seem all that shocked. If anything, he looked somewhat relieved and Dillon found himself remembering what Meg had said about the truth being the only thing that made any real sense.

She'd obviously been right.

At least as far as his dad was concerned.

Dillon shifted his attention to his mother. While she hadn't been able to move, she'd heard every word. Dillon had made sure of that. He fought down his own fear, lifted the trancelike veil and waited for her reaction.

She took one look at him, let out a shriek and passed out cold.

It wasn't exactly the *"It's okay. I love you anyway, son,"* he'd been hoping for, but at least she hadn't gone into cardiac arrest.

"Give her some time," his father clapped him on the shoulder as he pushed to his feet.

"What about you? Are you all right with this?"

"I don't know." The man shrugged. "It's pretty unbelievable. At the same time, your mother's been living in a tent for three weeks straight now, so I'm not beyond buying the impossible." His gaze collided with Dillon's and worry lit his expression. "I just want you to be okay."

"I am."

"Good because I was afraid I was going to have to zap you with the stun gun. I still haven't figured out how to do it without goosing myself."

Dillon helped his father load his mother into the car for yet another trip to the E.R. for smelling salts. And possibly a mental evaluation should she start spouting off about the story he'd just told them.

But it was a chance he had to take. He was through playing it safe and worrying over each and every consequence. No more being scared.

No, he was facing his fears and acting on his feelings for the first time in his life.

He only hoped Meg was ready to do the same.

He fought down a rush of uncertainty, climbed onto his motorcycle and headed into town.

MEG IGNORED THE URGE to throw her hands into the air, or better yet, slide them around Honey Harwell's neck.

The young girl stood center stage in the back dressing room. It was almost seven and Elise had yet to return. Other than Terry and Hank who were once again having words in the back alley, Meg and Honey were all alone.

Meaning no one would hear if she decided to get physical. That, or wash the girl's smart mouth out with a little heavy-duty soap.

She resisted the appealing thought and summoned her patience. "Let's try this once again. It's the perfect cut and color."

"It sucks. It more than sucks. It royally sucks."

Where was a good bar of Ivory when she needed one?

Meg drew a deep breath and tried a different approach. "It

doesn't suck as much as the others, right? I mean, they sucked so bad they reeked," she reminded the girl of her earlier comments.

Honey seemed to think. "I hate this. I want to go home."

"Then try the dress on again because that's the only way you're getting out of here. Your mother said to pick something by the time she got back or she was taking your iPod."

"This bites," Honey breathed as reached for the dress.

Amen.

Meg pulled the curtains on the dressing room and debated whether or not to pick up the phone and call 911.

"…over, I'm telling you." Terry's voice carried from the partially open back door where she stood with Hank—again. "Can't you just leave me alone?"

"But I love you, baby. You mean the world to me. All those other women didn't mean crap."

"I don't care about them. That's the past. I've moved on. So should you."

"But you can't just make love to a man and then turn your back…"

Meg bypassed the phone and retrieved a small can of Mace she kept under her cash register. She'd promised Terry to let her handle Hank her own way. As long as he kept a mild tone of voice and didn't get physical, Meg intended to keep that promise. But at the first sign of real trouble, she was giving him a face full.

She was just about to head back into the dressing room to check on Honey when she heard the rumble of a motorcycle. She turned in time to see Dillon pull up to the curb in front of her shop and kill the engine. Muscles rippled and bunched as he climbed off the sleek black chopper.

Her heart shifted into overdrive as the bell on the front glass jingled.

He wore a pair of jeans and black T-shirt. His jaw was set, his face determined. Emotion blazed in the deep green depths of his eyes, so fierce and telling and—

No!

Panic bolted through her and she opened her mouth before he had the chance. "Don't say it."

"Don't say what?" He arched one blond brow and stepped toward her.

She took a step back. "Don't say what I think you're here to say."

"I told my folks."

"You'll just ruin everything," she rushed on before his words registered and she caught herself. "Come again?"

"I told them and they were okay with it." He shrugged. "At least my dad was. The verdict is still out on my mom. I realized something yesterday. For all my newfound boldness, I've still been holding back. Afraid." His eyes glittered with a knowing light. "Just like you."

Before she could blink, much less open her mouth and voice the denial that sprang to her lips, he was standing in front of her. Large, strong hands cradled her face. "Don't be scared."

He touched her so softly, so tenderly that her throat tightened. "I'm not afraid of you," she finally managed to whisper.

"No." He forced her gaze to meet his. "You're afraid of you."

His words sank in as he stared down at her, into her. He saw the frantic thoughts that raced through her head. The anxiety. The denial. The fear.

She fought against the notion and stumbled backwards, away from his warm hands and his probing stare. "I am *not.*"

"Yes, you are." He let his hands fall to his sides, but he didn't look the least bit happy about it. His fingers clenched and it was all he could do no to reach for her again. "You're afraid to let go, to fall in love, to *be* in love. Because if you don't put yourself out there, you can't get hurt." His gaze darkened and suddenly she saw herself sitting on the floor in the kitchen, Babe in her arms, the policeman lingering nearby. "If you don't have anything, then you can't lose it. That's why you're afraid of love."

Her throat constricted and a rush of tears burned the backs of her eyes. She blinked and fought for her voice. This was crazy. He was crazy. "I love a lot of things. Babe. My grandparents."

"You loved them *before* your father died. But since, you haven't let yourself get close—really close—to anyone. You're afraid, all right. Afraid to live, to love, to be yourself. That's why you've tried so hard to change all these years. You want to forget the woman you were, to bury the past."

"I wasn't a woman back then. I was a tomboy."

"You were a woman, all right. One hundred percent. And you could hold your own against any man. You still can. The difference is, you were comfortable in your own skin then and you're not now. Because being in that skin reminds you too much of your father, of your loss, of your pain." He reached for her again, his hands catching her shoulders, sliding up her neck, cradling her cheeks. "You have to let it go, baby. You can't keep running and hiding. Just let go."

She wanted to. She wanted to slide her arms around his neck and give in to the flood of emotion that threatened to blind her.

But she'd been holding back for so long, fighting so hard, that her instincts kicked in and she held tight to the denial racing through her. "You're crazy. You don't want to face the fact that I don't have feelings for you and so you're making all of this up to ease your wounded ego."

"If that's the truth, then look me in the eyes and tell me you don't have feelings for me," he countered. His hands splayed on either side of her face, anchoring her in place, forcing her to face him. To face herself. "Tell me you don't love me the way that I love you."

"I…" She tamped down on the anxiety pumping her heart faster and fought against the urge to turn her face into his palm, to kiss the throbbing pulse beat on the inside of his wrist, to lose herself in the man towering over her.

It would be so easy to give in.

To wind up on the floor, raw and open and heartbroken.

"I don't love you," she said, forcing the words out. And then she did what she should have done instead of propositioning him that night at the motel.

She turned her back on Dillon Cash and walked away.

DILLON BARELY RESISTED the urge to throw her over his shoulder, take her back to his place and love her until she stopped denying him and finally accepted the truth.

He wouldn't manhandle her because that's what she wanted—a convenient excuse to dismiss what she felt as lust.

But it was more, even if she refused to admit it.

He watched her disappear into the back and forced himself to turn. He pushed through the door and strode toward his motorcycle. He was about to climb on, to get the hell away before he buckled and gave in to the emotion welling inside of him, when he heard the raised voices coming from around back.

"…can't do this to me. Not again."

"Come on, Hank. Settle down."

"It's you who needs to settle the hell down. You can't play with a man's emotions like that."

It wasn't so much what the man said that distracted Dillon from his own damnable feelings and drew him around the side of the building. It was the threatening edge in his voice.

A few steps later, Dillon rounded the back of the boutique. His gaze sliced through the darkness in time to see the man reach for Meg's assistant.

In the blink of an eye, Dillon reached them. He caught one of the man's hands before it slid around the woman's throat.

"What the—"

"Leave her alone," Dillon cut in.

"Get lost," the man growled, pulling and tugging against Dillon's viselike grip. "This ain't none of your business. This is between me and my woman, here."

Dillon arched an eyebrow at Terry Hargove. Fear lit her eyes and she quickly shook her head.

"She's not your woman," Dillon told the man, squeezing

just enough to make his point. Bones cracked and the man shrieked. "Is she?"

"N-no," the man bit out when he finally seemed to find his voice.

"Good. Now get the hell out of here. And don't come back." Another squeeze and then he let go.

The man scrambled from the alleyway and Dillon turned back to the frightened woman. "You didn't see that," he told her. She looked startled at first, and then her body seemed to relax. Her eyes glazed over as she stared into his eyes. "Go back inside and forget what just happened. Forget about him."

She nodded and Dillon had half a mind to recruit Terry for his cause. A few persuasive thoughts and he could easily have the woman trying to convince Meg that he was the greatest thing in the world.

The trouble was, he wanted Meg to come to that conclusion herself.

To want him of her own free will.

To want him enough to admit it.

And so he tamped down his own desperation and watched Terry disappear through the back door. Hinges creaked and the lock clicked. He forced himself to turn away.

He'd risked it all and he'd lost.

The realization made his gut clench. Hopelessness rushed through him, so thick and consuming that he barely heard the footsteps behind him.

The sound pushed its way past the thunder of his heart and the hair on the back of his neck prickled. Anxiety slithered up his spine. He stiffened and his surroundings faded into a red haze as his survival instincts kicked to life. A growl vibrated up his throat and he whirled, ready to fight to the death.

But it was too late. He barely caught a glimpse of two shadows before he felt the stab in his neck. Pain gripped him, fierce and consuming. His muscles tightened. The ground seemed to shake.

And then everything went black.

19

SHE *WAS* AFRAID.

Meg finally admitted the truth to herself as she stood in the dressing room fifteen minutes later, trying to talk Honey Harwell into trying on dress number nine again since eight had failed like all the others. She saw the wistful look on the girl's face, the hidden longing, and she knew then that Honey wasn't turning down everything Meg showed her because she didn't like it.

No, she was turning down this particular dress because she liked it too much.

Because she loved it.

Just the way Meg was turning down Dillon. Running from him. Hiding.

Because she didn't want to take a chance, to fall in love, to end up brokenhearted and alone.

The truth crystallized as Honey ran her fingers over a row of buttons, her touch lingering a little too long before she made a face.

Yes, Dillon was right.

Meg was still the same person deep down inside, still nursing the same hurt, still scared.

Still alone.

And Dillon was still there.

Holding her. Helping her. Loving her.

He always had been.

And while she had no clue what tomorrow would bring—his salvation or an eternity as a vampire—suddenly it didn't matter. All that mattered was telling him that she loved him today.

Right now.

"It's yours," Meg told Honey as she set aside a stack of dresses.

"Excuse me?"

"I know you like this dress. You know you like this dress. So why don't you just admit it and end the misery for both of us?"

Honey popped a bubble with her gum, licking the sticky whiteness from her lips. "You're crazy, lady."

"And you're in denial. There's nothing wrong with wearing pretty things. Just like there's nothing wrong with wearing sweats and a lucky Cowboys T-shirt." When Honey's disdain turned to bewilderment, Meg rushed on, "Stop being afraid of yourself."

"I'm not afraid of anything."

"Yes, you are. Face it so you can get past it."

"What the hell do you know?"

"More than you can imagine." Her own hurt bubbled up deep inside her, but she didn't tamp it back down. Instead, she let it come, embracing it. Her eyes burned and the tears that had threatened her earlier slipped down her cheeks now.

Honey stiffened. "Geez lady, you don't have to get all emotional. I—I didn't mean to hurt your feelings."

Meg leveled a stare at the girl. "Do you really want to miss your one and only senior prom?"

"Maybe," Honey finally said after a long, contemplative moment. "I don't know."

"Then that means there's a part of you that wants to go." She wiped at her tears. "So take that dress and go. My treat."

An eager light glimmered in her eyes before fading into cold determination. "And look like the rest of my sisters? I have enough trouble getting my mom to notice me without blending in with the bunch."

"Is that what this is about, Honey Harwell?"

The familiar voice filled the room and Meg turned toward the curtained doorway to see Elise standing there.

"You're acting like a mule because you want my attention?"

"Hardly." Honey tossed the dress back at Meg. "The last thing I need is you hounding me."

It was the last thing she needed, and the one thing she desperately wanted.

Meg knew it and, thankfully, so did Elise.

The woman took one look at her daughter, grabbed the dress and thrust it at the young girl. "Put it on."

"I already hate it."

"Then we'll try on more until we find one that you don't hate. And we'll keep trying if we have to spend every single day here from now until prom." She smiled at her daughter. "That, or you could take this one and we could head over to the diner for a couple of diet sodas."

"Without Katy or Ellen or Marjorie or Sue?"

"Just us."

Excitement fueled the young girl's gaze as she motioned to dress number eight. "I'll take this one. And those gold shoes and the earrings I saw in the front window. And that necklace in the front case."

One problem solved. One to go.

Meg promised Elise to have everything boxed up and delivered tomorrow, then bid the mother and daughter goodnight. She was just about to lock the front door and see what she could do about tackling problem number two when she spied the black motorcycle still parked at the curb.

Hope flared, only to die a quick death when she walked outside. Fear slithered up her spine a split second before she heard the grumble of an engine. She turned toward her left in time to see a car pull out of the driveway behind the storefront next to hers. The Buick crept onto Main Street and headed North, away from her.

A strange sense of déjà vu swept over her and her mind rushed back to the parking lot at The Roundup. She saw the familiar blue paint and tinted windows.

Her hands and feet started to tingle and she knew then that something was desperately wrong.

Even before she heard Dillon's desperate voice.

Get help.

But she didn't have time. Despite the car's slow, steady pace, it was already near the main intersection of town. Once it turned onto the highway, it would pick up speed and be God knows where by the time she called Jake and Garret. While she had no doubt they would find him, they might not make it before…

The thought trailed off and fear rushed through her. Time sucked her back, paralyzing her for a brief moment.

The worst day of her life.

Not this time. Not if she could help it.

"Call Nikki Braxton," Meg told Terry as she rushed inside and snatched up her keys.

"What for?"

"Tell her Dillon's in trouble and he's headed for the interstate."

"Dillon? Dillon Cash? But he was just here."

"You saw him?"

"Yes." She seemed to think and the lightbulb that had clicked on in her head dulled. "I guess not. Where are you going?" Her voice followed Meg as she rushed back out the door.

"To help Dillon."

I'm coming. She sent the silent thought, climbed into her car and took off after the Buick.

MEG'S VOICE WHISPERED through his head, coaxing him from the smothering blackness that held him immobile.

They hit a bump and his body bounced, shaking him from the lethargy and jerking him back to reality. To the vinyl seat beneath him and the duct tape binding his wrists and ankles, and the voices coming from the front seat.

"Can't you drive any faster?" a woman's voice asked.

"You want me to get stopped?" The question was deep and inexplicably male. "There are state troopers up and down this road. The last thing we need to do is get pulled over with a body in our backseat."

"A vampire," the other voice corrected. "There's a big difference. You saw for yourself last night."

"Yeah, well I still ain't one-hundred-percent convinced, and I won't be until I'm holding one of those fangs in my hand. Until then, I'm taking this as if we were in the middle of a bona fide kidnapping. Any kidnapper worth his salt knows you don't speed when you got someone hog-tied in your backseat."

"So don't speed. But you can at least go the friggin' speed limit, can't you? That damned dart will wear off before we even get back to the motel at this rate."

But it was already wearing off, thanks to last night, Meg's sweet blood, and the voice that whispered through his head.

Hold on, she chanted. *Just…hold…on… There. I see them.*

Panic bolted through him. The last thing, the very last thing he wanted was for Meg to catch up to them while he was tied up and defenseless. She would wind up in the backseat next to him, at the mercy of whoever sat in the front seat.

He fought against the numbness and willed his hands to move. His fingers flexed and tightened. The tape snapped as easily as toilet paper.

"I hope you're right about this," the man muttered. "If we go to all this trouble and all we get is a couple hundred dollars, I'm going to be pissed."

"Just hush up. That grilled cheese sandwich with the Jesus image went for eight thousand dollars on eBay. You think a real vampire fang won't go for at least ten?"

"*If* it's real."

"It's real, already. You saw yourself last night at that honky tonk. Didn't I tell you?" the woman muttered. "I told you even before we headed down here. This guy's a vampire, all right. I knew it when I first saw the blog. I told you then, didn't I? The stuff he mentioned… Well, you just can't make shit like that up."

The words sank in and the truth dawned. Dillon knew then that he hadn't drawn the attention of vampire hunters, or even the Ancient One.

Not yet, that is.

No, he'd drawn a couple of crazies who wanted to auction off his fangs on eBay.

As ridiculous as it was, he couldn't deny the pain piercing the side of his neck where they'd shot him with another tranquilizer dart. To render him unconscious so they could take him to some seedy motel, tie him to a bed, rip out his fangs and make their fortune on the damned Internet.

Like hell.

He summoned his muscles to cooperate and eased up just enough to peer over the seat. His gaze dropped to the tranquilizer gun sitting on the cracked vinyl between them, right next to a pistol and a giant-size set of pliers.

Make that dangerous crazies.

"Holy shit," the driver muttered and swerved.

Dillon hit the seat and hissed as a wave of pain swamped him. He fought against the heat that needled him and focused on the voices.

"What's wrong?" The woman demanded.

"There's a car following us."

She shot a nervous glance over her shoulder. "Okay, fine, but don't put us in the nearest ditch. Just stay calm." She twisted back around and motioned to the right. "Pull over."

"But someone's on to us."

"And we need to take care of it. Now *pull over*."

The car started to slow and the pain eased enough for Dillon to focus.

A few bumps and they pulled off onto the shoulder.

Headlights blazed in the rearview mirror as Meg skidded to a stop behind them. She scrambled from behind the wheel.

Metal clicked as the woman fed bullets into the gun and cocked the trigger.

"Dillon!" Meg's frantic voice filled the air at the same time that Dillon reached over the seat and snatched the gun from the woman's hand.

"What the—" The question faded into a loud *crack* as the gun exploded.

The windshield shattered. The man and woman took one look at him and screamed. They scrambled from the front seat, rushed past Meg and headed for the surrounding trees.

Dillon had half a mind to go over him, but then he caught the distant rumble of motorcycles and he knew the cavalry was on its way. Jake and Garret would find the crazies soon enough and dissuade them from ever again pulling such a stunt.

Right now, Dillon had more important things to tend to.

"You're okay," Meg breathed as he climbed from the backseat and stared down at her. Her hands went to his face in a quick search-and-discovery mission before he could even answer.

He caught her hand and held it over his heart. "That depends on who's asking?" She gave him a puzzled look and he added, "If it's my friend, I'm fine. All parts present and accounted for. If it's my lover…" He let his voice trail off as he studied her face, searching for the truth, praying with all his heart that she didn't block him out this time.

He needed to know in the worst way.

As if she sensed his desperation, she stared up at him, meeting his gaze. Her eyes gleamed, shining with a love so fierce that it hit him like a sucker punch to the gut and he knew.

Deep in his heart, he *knew*.

"You were right," she said. "I was scared. I still am, but I'm willing to face that fear if it means being with you." She swallowed. "I love you, Dillon. I always have."

"Even when I couldn't kiss worth a crap?"

"Even then. I just didn't realize it." She read the doubt that still niggled at him and her hand touched his cheek. "You have to trust me just like I have to trust you."

He held her hand to his cheek. "I do. I love you."

"Even when I couldn't kiss worth a crap?"

When he hesitated, she gave him a playful punch. He caught her in his arms and drew her close. "Even then," he assured her. "I know the future seems uncertain, but everything will work out."

Her gaze met his. "We'll work it out."

He nodded. Whether it meant joining as man and wife and growing old together, or spending an eternity. Either way, they would be together. Now. Always.

"So which is it?" He eyed her. "Are you my lover or my friend?"

"Both," she murmured, and then she kissed him.

Epilogue

GARRET SAWYER STOOD off to the side of the deserted highway and eyed the man and woman standing catatonic in front of him. Thanks to their recent escape attempt, their clothes were ripped. Dirt caked their skin and leaves stuck to their hair. But they were here. Present and accounted for.

Which meant Garret and his buddies were safe.

For now.

Both the man and woman were repeat offenders recently released on bail. The man had a rap sheet longer than a first grader's list to Santa. The woman had been in and out of the system since she was twelve. Neither had ever committed anything more than a misdemeanor, except for an assault charge when the woman had gotten into a fight with her bigmouth neighbor and pelted her with a paintball gun.

They were small-time crooks who'd figured they'd get their hands on some righteous cash by selling real vamp fangs on the Internet.

A crazy scheme that wasn't the least bit funny.

He fought down the urge to grab them both, slam their heads together and knock some sense into them. But Garret Sawyer hadn't been around forever by losing his temper. He settled for something even more effective.

"Climb back into your car," he said, biting out the words, carefully, clearly, staring deep into the man's eyes. "Go back to wherever it is that you came from and forget all about us. You weren't here. We weren't here." He gave the guy one last sweeping glance. "And for Christ's sake, do something good for your fellow man."

When Jake arched an eyebrow at him, Garret shrugged. "As much trouble as these two have gotten into over the years, I figure they owe society big -ime."

He nailed the woman with a stare and repeated his spiel. A quick motion with his hands, and the couple scrambled into their damaged car. The engine roared, the Buick shifted into gear and just like that, everything went quiet.

"It's late," he murmured as he watched the headlights disappear in the distance. "We'd better get back to town." He turned back to his friends, but they'd already taken the hint and were bailing.

Dillon, still weak from the recent tranquilizer attempt, slid his arm around Meg and let her guide him toward her car. Nikki and Jake walked hand in hand to the custom-made chopper parked next to Garret's classic Harley.

Isolation slithered around him and yanked tight. A feeling he'd had more than once in the two hundred plus years that he'd been a vampire. Always standing on the outside and never really fitting in. It came with the territory.

And it had never really bothered him.

Until now.

You've smelled one too many exhaust fumes, buddy.

He stiffened and turned toward the Harley he'd spent the past month restoring. The bike's frame gleamed neon blue in the darkness, the chrome handlebars a nice contrast with the vivid color. A black-and-silver skull wrapped around the fuel tank. It was an original and the inspiration for one that Garret was working on right now for an investment banker out of Austin. A job he had to finish in the next two days, otherwise he lost the bonus he'd been promised.

And Garret didn't like to lose. He took his work seriously. Even more, he liked his work. It passed the time and that in itself was a godsend to a man who'd already been around one hundred and eighty years too long.

A temporary situation, he reminded himself.

While Dillon hadn't managed to lure out the Ancient One this time, the young vamp was onto something with his research and his blog. A little legwork from Jake and Garret to follow up on his leads, and they would be able to narrow things down considerably.

It was only a matter of time.

Hope fired inside of him, a feeling that was quickly snuffed out when he gripped the handlebars and started to straddle the leather seat.

A whisper of awareness drifted down his spine. He stiffened and his fingers clenched. His nerves shifted to red alert. Garret knew then that while Dillon had sensed his attackers rather than another bloodsucker, there truly was a fourth vampire in Skull Creek.

But it wasn't the Ancient One.

The realization should have eased the sudden pounding of his heart and the frantic tightening in his stomach.

It made it worse.

Because what lurked nearby was much more dangerous than a centuries old monster with annihilation on his mind.

His groin tightened and his nostrils flared. The truth hit him. *Her.*

The first woman he'd ever loved.

The only woman.

"Long time no see, Garret," her soft, familiar voice slid into his ears.

But it wasn't nearly long enough.

Because Viviana Darland hadn't just taken his heart way back when. She'd taken his soul, as well. And her presence in Skull Creek could only mean one thing.

They were in for trouble.

Big, *big* trouble.

* * * * *

COME TOY WITH ME

BY
CARA SUMMERS

Cara Summers has written more than thirty stories, and this year she has been awarded the *Romantic Times BOOKreviews* Career Achievement Award for Series Storyteller of the Year. *Come Toy with Me* is her fifteenth Blaze® novel, and she's looking forward to writing many more. Her next project for Blaze will be a two-book WRONG BED mini-series, involving identical twin sisters. Look for it in July 2010. When Cara isn't writing books, she teaches in the writing programme at Syracuse University.

To my sister Janet – my biggest fan and supporter.
I love you and I wish you all the best as you
begin a new chapter in your life.
You go, girl!

1

"IF YOU HAVE PLANS for Christmas, cancel them."

Retired Colonel James McGuire fired the order at him the moment Dino Angelis strolled into the office on the top floor of the Merceri Bank Building. Dino took his time walking across the expanse of Oriental carpet as he studied the tall, gruff-spoken man standing behind the carved oak desk.

Admiral Robert Maxwell, Dino's boss, had described his oldest and dearest friend accurately. James McGuire was a tall, lean man in his early sixties who despite his white hair appeared to be several years younger. McGuire had retired from the army two years previously and married his second wife, Gianna Merceri, who would one day inherit the Merceri banking fortune. Since then he'd worked as a VP for the New York City branch. Though he was wearing an impeccably tailored business suit, the colonel's bearing and tone of command marked him unmistakably as ex-military.

"Much as I hate to ruin anyone's holiday, this job may take longer than either one of us would like," McGuire continued.

Dino sighed inwardly. Okay, so his hunch that he wouldn't make it home for Christmas had been right. Ninety percent of the time what his family referred to as his premonitions were extremely accurate. They'd saved his life on more than one occasion. But this would make three Christmases in a row he hadn't been with his family, and his cousin Theo was getting married on December 27th.

Not for the first time, Dino asked himself if there'd been some way of getting out of this assignment that he'd overlooked. But Admiral Maxwell owed Colonel McGuire a favor, and Dino owed his admiral, big-time. For the last two years he'd worked in special operations under Maxwell's command. Three months ago, he'd been shot on one of his missions. A bullet had come within an inch of his spine. Recuperating in hospitals in Germany and later in D.C. had given him time to reevaluate how he wanted to spend the rest of his life. He'd joined the navy because he loved the sea. He'd wanted adventure and to see the world. Plus, he'd sensed it was what he was supposed to do. Now, he wanted a job that wouldn't isolate him so completely from his cousins, his uncle and his mother. He missed the closeness, the connectedness he always found with his family. Admiral Maxwell had not only understood his decision, but he'd worked hard to expedite Dino's discharge, and Dino liked to repay his debts.

So he had committed to do a job that he knew nothing about—except that it involved McGuire's family. Of course, Maxwell had used that information as part of the bait. He knew that for Dino, family was important, given it was one of the main reasons he wanted out of the navy. McGuire also knew Dino had expressed an interest in getting into some kind of investigative or security work when he returned to civilian life and that this assignment would be a good opportunity to give it a whirl.

To make the job even more tempting, the admiral had even given Dino the business card of an old navy buddy, Jase Campbell, who was now running his own security firm in Manhattan. Dino had done his first two special ops missions for Maxwell with Jase at his side, and they'd found their styles complementary. Jase was a meticulous planner, and Dino was good at improvising and going with his hunches.

McGuire made a stabbing motion with the unlit cigar he held in his hand. "The truth is this problem I want you to solve for me may stretch into the new year."

Good thing he hadn't promised his mother that he would make it home. Of course Cass Angelis probably already knew not to expect him. Psychic powers ran strong, especially in the women on his mother's side of the family. His mother claimed the psychic abilities could be traced back to the Oracle at Delphi, and hers were particularly powerful.

When he'd been a kid, he'd been hard pressed to get away with anything. She'd always known what he was up to. But his own hunches had kept him out of scrapes on more than one occasion. Recalling that, Dino bit back a smile and refocused his attention on the colonel.

"Perhaps you could tell me exactly what kind of a job you're offering. Admiral Maxwell said that it had something to do with a family problem, but he didn't offer any details."

Maxwell had been apologetic about that. He'd explained that his friend McGuire hadn't been forthcoming. All he'd said was that he'd needed the best man Maxwell could come up with. Dino figured that whether or not he was Maxwell's "best" man was debatable. What couldn't be argued was that he was available. With his discharge papers from the navy due to come through within the next month, he'd just been pushing papers for Maxwell at the Pentagon.

Frowning, the colonel gave Dino a brief nod as he set the cigar down on the desk. "A family problem. I suppose that's one way to describe it. My—"

The intercom on his phone interrupted him and a brisk

female voice spoke. "Colonel, your daughter is returning your call. She's on line three."

"Thank you, Margie." As he reached for the phone, McGuire met Dino's eyes. "I have to take this."

Taking advantage of the opportunity, Dino glanced around the room, absorbing the details. The wall behind him was made of glass and offered a view of the waiting area—a one-way view that allowed Colonel McGuire to see anyone who stepped into the lobby. He wondered how long the colonel had been studying him while he'd been cooling his heels in the lobby.

Through the wall-to-wall window behind McGuire, Dino could see a wintry view of Central Park. The trees were bare of leaves, the ground a dismal brownish-gray, and a serious snowstorm was promised tomorrow. Over a foot of snow was being predicted and Manhattanites were looking forward to a white Christmas. Now that it was almost certain that he was going to be in the Big Apple for the holiday season, Dino was looking forward to it, too. San Francisco had never offered much in the way of white Christmases.

Bookshelves lined the wall to his right, and a large portrait of a woman graced the wall to his left. The brass plaque beneath the painting read: Lucia Merceri. Admiral Maxwell had mentioned her, describing her as the grand matriarch of the Merceri family, a woman with a will of iron. Though she lived in a villa outside of Rome, Lucia kept close track of her family members in New York. In the painting, she wore a black suit, her white hair was pulled up into a ballerina's knot, and she carried a walking cane in her right hand. But it was the dark, piercing eyes that captured Dino's attention. This was a woman who took no prisoners.

"Cat, darling, I need to see you today. How about lunch?"

At the abrupt change in the colonel's tone, Dino shifted his gaze back to him and was struck by how much his stern expression had softened.

"I know how busy you are. A toy store at Christmas—it must be total chaos. But don't you need a break? I thought I might lure you out to that place on Forty-fifth Street you like so much. You have to eat."

Dino knew that Cat McGuire was the colonel's only child by a first marriage. According to Admiral Maxwell, Nancy McGuire had died of MS when Cat was ten, and during the next eight years until Cat had entered college, the colonel had made sure that his daughter had been with him on every assignment barring those that took him directly into combat zones. Even then, McGuire had tried to station his daughter in a place where he could visit her as frequently as possible.

"A delivery?" Disappointment laced the colonel's tone. "I know there are only five shopping days left until Christmas— yes, right, four and a half. But can't one of your employees sign for it?"

The almost wheedling note in the colonel's voice surprised Dino. This man was a sharp right turn from the one who'd fired orders at him a few minutes ago. McGuire chose that moment to glance at him and wave him into a chair. It was only then that Dino realized he'd been standing at attention ever since he'd stopped in front of the desk.

But Cat McGuire evidently didn't take orders from her father. In fact, she seemed to be doing most of the talking.

Intrigued, Dino settled himself in a comfortable leather chair and stretched out his legs. His admiral's close relationship with McGuire could be traced back to the fact that they'd grown up together in Toledo, Ohio, and graduated from the same high school. Though one had gone to Annapolis and the other to West Point, their friendship had never faded. Maxwell was even Cat's godfather.

The admiral had shown him a framed photo of his god-daughter. The moment he'd glanced at it, Dino had experienced a heightening of his senses and he'd known the same way he supposed his mother knew things that the Fates were offering him something he shouldn't walk away from.

It had been the same when he'd been working special ops under Admiral Maxwell. He'd always sensed which ones to volunteer for. The danger that had lain in wait for him on his last mission had come to him in a vision. On the rare occasions that he experienced one, the image always flashed into his mind like the negative of a black-and-white photo. His pre-knowledge had probably saved his life.

When he'd been looking at Cat's picture, he'd also experienced a very strong attraction. He'd tried to rationalize it. After all, it had been a long time since he'd had a woman in his life. The kind of work he'd been doing for the past two years hadn't left time for anything personal. And she was definitely pretty with long red-blond hair and fair skin. The hint of cheekbones suggested strength and the set of her chin spoke of stubbornness.

But it was her eyes that he'd stared at the longest. They were oval-shaped and in the photo they were a glorious mix of gold and green. Cat's eyes. A man could get lost in them.

Warning bells had sounded in his mind. He was starting a new phase of his life. He wanted more contact with his family, and he needed to find out if the skills he'd been honing in the navy could be translated into a career in the private sector. That was a lot for a man to have on his plate.

It was the wrong time to become involved with a woman—especially one who pulled him the way Cat McGuire did.

Colonel McGuire picked up the cigar again and tapped it on the desk. "If lunch is out, let's meet for drinks once you close up shop…eight o'clock? I thought you closed at seven."

There was a pause, then the colonel continued, "Eight it is. How about meeting me midtown at the bar in the Algonquin?"

The cigar tapped in a faster rhythm. "All right, Patty's Pub it is—right across from your store. Eight o'clock."

When he hung up the phone, McGuire sank into his chair and sent Dino an exasperated look. "Ninety percent of the people I negotiate with are easier to manage than she is. I swear she lives and breathes that store."

"The Cheshire Cat."

"Yes. *Alice in Wonderland* was her favorite book when she was little." Setting down his unlit and unsmoked cigar, he narrowed his eyes on Dino. "Did my friend Maxwell fill you in on the name of the store?"

"No. I looked it up myself." He'd been curious about it, as well as its owner, so he'd paid it a visit early that morning. Merely as a little reconnaissance mission, he'd told himself. The more you knew before you took on a job, the better.

The Cheshire Cat hadn't opened yet, but he'd checked out the display windows and found himself charmed by the thematic way the toys were arranged in each one. One told a story of pirates, and the other featured a battle between a dragon and a valiant knight.

Then beyond the artfully arranged toys his attention had been caught by Cat McGuire hurrying down a wrought iron spiral staircase in the center of the store. Once she reached the bottom, she'd flown to the door and pulled it open.

Dino had experienced an even greater heightening of his senses than he'd felt when he'd looked at her photo. And no wonder. She'd been pretty enough in the picture, but in person, she was stunning. And tall. In the boots she was wearing, she had to be nearly five ten.

Though Dino had known he was staring, he couldn't seem to stop. She'd fastened her hair back from her face with some feminine bit of magic, and red-gold curls had tumbled to her shoulders. He'd wondered if they would feel warm to the touch. Silver hoops had hung from her ears, and the dark blue sweater she'd worn belted over a long flowing skirt had him thinking fancifully of gypsies dancing in the firelight.

As customers filed into the Cheshire Cat, her gaze had met his—for just an instant. He'd felt the impact like a swift, hard punch in the gut. Then his mind had emptied and all he'd been aware of was her eyes. He'd read the same startled response in them that he was feeling—a reckless, nearly overpowering desire. Then the green had darkened to the color of the Mediterranean Sea at twilight, completely alluring. What color would those eyes turn when a man made love to her? When he was inside of her?

Before he could get a handle on his thoughts, an image had flashed into his mind—he and Cat standing against a wall. Except for a few wispy pieces of lace she was naked, her bare legs wrapped around him. And he was thrusting into her, pulling out, thrusting in again.

Recalling it now, his whole body hardened, his blood heated.

"I checked you out, too," McGuire was saying.

Dino ruthlessly reined in his thoughts. But he had less luck controlling his body's reaction to the image fading from his mind.

"I don't mind telling you that I specifically asked Bobby to find me an army man."

Dino met McGuire's eyes steadily. "Admiral Maxwell told me to tell you that with a navy man you're trading up."

McGuire grinned, then broke into a full belly laugh. The sound filled the room, and Dino felt the corners of his mouth curve.

"That sounds like Bobby," McGuire said. Then his expression sobered. "I trust Bobby to have chosen the right man, and that means I trust you with my daughter's safety."

Dino once more felt that heightening of his senses. Hadn't he known from the beginning that the job would be about the daughter? Wasn't that precisely why he'd gone to the store to check her out? And considering his intense reaction to Cat as a woman, he was going to have to be very careful.

"Why don't you tell me exactly what it is that you want me to do?"

The colonel met Dino's eyes directly. "You already know that my daughter Cat owns and runs a toy store in Tribeca. She's been doing it for a year and a half now. Before that, she was in the toy department at Macy's and worked her way up to head buyer."

McGuire picked up his cigar yet again, but still made no move to light it. "The fact that Cat's in retail is a problem for my wife's family, especially for my mother-in-law, Lucia Merceri."

McGuire gestured to the portrait that Dino had studied earlier. "That woman is a true matriarch. She runs her family with the verve and determination of a five-star general. When Cat met her at Gianna's and my wedding, she likened her to the Queen of Hearts in *Alice in Wonderland*."

Dino was beginning to wonder where McGuire was headed.

"Ever since we married, Lucia has been pressuring my wife, Gianna, to find a suitable husband for Cat so that she can take her rightful place in New York City society. Lucia believes that women have a duty to produce a family, to contribute to the community, and that they should leave the business world to men. Unfortunately, she's influenced my wife's thinking in that direction, too."

"I take it Cat disagrees."

"That's putting it mildly. But between us, we can usually handle Gianna."

Dino frowned. "Does this job have something to do with running interference between your wife and your daughter? Because if—"

"No." McGuire raised a hand, palm outward. "I can handle that part myself. I'm getting to be quite good at it although at times it's a little like moving through a minefield. The trouble my daughter is in has to do with that shop of hers."

Dino merely raised his brows.

"The Cheshire Cat imports and sells unique toys. There's nothing in the place that you would find in one of the big chain stores or even in the more upscale department stores. Almost everything is one of a kind. About a year ago when Cat was still doing a lot of traveling, she discovered a town in Mexico, Paxco, where doll- and toy-making are highly revered and a local cottage industry. She signed a contract with the craftsmen, and in the past year, has imported a number of products from Paxco.

Dino said nothing. For the first time since he'd walked into the office, he heard worry in the colonel's voice.

McGuire picked up his cigar and jabbed it at the air again. "That's where the trouble is. Someone has taken advantage of my little girl."

"How?" Dino asked.

"Some bastard is smuggling drugs into the country in those toys. Cocaine."

Dino thought for a minute. How much cocaine could be smuggled in toys? "It must be a rather small-scale operation."

McGuire's expression turned very grim. "Small, but very profitable. My contacts at the CIA tell me that the cocaine is premium quality and the person running the operation targets a select group of clients who are willing to pay very generously for high quality and the guaranteed discretion of the distributor."

Dino nodded thoughtfully. "The rich folks don't have to lower themselves to rubbing elbows with someone on the street."

"Exactly. But drugs aren't the worst of it. The profits from this little enterprise are being used by a terrorist group out of Latin America to help establish a cell in this country. That's brought in both Homeland Security and the feds—which means the whole situation's got cluster fuck written all over it."

Dino silently agreed. "Does your daughter know about the smuggling?"

The colonel shook his head. "I thought about telling her, but I know her too well. She'd be furious that someone was using her shop that way. There's no way I could convince her to keep her nose out of it. She'd start poking around, and that could put her in even more danger."

"What else did your CIA informants tell you about the operation?"

"Someone on the other end in one of those small towns is loading the drugs into the toys just before they're shipped here."

Simple, safe, Dino thought. And a toy store was a good cover. "There has to be someone in the store who knows which pieces have the drugs in them."

"Yes." McGuire tapped his cigar on the desk. "And the feds' prime suspect is my daughter. They think she's part of a damn terrorist smuggling ring."

Dino kept his eyes steady. "Is she?"

McGuire's color heightened, but there was no other sign of his brief struggle for control. His voice was flat and firm when he spoke. "No. She's not. From the time she was a little girl, she's dreamed of running a toy shop—a place where she could make children's dreams come true. That was her mother's dream, too. Nancy even designed some dolls. It was something they shared before Nancy passed. Cat's not involved in this criminal enterprise, but someone else in that shop has to be."

"Any idea who?"

"She has two full-time employees. Her assistant manager is Adelaide Creed, a retired accountant, and Cat looks on her as a second mother. And she often speaks of her buyer, Matt Winslow, as the brother she never had. She also has a part-time employee, Josie Sullivan, a sixty-five-year-old retired school-teacher. Any one of them is close enough to the business to be involved. Hell, they could all be working together."

"I assume you've run background checks on each of them, and none of them has an urgent need for money, or a sudden influx of the same."

McGuire nodded. "I used a man your boss recommended—Jase Campbell. He researched their finances and found nothing out of the ordinary. On top of that they each appear to be stellar citizens. Josie was given an award from the mayor for excellence in teaching, and Matt is going to school at night to get his MBA. When she first retired from her career as an accountant, Adelaide Creed worked for Congresswoman Jessica Atwell. When the governor appointed Atwell Attorney General, Adelaide applied for work at the Cheshire Cat."

"So you have no leads."

"None. And my informants tell me that the feds expect to move on the operation any day. This whole thing is about to come crashing down on Cat's head."

"And my job is to bodyguard her?"

"Not just that. You'll be on the inside. I want you to take a look around and find out who's on the receiving end of the stolen goods. Maybe you can even get a lead on the mastermind behind the whole thing. According to my sources, the feds don't have much of a clue there. Bobby claims you're one of the best operatives he's ever had under his command. He says you have a special kind of sixth sense when it comes to investigations."

Thinking it was better not to comment on that, Dino said, "Isn't the sudden appearance of a bodyguard going to raise the suspicions of whoever is involved?"

Dino watched some of the tension in the older man ease.

"Not if your cover story is good enough. And yours is excellent."

Noting the gleam in the colonel's eyes, Dino had a hunch that he wasn't going to like it.

"You're my daughter's new fiancé."

2

THE FIRST FIVE BEATS of silence that followed his announcement allowed James McGuire a moment to study the young man sitting across from him. Dino Angelis looked perfectly at ease, his elbows resting on the arms of the chair, his legs stretched out and crossed at the ankles. McGuire had seen the same kind of seeming relaxation in jungle cats while they watched their prey. And like those cats, he wagered that Dino Angelis could move quickly enough when he was ready.

He agreed with Bobby—Angelis was smart. So far, his questions had been perceptive and to the point, his comments insightful. The man didn't believe in wasting words. For a split second, right after he'd said the word *fiancé*, he'd read surprise in the younger man's eyes. Other than that Angelis hadn't revealed much of anything he was thinking since he'd ambled into the room. He'd make a formidable opponent in a poker game.

As the five beats stretched into ten, McGuire said, "Any questions?"

Dino raised one finger. "Who's going to believe in a fiancé who turns up out of the blue?"

Once again he'd zeroed in on a key point. McGuire opened a drawer in his desk and pulled out a manila envelope. "Got it covered. This is your complete history with my daughter—

from first meet to secret weekends here in Manhattan at the Waldorf to the night that you popped the question on the skating rink at Rockefeller Center. Melted my little girl's heart. She loves to skate—could have competed nationally if we hadn't had to move around so much. Your relationship has been hush-hush so far, but Cat's invited you here for Christmas to publicly announce the engagement and to meet her family. You have a two-week leave from the Pentagon."

"Where am I going to be staying? I can't do a very good job of protecting your daughter if I go back to my hotel room every night."

McGuire opened the envelope and pulled out a key. "Cat's apartment building is a co-op. A few months ago, the apartment next to hers became available, and I bought it for her as a surprise Christmas gift, figuring she could expand the space she has now. You can stay there. Both apartments overlook a courtyard that connects the building to the block the Cheshire Cat is on. As far as Cat's employees are concerned, it will appear that you're staying with her. You'll have a day to memorize your background story before you drop in at the shop and surprise my little girl."

"How is your daughter going to react to all this? Won't she want to know why you've hired me to act as her bodyguard?"

"I'm not going to tell her that part."

"Then why would she agree to this fake fiancé masquerade?"

"I'm going to persuade her to cooperate over drinks this evening."

Dino's eyes narrowed. "You think she'll agree?"

McGuire kept his smile easy, confident. There *was* still that little obstacle to overcome. Cat was her father's daughter. She could be stubborn when she wanted to.

"Cat has a weakness for wanting to please her father—

especially at Christmastime. And the fake engagement is the only way to protect my wife and daughter from Lucia Merceri."

Dino inclined his head toward the portrait on the wall. "I'm not following. What part does your mother-in-law play in all of this?"

"Nothing in the drug smuggling part. But the old battle-ax is the prime mover in the fake engagement scenario." McGuire leaned back in his chair. "Just about the time I learned about the danger my daughter is in, my wife came to me in tears. It seems that over the past year, her mother has been asking for progress reports on what Gianna is doing to get Cat 'settled.' Turns out my wife has been placating her mother with stories, telling her that Cat has been seeing someone secretly. Gianna told Lucia she discovered the trysts by accident and she hasn't wanted to get involved because she was afraid of jinxing it."

"An interesting story," Dino commented.

"Yeah. In my wife's defense, I have to say that she's been focused on her daughter Lucy's pregnancy and didn't have much time left over to run a campaign to get Cat a husband. So she made up a whopper. And Lucia's been fascinated by it. Last week she announced that she was coming over here to celebrate Christmas with us, and she wants to meet the man Cat is seeing. My wife is in a panic about what her mother will do when she discovers the lie. It won't take Cat long to figure out that if she goes along with this masquerade, she can bring some peace to the family during the holidays, and her stepmother will owe her. Christmas is a special time for Cat. She wants to make everyone happy. And Lucia is flying back to Rome on New Year's Day. Crisis over."

Dino studied the colonel. "So the fake engagement is supposed to fool your mother-in-law until New Year's Day?"

"It could actually last a bit beyond that, depending on how the drug smuggling problem is resolved. I'm leaving the story about your eventual breakup in Gianna's capable hands. Apparently my wife can lie like a trouper."

Dino unfolded himself from the chair and picked up the key and the envelope. "If that's all, sir, I'll take this back to my hotel room and go over the specifics."

McGuire rose and extended his hand. "Good, good. You'll report for duty at the Cheshire Cat tomorrow no later than eleven hundred hours."

"Yes, sir."

McGuire waited until Dino had his hand on the doorknob. "One more thing."

Dino glanced back.

"It's not part of the job, but it would be great if you could get Cat to relax and have a little fun. The girl is so focused on her store that she doesn't take time to smell the roses anymore."

"I'll see what I can do."

McGuire managed to hold in his sigh of relief until he'd watched the elevator doors slide shut on Dino Angelis. That had gone almost too smoothly. Then he took his cell phone out of his pocket and dialed a familiar number at the Pentagon.

"Jimmy, you've called to tell me you owe me fifty bucks, right?" Bobby Maxwell asked.

Grinning, McGuire sank into his chair. Bobby had always been a bit cocky, so he kept his tone serious. "You haven't won the bet yet. They haven't even met. And first things first. My daughter's in danger. That's his primary mission."

"A little adventure is just what they need. It'll bring them closer."

"It might turn out to be more than a little adventure."

"Angelis has the best instincts of any man I've ever

trained." Bobby's tone too had turned serious. "If there's something going on in your daughter's store, he'll spot it. And he'll know what to do."

"I hope you're right."

"I am. And I'm also right about the fact that he'd make the perfect man for our little girl."

"We'll see," was all McGuire said. But he was already hoping that his friend Bobby would win the little wager they'd made. He too thought that Dino Angelis just might be the perfect match for Cat.

CASS ANGELIS' CELL PHONE RANG just as she was about to leave the tower room in her house. A glance at the caller ID had joy bubbling up inside of her. "Dino?"

"You probably already know I'm not going to make it home for Christmas."

She'd sensed that much last night. She'd also sensed there was more, but the images she'd seen in her crystals hadn't been clear. Except for the woman—tall with reddish hair and stunning green eyes. Turning, Cass moved to her desk and sat down. The client who was due any minute would have to wait. Cass could hear traffic noises in the background on the other end of the line.

"I'm in Manhattan on a job. I couldn't say no."

"I understand." And Cass did in spite of the band of pain that tightened around her heart.

For a moment, there was silence on the other end of the line, and Cass waited. Of all of her "children," her son Dino had always been the most reserved.

Twelve years ago when her husband Demetrius and her sister Penelope had been killed in a freak boating accident, Cass and Dino, her brother-in-law Spiro and his four children,

Nik, Theo, Kit and Philly, had moved into the huge house Cass's father had built. From that day on, Cass had raised her nephews and niece as her own, and Dino had come to regard them more as brothers and kid sister than cousins. Dino had been the only one who'd had a desire to see the world, the only one who'd moved away from San Francisco.

"There's a woman," Dino finally said. "I sense that the Fates have put her in my path for a reason. And I had a vision about her."

The redhead, Cass knew. "You'll figure it out."

Dino laughed then, and Cass's mood suddenly lightened. "You've been saying that to me for as long as I can remember."

"A mother's job," Cass replied. "And I don't recall that I was ever wrong."

"I'll get home as soon as I possibly can. My discharge papers are coming through in a couple more weeks. That was supposed to be your Christmas present."

"Well." She hadn't seen that, hadn't even allowed herself to hope for it. "I'll have a surprise for you too—when you get here." She wanted Dino to meet Mason Leone, the man she'd been dating, in person before she told him that after all these years, she'd fallen in love again.

The traffic noises grew louder. "I have to go. I'll try to keep in touch. Love you."

"Love you, too," Cass said, but Dino had already disconnected.

A quick glance at her watch told Cass that she still had a few minutes before she had to go down to her office. Crossing quickly to her desk, she took her crystals from a drawer. Midnight was usually the hour when she could see things more clearly. But she simply couldn't wait.

Sinking into her chair, she cleared her mind and waited.

One by one the crystals began to glow in her hands. In their centers, mist blossomed, parted, then closed again. In one, she saw Dino in his full dress uniform dancing with the redheaded woman she'd seen before. Around them, lights twinkled. As the mists thickened in one crystal, they thinned in another.

Cass glimpsed a doll this time, with a porcelain face and a red silk dress. When her attention was drawn to a third crystal, Cass felt fear knot in her stomach. She could see the red-headed woman again, but she was no longer with Dino. She was in a dark place, and she was facing the barrel of a gun. The shot that rang out nearly had Cass dropping her crystals.

In spite of the client who was waiting for her, Cass sat where she was for a few more minutes while fear warred with joy inside of her.

Dino and the woman would be facing serious danger, but Dino had been right. The Fates were making him an offer, and if he chose to accept it, he would find his true love.

ON HER WAY DOWN from her office, Cat took a moment to breathe and glance around her store. A toddler clutching his mother's hand had decided to sing along with the rendition of "Jingle Bells" pouring out of the sound system. Another child was busily plucking ornaments off the Christmas tree she'd set up in one of the corners. Cat grinned. She had to retrim that tree almost every night, but it was worth it.

The bell over the Cheshire Cat's door jingled. From her vantage point halfway up the spiral staircase in the center of her store, Cat spotted Mrs. Lassiter and Mrs. Palmer, two of her most loyal customers. No doubt they were here to pick up their dolls. She dashed down the rest of the stairs. Just as she reached the two women, the bell jingled again, and more customers pushed their way into the store. Cat briefly shifted her gaze to the newcomers, and she immediately recognized them as two sisters, Janey and Angela Carter. They had also ordered the dolls. Cat sent them what she hoped was a welcoming smile.

"I came to pick up my granddaughter's doll," Mrs. Lassiter said in a voice that carried. "It's one of the special ones you ordered from that place in Mexico."

"Yes. From Paxco, Mexico." Cat did her best to project calm reassurance. "I'm sorry, but they haven't arrived yet. I expect them—"

"You said they'd be here today. What's the problem?"

Ignoring the nerves dancing in her stomach, Cat smiled. "No problem."

"When will they arrive?"

Cat wished she knew. "I'm hoping tomorrow. Thursday at the latest."

The bell over the door jingled again, and a portly white-haired man entered and looked around. Cat was sure she'd never seen him before, and yet there was something about him that was familiar. He crossed to Adelaide and cut rudely into the line in front of her counter. Someone voiced a protest, and for a moment Adelaide lost her usual pleasant expression. She even dropped a toy soldier she was about to ring up. Then she said something to the man and pointed in Cat's direction. As he strode toward her, Cat suddenly figured out why he might look familiar. With his white hair and mustache, and the narrow unframed spectacles that sat nearly on the end of his nose, he reminded Cat a bit of Santa Claus.

Oh, how she wished he were. Where was Santa when you needed him?

"But you're not sure?"

Cat shifted her gaze back to Mrs. Lassiter. Worry outweighed the annoyance in the older woman's voice now, and

Cat could see the same concern reflected in Mrs. Palmer's face, as well as in the Carter sisters'.

The shop was packed. It was Christmas week in Manhattan *and* lunch hour—that time of day when both locals and tourists poured into stores with one purpose—to finish their Christmas shopping.

And her father had wanted her to join him for lunch in midtown? Right. Her family didn't really have a clue about the kind of pressures that built once you combined Christmas, children and toys.

Cat met the worried gazes in front of her one at a time. "I'm confident that the dolls will arrive in the next two days." They had to.

Out of the corner of her eye, she saw that her assistant Adelaide had fully recovered from her encounter with the Santa Claus man and was ringing up a fairly hefty sale for a young couple. Tourists. The man had a camera slung over his shoulder and the woman was unfolding a street map.

"So the bottom line is that you have no idea whether or not the doll I ordered will arrive by Christmas Eve." This time it wasn't Mrs. Lassiter who spoke. It was the Santa Claus man. His voice carried and several customers who'd been browsing nearby stopped to stare in his direction.

"You said the dolls would be here no later than today," Mrs. Lassiter chimed in. "Don't we have a free trade agreement with Mexico? Would it help if I called my congressman?"

Cat turned the full wattage of her smile on the small group gathered in front of her and kept her voice calm. "I don't think it's time to panic yet. I only learned yesterday afternoon that the delivery of the dolls might be delayed a day or so. *Might* be. They could be on their way right now. Each doll is handmade, and a few of them weren't quite ready for shipment. I told them to ship the ones that were immediately." What she didn't add was that Juan Rivero, who'd called her with the bad news, had answered her by saying that they only needed one more day. And then he'd hung up.

"In the meantime, my buying assistant, Matt Winslow, flew to Paxco, Mexico, late last night. I'm hoping to hear from him any time now."

She should have heard from him already, even with the time difference. And Matt wasn't answering his cell. Cat concentrated on the unhappy faces in front of her and firmly pushed that worry out of her mind.

"Worst case scenario, they'll express ship the ones that are ready today, and Matt will personally bring back the dolls that are holding up the shipment with him."

"You're sure?" This question came from a very worried Mrs. Palmer.

"My granddaughter Giselle is expecting Santa to bring her that doll for Christmas. I showed her your brochure and that doll is the only one she wanted," Mrs. Lassiter said. "I don't want her to be disappointed."

"It's the same with my daughter." In contrast to Mrs. Lassiter's confrontational expression, Mrs. Palmer's eyes held a great deal of worry and sadness. Her black wool coat was off the rack and was growing threadbare at the sleeves. "That doll was the only gift Mandy asked Santa for."

Cat's heart twisted. Both Mrs. Lassiter and Mrs. Palmer frequented her store. And because she made it a habit to learn as much as she could about her customers, Cat was aware of the number of visits that Mrs. Palmer and Mandy had made to the Cheshire Cat to choose that one special gift. If it didn't arrive, Cat wagered there would be nothing else under the tree.

But the shipment *would* arrive. She'd been chanting that

sentence to herself like a mantra all day long. The unique dolls that were now being finshed in the small town of Paxco, Mexico, were even more special to Cat because she'd asked the craftsmen to create them from a design of her mother's. She'd taken twenty-four orders and added on one she intended to give her father. That had been in mid-November.

"The dolls are going to get here," Cat assured the group in front of her. Her gaze lingered on the Santa Claus man. With his index finger, he shoved his glasses to the bridge of his nose and met her gaze for a moment. Once again, something tugged at the edge of her mind. She knew that she'd never seen him in the store and she wondered who had taken his order.

"You can track the shipment, can't you?" The question came from the Santa Claus man in a calm voice.

Cat beamed a smile at him. "Absolutely. Just as soon as I get a tracking number." Matt was supposed to phone her with that information. "Tell you what. I have a list of all your names and your phone numbers. I'll call you just as soon as I get some news from my assistant. It should be before the end of the day. First thing in the morning at the latest."

In her peripheral vision she saw that Adelaide had stepped away from the counter to assist a customer, and there was now a line at the checkout station. Matt was supposed to be here working today, but though she needed him badly, she needed him in Paxco more.

She masked her relief as the small crowd in front of her began to drift away—all except for the Santa Claus man who stepped forward and handed her a card.

"I'd appreciate a call the moment you get the tracking number."

She glanced down at it, noted the ritzy address on East 70th and the name. George Miller. It didn't ring a bell. She glanced back up at him. "Have we met before, Mr. Miller? You look familiar to me, but I can't quite place it."

He gave her a smile that didn't quite reach his eyes. "No. I would have remembered if we'd met before, Ms. McGuire." He turned to exit the shop.

Cat tucked the card into her pocket, took out the notebook she always carried with her, and jotted down a reminder to personally call each customer who was waiting for a doll just as soon as they arrived.

One crisis postponed, she told herself as she moved as quickly as she could toward the checkout counter. As she did, she brushed by Adelaide.

Pitching her voice low, Adelaide said, "Nicely done. You're better than anyone I know at defusing panic attacks."

"I didn't do so well on my own," Cat murmured.

Adelaide shot her a quick sideways glance. "At least no one brought up the Nor'easter that's due to arrive tomorrow. If they close down the airports…"

Cat clamped her hands over her ears, and Adelaide's rich laugh filled the shop. She was a round, comfortable-looking single woman in her late fifties who combined a love of children with an accounting degree from Sarah Lawrence. In addition, she had a personal warmth that reminded Cat of Paula Deen, one of the most popular chefs on the Food Network. Adelaide had retired early from a lucrative job at Price Waterhouse and referred to her work at the Cheshire Cat as her little mad money job.

Adelaide patted Cat's shoulder. "Just teasing. These winter storms are never as bad as the predictions. It's all hype."

"From your mouth to God's ears," Cat said. Then she added, "The man who cut into your checkout line earlier— George Miller—did you take his order for one of the dolls?"

"No. I've never seen him before. Have you?"

Cat shook her head. "But there's something familiar about him."

Out of the corner of her eye, Cat spotted the beginnings of a protest at the checkout counter. Dashing forward, she beamed a smile at the man who was first in line and rang up the sale. While he was signing the credit card receipt, she pulled her cell phone out and speed-dialed her neighbor.

Josie Sullivan was a retired schoolteacher in her early seventies who'd moved into the apartment below Cat's about a year ago. She had an ethereal air that reminded Cat of one of Tennessee Williams' southern heroines. But beneath her seemingly fragile exterior, Josie had an energy and an iron-willed determination that must have served her well in a third-grade classroom.

It certainly worked when she was steering customers toward a sale. Off and on over the past year, Josie had been filling in at the store during what Cat had dubbed the "crush hours." Since their apartments were in the building that shared a courtyard with the Cheshire Cat, Josie could make it to the store on a moment's notice. All she had to do was exit the back of their building, cross the courtyard and take a shortcut down an alley. The arrangement was working out so well that Cat was going to offer her a more permanent part-time job right after the first of the year.

"Cat, tell me you desperately need me in the store," Josie said the instant she picked up her phone. "I'm simply bored to death."

Cat smiled. "I desperately need you in the store." Then she held out her hand to the harried-looking woman who was next in line at the counter. "Sorry you had to wait. Let me take that for you."

BY EIGHT O'CLOCK, Cat's head was aching and her feet were killing her, but she was finally able to lock the front door of her toy store. Even though the Cheshire Cat officially closed at seven, the shop had still been filled with shoppers. During the week before Christmas, one had to go with the flow, but she'd insisted that Josie and Adelaide leave at seven. On Thursday they would close at 6:00 so that they could all attend the big charity ball her stepmother chaired each holiday season.

Cat had bought tickets for all of her employees, hoping to placate her stepmother. Gianna Merceri McGuire was not going to be pleased when Cat arrived without a date in tow.

A date. In the past year and a half, the concept had become foreign to her. The last time she'd gone out with a man she'd still been working at Macy's.

It was then that she once more recalled the stranger who'd been standing at the edge of the small crowd on the sidewalk that morning. He'd been teasing his way into her mind all day. This was the first opportunity she'd had to think about the odd reaction she'd had to him.

No, *odd* wasn't the precise word. She'd never had such an intense reaction to a man in her life. Not even to the men she'd taken as lovers. Cat frowned as she recalled that moment when his eyes had collided with hers. The contact had been as intimate as a touch. She hadn't been able to think or move. All she could do was feel. Desire—raw, primitive, compelling— had filled her. And in that instant, an image had formed in her mind of the two of them naked, their legs tangling as they rolled across a floor.

Which was absolutely ridiculous. He was a complete stranger. She'd barely caught a glimpse of him.

But she had no trouble picturing him now. He'd been big, broad-shouldered and tall. He'd had a strong face, like a warrior. In the black leather bomber jacket and jeans, he'd looked tough. Not her usual type. But that hadn't stopped her from imagining their bodies locked together.

Fisting her hands at her side, Cat pushed the image out of her mind. There had to be a rational explanation for what she'd felt—what she was still feeling. First of all, she hadn't slept much the night before. And he was a man who would stand out in any crowd. Her body had obviously been trying to tell her something. Devoting all her time to making the Cheshire Cat a success had left a void in her life. That had to be it.

She'd better get back into the dating scene. Nothing serious. But some simple, uncomplicated sex held a certain appeal. Pulling her notebook out of her jacket pocket, she jotted a note to herself. *New Year's resolution #1: Start dating again.*

And the plan would have certain benefits. Next year she might have an escort for Gianna's charity ball. Her stepmother wanted her in a serious relationship with a "suitable" man— suitable meaning someone with the proper social standing. Cat wasn't about to walk down the path that Gianna had all mapped out for her, but a date now and then, someone to see a movie with—that would be enjoyable.

Right. Who was she kidding? When she'd looked into that stranger's eyes this morning, going to a movie with him had been the last thing on her mind. She'd thought of sex, raw, wild, incredible.

Tucking her notebook back into her pocket, Cat firmly pushed all thoughts of the attractive stranger, the upcoming ball and the questions she would have to handle from her step-mother firmly out of her mind. She had much bigger problems.

Those missing dolls. Striding to the small space behind the cash register, she opened a manila folder and thumbed through the orders she'd removed from her files earlier in the day.

Twenty-four children were going to be disappointed if Matt Winslow didn't get the shipment out of Paxco. And right now twenty-four unhappy customers were waiting to hear from her—and she didn't have any news to give them. Closing the folder, she tucked it into her tote bag.

She hadn't been able to get through to Matt all day, and he hadn't answered any of the messages she'd left on his voice mail. She also hadn't been able to contact Juan Rivero, the man who'd called her yesterday to tell her the shipment of dolls might be delayed.

Taking out her cell, Cat punched in Matt's number again. Listening to the rings, she paced back to the window and scanned the street for her FedEx man. There was still a chance…. But the only truck she spotted was delivering soft drinks to the bar across the street.

Cat closed her eyes and swore under her breath. The *same* bar where she was supposed to be meeting her father right now! Whirling, she dashed back to the counter and grabbed her tote. She was about to close her cell, when she heard the faint voice in her ear.

"Cat?"

She raced to the second step of the spiral staircase where reception for her cell was usually clearest.

"Matt, where are you? Tell me you've shipped the dolls."

The only reply she received was a burst of static.

"Matt? Are you there?"

"Bad…"

"What?" Please not bad news, Cat prayed.

"Connection…terrible."

He was right about that. His voice was fading in and out. Cat bit back on her impulse to ask him why he hadn't called all day. Only one thing mattered now. "Tell me you shipped the dolls."

"…tomorrow…Thursday…"

There was another burst of static. Which was it? Did he mean that they wouldn't ship until tomorrow? Or that they would arrive tomorrow? Thursday was two days from now. Cat swallowed her disappointment. Starting tomorrow afternoon, there could be delays because of that Nor'easter moving up the coast.

"…want to be there…to open them. Need to…"

"Did you ship all of them?"

There was another burst of static and then the connection was broken. Cat punched in Matt's number again, but this time she was transferred to his voice mail.

"Call me back with the tracking number," she said.

She'd feel better once she had something more concrete to go on.

In the meantime, her father was waiting, and tardiness had always been an issue with him. She set the security alarm, locked the door behind her, dashed toward the curb and quickly threaded her way through traffic to Patty's Pub. Through the window, she spotted her father already seated at one of the tables.

For the first time all day, she had time to wonder just what urgent matter had brought her father all the way down to this end of town.

THE PHONE RANG, and the hand that reached for the receiver trembled slightly. *Breathe. Don't panic.* "Hello."

"Where are the dolls?" The voice on the other end of the line was soft and chilling.

A shudder was ruthlessly suppressed. "They've been delayed. They should arrive tomorrow—Thursday at the latest."

The long silence caused a fresh flutter of panic.

"You'll be in the shop when the shipment arrives?"

"Yes. Of course."

"I'll expect the doll I ordered no later than Thursday. Otherwise…"

The line went dead.

3

JAMES MCGUIRE ROSE as his daughter threaded her way through the packed restaurant. The crowd was a lively one, and the noise level nearly succeeded in muting the tinny-sounding Christmas carols that poured through the speakers. He'd arrived half an hour early and tipped the hostess to find him a table.

This wasn't the type of place he would have chosen, but he'd learned years ago to pick his battles with his daughter. And a pretty little waitress named Colleen had informed him that the Mulligan's stew here had been written up in the *Zagat's* guide.

A rush of love moved through him when Cat wrapped her arms around him in a warm hug. When he drew back, he held on to her for a moment and studied her face. Just as he'd suspected, there were circles under her eyes. Even as a child, she'd always given every project she worked on her all. It was high time she had something in her life besides that toy store. "It's been too long, little girl. You have to get away from that store sometimes. I miss you."

"You could always come down to this end of town and visit me in the Cheshire Cat," she said.

McGuire winced a little. "Touché. One guilt trip deserves another. Sit down. I ordered you a glass of your favorite wine. Pouilly-Fuissé, right?"

"Right."

"Colleen here recommended the Mulligan's stew, so I took the liberty of ordering that, too. I'll bet you didn't take time for lunch today."

Cat narrowed her eyes on her father. "You want something. Why don't you just come out with it?"

"Now, Cat, can't you believe your dad just wanted to see you?"

Her eyes narrowed even more. "Maybe when pigs fly."

He threw back his head and laughed. "Never could put one over on you, could I?"

"Maybe when I was six."

He raised his glass. "At least take a sip of that wine. It costs the earth."

Cat's brows shot up as she reached for her wine. "And that single malt Scotch you're drinking doesn't?"

He merely smiled as he touched his glass to hers. "To a very happy holiday season."

Cat sipped her wine. "You've got that gleam in your eyes. You're up to something. If you came all the way down here to make sure I'm going to Gianna's big charity ball on Thursday, I'll be there. I also bought tickets for Adelaide, Josie and Matt. He should be back from Mexico by then."

"Mexico?" He had to tread carefully. He wasn't supposed to know much about her store.

She smiled as she took another sip of wine. "He's in this little village. I've told you about Paxco, haven't I?"

"Remind me," he said. She actually started to glow when she talked about her business. It was something she rarely spoke of when the family gathered because of Gianna's preference that she get out of retail. His wife had even gone so far as to offer her a job at Merceri Bank.

"Matt had to fly down there yesterday because this one shipment of dolls has been delayed. If it doesn't get here, there are going to be twenty-four little girls who won't get what they want from Santa."

No wonder she was worried, McGuire thought. Her mother had died on Christmas Eve, and ever since then, Cat had put a lot of effort into making sure that everything was perfect at Christmastime. He'd done the same for her. But he couldn't read any sign that she suspected something other than doll-making was going on in Paxco. He placed a hand over hers. "Don't worry, little girl. They'll get here."

She lifted her chin. "I know that, and that's exactly what I told my worried customers. I'm hoping they shipped today and they'll arrive tomorrow or Thursday. Friday at the latest."

She sipped more wine. "Still, I'll feel better when Matt calls back and gives me a tracking number. The connection I had with him was very bad."

McGuire studied his daughter. He didn't like it one bit that one of the shipments from Paxco was delayed. If something happened to prevent the drugs from arriving, or even worse, if someone at the other end had gotten greedy, it might very well increase the danger to Cat.

Thank heavens, Dino Angelis would be at her side beginning tomorrow morning.

"About Gianna's ball…"

Cat met his eyes. "I told you I'll be there."

"But you don't have a date."

"And just how do you know that?"

Hearing the thread of annoyance in her tone, he took a drink of his Scotch. "A smart army man never reveals his sources."

Cat regarded him steadily as she took another taste of wine.

"All I want is a favor. I'd look upon it as your Christmas

gift to me. And you can check Gianna off your list at the same time. I'm offering you a two-for-the-price-of-one deal."

She still said nothing. McGuire wondered not for the first time why she couldn't have taken more after Nancy than him.

"C'mon, Cat. Your daddy shouldn't have to beg."

Cat threw up both of her hands. "Okay. I'm not agreeing to anything yet. Just what is it that you want me to do?"

"Just get engaged for Christmas."

CAT STARED at her father. She sincerely hoped that her mouth hadn't dropped open because she knew that was just the reaction he was hoping for. Her mom and dad had always played chess together, and after her mother had died, she'd asked her father to teach her the game. But even after she'd joined the chess team at school, she'd never been able to beat him. He was a master strategist. Just what was he up to? "You're joking."

"I couldn't be more serious."

She glanced at his drink. "How many of those did you have while you were waiting for me?"

He shook his head sadly. "Is that anything for a respectful daughter to ask her father?"

She sipped her wine and leaned back in her chair. "Are you going to tell me what you're up to?"

"Thought you'd never ask. Gianna has gotten herself into a little scrape." He told her the same story he'd told Dino Angelis and watched her eyes widen. Unlike the navy captain, she'd had the experience of meeting Lucia Merceri.

"So the Queen of Hearts is going to arrive tomorrow and catch her daughter in a lie?"

"Unless I solve the problem."

"How?"

"It's simple. I've hired you a fiancé for Christmas."

"You've what?"

Several people in the immediate area sent glances her way, so Cat clamped down on her emotions and hissed, "You've hired me a fiancé? And where, pray tell, did you get him—some kind of escort service?"

Colleen appeared at their table and set down two bowls of Mulligan's stew. "Is there anything else I can get you?"

Cat managed a tight smile. "No." But she would have liked to order a bucket of cold ice water to pour over her father's head.

As if sensing the tension at the table, Colleen's bright smile wavered. "Enjoy your meal." Then she scurried away.

"You've scared that poor little waitress."

Keeping her voice pitched low, Cat leaned forward. "Don't you put that on me. If you don't tell me what you're up to, you may end up wearing what's left of my very expensive wine."

He spread his hands, palms outward. "I'm just trying to make everyone happy for Christmas."

He wasn't lying about that. If anyone had ever captured the essence of the spirit of Saint Nick, Colonel James T. McGuire had. From the time she was little, even before her mother's death, he'd always tried to figure out what she wanted most and then he'd put all his efforts into getting it for her. Within reason, of course. But since he'd married Gianna, he'd shifted his focus to his wife.

"I thought Gianna already had her Christmas wish. Lucy is due to deliver little Merry any day now."

"She's trying to hold off until after the charity ball."

That didn't surprise Cat. If Lucy managed to pull it off, her stepmother would have all her family around her at the ball and still have her first granddaughter by Christmas.

Her father laid his hand over hers. "Lucia Merceri will only be in town until New Year's Day. And as soon as little Merry arrives, her attention will be diverted."

She managed not to grit her teeth. "And how is Lucia Merceri going to react when she discovers the whole thing was a trick?" Cat jabbed a finger in his direction. "I wouldn't want to be in your shoes when she figures out we lied to her." She frowned. "Matter of fact, I wouldn't want to be in *my* shoes."

"Not to worry." Her father picked up a fork and dug into his stew. "We've got that all worked out. Gianna will just weave her mother another story. A month from now, you're going to have a falling-out with Navy Captain Dino Angelis."

Cat had scooped up a bite of her stew, but the fork slipped from her fingers and clattered back into the bowl. "A month? You can't expect me to carry on this masquerade for a month. I won't."

Her father wiggled his fork at her. "Relax. You'll get through the month just the way you got through the last month—the secret dating and engagement part."

Cat's hands fisted on the table. "The secret dating and engagement part?"

Her father took a manila envelope out of his pocket and pushed it toward her. "The back story is all in there—exactly what Gianna told her mother—from the first time you met to your romantic trysts at the Waldorf right up to when he popped the question on the skating rink at Rocke-feller Center."

Cat's eyes narrowed. Her father knew her weaknesses. She loved to skate, but she barely had time for it anymore. "He doesn't skate."

Her father beamed a triumphant smile at her. "He was captain of his hockey team in high school."

She wanted to bang her head on the table. He was outmaneuvering her at every turn. "And just where did you dig up this navy captain who skates?"

"Captain Angelis works for your godfather, Admiral Maxwell. I've already filled the captain in on his back story."

"And he agreed to go along with this charade?"

"Your godfather persuaded him."

Bribed him, Cat thought. Though she'd experienced first-hand just how persuasive Uncle Bobby could be. He was almost as gifted as her father was at making people dance to his tune. She could feel herself weakening.

"Captain Angelis has a two-week leave which he intends to spend with you meeting your family. But who knows? Something might come up, and Bobby could call him back early. The important thing is that we get through the Christmas season and send Lucia Merceri happily back to Rome."

Cat liked Gianna, and she could fully understand the desire to placate Lucia. The woman was scary. She reached for her wine, took another sip, and gave up. "Okay. I'll do it."

"Atta girl. I knew you'd come through for your old dad." Her father dug into his stew. "Eat up. You're wasting away."

Cat ate a carrot, then said, "When do I get to meet Navy Captain Dino Angelis?"

"Tomorrow morning. He's scheduled to arrive at The Cheshire Cat no later than eleven hundred hours."

Cat shifted her attention from her stew to her father. "The store is going to be packed with customers. Shouldn't we meet privately first?"

"When?"

Cat sighed. He was right of course.

"Besides," he continued, "you'll have plenty of time to talk. I've arranged for him to stay in the apartment next to yours."

"He's staying in my building? What about the Waldorf? Isn't that where you said we had our little romantic trysts?"

Her father's brows shot up. "That was when you were keeping your relationship a secret. There's no need for that anymore. Now your job is to convince everyone that your relationship is real. He'll be able to walk you home at night. To all outward appearances, he'll be staying with you." He cleared his throat. "Which is what I assume would be happening if he were your real fiancé."

He reached over and patted her hand. "Besides, with your busy schedule, you wouldn't have any time to go uptown anyway. You couldn't even meet me for drinks at the Algonquin."

Cat mulled it over in her mind.

"The two of you are going to have to spend time together. Lucia Merceri is a sharp woman. She'll be grilling you separately on how you met, when you first fell in love."

Cat stifled an inward sigh.

"Spending time together will give you time to get your stories straight. Make sure you're on the same page. And think of the upside."

Cat's tone was dry. "If there's an upside to this, don't keep me in the dark."

Her father grinned at her. "You'll have an extra person to help out in your store just when you need it the most."

For the second time in as many minutes, Cat badly wanted to bang her head on the table. But she didn't. Her father was right, of course. She could use some help in the store. But he wasn't going to have it all his way. "This navy captain can move in for eleven days. That will get us to New Year's Day. Then Uncle Bobby is calling him back to the Pentagon."

"Deal."

James McGuire held out his hand, and Cat shook it.

4

FROM HIS POSITION in the short alleyway that ran along the side of the Cheshire Cat, Dino had a clear view of the window in Patty's Pub that framed Cat McGuire and her father. When he saw father and daughter shake hands, he knew that his fate had been sealed. He dug his hands deeper into the pockets of his bomber jacket. The sky was clear and the temperature was hovering at the freezing mark. But watching Colonel McGuire persuade his daughter into accepting a fake fiancé had proved highly entertaining.

Dino had arrived while Cat still had customers in her shop—so he could familiarize himself with the area, he'd told himself. Along with his detailed cover story, McGuire had provided a hand-drawn map, so Dino knew that the alleyway emptied into a courtyard that backed into Cat's apartment building and that Cat used it to get to and from work. Not the safest route, he mused.

McGuire's conversation with Cat had not gone smoothly. His daughter had a temper. He'd read it in her body language and in her gestures. There was a lot of raw, pent-up passion in Ms. Cat McGuire, and he knew that was part of the reason he was drawn to her.

Keeping Cat safe was a trickier assignment than any he'd ever taken on under Maxwell's command. It would have been a far easier task if he were just going to be her bodyguard. But the other role McGuire had required—acting the part of Cat's head-over-heels-in-love fiancé and lover—was going to challenge his ability to remain coolly objective.

Even through a plate glass window and at a distance of some fifty yards, he felt the steady beat of desire in his blood. For the first time in his life he wondered if he would be able to control it. He wanted her with an intensity that he couldn't fathom. Nothing, no one had ever pushed him to the edge like this.

Oh, he might tell himself that he had a job to do, and mixing business with pleasure would distract him and possibly jeopardize Cat's life. But no amount of lecturing could erase the vision that he'd had earlier of the two of them making love. Was it a premonition of the future or simply a fantasy? He'd always believed that the Fates offered choices, but he was beginning to wonder if he was going to be able to make the right one where Cat McGuire was concerned.

The other problem—as if his intense attraction to Cat wasn't enough—was he had a strong feeling that James McGuire hadn't told him everything. And going into an operation without all the intelligence that was available was dangerous.

That was why he'd contacted his navy buddy Jase Campbell right after he'd spoken with his mother. Dino not only needed some backup, he also needed Jase's high-tech expertise.

The question was what was McGuire hiding? The most obvious answer was that Cat McGuire was up to her neck in a highly profitable smuggling operation. James McGuire might not believe she was involved—but his opinion was biased.

Dino had to make sure that his wasn't. Cat McGuire might not be aware of the fact that the profits were being funneled to terrorists, but she was the obvious prime suspect to be on the receiving end of the smuggled drugs.

Otherwise, how could it all be happening under her nose? Unless she was stupid, and Dino didn't think she was. Neither did the feds.

At least McGuire hadn't lied about that. There was at least one other person watching Cat and her father tonight. Dino had spotted the man huddled in the doorway of the shop next to the Cheshire Cat when he'd strolled down the street and into the alley. The guy had been too well dressed to be homeless, and he hadn't even bothered with some kind of disguise. Of course, the feds had never been known for their creativity. He himself had brought along a camera, a guide book, plus a shopping bag stuffed with gifts.

When a tall figure moved in the shadows at the mouth of the alley, Dino closed a hand around the gun in his pocket and slipped behind one of the Dumpsters that flanked the alleyway door to Cat's toy store. It wasn't the fed he'd spotted earlier. That guy had been shorter, stockier. He listened, not breathing, for any sound at all. An engine grumbled as a truck rolled past on the street.

The voice when it came was low-pitched and uncomfortably close. "I come in peace. Don't shoot me."

Dino drew his hand out of his pocket. Jase Campbell could move more quietly than anyone he knew. "That was a risky move. I might have shot you."

"Nah." There was a wealth of humor in Jase's hushed voice. "I would have taken you down before you ever drew your weapon. Remember that time in Afghanistan?"

"Yeah." Dino never forgot the times he'd almost bought it. "You saved my life."

"It was a mutual saving that time. Your hunches and my moves. They're a pretty unbeatable combination."

"I hope so." Dino moved out from behind the Dumpster to

where he could once more see Cat and her father. They were eating, and the tension he'd seen earlier had eased. "I need more than your pretty moves this time around. I need your high-tech expertise. Any possibilities on who's leaking information on an ongoing CIA investigation to Colonel James McGuire?"

Jake's chuckle was low-pitched as he materialized out of the darkness. "No proof. But I have a prime suspect. You know, there's a nice little pub across the street. We could have a beer while I report."

"My job and her father are sitting in the window right beneath the Guinness sign."

Jase turned to look and gave a soft whistle. "She's certainly a looker. I wouldn't mind playacting the part of her fiancé."

"You want to bodyguard someone who can't know you're bodyguarding her?" And touch her and kiss her in public and still retain a clear head?

Jase sighed. "There's always a catch to these dream jobs."

"That's where you come in. I need a second set of eyes." He'd filled Jase in earlier on everything he knew about the case—which was limited to what McGuire had told him. Jase was going to provide backup twenty-four-seven. "There's a fed in the doorway next to her shop."

"Not anymore. He took off when I asked him for a match."

Dino grinned. "He'll be back."

"Hopefully, he'll find a more, shall we say, subtle hiding place."

"Where's your man stationed?"

"He's already in her apartment building. I figured you and I could see she got inside safely. You think the danger is imminent?"

"I don't think anything yet. I'm not even willing to believe she's as innocent as her father says she is. I'm just playing it safe. Drugs, money and terrorists. There could be some pretty ruthless people involved in this."

Cat and her father had risen from their table and were pulling on coats as they threaded their way to the door of the pub.

"So who's your prime suspect at the CIA?"

"You're going to love this. Jack Phillips, Cat's uncle and McGuire's brother-in-law by his first wife, is a career man at the CIA. He's never risen up through the ranks because he has a reputation of being a bit of a rogue. He and McGuire aren't on the best of terms, but I figure Phillips might be feeding information to McGuire to ensure his niece's safety."

When Cat and McGuire appeared at the mouth of the alleyway, Dino and Jase faded back behind the Dumpster.

"You know, little girl, you should never take this shortcut alone at night," McGuire said as they passed.

"Daddy, this is a safe neighborhood. Everyone uses this alleyway."

As the voices dwindled, Jase said, "You're going to have your work cut out for you."

In more ways than one, Dino thought. "Let's go have that beer."

CAT LET HERSELF INTO her apartment and flipped the switch that turned on the Tiffany-style lamp in her living room. The switch also turned on twinkling lights on the small Christmas tree on the narrow table behind her sofa.

Dropping her tote on the coffee table, she avoided the sofa. If she sat down, she might be tempted to close her eyes—and then it would be all over for tonight. Exhaustion had slammed into her the instant her father had seen her inside the building and turned to walk back across the courtyard.

She reached the window in time to see him stride out of

the alleyway into the street. A rush of love overtook her. Would there come a day when he couldn't talk her into whatever he wanted her to do?

A fake engagement was the last thing she needed on her plate right now. She had a delayed shipment of dolls, and an assistant buyer who couldn't seem to find a way of contacting her. And twenty-four children might be disappointed for Christmas.

Just thinking about that had a band of pain tightening around her heart. Christmas should be a time of joy, especially for children.

Cat straightened her shoulders. Giving in to worries and anxiety attacks had never been her way. It had never been her mother's way either. She focused her attention back on the courtyard. Magnolia, lilac, and dogwood trees that would bloom beautifully in the spring were now strung with tiny white lights that twinkled like stars.

Christmas was a time for miracles. She'd always believed in that. Those dolls were going to arrive. Tomorrow.

She shifted her focus back to the tall figure of her father still standing in front of the alleyway. She could see the Guinness sign blinking over one of the windows at Patty's Pub. It was going to be tricky catching a taxi at nearly eleven in this section of town. She should have reminded him to call for one when they were having an Irish coffee.

Then a limo pulled up and Orlando, the Merceri family's chauffeur, stepped out. Cat kept forgetting how much her father's life had changed since he'd married Gianna Merceri. But she was so happy for him. She was well aware of how much he'd loved her mother and of how close they'd been. But he loved Gianna, too.

Her lips curved in a smile. Anyone who could find that kind

of love even once was lucky, so she figured James McGuire was doubly so.

Hopefully, one day she'd share in that luck. But right now she had problems to solve: try Matt one more time, check the weather report on the storm that was forecast to slam into Manhattan, and read over the scenario she was supposed to enact starting tomorrow with her never-before-seen fiancé.

For just a second, she rested her head against the window-pane. Well, she'd make it through this. Eleven days wasn't that long. And her father was right—she could use an extra pair of hands in the store.

She might even be able to talk her make-believe fiancé into donning a Santa Claus suit. Cheered by the idea, she was about to turn away from the window and reheat some morning coffee when her eye was drawn to the two men sitting in Patty's Pub beneath the blinking Guinness sign.

Suddenly her senses went on full alert. No. *Full alert* was way too tame a description for the entire-body meltdown she was experiencing. That man—not the one with longish blond hair in a thick black sweater—but the one with hair the color of coal in the black bomber jacket. She'd seen him before.

Racing into her bedroom, she snatched her binoculars off the top shelf of her closet and dashed back to the window. Yes. Yes, it was *him.* She'd only had that brief glimpse of him, but she remembered that slash of cheekbone and that impression she'd had of warriorlike strength. He was definitely the same man she'd seen standing at the edge of the small crowd of cus-tomers she'd let into her shop that morning. The same man who'd liquefied her knees and sent her thoughts flying away.

Just looking at him through the binoculars had her heart skipping a beat and her throat going dry. And then the same fantasy that had been teasing at the edges of her mind all day suddenly flooded it. The two of them naked, their bodies locked together and rolling across the floor. A baffling need arose in her to get closer to him—to just go over to Patty's Pub and…what? Jump him?

No. For a moment, she lowered the binoculars and closed her eyes. Then she made herself take deep breaths. She had to get a grip. This kind of reaction wasn't like her at all. She was a rational, sane woman. So she was going to figure out a way to handle it.

Raising the glasses, she looked through them again. First, she was going to take a more objective look. He was leaning against the back of the booth, seemingly relaxed, yet she sensed a kind of leashed intensity in him.

The man with the lighter coloring was more animated. As Cat watched, he threw back his head and laughed. Friends, she thought. And both strangers to the neighborhood.

Her gaze returned to Mr. Tall, Dark, and Intense as he lifted a glass of Guinness and took a long swallow. She focused in on his hands—the wide palms, the long fingers—and her thoughts drifted to what they might feel like on her skin. Every nerve in her body began to throb, her heart skipped another beat, and the same irrational need arose in her to go to him. She'd never had this strong an attraction to a man before.

"Who are you?" she murmured.

As if he'd heard her speak, he turned and looked straight at her. Cat felt the impact of his gaze right down to her toes. And she froze. He knew she was looking at him through binoculars, for heaven's sake. She thought of that moment in Hitchcock's *Rear Window* when Raymond Burr had caught Jimmy Stewart doing the same thing.

A hot wave of embarrassment shot through her, freeing her

from her momentary paralysis. She jumped away from the window and jerked the shade shut. Then she dropped the binoculars on the sofa, and because her knees still felt a little weak, she sat down.

What in the world was happening to her? For the last few minutes she'd been ogling a man as if she were some hormone-driven teenager. More than that, she couldn't seem to rid her mind of the fantasy of having sex with him. Wild, wonderful sex. With a little groan of disgust, she rested her head against the back of the sofa. She had to be working too hard.

When she felt her eyes drifting shut, Cat immediately straightened up. She still had things to do. Snagging the remote, she turned the TV on to a local news station and frowned all the way through the weather report. Not only was the smiling blonde tracking a Nor'easter heading up the coast, but she was also pointing to another storm gathering force over Chicago and pushing through Michigan. Both were due to hit Manhattan sometime tomorrow morning. The banner headline beneath the weather map read The Perfect Storm in red block letters.

But the dolls could already be on their way. Matt had said *tomorrow*. He could have meant the delivery date and not the shipping date. Maybe he'd meant Thursday at the latest. *Please*.

The weather banner was replaced by *Attorney General Jessica Atwell testifying in front of Congress about New York State's new Keep Our Kids Off Drugs program.* For a moment, Cat studied the older woman. She was on television all the time lately due to the success of her antidrug campaign. Adelaide had volunteered in Jessica Atwell's campaign headquarters until the governor had tapped her for the A.G. job. Now with all the publicity Atwell was garnering, there was speculation that she was going to make a run for the Senate. Cat sincerely hoped that Adelaide wouldn't decide to go back and work for her old boss.

Yawning, she turned off the TV. That was a problem for another day. She had plenty on her plate right now. Cat pulled the manila envelope her father had given her out of her tote. After the weather report, maybe the background information on her temporary fiancé would look good by comparison.

On the top of the sheaf of papers she pulled out was a photo of Captain Dino Angelis.

Once again, Cat's heart skipped a beat and her throat went dry. It was *him*—the same man who'd stood outside her shop that morning, the one who was right now having a beer in Patty's Pub. The very same man who'd been toying around at the edges of her mind all day.

And she'd been fantasizing about toying with him. A lot. And tomorrow, he was going to walk into her store and play the part of her fiancé?

No. Cat shook her head firmly. No way. No how. Her life was complicated enough already.

Rising, she rounded the coffee table and paced to the door. She had half a mind to grab her jacket and go over to Patty's Pub and confront him. What had he been doing in the neighborhood this morning and again tonight?

Checking her out?

Whirling, she grabbed the binoculars, strode back to the window, and threw up the shade. The table beneath the Guinness sign was empty. Cat wasn't quite sure whether it was relief or disappointment she was feeling.

Turning, she flung herself down on the couch, then reined in her temper and made herself take several deep, calming breaths. All she had to do was think it through. For starters, she'd given her father her word that she'd play her part in the fake engagement. And she'd always been a woman of her word.

The fact that she was incredibly attracted to the man she was playacting with was just a little bump in the road. In business, she handled those on a daily basis.

And if Navy Captain Dino Angelis *had* been checking her out on the off chance that his role as her fake fiancé was going to have some side benefits? Cat allowed herself one grim smile. Well, she'd just lay out the ground rules for him the moment they met.

In the meantime, Cat pulled the rest of the papers out of the envelope. She'd learn as much as she could about Captain Angelis.

Problem solved.

DINO WAS LEAVING a tip for the maid when his cell phone rang.

"Did I wake you?" Colonel McGuire asked.

"I'm about to leave the hotel."

"You're not due to arrive at the store until 11:00—two hours from now."

Dino didn't tell McGuire that ever since he'd awakened, he'd been feeling a sense of urgency about getting to the Cheshire Cat. Instead, he said, "I have an errand to run."

"An errand?"

"It occurred to me when I was studying my assigned part last night that a crucial prop is missing from the little play you've cast me in." And he'd taken care of it shortly after he left McGuire's office the day before. It was the one detail that the colonel had overlooked.

The brief silence on the other end of the line had Dino biting back a smile.

"A prop?" McGuire asked.

"If we want everyone to believe that Cat and I are engaged, she should have a ring. I didn't give her one when I proposed at Rockefeller Center because we decided to keep the engagement a secret for a time."

Two more beats of silence, and then McGuire cleared his throat. "Good thinking. Of course, she needs a ring. It's the first thing my mother-in-law will notice. Bobby may be right about you."

Let's hope so, Dino thought. Because in spite of everything that McGuire had outlined, the whole charade could go up in smoke, depending on how the scene played out when he walked into the Cheshire Cat.

She'd seen him twice now, so he wasn't quite sure how he was going to play it. Not that he was overly worried. Improvising on the spot had saved his neck many times.

Shouldering his suit bag and his duffel, Dino stepped out into the hall and strode toward the elevators. "Is there something special you called about?"

"Yes. Yes, there is. When I met with Cat last night for drinks, she was worried about a shipment of dolls from that town in Mexico. Paxco. It's been delayed. Could be something's gone wrong on the other end. And if the drugs are in that shipment, she could be in more imminent danger than I thought."

"Then the sooner I get over there, the better."

"Yes. Ri—"

Dino disconnected the call, speed-dialed Jase, and filled him in on the delayed shipment.

"You want me to send someone down to Paxco?" Jase asked.

"No—we don't want to tip off anyone down there. It might panic whoever is on this end. Where is Cat right now?"

"In the Cheshire Cat. She went in at 8:00 a.m. She let in a

woman who fits the description of her assistant manager ten minutes ago."

Dino glanced at his watch. "I'm due there at 11:00, but I'm going to arrive early."

"Got one of your feelings?"

"Yeah." And it was growing stronger with each passing moment.

WHEN THE BELL over the door of her shop jingled, Cat whirled around, nearly dropping the stuffed dragon she'd pulled down from the shelf.

It wasn't him. And it wasn't disappointment she was feeling.

"Easy does it," Adelaide murmured, taking the dragon from Cat to ring up the sale. "The FedEx man never gets here until almost noon."

Earlier, Cat had filled Adelaide in on Matt's garbled message and her hope that the dolls might arrive that day.

"In this weather, all deliveries will be slowed down, so I'd relax if I were you."

Relax? That was a laugh. It wasn't the possible arrival of the delayed dolls that had her heart racing every time someone stepped into the store. Navy Captain Dino Angelis wasn't due until eleven o'clock, an hour and a half from now, and her nerves were already stretched to the breaking point.

In spite of her resolve, she'd dreamed of him, awakened thinking of him. Even after a cold shower and two cups of coffee, she hadn't been able to completely rid her mind of him. Or the fantasies that had filled her dreams during the night. Bottom line, she'd never wanted a man the way she wanted Dino Angelis. How could he affect her this way when they hadn't even met? Hadn't touched? What would it be like when he did lay a hand on her? A shiver of anticipation moved through her. He'd have to touch her, and she'd have to touch him back if they were going to carry off this masquerade. Just the thought had her blood heating, her heart pounding.

Get a grip. Cat glanced around the store which had been teeming with customers ever since she'd opened the doors. Josie was standing behind a table in the far corner offering gift wrap services, and Adelaide was ringing up purchases, leaving Cat free to help customers find that special last-minute gift.

Outside, a good six inches of snow had accumulated on the sidewalks, and as if in celebration, a string rendition of "White Christmas" was flowing out of the speakers. Through it, she caught snatches of conversations. The hot topic seemed to be the storm.

"Looks like everybody had the same idea…"

"…finish my list and get home."

"…catching the 11:00 train out of the city. Otherwise I'll be stuck here."

"The way the weatherman was talking…"

"…expecting to shut down the airports."

When her cell phone rang, Cat dug it out of her pocket and hurried to the spiral staircase to take the call.

"Cat?"

Relief streamed through her at the sound of Matt's voice. "Where are you?"

"I've been stuck in Chicago since 2:00 a.m. The damn storm closed down the airport, but I'm due to fly out in a few minutes. That should get me in before the brunt of the Nor'easter hits Manhattan. According to the weather channels, it's going to be bad."

Cat glanced out the windows. "It's already snowing heavily here. What about the dolls?"

"They aren't there yet?"

"No."

"They will be. I've been tracking the package on my Palm Pilot and they arrived safely at JFK this morning."

Relief was so strong that Cat sat down on one of the steps. "You're sure?"

"Grab a pencil and I'll give you the tracking number."

She dug into her pocket for her notebook. "Go ahead."

When she'd jotted it down, Matt continued, "I wanted to be there when they arrived. They've really brought your mother's design to life, and the workmanship is exquisite. But do me a favor and don't open the box until I get there. There's something I have to explain. Will you promise to wait?"

Cat frowned. "I—"

"Gotta go. They're starting to board my plane. Barring any more delays, I should be at the store shortly before noon."

Matt disconnected and Cat frowned at the phone. She didn't think she could wait for Matt. Once those dolls arrived, she was going to open the package and start calling customers.

The sudden jingle of the bell over the door had her jumping to her feet.

It wasn't *him*.

Instead, it was Mrs. Lassiter. As the grim-faced woman walked toward her, Cat sent her a warm smile. It wasn't returned.

"Are they here?"

"Not in the store, but they touched down at JFK early this morning and I have the tracking number. Our FedEx man usually doesn't get here until around noon." She glanced out the window. "Weather permitting."

Mrs. Lassiter's frown faded, and Cat could almost see relief pouring through her.

"Could I have the tracking number?"

"Absolutely." Pulling her notebook out, Cat read the number off.

She'd just seen Mrs. Lassiter out the door when she remembered she'd promised to call the Santa Claus man. Digging her notebook out, she located the card he'd given her, then hurried behind the counter to dial it.

The call was answered on the second ring.

"Yes?"

Due to the noise in the store, Cat wasn't sure she recognized the voice. "This is Cat McGuire from the Cheshire Cat, and I'm calling a Mr. George Miller."

"Have the dolls arrived?" The tone was clipped and brusque.

"Not yet. But they've landed at JFK, and I have a tracking number for you." Cat read it off.

The phone went dead without a thank-you. Frowning down at it, Cat decided to revise her opinion of Mr. Miller. He was a bit rude to remind her of Santa Claus. But he definitely did remind her of someone.

"Problem?" Adelaide asked.

"I just passed the tracking number for the dolls on to Mr. Miller—that man who cut to the front of your line yesterday, and he's still rude. You're sure you never saw him in the store before?"

Adelaide laughed. "Someone like that—I think I'd remember."

"Well, the computer says he paid for a doll." Cat shrugged. "Matt probably took the order. I'm going to go up to my office for a few minutes. Maybe some of our other customers would like to know that the dolls are at least in the city."

She was on the first step of the stairs when the bell over the door jangled again. Even before she turned around, she could feel him. Turning, she watched Navy Captain Dino Angelis walk into her store.

Beneath the leather bomber jacket, she caught a glimpse of a uniform. A suit bag and a duffel were slung over one shoulder and he carried two grocery bags in his arms.

Here he is. That was the one errant thought that tumbled into her mind before it went blank. A sound filled her head— a rush of white noise that blocked out conversations and the current Christmas carol pouring out of the speaker.

He'd already negotiated half the distance to her, and Cat badly wanted to run. But not away. She felt a pressure in her chest and a strong tug in her belly. If she could have moved, she was very much afraid that she would have run into Dino Angelis' arms.

When he reached her, he dropped everything he was carrying. Now that he was close enough to touch, she fisted her hands at her sides so that she wouldn't lift them to his face. But she wanted to. She'd always thought of herself as a sensible, clearheaded woman. What she was feeling was neither of those things.

This close, the lean face seemed even stronger, and she noted the faint scar beneath his left cheekbone. A warrior's scar.

But it was his eyes that fascinated her. They were the darkest shade of gray she'd ever seen. She thought of black smoke from a fire—the kind that disoriented you, tricking you to move toward the flames instead of away. And there was that intensity in the way he looked at her. She'd been aware of it when he'd stood in front of her shop and again when he'd glanced up from the window of Patty's Pub. It was as if he could read what she was thinking. How could that be?

"I missed you."

Cat wasn't sure whether he'd said the words aloud or she'd

read his lips. Or perhaps she'd spoken them. But how could she miss a man she'd never met?

His hands closed over her upper arms, and then he touched his mouth to hers. It was just the briefest meeting of lips, but his scent surrounded her. He smelled faintly of the sea. And then she caught the first hint of his taste—dark, delicious—and an aching hunger filled her.

Later, much later, she'd wonder what she'd been thinking. She was standing in the middle of her shop, surrounded by customers. But she couldn't think, not when every pulse point on her body had begun to throb, not when greed was building so quickly. So she wrapped her arms around him and pressed her mouth fully to his.

The second taste of him was even better than the first—raw and hot and wonderful. She heard his moan, felt his hands tighten on her arms, and she experienced a whirl of pleasure so sharp that she had to cling to him for support. Suddenly, inexplicably, there was nothing but him. She wanted nothing but him.

IT WAS THE JINGLE of the bell over the door that finally brought Dino to his senses. Even then, he had to call upon all of his willpower to gently unwrap Cat's arms and set her away from him. Baffled, he stared down at her and something akin to fear shot up his spine.

Kissing her had been one of several scenarios he'd considered, thinking that it might be the best way to get over that first awkward moment and at the same time to convince the people she worked with that their "secret" engagement was real. But once he walked into the store and saw her, the kiss had become a certainty. As he'd moved toward her, he'd felt as if his will had been snatched away from him. He'd simply had to taste her.

In the twenty-four hours since he'd first seen Cat McGuire, he'd wondered what it might be like. But nothing had prepared him for the explosion of passion he'd tasted in that avid mouth and felt in that strong, lean body. Nor had he anticipated the strength of his own response—the sharp rush of desire and the burning ache that had driven him to the edge of his control.

He'd never wanted any woman the way he wanted Cat McGuire. He let his gaze drift over the clouded gold-green eyes, the tumbled hair, the lips still swollen and wet from their kiss. Hell. He wanted her right now. No woman had ever exerted this kind of power over him.

But he had a choice. Didn't he?

The bell jingled again over the door of the shop, and he saw awareness creep into her eyes. He sensed in the same instant that the only sound in the store was the bluesy sax playing "I'll Be Home for Christmas."

Gathering his thoughts, Dino wrapped an arm around Cat's shoulders and drew her close to his side as he turned to face a sea of curious faces. He flashed them a smile.

"I wish I could apologize, but I'm Cat's fiancé, and I've missed her."

5

_____

"I THINK THAT WENT WELL." Taking out the key McGuire had given him, Dino unlocked the door of the apartment next to Cat's and led the way inside.

Cat followed him into the room, closed the door and leaned back against it. The space was an exact copy of hers with a small kitchen to the left, bedroom and bath to the right, and a small living room in the center.

He crossed to the sofa in a stride and a half. Setting his duffel, suit bag, and grocery bags on the floor, he slipped out of his bomber jacket and then stepped to the window that overlooked the courtyard. Outside, the heavily falling snow totally obscured the view. But the view Cat was looking at was inside the apartment. Even from the back, the man was beautifully built. The uniform fit like a glove over broad shoulders, narrow waist and hips. When she found herself staring at his butt, she shook her head to clear it. They had important business to settle.

"You think it went _well?_" She purposely hadn't talked to him on the walk across the courtyard or up the three flights of stairs to the apartment. And her silence wasn't due to the howling wind or the blowing snow. She'd learned a long time ago to give her temper time to cool before speaking. But in all fairness, it wasn't Dino Angelis she was angry at. It was herself.

For those few moments when he'd kissed her, she'd lost track of everything but him.

He glanced over his shoulder at her. "I believe Adelaide and Josie have bought fully into our secret engagement story."

"That's why you kissed me?"

"It seemed a quick and effective way to convince them."

How could he stand there talking about it so coolly when she'd been entirely swept away by that kiss? She'd lost track of where she was—who she was. While his mouth had been pressed to hers, devouring hers, all she'd known was a need that threatened to consume her.

Every rational thought had drained out of her mind—and what had poured in was *him*. His taste, his touch, the feel of that rock-hard body pressed against hers. She'd never experienced anything like it. Even now, looking at the lean length of him, desire flared again—hot, urgent, necessary.

Get a grip, Cat! There had to be a way to handle this. She narrowed her gaze on him as he shifted his attention to the brown bags.

"I stopped in the little grocery store on the corner and picked up provisions. They're predicting that this storm will shut down Manhattan before the afternoon is over. I got plenty for both of us—if you want to borrow."

He glanced around, then carried the bags through the archway into the small galley-shaped kitchen.

She watched while he unloaded food and wine, storing some of it in the refrigerator and tucking the rest away in cupboards. It looked like a lot of stuff to her and it drove home the point that he was here to stay. Until New Year's Day, she reminded herself.

His movements were slow, precise. How could he appear to be so cool and collected while she felt hot and wired? It had been the same way in the shop. Temper bubbled up as she recalled the easy way he'd introduced himself to Josie and Adelaide while she'd stood there focusing all her attention on getting some feeling back in her knees.

Within minutes, Dino Angelis had charmed the two older women into accepting the romantic story of their secret engagement. Two of her regular customers had congratulated her, and Adelaide had insisted that Cat take Dino to her apartment and get him settled in. She and Josie could manage for a while on their own.

After folding the bags and storing them, Dino turned, leaning a shoulder against a cupboard. "Convincing Josie and Adelaide was only part of the reason why I kissed you."

He was looking at her in that intent way again, and it made her toes curl. It suddenly occurred to her that they were standing as far apart as they could get in the small room. And he'd been the one who'd created the extra distance by moving into the kitchen. Perhaps he wasn't as cool as he wanted her to believe.

"What was the other part?"

"I also kissed you because I wanted to. I'd been thinking about doing it ever since I first laid eyes on you outside your shop yesterday morning."

Me, too, Cat thought. And she'd fantasized about doing a lot more than kissing. Right now, she was thinking about walking to him, unbuttoning that shirt and getting him out of it. Reaching behind her, she closed one hand around the doorknob to anchor herself. "Don't do it…again."

A smile curved his lips, and Cat saw a dimple flash on his right cheek.

"Now that we know what it's like, we're both going to want to do it again."

She already did. What was wrong with her? Pressing her palms flat against the door behind her, she straightened her shoulders and pushed herself away. "We're adults."

"Agreed."

"Reasonable, intelligent adults. We don't have to act on our impulses."

"No argument there."

But…

Though neither of them spoke the word aloud, it hung in the air between them. And Cat knew that if one of them moved toward the other right now, being reasonable or intelligent or even an adult wasn't going to matter.

Temper surged through her again. "I don't want to feel like this."

"The Fates don't always offer what we're looking for."

She frowned at him. "The Fates?"

His eyes were steady on hers. "I was raised in a Greek family. We believe strongly in the Fates and the choices they offer us. Sometimes they surprise us."

Dino Angelis was a surprise, all right, and Cat wasn't at all sure that she had a choice where he was concerned.

That scared her. She was used to having some control over herself. Her life. She ran her hands through her hair and began to pace. "Look, I don't have time for this. I don't even have time to think about this right now. I should never have agreed to this charade of my father's."

"Are you thinking of backing out?"

Her chin lifted as she turned to meet his eyes. "No. I agreed to do this fake engagement thing, and I keep my word."

For the first time she wondered if he was any happier about the situation than she was. She'd read in the background information her father had provided that he had family in San

Francisco—family he wouldn't be joining for Christmas. "Are *you* thinking of backing out?"

"No. I keep my word, too."

Cat studied him for a moment. "It's got to be hard for you. Don't you want to spend the holidays with your family?"

"Yes."

"Then why did you agree to do this?"

Dino met her eyes. "Sometimes, I can just feel things and know that they're right. When your father asked me to take this job, I knew that I was meant to do it."

"So you're saying it was fated? Inevitable?"

"I suppose."

Fate. Inevitability. Hadn't she felt a similar way when she'd first opened the Cheshire Cat? And when he'd walked into the store earlier, hadn't her first thought been—*Here he is?* No, she couldn't allow herself to think that way.

"I didn't expect…" She raised her hands and dropped them. "…everything to be so…complicated."

"Complicated is one word for it." He straightened from the cupboard. "If it will help, now that we've established the credibility of the engagement, I can promise that I won't grab you and kiss you again. When we kiss the next time, it will be a mutual decision."

There was something in his tone and in the way he looked at her that made her believe him. Some of her tension eased.

"I'm going to stow my things, and we'll get back to the Cheshire Cat."

She led the way down a short hallway to the right. "The bedrooms and bath are this way. This apartment has the same floor plan as mine." When they reached the bedroom, she stood aside and let him enter.

He unpacked his suit bag and hung a dress uniform on the

clothes tree in the corner of the room. Then he dropped his duffel on the foot of the bed and unzipped it. "Before we go back to the store, I have something for you."

Cat recognized the trademark blue of the designer jeweler the moment he pulled the small box out of his bag, and her heart took a little tumble. He opened it and held it in his out-stretched hand as he walked to her.

Her throat was dry as she stared down at the ring. A marquise-cut emerald caught and reflected light in an oval ring of diamonds. He lifted her hand and slipped the ring onto her finger.

Something touched her then—more than the warmth of his hand, the firmness of his grip. She felt a sense of rightness. Of inevitability?

A bubble of panic rose. This was a make-believe engagement with a man her father had maneuvered into taking her on as a job. James McGuire had no doubt provided the ring as window dressing—along with the background story he'd given them both. Still, she said, "It's lovely."

"It fits?"

She nodded. For the life of her she couldn't seem to take her eyes off of the ring. Nor could she find the strength to pull her hand out of his.

"I chose the emerald because of your eyes, but I had to guess at the size."

She met his eyes then. "You bought this ring?"

He nodded. "I believe it was the only detail that your father missed. But I figured it might be a telling one. From what your father has said of Lucia Merceri, a missing engagement ring would catch her attention."

Wincing, Cat nodded her head. "She'd pounce on it like a hungry dog on a bone, and she wouldn't let go until she had an explanation."

"The more I hear about this woman, the more curious I am to meet her."

Cat nearly smiled as she met his eyes. "Be careful what you wish for."

Dino glanced back down at their joined hands. "The ring looks good on you. In my experience, it's often the small things that make an operation go south."

An operation. The two words brought Cat out of her little trance and stiffened her spine. Oh, the ring was a telling detail all right. It was a symbol of their fake engagement—designed to fool everyone. She'd do well to remember that.

Pulling her hand out of Dino's, she said, "I need to get back to the store."

"Of course." Placing a hand on the small of her back, he guided her out of the room and down the short hallway. "When we get back there, put me to work. For the length of our engagement, I'm at your service."

DINO SAT BACK on his heels and blew out a long frustrated breath. Cat McGuire had taken him at his word and assigned him a challenging task. The moment they'd gotten back to the store, she'd escorted him up the circular iron staircase to a large room on the second floor that she used as an office. Then she'd asked him to put together a dollhouse that she'd promised a customer before closing that day. He'd noted that the dollhouse had been shipped from Paxco, Mexico.

As far as he could see, the package hadn't been tampered with, and there'd been nothing in it but the promised dollhouse, which was as tricky to assemble as a thousand-piece jigsaw puzzle. He was halfway through when she appeared at the top of the stairs. "Is it finished?"

"Just the first floor."

She dropped to her knees, selected one of the wall pieces that surrounded him and snicked it easily into place.

"I can see you're an expert," Dino said.

"Practice makes perfect. I've done quite a few of these. My first one took me over three hours."

Dino picked up a second piece of wall. When it didn't immediately slide into place, her hand covered his.

"Sometimes, you have to finesse it like—" She broke off when his fingers closed around hers. The piece of dollhouse clattered to the floor.

Dino hadn't been conscious of taking her hand. It had just seemed to happen. Her fingers were slender but strong, and they returned the pressure of his.

They touched nowhere else, but they were close, their knees nearly brushing, their bodies leaning toward each other. In that moment, he recalled exactly what her body had felt like when it had been pressed to his—the melting softness, the heat. God, he wanted to touch her. He wanted to slip that sweater over her head and let his hands slowly, very, very slowly mold every inch of her. He wanted to feel the silky texture of that bare skin beneath his fingers.

When his gaze dropped to her mouth, he remembered exactly how she'd tasted, the initial tartness, then the incredible depth of the sweetness. Hunger built fiercely inside of him. Her lips were parted, moist and so close that he could feel her breath mingle with his. He shifted his gaze to her eyes. They were wide and clouded with the same desire that he was feeling.

If either of them moved…

He could have her, Dino thought. They could have each other. Right now. Right here. In seconds, he could make the vision that had been tempting him, tormenting him ever since he'd first seen her, a reality.

But that wasn't what he'd promised her. He'd told her he wouldn't grab her and kiss her again. Summoning up all his control, Dino released her hand, picked up the piece of wall and slipped it into place. "I can take it from here."

"I—yes." She scrambled to her feet. "Right. I'll get back to work."

She was as rattled as he was. He took some satisfaction in that as he watched her descend the stairs. He wanted her way too much for comfort, and he was beginning to think way too much for his own sanity. How many more times was he going to be able to draw back before he took what he wanted?

CAT DIDN'T KNOW how she made it to the bottom of the stairs. Layers of mist still clouded her brain, and her legs felt as if they'd dissolved below the knees. The Cheshire Cat was filled with customers, laughing, talking, but all she could hear was the loud hammering of her pulse. She wondered why everyone in the store didn't turn and stare at her.

Gripping the stair railing, she drew in a deep breath and willed her brain cells to click back on again. They'd begun to go into meltdown the instant Dino's fingers had gripped hers.

For heaven's sake, all he'd done was take her hand in his. There'd been no other point of contact between them, and yet it was as if he'd touched her everywhere. She'd imagined exactly what it would be like to have those hands on her bare skin, her shoulders, her throat, her breasts. She'd felt the hardness, the urgency, the ruthlessness. An almost unbearable thrill had moved through her.

And when he'd nearly kissed her again... Lord, she'd wanted him to. More than that, she'd willed him to. Even though she knew that if his mouth had taken hers, neither one of them would have stopped with a kiss. They would have made love right there on the floor of her office without any care at all for the fact that just below, her shop was filled with customers.

Gathering her scattered thoughts, Cat focused her gaze on her store, her customers. But even as she stepped off the stairs and managed a smile for one of them, she wondered how much longer she would be able to resist what she was feeling for Dino Angelis.

BY FOUR O'CLOCK THAT AFTERNOON, Dino was ready for a break. He felt as if he'd been on a particularly demanding set of maneuvers. After finishing the dollhouse, he'd taken the time to search her office. She kept the space militarily neat. The desk was large, free of clutter, and the paperwork in the two filing cabinets all related to her toy business. There was a small refrigerator stocked with bottled water and a carved oak cabinet that contained a bottle of good brandy and four glasses.

Over her desk, there were a series of sketches, each one of a different doll, and they were all signed by Nancy McGuire, Cat's mother.

At noon, Cat had asked him to run across the street to the pub and bring back sandwiches—which the three women had somehow managed to grab bites of between customers. Though he hadn't liked leaving Cat in the store, the errand had allowed him to spot the location of the federal agent. He was across the street today, but he was still standing out like a sore thumb. Dino hadn't been able to spot Jase's man, which had reassured him.

His most recent assignment had been to clean up her back storeroom. As far as he could tell the small space was used mostly for stashing deliveries until the toys could be unpacked and put out on display. From the buildup of clutter, he surmised that it might have been a week or more since anyone had had time to put the room in order. Small wonder if the Cheshire Cat had been as busy in the past two weeks as it had been today.

Opened boxes had been piled everywhere. None of them had been shipped from Mexico. Adelaide and Josie had dashed in frequently to grab an armload of dragons or pirate ships to replenish the ones that were flying off the shelves. Cat had so far stayed away. That was making it easier for him to keep his mind on his real job.

While cleaning, he'd taken time to check out her security system. While it was a good one, he figured that someone with Jase's expertise would be able to bypass it without much trouble.

There were two entrances. The one at the front of the store and the one in the storeroom that led out to the alley that ended in the courtyard of her apartment building. If he were going to break in, he'd use the alleyway entrance.

So far, there'd been no sign of the delayed shipment of dolls. Gut instinct told him they were the key. They had to be. And the longer the dolls were delayed, the more danger Cat might be in.

Taking one last look out into the shop to assure himself that Cat was safely involved with a customer, Dino propped open the side entrance to the store, grabbed an armful of collapsed boxes and made his way to the Dumpster.

Cat entered the storeroom just in time to watch Dino exit. When she caught herself staring at his backside, she shook her head in disgust. Since she'd fled down the stairs from her office, they'd mostly managed to avoid each other. But that hadn't kept him out of her mind. And in spite of how busy she was, she'd caught herself more than once looking for him. At him. Each time she did, memories and sensations came flooding back and she wanted him more. Her body wasn't paying one bit of heed to any resolutions she might have made.

Shaking her head to clear it, she tried to remember what she'd come into the storeroom for. First baffled, then annoyed, she scanned the shelves for a clue that would trigger her memory. And there it was. The toy soldier. *That's what you came for—a* toy *soldier, not a real one.*

It was on the very top shelf, of course. Grabbing the ladder, she edged it along the floor to a spot directly below the toy, and then scooted to the top rung. But it was just out of reach. Rising to her toes, she stretched her arm to its full length and closed two fingers around the rifle.

Beneath her, the ladder swayed and teetered. Getting a firmer grip on the soldier, she fought for balance. She was losing the battle and praying that she wouldn't break something when the ladder suddenly steadied and two large hands closed firmly around her calves.

"Steady now?" he asked.

"I'm fine."

Still he took her arm and guided her to the floor. Cat could feel the pressure of each one of his fingers just below her elbow. They burned her skin like a brand. A longing filled her to feel his hands move over every inch of her. And to have her hands on him. His throat was at her eye level, and she could see the rapid beat of his pulse. Her own raced to match its rhythm.

Thoughts drained away and a noise filled her mind—the sound of the wind before a storm. She should step back. Dimly, she was aware of a pressure building inside of her. Hunger was too tame a word. This was greed. Irrational. Compelling.

Once again, it was Dino who broke the contact, dropping his hand and backing away. "You should be more careful."

"Yes." She couldn't have agreed more. Her reaction to the man might confound her, but one thing was becoming crystal-clear. Whenever she came near him, she wanted him. It was that simple. That primitive. That inevitable?

"Thanks for the help."

"No problem."

Oh, yes it was. But it wasn't fear that moved through her as she walked into the front room of the shop. It was a wild thrill.

FIGHTING AGAINST THE URGE to go after her and drag her back into the storeroom, Dino waited five beats before he moved to the doorway. She was handing the toy soldier to an excited customer.

What in hell was he going to do about what he was feeling for Cat McGuire? If this were an op, he'd have a strategy in place by now. His mind and his body would be working in harmony. But with Cat, what his mind was telling him to do was at total odds with what he wanted to do.

She was…well, she was something he'd never experienced before. He'd known from the moment he'd first seen that photo of her that something might happen between them. But he'd never anticipated the power of their attraction, nor the way it was escalating. On both their parts.

Each time he touched her, his control was being stretched to the breaking point. Soon, Dino knew that he wouldn't be able to back away. And the worst way to address the problem was to stand here staring at her like some totally bewitched adolescent.

Turning back into the storeroom, Dino tried to find something else to do. But the room was already neat. He'd stacked boxes against one wall and placed the toys he'd unpacked on the shelves that lined two walls. In the process he'd unearthed a small refrigerator stocked with soft drinks and bottled water. Next to it was a narrow table and two chairs. On the shelf

above the fridge was a teakettle and one of those fancy cof-
feemakers that produced one cup at a time. His mother had a
similar one in her office so that she could always offer her
clients fresh brewed coffee.

On a slow day, Dino could picture Cat racing in to grab a
drink or a quick cup of coffee. What he couldn't picture her
doing was sitting down at that table. The thought had him
frowning slightly. The woman worked tirelessly, and she never
seemed to walk when she could run. Then, because he could
no longer help himself, he moved back to the doorway and
glanced out into the shop. Just as he'd suspected. Even now
she wasn't still. She was leaning against the counter scribbling
in the small notebook she carried in the pocket of her skirt.
There was only one harried-looking shopper left in the store.

Customers had thinned steadily since noon. Outside, the
falling snow was so thick that it blocked the lights of the pub
across the street. Cars and trucks on the street progressed at
a snail's pace. But they were still moving. Cat had sent Josie
home at one and insisted that Adelaide leave shortly after that
so that she could take the subway uptown before the rush hour
backed everything up.

Both women had protested vehemently.

"You'll need help when those dolls arrive," Adelaide
had argued.

"Dino can help me," Cat had countered as she'd handed
Adelaide her coat.

"What about the phone calls? You promised to call
everyone as soon as the dolls were here."

"I can do those. Now go."

Josie had been an easier sell, but she'd reminded Cat that
she could be back at a moment's notice if she was needed.

Dino had to wonder if Adelaide's and Josie's reluctance to

leave had anything to do with the fact that the dolls hadn't been delivered yet and they wanted to be in the store when the FedEx man finally arrived. Each seemed to sincerely care about the shop and the customers. And he'd observed enough of Cat's relationship with Josie and Adelaide to know that she trusted them both implicitly. Either one of them might be the "inside man" who identified the toy carrying the drugs and made sure it got to the person behind the operation.

His gaze returned once more to Cat. As if she felt it, she glanced up, and in the moment that their eyes met and held, Dino once more became aware that the clock was ticking. He was simply not going to be able to keep a handle on what he was feeling for her much longer.

AS SHE LOOKED INTO HIS EYES, Cat felt a pull as strong and inexorable as the pull of the moon on the oceans. Her skin was tingling, her pulse pounding. And all he was doing was watching her. What would happen when he touched her? Really touched her? Her time for deciding what to do about Dino Angelis was running out. If they'd been alone in the store, she might have gone to him right then and done what she'd been fantasizing about doing all day.

She dragged her eyes away from Dino's to check on her lone customer. The woman, a stranger, was currently in a relaxed browsing stage. A shopper at heart, Cat decided to give her new customer five more minutes before offering to help.

She resisted the urge to look at Dino again. She knew he was still in the doorway to the storeroom because she could feel the heat of his gaze on her skin.

Think of something else. The dolls.

The man was even distracting her from what had been the topic most on her mind before she'd met him. In spite of the earlier crush of last-minute shoppers, she'd managed to keep track of her package from Paxco. And it was on its way. As soon as the dolls arrived and she'd notified the people who'd bought them, she and Dino Angelis would be going back to her apartment building. Once inside, they *could* go their separate ways. The curtain would descend on their little act until the next day. It was the simple solution.

So why did she suddenly want complicated?

Cat nibbled on the end of her pencil and frowned. In other situations in her life, business, family, she could always figure something out. She even knew how to handle her father.

Glancing back down at her notes, Cat reviewed the list she'd made. Writing things down always helped her to think more clearly. #1—*I'm* extremely *attracted to Dino*. Cat drew a second line under the word *extremely*.

#2—*I really, really want to have sex with Dino Angelis.* Hot, uncomplicated, outrageous sex. He'd shown her so much with one kiss. Was she going to be able to live without knowing more about what he could do to her?

Or about what she could do to him?

#3—*If I pass on this opportunity, will I ever have another chance?* She thought of what Dino had said about the Fates offering surprises. Well, Dino Angelis might be the biggest surprise she'd had in her life so far. He'd already stirred things in her that she'd never felt before.

It was a fake engagement. In Dino's words, an operation. It couldn't go anywhere—so what if they decided to simply enjoy each other? What on earth could be wrong with that? They were both adults. She tapped her pencil on the page of the notebook. Reasonable and intelligent adults.

Her lips curved when she realized she was using the same

argument she'd used with Dino earlier—only this time for a different outcome.

Her gaze dropped to the ring she wore on her finger, and something tightened around her heart. The problem was that the ring didn't feel fake. She fisted her hand. In fact it felt just right.

#4—*I like him.* Until yesterday morning he'd been a complete stranger to her. And though she still didn't know much more about him than her father had detailed in the file, she felt she was coming to know him. For starters, he was a hard worker. And he hadn't objected once during the day as she'd ordered him around.

Cat tapped the eraser of her pencil against her bottom lip. He hadn't complained when she'd shown him the dollhouse. And there was something about his presence that inspired... what? Confidence? Now that she'd gotten a little distance and some perspective, she had to admit that his entrance into the shop and the way that he'd kissed her had been a stroke of genius. Adelaide and Josie had bought into the secret engagement one hundred percent. And they were completely charmed by him.

Cat frowned down at her notes. Why did she suspect that liking him was going to complicate things?

Stop overthinking it.

Dragging her eyes away from her notes, Cat glanced around her store. Hadn't she spent the last several years of her life focusing on her career and achieving her dream of owning her own toy store? Maybe her father was right for once, and she ought to take some time to smell the roses. Or to just simply enjoy Dino Angelis.

She let her gaze drift to the door of the storeroom. Dino had his back to her, as if making one last check on the cleanup he'd done. From the front the man was a knockout, but his backside came in at a close second. She felt that pull again, strong, sure, and an aching need moved through her. Of all the toys in her store, Dino Angelis was the one she wanted most from Santa.

"Miss?"

Reining in her wandering thoughts, Cat focused on the worried-looking woman standing in front of her.

"I just can't decide. My son David is seven. He's a reader, does well in school. He doesn't go in much for sports. Do you have any suggestions?"

"Do you think he might like a magic set?" Cat led the way to the front of the shop where she'd displayed a selection of beginning magician kits. "I sell a lot of these to young boys who are smart and have a serious turn of mind."

DINO WATCHED Cat escort her last customer to the door. The woman's harried expression had been replaced by one of delight.

"I can't thank you enough, Ms. McGuire. It's the perfect gift for my David."

"Most days I have the best job in the world," Cat said as she opened the front door. "I hope that you and your family have a lovely Christmas."

In the brightly colored green sweater and print skirt, Cat reminded Dino a bit of a butterfly. They were elusive, hard to capture, but definitely worth the chase. He desperately wanted his hands on her. He recalled the way she'd felt in his arms— slim, supple and strong. He wasn't sure what he was going to do when they finally returned to the apartment building. Go their separate ways? That would be the smart move. But he wasn't sure he'd be able to make it.

The rush of cold air from the open door did nothing to diffuse the heat that arrowed through him as a seductive fantasy blossomed in his mind. The lights were low, and there was music playing—something muted on a saxophone. She was standing only a few feet away. Slowly, she pulled the sweater up over her body, revealing that pale, delicate skin one inch at a time.

What she wore beneath it, the froth of white lace and silk that barely covered her breasts, had his breath backing up. Her flesh was smooth and delicate as alabaster. For a moment he simply let his eyes absorb her while the need to touch her grew into a burning ache. He could vividly imagine the contrast between the slight roughness of the finely crafted lace and the petallike softness of her skin.

In his mind, he reached out to trace a finger over the swell of flesh above her bra when Cat suddenly vanished through the door of the shop.

Dino blinked, refocused. But his eyes hadn't deceived him.

One second she was there and the next, all he could see was a swirl of blinding snow. Panic streaming through him, Dino raced for the door. "Cat!"

6

WHEN DINO CRASHED into her, the impact unbalanced both of them. Gripping her shoulders, he staggered back against one of the display windows, pulling her with him.

Cat struggled to break free. "He's here."

"Who's here?" Dino shifted in front of her as he peered through the blinding snowfall.

Cat wiggled out from behind him, pointing into the street. "Ted. The FedEx man."

Dino made out the shape of a truck that was double-parked in front of the Cheshire Cat. Swiping snow off of his eye-lashes, he finally saw the darker shape of a man moving toward them. Once more he pushed Cat behind him.

"Cat McGuire?" a gravelly voice asked.

"Who wants to know?" Dino asked.

"That's me." Cat spoke at the same time and this time she didn't wiggle. She gave Dino a good hard shove and stepped around him.

The man was close enough that Dino recognized a delivery man's uniform, but they were easily come by. He was carrying a large box, poised on his shoulder in much the same way a skilled waiter would balance a tray.

Even as Dino inserted himself between Cat and the delivery man, Cat said, "You're not Ted."

With one hand Dino gripped Cat's arm firmly. He slipped his other one into the pocket of his jacket and closed his fingers around his gun.

"No, ma'am. Ted ran into some trouble. Could you sign here?"

"Do you have some ID?" Dino asked.

"ID? Look, buddy. Go check my truck. There's an 800 number. In the meantime, I've got a delivery from Mexico." He set the box on the ground and passed an electronic signature pad to Cat.

The wealth of tiredness in the man's tone did more to convince Dino than anything else that he was looking at a true FedEx delivery man. "What kind of trouble did Ted run into?"

As Cat scrawled her signature, the man elaborated. "He got held up. Can you imagine that? You live here in this city, and eventually you see everything. He'd just gotten a signature when two thugs in a van pulled up alongside of him, pointed a gun at him, and told him to open the back of his truck."

"They robbed him?' Cat asked.

"Nah. Luckily, some concerned citizens witnessed the attempted robbery and dialed 911. Not that there would have been a quick response in this weather. But one of our mounted policemen happened by, and between the angered witnesses and the horse and the fact that the policeman was armed, the two men jumped in their van and took off. This city gets a bad rap a lot of the time, but those people were pissed. I mean there were probably Christmas presents in there."

"There were," Cat said as she handed him her signature.

"Ted was pretty shook up, as you might imagine, and since I was nearby when he called the incident in, I offered to deliver some of his packages."

"You're a true Good Samaritan," Cat said. "This box contains a Merry Christmas for twenty-four children."

"Happy holidays," the man said as he disappeared into the thickly falling snow.

Dino shouldered the box. "Let's get this inside." Carrying it half propped on his shoulder the same way the delivery man had, he urged Cat back into the store.

"I'm assuming you want to unpack these now," he said.

"Definitely. I've been so worried about them that I won't be satisfied until I know they're all here. Then I promised to call each person who ordered one of the dolls and give them the good news."

Her eyes shifted to the shop window. All she could see was a blur of snow. "The worst of this is supposed to be over by midnight."

"Why don't you lock up the store and set the alarm while I carry these upstairs? Your office offers the most space, and you wouldn't want anyone just wandering in while we're working."

No, she didn't. Cat studied Dino as he strolled to the spiral staircase and climbed them. She opened her mouth, and then shut it. What he'd said about locking up was smart. She was sure she would have thought of it. Eventually. Once she'd assured herself that the dolls were all here. But something in the way he'd said it had set her nerves a bit on edge.

Turning, she flipped the Open sign to Closed, then locked the door and turned the alarm on. Hurrying to the storeroom, she checked the locks on the door that opened onto the alley and made sure the security system was activated there also.

No, it wasn't that he'd reminded her to lock up that had her nerves jumping. It was the way he'd grabbed her out in the street and shoved her behind him—almost as if he'd believed she was in some kind of danger.

Which was totally ridiculous. She swept her gaze around the Cheshire Cat as she strode to the spiral staircase. What safer place could there be than a toy store? The fact that some Scroogelike thugs had tried to rob a FedEx truck four days before Christmas was just one of those crazy things that happened in Manhattan.

As for Dino's overly protective attitude, she could probably lay the blame for that on his military background. Her father often displayed the same annoying traits.

Her nerves a bit more settled, she ran up the stairs and discovered that Dino had already opened the box and was holding up one of the dolls. Moving toward him, she held out her hands. "Matt was right. They are more beautiful in person."

He gestured to a framed sketch over her desk. "It's the same doll, isn't it? Did you design it?"

"No, my mom did."

"You must be so proud."

"I am." Something in her throat tightened as she took the doll. It had a face of delicately painted porcelain. The brunette hair was pulled back and then fell in curls almost to her waist. The silk dress was a rich shade of red. "It's been my dream to bring one of her sketches to life. But it wasn't until I discovered these wonderful craftsmen in Paxco, Mexico, that I was able to accomplish it. Next year, we'll add a second design and people can begin to collect."

"Take a closer look," Dino advised.

Turning the doll over, Cat saw that an inch of lace had pulled away from the hem of the dress, and the pantaloons beneath the dress were soiled. Frowning, she thought fast. "I can fix it. Let's check the rest."

It wasn't until they'd unpacked all of the dolls and matched them to the order slips she'd retrieved from the file in her tote bag that Cat relaxed.

"I count twenty-five," Dino said.

"And twenty-four are in pristine condition. Thank heavens I ordered one for myself at the last minute. I can take the one with the torn lace and repair it. I'm going to surprise my father with it. He's so hard to buy for."

She picked up the damaged doll and examined it. "Maybe this one delayed the shipment. Matt may be able to explain it when he gets here."

"Matt?" Dino asked.

"Matt Winslow is my assistant buyer. I sent him down to Paxco the day before yesterday, the moment I learned about the delay. He got stranded at O'Hare overnight, but when I talked to him last, he was boarding a plane for JFK. He was supposed to get here at noon. Things have been so hectic that I completely forgot."

"Any planes coming into JFK or LaGuardia were probably delayed," Dino said. "Did Matt know you'd ordered the extra doll?"

"I never mentioned it to him. I told him to ship whatever dolls were ready." She recalled her earlier conversation with him. "He asked me to wait for him before I unpacked the dolls. He seemed concerned about something. Perhaps because this one was damaged." As she spoke, she carefully stored it in her purse.

DINO RESTED HIS HIP against her desk and willed himself to ignore the stab of jealousy her words and the expression on her face had caused. For the first time, he wondered what kind of a relationship she had with Matt Winslow. Certainly not a serious one if she'd agreed to the pretend engagement with him.

She stepped toward him and set her tote on the desk. They were standing so close that he could reach out and touch her.

Keep your mind on the job. He carefully tucked his fingers in his pockets. "What's he like?"

She met his eyes as she considered. "Matt is very business-focused. He's smart, good-looking, and he thinks in creative ways."

How creative, Dino wondered. Creative enough to put the drugs in the damaged doll? Dino very carefully avoided looking at her tote bag. He let himself consider reasons why the dolls hadn't shipped on time. Perhaps the drugs had been delayed on the Mexico end and the last-minute rush had caused one of the dolls to be treated carelessly. The soiled pantaloons and torn lace would make it easy for someone on this end to identify it. Is that why Winslow had wanted to be present when the shipment was opened? The condition would delay the sale of the doll—perhaps until the customer it was meant for walked into the store.

"I'm lucky to have Matt," Cat continued as she settled her hip on the desk. She nearly brushed against him as she did.

Dino tucked his hands deeper into his pockets.

"But working for me is just his stepping-stone to something bigger."

"Bigger like what?"

She laughed, and as the bright bubble of sound filled the room, Dino realized two things. He'd never heard her laugh before. And he wanted to hear the sound again—and often.

"Matt wants to be a millionaire someday. He's not going to accomplish that here at the Cheshire Cat."

For a moment as he looked at her, Dino felt every thought drain out of his head. Maybe it was the way she was smiling at him. Or perhaps it was her eyes. Lit with laughter, they reminded him of that shade of green that was so peculiar to the color of the sea around the Greek Isles. Whatever it was, he felt abruptly and completely enchanted. Unable to stop himself, he reached out and touched just the ends of her hair, rubbing a curl between his fingers. In spite of the fiery color, it felt cool against his skin.

She'd stopped talking and he recognized the growing sensual awareness in her gaze. When she moistened her lips, he nearly broke his promise not to grab her and kiss her again.

"I've been thinking," she said.

"About what?"

She lowered her eyes to his mouth, then raising her hand, she brushed one finger along his bottom lip.

"I've been thinking about kissing you again. But first…"

Abruptly, she dropped her hand and strode to the center of the office.

Dino came very close to breaking his word. His lip burned where she'd touched him. How hot would they both burn when he kissed her again?

She whirled back to face him. "I want to do more than kiss you. I want to have sex with you."

WHEN HE TOOK A STEP toward her, she wanted badly to just shut up and run into his arms. But she held up both hands. "First, let me finish." She drew in a deep breath. "I've thought it all through. I even listed the main points in my notebook."

His brows shot up. "That's what you were writing about?"

She nodded. "I want you to know up front that I understand the ground rules."

"Ground rules?"

Cat waved a hand, nearly losing her train of thought when light sparkled off her engagement ring. "That this is just an operation to you. To me, too. At my father's request, orders really, we're pretending we're engaged until the holidays are over. It's kind of like being Cinderella at the ball. Poof. Everything goes back to normal at the stroke of midnight on New Year's Eve. You'll go back to working for my godfather at the Pentagon, and I'll go on with my life here. I can live with that. But…"

"But…?" He waited in that quiet, intense way he had, and her thoughts threatened to spin away.

Ruthlessly, she gathered them. "But no one has ever made me feel the way you do." She took a tentative step toward him. "I want to know what else you can make me feel. I want to know what I can make you feel."

The heat in his eyes gave her the courage to continue. "You talked about the Fates offering choices. I suppose that the safer option would be to try to keep our distance."

Anxiety had her turning to pace. "Normally, I choose the safer path. I'm not much of a risk-taker." She whirled to face him. "But I don't want to keep my distance. I don't see any reason why we can't enjoy each other. Maybe the Fates are offering us an opportunity to give each other a Christmas present."

"A Christmas present?"

Her heart was beating so fast Cat wondered if he could hear it. She drew in a deep breath and let it out. "I was thinking earlier that of all the toys in my store, you're the one I most want to play with."

"You're sure?"

Nerves danced in her stomach, but as each second ticked by, she became even more certain. "Yes."

He moved toward her then in that slow gait that ate up the ground. *Thank God,* was all she could think. But he stopped when she was still out of arms' reach.

Suddenly, her temper surged. "Do you feel the same way about this or not?"

"Oh, we're on the same page."

"Then why don't you grab me and kiss me. You have my permission."

"First, take off your sweater. While you've been jotting down pros and cons in your notebook, I've been fantasizing about seeing you naked."

Suddenly both her temper and her tension eased. She shot him a smile that widened when she saw the gleam of amusement in his eyes. Slowly, she unbuckled her belt and dropped it to the floor. "The difference between the male and the female mind?"

He nodded. "We're simple creatures at heart."

Maybe that was true for most men, but Cat didn't believe that of Dino Angelis. Not for a moment. There were layers to him that fascinated her every bit as much as the physical attraction.

Cat slipped her hands beneath the edge of her sweater and drew it slowly up and over her head. The slight scratchiness of the wool rubbing over her skin was erotic, but when he dropped his gaze slowly from her throat to her waist, she felt singed.

"I was imagining white lace, but the pale green is very nice."

"Thanks. Now it's your turn." She moved to him and began to unbutton the shirt of his uniform. "I've been thinking about doing this all day." When the last button had been freed, she slipped her fingers beneath the shirt, running her hands over his skin as she shoved it down his arms. The garment had a tailored fit, and as she'd watched him lift and carry during the day, she'd gotten a good idea of the planes and angles of his upper body. Still, looking at his bare skin, her palms went damp.

"Problem?" he asked.

"Yes," she managed. "You still have too many clothes on."

"It's your turn again."

She hadn't thought it was possible to get any hotter without turning into a puff of steam. But she'd never stripped for a man before—never helped a man to strip for her.

Getting into it, Cat ran her fingertips from her throat, over her breasts to the waist of her skirt. Then she unhooked it, wiggled her hips and let it slide to the floor.

The quick catch of his breath sent a fresh thrill of pleasure through her. She knew what he was looking at. She had a weakness for expensive lace underwear, and she favored thigh-high stockings. She'd chosen the sea-foam green in honor of the Christmas season. The high boots were for fashion, as well as protection against the inclement weather.

For ten humming seconds, Cat didn't think Dino was going to be able to unglue his gaze from her legs. When he finally met her eyes, she thought she just might melt into a puddle of lust.

"I thought I was going to be able to prolong this." He moved then, closing the distance between them. When he gripped her waist, and lifted her, she felt like a featherweight. "Hold on."

She wrapped arms and legs around him, her head spinning as he strode to the wall and pressed her against it. His mouth covered hers for one drugging kiss. She sank into it. If she were offered a choice between survival and this, she'd choose this.

No man had ever had this power over her. No one had ever made her feel this helpless. But it wasn't fear that streamed through her, it was delight as he ran his hands over her in one possessive sweep, pressing here, molding there. He slipped fingers beneath her thong and she nearly came when he penetrated her heat.

She quivered, moaned his name, then cried out in shocked protest when he lifted his mouth from hers. Desperate, she arched helplessly, trying to get closer to him as he rained kisses over her face, her neck, and closed his teeth around one nipple through the lace of her bra.

"I can't seem to get enough, can't seem to get a grip on control where you're concerned."

His words were a hot breath at her ear.

"No problem." She tried desperately to pull his mouth back to hers. "Kiss me again."

He pressed her more firmly against the wall, and she felt the hard strength of his desire pushing into her center. Helpless, she pumped against him. But she couldn't get close enough, not with the fabric of his trousers separating them.

"I need some help." His voice was ragged.

Together they jerked at his belt, yanking the snap of his pants open and dragging down the zipper. As he struggled to shove the fabric down his hips, she wrapped her hand around the hard length of him, guiding him toward her.

"The condom."

"What?"

"In my back pocket."

Condom. Cat tried to wrap her brain around the concept as she reached around him and pulled it out. Together, they fumbled to sheath him.

"Now. For heaven's sake, now!"

She wasn't sure if she'd shouted the words or just thought them. Finally, just when she wasn't sure if she could survive another second, he drove into her. His thrusts were fast, hard. Glorying in it, she moved with him.

"Again. Again. *More.*"

This time she was almost sure he'd said the words, over and over until they became a chant in her head, a beat in her blood.

He battered her against the wall, they battered each other until the orgasm ripped through her. She was still shattering into small pieces when she heard his cry of release.

7

WHEN HE COULD FINALLY THINK again, Dino had no idea how Cat had ended up sitting on his lap on the floor, her head snuggled against his neck. Her hand rested against his bare chest, and the emerald caught and reflected the lights from the Christmas tree.

It was just a symbol of their temporary arrangement, he told himself. That was why it looked so right on her finger—because it was right for now. Just as making love with her was right for now.

No regrets, Dino promised himself. He'd chosen to take what the Fates, what Cat had offered. And he wouldn't lie to himself. Making love with her once wasn't going to be enough.

"I think that went well," Cat said.

Realizing that she'd repeated the exact words he'd used after he'd kissed her that first time, Dino threw back his head and laughed. When she joined him, he pulled her close in a friendly hug.

"Touché. And it did go well." He drew back from her then and met her eyes. "But I'm thinking there may be room for some improvement." He traced a finger down the side of her neck. "We could give it a shot."

Downstairs, someone pounded on the door.

"Ignore it," Dino murmured against her mouth.

Cat pressed both of her hands against his chest. "I can't. Technically, the store should still be open."

The pounding grew louder.

"And I left all the lights on."

With a sigh, Dino eased her off his lap, and they both reached for clothes. Dino finished dressing first and hurried down the stairs. He could make out two figures huddled in front of the door.

"It's the Santa Claus man and Mrs. Lassiter. I know they're both anxious to get their dolls, but how in the world did they make it back here in this storm?" Cat said from behind him as she punched numbers into the alarm pad.

"Santa Claus man?" Dino asked.

"When he walked into the store yesterday, I thought there was something familiar about him, and I decided it was because he looked a bit like Santa. His real name is George Miller."

"He isn't a regular customer then?"

"No."

"What about the woman?"

"Mrs. Lassiter is in here all the time. And she's evidently desperate to get her doll. They both must be to come out in this storm."

Dino opened the door, and a tall woman and a portly man entered the store.

"I came to pick up my doll." The man spoke directly to Cat. "You're supposed to be open until seven."

"I closed early because of the weather. How did you know the dolls had arrived?" Cat asked.

"You gave me the tracking number," Mrs. Lassiter said.

"Right," Cat said. "And then I called and gave it to you, Mr. Miller. You'll have to forgive me. It's been a long day. I'll get them for you."

As Cat hurried up the stairs, Dino studied Mr. Miller. The white hair and mustache along with the glasses did create a certain resemblance to Santa Claus. What interested Dino even more was that Cat wasn't familiar with him.

"Do the two of you know each other?" Dino asked.

Miller glanced at the woman next to him. "No. Why?"

"You both arrived at the same time."

Mrs. Lassiter flicked Miller a glance. "Coincidence."

"How did you both manage to make it back into the city?"

"I decided to stay at a friend's in the city overnight," Mrs. Lassiter said. "Who knows how long it will be before they clear away all this snow. The doll is very important to my granddaughter."

"And you, Mr. Miller?" Dino asked.

Miller pushed his glasses up on the bridge of his nose and studied Dino. "I live in the neighborhood."

Cat raced down the stairs carrying dolls and two Cheshire Cat gift bags. "Here they are."

She handed a doll to each customer so they could see them before she put them into the gift bags. "Merry Christmas. I hope you don't have far to go in this weather."

"You'll be open tomorrow?" George Miller asked.

"Yes." Cat opened the door for them. "The snow is supposed to stop at midnight. I'm sure that by tomorrow, New York City will be back to business as usual."

Dino thought hard. He didn't like the fact that two of the dolls were leaving the shop before he'd had a chance to search them. He'd been hoping to sneak back into the Cheshire Cat tonight and accomplish that. He hadn't anticipated that two customers would come early.

He studied Cat as she reset the alarm. If she had handed over the drugs just now, how had the doll been matched with

the right customer? They were all identical, each a faithful
match to the drawing over her desk, and when he and Cat had
worked, side by side, unwrapping each doll, she hadn't shown
favoritism to any one, hadn't looked for any special markings.
She'd simply pulled them out of the box and lined them up
in the order in which they'd been unpacked.

Dino shoved his hands into his pockets. Was he actually
considering the possibility that she was involved? Perhaps that
was a sign that he had at least some objectivity left where she
was concerned. But while they'd unpacked the dolls, he *had*
looked for markings, and he'd found none.

The only doll that had been different was the one she'd
stuffed into her tote. Watching her re-alarm the system, Dino
went with his gut instinct. Even if the doll in her tote did contain
the cocaine, Cat McGuire wasn't involved. Everything he knew
and sensed about her as a person told him that she wouldn't have
used her mother's dolls in this kind of an operation.

THE PHONE RANG. A glance at the caller ID brought on a surge
of panic. It rang again. Ignoring it wasn't an option.

"Yes?"

"You were supposed to be there when the shipment of
dolls arrived."

Lying wasn't a good idea when the voice at the other end
of the line was this emotionless. "I couldn't be there. This
weather—"

"I don't tolerate excuses."

The flat tone of the statement had fear joining the panic.

There was a beat of silence, then, "The dolls are in the shop
right now. I want you to get me mine."

"How?"

"I'm going to give you a number to call. 758-3712. When

the man answers, tell him what you need. Remember, there are consequences for failure."

The line went dead.

Breathe. There's still a way to solve the problem. Just dial the number.

The fingers that punched the numbers into the phone trembled.

INCOMPETENT BUNGLERS. That's what they all were. First down in Paxco and now at the toy store. For nearly a year, the operation had run without a hitch, and suddenly people were dropping the ball right and left.

Fury welled up. It never paid to depend too much on others. As soon as the going got a little rough, they began to panic. And then the mistakes always multiplied. Temper bubbled up again.

Walk off the anger. It will only cloud the issue. It's your cool head that's gotten you this far. Think.

It wasn't too late. There was still time to get the drugs before the danger became too great. But there was no doubt the threat of exposure was growing. Cat McGuire was a smart woman. Perhaps too smart. If she started to put two and two together…

Anger faded abruptly as a plan formed. There was a way to eliminate the problem. The hand that punched numbers into a cell phone was as steady as a rock.

DINO CLOSED CAT'S BEDROOM DOOR and moved quickly through the small apartment to the kitchen. He'd left her in the bathroom drying her hair. The temptation to linger and watch while she did it had been strong. But he'd already given in to too many temptations where she was concerned.

He hadn't been able to prevent himself from joining her in the shower. He'd watched her eyes darken to a deep emerald green when he'd carefully laid the condom in the soap dish. A fresh wave of heat engulfed him as the memory seared through his mind.

"I'm not going to make it out of here without having you again," he'd said.

"Fine with me."

He'd taken the soap from her hands and rubbed it between his own. "But first, I'm going to wash you slowly from head to toe."

And he'd delivered on his promise. At last, he'd had his hands on her skin, something that he hadn't taken much time to do when they'd made love in her office. He'd lathered her neck and her breasts. Then he'd lingered for a while on her bottom before he'd thoroughly explored the slick, silky skin of her legs. Her eyes had misted over and her breath had become ragged before he'd finally slipped two fingers into her and made her come, once, then twice. Then again.

The water had turned cold before he'd put on the condom, lifted her and buried himself in her. He'd struggled to keep his thrusts slow, but she'd dug her nails into him, cried out his name, and he was helpless to do anything but drive them both into the madness.

With a frown, Dino shook his head to clear it of the memory. The woman had completely enchanted him. When he wasn't making love to her, he was thinking about it. And his need for her was already interfering with the job he had to do. He glanced back at the bedroom door. He couldn't be near her and not want her. But his job was to keep her safe, not naked and beneath him.

And that was only part of the problem. Her proposition had been for uncomplicated, "poof, it's over at the stroke of midnight" sex. But when he'd slipped that ring on her finger, something had clicked for him. And each time he made love to her, it clicked again. But that wasn't something he could think about now.

Shaking his head again, Dino wondered if he would ever be able to completely rid his mind of her. Then he pulled his cell phone from his pocket. He could still hear the hum of the hair dryer, but he had no idea how long it would take her to finish. This might be his only window of opportunity to call Jase. Dino punched the numbers in.

"Yes?"

"I don't have much time. Two names—Lillian Lassiter and George Miller. Check them out." During the process of helping Cat call all of her customers who'd ordered dolls, he'd noted the full names on the order slips.

"Are those the two I saw visit the store after you closed?"

Dino's brows shot up. "Right. I thought you had one of your best men assigned to the store tonight."

"One of my best men is stranded in the Bronx, so you're stuck with yours truly. Nothing is moving in this mess."

Dino moved into the living room to assure himself that the hair dryer was still running. A glance out the window told him that the storm was still at full throttle.

"As you no doubt saw, the FedEx man delivered the dolls, but I didn't have a chance to search them for the drugs."

"I can handle that. It will get me out of the cold."

"Be careful. You may not be the only one checking them out."

"Got one of your feelings?"

"Maybe. Watch your back and keep me updated. The next time you call, you'll be my cousin Nik."

"You got it."

The moment, Dino pocketed his cell, he strode back to the kitchen. They'd stopped at his apartment earlier, and he'd picked up what he'd need to fix them a meal. He couldn't risk searching the doll in her purse until later when she was sleeping.

CAT LOOKED AT HERSELF in the full-length mirror. How did one dress to have a home-cooked meal with one's lover?

She'd decided against work clothes, but she certainly wasn't going to wear the sweats she wore on the rare occasions when she lounged around the apartment. So jeans and a red silk shirt it was—she refused to change again.

Impatient with the fact that her hair was still damp, she'd pulled it into a ponytail and fastened it with a red scrunchy. Not the most glamorous hairdo, she decided, but it would have to do. Stepping closer to the mirror, she studied her image more closely. When was the last time she'd dressed with a man in mind?

And Dino Angelis was no ordinary man. She grinned at her reflection. In fact, he might be the very best Christmas present she'd ever given herself. Her body was still tingling at several pulse points from how he'd touched her in the shower. She'd known that making love with him would be incredibly exciting, but she hadn't anticipated the half of it. Nothing, absolutely nothing had come close to what she'd done, what she'd discovered with Dino.

She'd never thought of herself as a particularly sensual person, but he had set her inner sex siren free. So much so that she couldn't wait to make love with him again. And why not? The dolls had arrived safely. By tomorrow, they would all be in the hands of their new owners. Wrapping her arms around herself, she twirled once in front of the mirror before she strode to the door.

The moment she stepped into the living room, she stopped short and her heart fluttered up to her throat. The scene Dino had created assaulted her senses. There was music, something low and bluesy, but she couldn't take her eyes off of the red checked tablecloth spread on the floor and the two fat candles burning on the coffee table. The only other lights in the room twinkled from the small Christmas tree.

When he'd said he'd cook a meal for her, she hadn't expected a picnic in December.

The scent coming from her kitchen pulled her like a magnet. But when she reached the archway, it wasn't the food that had her mouth watering. It was the man. He was wearing coal-colored jeans, a black turtleneck sweater, and his feet were bare. Unlike his uniform, these clothes fit him like a second skin and incredibly, her palms began to itch. In her mind, she pictured him without the clothes and her insides went into a meltdown.

Get a grip. She shifted her gaze to his hands as he moved chicken breasts from a skillet into bowls and ladled sauce over them. Although the aroma drew her, all she could think about was how those wide, hard palms had felt on her skin. What those long fingers had felt like as they'd moved inside of her.

He didn't have to kiss her or touch her to make her want him. He just had to *be*.

How in the world can you want to jump him so soon after what you did to each other in the shower?

"Can I help?"

He turned and slowly swept his eyes over her. "You could pour some wine."

If he continued to look at her like that, she was going to drag him to the floor. And if he could tell what she was thinking, he'd suspect she was a nymphomaniac.

With an effort to control herself, Cat moved to the uncorked bottle sitting on the counter and tipped wine into two waiting glasses. Turning, she watched him sprinkle some freshly chopped herbs on top of the chicken breasts, then place a knife and fork in each bowl. When he'd finished, she handed him a glass, then took a sip of her own.

Say something. Anything.

"When you said you were going to whip something up, I didn't expect gourmet fare. Did the navy teach you to cook like this?"

"No. All the Angelis men can cook. My cousins and I grew up in our family's restaurant, The Poseidon." Leaning a hip against the counter, he took a drink of his wine. "You'd like it there, I think."

Cat knew from the file her father had given her that Dino had lost his father and aunt in a boating accident when he was eleven and that his mother and uncle had blended the two families.

"My uncle was hoping that one of us would eventually take over the restaurant and continue in the family business, but it didn't happen. However, there's still hope. My cousin Nik has married a caterer, and last year my uncle Spiro married Helena, a five-star chef from Greece. So there's still a good possibility that an Angelis will take over The Poseidon one day. My mother who has strong psychic powers predicts that Angelises will run the restaurant for some time."

"Your mother has psychic powers?"

Dino nodded. "She has a very successful practice in San Francisco."

Cat tilted her head to one side and studied him for a moment. "You said earlier that you accepted the job my father offered because you had a 'feeling' that you should. Do you have psychic powers, too?"

Dino shrugged. "Sometimes I get hunches. It seems to run

in the family. All of my cousins seem to have inherited some kind of power. Philly's is the strongest. She has a special gift with animals."

He handed her his glass, then balancing a loaf of bread on one of the bowls, he lifted them. "This isn't really picnic fare, but there's no place in your apartment to eat."

"You noticed." Cat led the way into the living room.

When they were seated with the steaming bowls in front of them, Dino broke off a piece of bread, dipped it into the sauce in her bowl and offered it to her.

Cat tried it and the flavors exploded on her tongue. Once she'd swallowed, she said, "What did you put in there?"

"Wine, garlic, oregano."

Eager now, she took the piece of bread he offered and dipped again. "It's marvelous."

"Where do you usually eat?"

She sliced into the chicken. "Restaurants mostly. Or I do takeout and eat it in my office or standing up in the kitchen."

She chewed and swallowed, and then sighed. "This is so good. If I thought I might be able to accomplish something like this, I'd take cooking lessons."

"I could teach you."

She grinned at him over the rim of her wineglass. "I'll give you fair warning. I've been known to burn water."

He met her eyes. "I love a challenge."

Trying to ignore the little thrill that moved through her, she set her glass down and cut another piece of chicken. "You know, we're still practically strangers."

"Ask me anything you want."

"You're very close to your family."

He handed her another piece of bread. "As close as brothers and a kid sister can be. We were raised in the same house, learned to sail and fish together. And fight together. Except for Philly. We kept her out of our fights. Mostly."

"I've often wished for a brother or a sister. Not that my father didn't try to fill a multitude of roles after my mother died. When my uncle Jack's around he tries to play big brother."

"What's your uncle like?" Dino asked.

"Hmm." Cat considered while she took a sip of wine. "My Uncle Jack is like Peter Pan—he never quite wants to grow up. And he's pretty good at playing big brother. It's just that you can't talk to your father or your uncle about boys. Or fashion."

She wrinkled her nose. "I learned early on not to take my father shoe shopping. He told me after our first shoe excursion that he understood for the first time why some soldiers went AWOL."

Dino threw back his head and laughed. As the rich sound of it filled the room, Cat felt her heart flutter again. It occurred to her that she felt very much at ease sitting here on the floor of her living room with this man she'd known for less than a day. In fact, she felt more at home than she ever had before.

Oddly disturbed by the thought, she turned her attention back to finding out more about Dino Angelis. "If you were so close to your family, why did you leave San Francisco?"

Finished with his meal, Dino leaned back against the coffee table and reached for his wine. "From the time I was a little boy, I had this feeling that I was meant to join the navy. I suppose it was partly because all the Angelis men are drawn to the sea. My father is descended from Greek fishermen and my mother's father was a ship builder in Sausalito."

Studying him in the flickering candlelight, Cat could easily picture him on the sea—hauling in fishing nets or at the helm.

She could also imagine him as a craftsman, running those capable hands over the helm of a sleekly crafted boat.

She recalled from her father's file that he'd worked special ops, and her first impression of him was that he looked like a warrior. Yet, today in her store, he'd played the role of a helpful fiancé perfectly.

Was being her lover just another part of the op for him? And why should that bother her? After all, she'd outlined the parameters of their relationship, hadn't she?

She stacked their empty bowls and carried them out to the kitchen. After rinsing them, she inserted them neatly in a dishwasher she rarely used. When she turned, she found he'd followed her with their empty wineglasses. He reached around her to place them on the counter, and his body brushed against hers.

The rush of heat was immediate and strong. This close, she caught his scent—her soap and something very male.

She moistened suddenly dry lips. "Playing a fake fiancé has to be a far cry from what you're used to. I'll bet you'll be relieved on New Year's Day when you can get back to working for my godfather at the Pentagon."

"Actually, Admiral Maxwell is expediting my discharge papers."

"You're leaving the navy? Why?"

"You could say I'm following one of my feelings again. I miss my family and I want more balance in my life."

She met his eyes steadily. "Do you always act on your feelings?"

"Almost always." He reached out to tuck a stray curl behind her ear. "Like right now, I want to make love to you again." Leaning down, he angled his head and nipped at her ear. "Have you ever made love in your kitchen?"

"No." But she placed both hands on his chest when he started to draw her closer. "I can't remember ever acting just on my feelings before. I don't understand it."

"Do you have to?"

"I usually like to. I prefer to have a goal so that I know where I'm going. I like to map out all the details. With you it's different. I don't want to think about the future and I don't want to consider the consequences. I just want to live in the present. You're a first for me, Dino."

"You're a first for me, too, Cat."

Hearing him say it and seeing the truth of it in his eyes, she felt a tight band inside of her ease. "I don't know where we're going."

"Neither do I." He took her fingers and raised them to his lips. "We don't have to. All we have to do for tonight is enjoy each other."

She smiled at him then. "I have one request."

His eyebrows rose. "Only one?"

"I want to touch you. All over. But first, I want you out of your clothes." She took his arm, running her hand from his shoulder to his wrist and linked her fingers with his. Then she drew him with her through the archway.

8

"I WANT TO SEE YOU NAKED," Cat said. "That's how I imagined you when I first saw you in the kitchen tonight."

"Really?"

"Oh, yes. And it's not a habit of mine to undress men in my mind." Pausing in front of the coffee table, she turned to study him. "Perhaps it's because I didn't get to see enough of you in the shower. That space is pretty confined."

Raising their linked hands, he pressed his lips to her fingers. "I didn't notice."

She pulled her hand free and slipped it beneath the edge of his sweater. "Let's get you out of this."

Together they pulled it off and dropped it on the floor. Watching the twinkling lights of the tree flicker over the golden tone of his skin, her desire for him sharpened and Cat fisted her hands at her sides. She had a plan. "As a navy man, you're used to following rules?"

"You could say that."

Slowly she shifted her gaze to his. "I only have one for you. You can't touch me until I'm through touching you."

"You're asking for a hands-off policy?"

"Exactly."

It had been a mistake to look into his eyes. The smoky heat she saw there was a mirror image of her own feelings, and for a moment she completely lost her train of thought. All she had to do was step forward, press her mouth to his, and she would once again experience that whirlwind of passion he could sweep her into. Fighting against the temptation, she shifted her attention to his lips and traced the shape of them with one finger.

When he drew it into his mouth and nipped it, an arrow of pleasure shot right to her toes. "The rules…"

"I didn't touch you. Yet."

Cat drew in a shaky breath and dragged her gaze determinedly to his shoulders. She ran her palms over them, absorbing the surprisingly silky texture on the surface and the hint of steel-hard muscles beneath. The contrast fascinated her as did the difference in their skin tones. Finally, she gave in to the temptation to explore his chest, grazing his nipples with her nails and then watching them harden.

Unable to resist, she leaned closer, gripping his waist for balance as she used her tongue and teeth first on one nipple and then the other. Each of his responses—his sharp intake of breath, the hiss of her name, the rapid beat of his heart—thrilled her.

Once again, she wanted to move closer, but remembering her goal, she fought off the urge. Instead, she ran her hands up to his ribs and around to his back.

"You have the sexiest back. I can't tell you how many times I caught myself staring at it today." That was the ticket, she thought. Just keep talking. She ran her nails lightly down his spine to his waist. "As soon as I have you out of the rest of your clothes, I want you to lie down on the sofa and I'll give your back the attention it deserves. But first…" She pulled open the snap of his jeans.

"I'm betting we don't make it to the sofa."

Cat didn't reply because it was taking all her concentration to lower his zipper. Biting down hard on her lower lip, she started to drag down the snug fitting jeans.

"Wait."

Stilling her hands, she glanced up in time to see him dig into his back pocket and drop condoms on the table.

"Three." The sight of them sent such an intense surge of heat through her that Cat was surprised she didn't just liquefy on the spot.

"Since I go with my feelings, I like to be prepared."

Cat sank to her knees and refocused her attention on tugging the jeans down his legs. Beneath them, he wore a pair of black briefs, stretched almost sheer, that clearly revealed the size of his erection. In some part of her mind that was still functioning, she knew that together, they managed to strip the jeans off, but she couldn't tear her gaze away from those briefs and what they were trying to cover.

Swallowing to moisten a dry throat, she said, "It's like a present."

"Consider it yours." Dino wasn't sure how much longer he was going to be able to follow Cat's rules. Then he simply stopped thinking when she traced a finger down the length of him.

"On Christmas Eve, I always snuck downstairs once everyone was asleep and I would touch each one of my presents, lifting each package and shaking them. It was torture knowing that I couldn't open them."

"You're a big girl now, Cat."

"Yes. I am." She drew down the briefs, and Dino stepped out of them.

For a moment, neither of them spoke or moved. Each time she exhaled, he felt the heat of her breath on his penis. And above the mournful sound of the jazz trumpet, Dino was certain he could hear the beat of his own heart. Or was it hers?

"It's going to blow my plan to hell, but I have to touch you." Then she closed a hand over him and milked him in one long pull.

"Cat—" He had to shift one of his feet to keep his balance.

"You like that?"

His only reply was a moan when she pulled her hand along the length of him again.

"Let's try this."

Dino came close to losing his balance again when her mouth closed around him. He couldn't breathe, could barely think. Yet, every one of his senses had sharpened. He was aware of the slow steady wail of the trumpet, of the way the Christmas tree lights brought out the darker red highlights in her hair, of the sharpness of her fingernails as she dug them into his buttocks. But mostly he was aware of how that hot, avid mouth was dragging him closer and closer to the edge of reason. And he was powerless to stop her.

He'd experienced desire before—the wild and reckless kind, the warm and needy kind. But no woman had ever made him weak. Helpless. His arms felt like lead. And when she began to suckle him, taking him deeper and deeper into the wet, hot recesses of her mouth, he felt the orgasm begin to build at the base of his spine.

But he wanted to be inside of her when he came—when they both came. The unbearable need for that intimacy gave him the strength to close his hands around the sides of her head and gently draw her away. He managed to maintain some control until he sank to his knees and they were face to face.

"I'm not through yet," she said.

"I don't always follow the rules." Then he crushed her mouth with his.

The kiss was desperate and demanding, exactly what Cat was craving. She heard the rip of silk, but later couldn't recall any other details of how her clothes had disappeared. All she could remember was those fast clever hands as they raced over her, pressing, possessing. She knew exactly what he was feeling because she was experiencing the same mindless pleasure. No one had ever set her this free with a touch. Reveling in it, she dug her nails into his shoulders to keep him with her when he tried to draw away.

"Condom," he said.

In the twinkling lights of the tree she watched him kneel and sheath himself. Then he made a place for himself between her thighs. Drawing him in, she wrapped arms and legs around him, then met him thrust for thrust. The storm built quickly until it far surpassed the one that had been battering the city all day.

"Look at me."

His face was above hers, filling her vision and her world. And she felt herself sinking into that dark, intense gaze.

Just before she did, she said, "Come with me."

Increasing the speed of his thrusts, he took them both over the edge.

DINO PAUSED in the doorway to Cat's bedroom, studying her sleeping form on the bed. It was the only time she was completely still. Since he had no idea how sound a sleeper she was, he'd waited, not moving, for fifteen minutes after her breathing had become steady.

She'd curled into him in sleep, throwing her arm across his chest as if to keep him there. Lord help him, he'd wanted to stay. Incredibly, he'd wanted to wake her and make love to her again. But the clock was ticking. This might be his only chance to search the doll Cat had tucked into her tote. And it was beginning to bother him that Jase hadn't called him back.

A glance at his watch told him it was nearly midnight, almost three hours since he'd talked to him. Surely, it wouldn't have taken the man this long to search those dolls.

He spotted Cat's tote on the narrow table behind the sofa. Shutting the bedroom door, he crossed to it, careful not to tread on the clothes they'd left scattered on the floor. The snow had stopped, and stars dotted a clear black sky.

Stepping closer to the window, he glanced down at the courtyard. Lights were twinkling on the trees, and a floodlight from the back entrance to the apartment building illuminated much of the area. Only the alleyway was shrouded in darkness. Still, Dino caught a movement near the door to the Cheshire Cat. Grabbing the binoculars he'd noticed earlier, he lifted them and focused the lens.

Two figures were fighting in the opened doorway to Cat's store. They were about the same height, both shorter than Jase, and appeared to be well matched. Locked in a fierce embrace, they tumbled onto the floor of the alley, rolled across it, each one claiming, then losing the upper position.

For an instant, they were out of sight behind a Dumpster. Then one scrambled to his feet and headed in the direction of the courtyard. The attempt at escape was prevented when the other figure took the first one down in a hard tackle.

Dino set down the binoculars and quickly pulled on his jeans and sweater. Where in the hell was Jase?

Damn! He'd left his shoes in Cat's bedroom. Moving quickly to the door, he eased it open, spotted his shoes near the foot of the bed, and retrieved them. He'd covered half the distance to the living room when Cat said, "Where are you going?"

He turned back. "I couldn't sleep. I thought I'd watch one of your movies."

She yawned hugely and threw back the covers. "I'll join you."

Dino thought fast while she pulled a robe out of the closet. "You should get some sleep. You have a busy day tomorrow."

She shot him a smile. "So will you."

By the time she'd closed the distance between them, Dino decided to go with the truth. "Look, I spotted two men fighting in the alleyway by your store. And the door to the Cheshire Cat is open. I'm going to check it out."

"I'll go with you."

"No." He grabbed her by the shoulders. "I'm trained to handle this kind of thing. You're not. You'll just get in my way. And every minute I spend arguing with you, they could get away."

EVEN AS HER HEART RACED, Cat stopped struggling and stared at him. There was something in his tone—the ring of command?—that had her saying, "Okay. Okay."

Feeling a bit numb, she stood in the bedroom doorway and watched as he grabbed his leather bomber jacket, then met her eyes again. His were cold as steel.

Suppressing a shiver, she wrapped her arms around herself. This was a side of Dino Angelis she hadn't seen before.

"Lock this door when I'm gone. Understand?"

She nodded. But as soon as he'd disappeared, it was the window she rushed to. Grabbing the binoculars, she focused on the alley. It was deserted, but the door to her shop was open. How—and then she saw him.

Not two men but one, sitting in the snow at the courtyard

end of the alley way, his back propped against the brick wall of a building. One of his hands was gripping his shoulder, and the twinkling lights on the courtyard trees winked on and off across his features.

The face was familiar. Cat's heart shot to her throat and lodged there. She allowed herself a few more seconds as the lights blinked on and off. The time only made her more certain. The man sitting in the snow was her uncle Jack.

And he was hurt.

Fear iced her veins, as questions spiraled through her mind. How? Why?

Where was the other man and where was Dino?

Dropping the binoculars onto the couch, she grabbed jeans, struggling into them as she half ran, half hopped into her bedroom. She dragged a sweater over her head, shoved her feet into boots and raced out the door.

It had to be a dream. A nightmare. She burst through the door to the stairwell and flew down the three flights. *Uncle Jack.*

What had he been doing in the alleyway? When she finally ran into the courtyard, the only man she saw was Dino. He was crouched down near the spot where she'd seen her uncle. As she reached him, she stumbled.

Strong hands gripped her shoulders and steadied her.

"I told you to stay in the apartment."

"I couldn't." Cat still stared at snow, at the impression where a man had been seated. "Where did he go?"

"Where did who go?"

"The man." She glanced down the alley way, but the snow had been so disturbed that no footprints were visible. "He was sitting right here. I was sure it was—"

She broke off the moment she saw it—the dark red stain right near the wall of the building. A fresh surge of fear moved through her as she tore her gaze away from it and met Dino's eyes. "That's blood, isn't it?"

"Yes. Who do you think you saw?"

"I thought—but I must have been mistaken. It doesn't make any sense. My mind's playing tricks on me." She clamped her lips together as she heard the hysteria rising in her voice.

Dino gave her a shake. "Who do you think it was, Cat?"

"My uncle Jack." Drawing in a deep breath, Cat gathered herself. It wouldn't do to fall apart. She had to think.

"Your uncle Jack Phillips who works for the CIA?"

"Yes. But he called me just a few days ago from Mexico. Surely, he would have told me if he was coming to New York."

"Why did he call?"

"To chat. He wanted to know how sales were going, if I was overworking myself."

"Do you know where in Mexico he called from?"

She shook her head slowly as she narrowed her eyes. "Why are you asking all these questions? And how do you know my Uncle Jack works for the CIA?"

DINO ANSWERED THE LATTER QUESTION and prayed it would distract her from the first one. "Your father mentioned it in your file."

"And you didn't see him when you reached the courtyard?"

"No. There was no one here." Dino glanced down the alleyway, but during the course of their fight, the two men he'd seen had crushed down a lot of the snow. "Did your uncle have the code to your security alarm?"

"No."

"But as a CIA agent, he probably possessed the skills necessary to bypass it."

Cat twisted out of his grip, her eyes narrowing further. "Just what are you suggesting?"

Dino jerked his head in the direction of her shop where the door stood wide-open. "Someone got into the Cheshire Cat tonight, and they didn't set off the alarm."

Before he could stop her, she was past him, running toward the shop.

"Cat." He followed and grabbed her hand, halting her as they reached the door. He couldn't send her back to the apartment because he couldn't be sure that she'd be safe there. Just as he couldn't be sure that Jase was in any condition to provide backup.

"I'm going to have to take you in there with me, but you're going to have to stay behind me and follow orders."

"This is my shop."

Even in the dim light, he could see her eyes glint with anger.

"And right now the man who hurt your uncle may be in there. Judging by the blood stains, I think we can presume he's armed."

Deliberately, Dino removed his gun from his pocket. "I want your word that you'll stay behind me and follow orders."

Her gaze had dropped to the gun and she swallowed hard. "All right. Yes."

Dino felt something twist in his gut. He'd meant to scare her and he had. But he shoved his feelings aside and, flattening himself against the wall, reached round to turn on the light.

The room was empty. Still using his body to shield Cat, he closed the door behind them.

"Reset the alarm."

He led the way across the room, gripping the gun with both hands. Dino's instinct told him that both men he'd spotted fighting in the alley were long gone. But he wasn't about to take any chances.

In the doorway to the front of the shop, Dino once again flipped on the light, then fanned the room with the gun.

"Stay here," he whispered to Cat. Then he moved forward, keeping his back to the wall. Finally when he'd checked every hiding place he waved her to him.

"Can you tell if anything's missing?" he asked softly.

Without saying a word, she moved to the cashbox behind the counter and checked it.

"The money is all here," Cat whispered. "There wasn't much. We do most of our business by credit cards." Then she glanced at the staircase. "But the dolls…"

"Stay here. I'll go up first and let you know when to follow."

He was halfway up when he heard the moan. Signaling Cat to stay where she was, Dino took the rest of the stairs in twos. He flipped on the lights and found Jase sitting by the filing cabinets holding his head in his hands.

"What happened?" Dino asked.

"Wish the hell I knew. I let myself in the front door, reset the alarm. I came up here to check the dolls." He nodded toward the shelves. "I started at the far end and checked each one. The heads are porcelain, the bodies cloth, and there's nothing to indicate that one of them was stuffed with anything different than the others. The last thing I remember before the lights went out is something that felt like a bee sting." Jase tapped his leg. "I'm figuring whoever it was took me out with some kind of hypodermic injection." He glanced at his watch. "That was two hours ago."

"You all right?"

"Yeah. Whatever drug he or she used has worn off. The blow to my pride might take a while to heal though." He flashed Dino a grin. "Of course, catching the person who did it would be the perfect pick-me-up."

Dino glanced around the room. "Maybe he was up here when you entered, heard you and hid." Jase Campbell wasn't a man who was easily taken by surprise. "There's room behind one of those filing cabinets."

Dino looked back at the shelves where the dolls were still neatly lined up and took a quick visual count. "They're all still there."

"Perhaps because none of them contains the drugs." Jase moved to the filing cabinets. "So he hides behind one of these and lets me search all the dolls for drugs. When I get close enough, he takes me out and leaves."

"What drugs?"

Dino drew in a deep breath and turned slowly to find Cat standing at the top of the stairs, her hands on her hips, her eyes flashing. She waved a hand at Jase. "Who is this man and why did he search my dolls for drugs?"

"Cat McGuire, this is Jase Campbell, an old navy buddy of mine. He owns his own security firm now."

Her foot began to tap and she bit out each word. "Why is he searching my dolls for drugs?"

"I asked him to."

Jase eased himself up from the floor. "I think this is my cue to exit."

Cat whirled on him. "Not until I find out what's going on here."

Jase inclined his head toward Dino. "He can tell you everything. I work for him." Then he turned to Dino. "I'm going to check around, see if the coast is clear. Then I'll be back and help you get her safely to the apartment."

Giving Cat a brief nod, he strolled toward the stairs and began his descent.

"Well?" Cat asked.

Dino drew a deep breath. This wasn't the way he'd intended to tell her, but he'd known from the moment he'd pulled out his gun in the alley that the time for keeping her in the dark was over. And there was no way to sugarcoat the truth. "Your store is under investigation. It's believed that someone is using the Cheshire Cat to smuggle cocaine in from Paxco, Mexico."

9

HER HEAD STILL SPINNING, Cat paced back and forth in her office, trying to walk off her anger. Dino had insisted on seeing Jase out so that he could make sure that the place was secure. She could hardly argue with that since more than one person had evidently been making themselves at home in her store tonight.

And she needed a moment to gather herself. To think. Her first reaction to what Dino had told her had been furious denial. There was still a part of her that wanted to believe that what he'd told her was impossible. But there'd been something in his eyes that had doubt and fear surging through her.

Whirling, she faced the beautiful dolls her mother had designed. Had someone used them to smuggle drugs? She didn't want it to be true. But Dino obviously believed that it was. He'd hired a security expert to search her dolls. The image of Dino in the alley, carrying that gun as if it belonged in his hand, came to her.

Okay. That much was understandable. He'd worked in special ops. He was used to dangerous assignments. But why had he brought a gun to the job of playing her dazzled fiancé? Then she recalled his strange reaction when she'd raced out of the store to meet the FedEx man—the way he'd shoved her behind him as if he were protecting her from danger. A suspicion formed in her mind.

She strode the length of her office again. Navy Captain Dino Angelis had a lot of explaining to do. But for now, she refocused on the people who'd broken into her supposedly locked store.

She tapped her fingers. There was Jase and the man who'd knocked Jase out. Dino had claimed he'd seen two men fighting in the alley. One of them must have been Uncle Jack and he'd been wounded.

Had her uncle been in the Cheshire Cat, too?

Why? And who had been fighting with him in that alley? Not Jase. He'd been unconscious in her office.

And why hadn't anyone called the police? She strode to her desk, but she didn't reach for the phone. Because the word forming a drumbeat in the back of her mind was *drugs*.

No, it couldn't be possible. She glanced again at the dolls she'd lined up on the shelves, each one sitting on a client's order form and waiting to be placed in a Cheshire Cat gift bag. They'd been created from her mother's design. How could someone have used them to smuggle drugs?

Quickly, she strode to the shelves and one by one she examined each doll, pressing and probing. But all she felt beneath the smooth cotton was the finely milled sawdust she'd been promised. Next she tested the weight of each one in her hands. They were all exactly the same.

And they were all still here. Surely, if one of them had contained drugs, it would be missing. Jase and Dino had to be mistaken. There weren't any drugs in her dolls.

But then why had her shop been broken into? Who had hurt her uncle Jack?

Think. She wasn't an idiot. Nor could she afford to be an ostrich and bury her head in the sand. The dolls on the shelves in her shop weren't the only ones that had arrived from Paxco,

Mexico, that day. Perhaps one of the other three contained the shipment of drugs. With a sigh, Cat sank into her desk chair and dropped her head into her hands.

That was the way that Dino found her when he climbed up to the office again. Something around his heart tightened. He wanted badly to go to her, take her into his arms and just hold her. Ruthlessly, he pushed his feelings aside. That might be what she needed, but it had nothing to do with the job he'd been hired to do.

Jase was going to check out the two apartments and make sure that his man was still on duty there. Then he would come back and help him get Cat safely back into her building.

After that, Jase was going to check more thoroughly into Jack Phillips' business in Mexico. Dino planned to have a little heart-to-heart with Cat's father on the same topic.

But no steps he took now mitigated the fact that he'd been in bed with Cat while someone had broken into her store. Jase had been drugged, and from the evidence, it looked as though her uncle had been wounded.

He'd already taken too many missteps where she was concerned. Still, he would have preferred to deal with the Cat who had stood at the top of the stairs a few moments ago, her temper flaring.

As if she'd read his mind, she straightened her shoulders, rose and whirled to face him. One look at the controlled fury on her face had relief streaming through him.

"I have a few questions for you, Captain Angelis."

"Fire away."

"Who are you really working for?"

"Your father."

"But he didn't just hire you to be my fiancé for the holidays and bring peace and joy to my family until Lucia Merceri flies her broomstick back to Rome. He hardly needed a navy captain trained in special ops for that, did he?"

"I suppose not."

Her hands fisted at her sides. "I feel so stupid. I should have suspected something. But you…you totally blindsided me."

There was angry accusation in her tone, and he sympathized with it entirely. "If it's any consolation, the blindsiding was mutual."

"Not just in the line of duty?"

"No." It was in that moment that Dino decided he was going to tell her everything. Not only was it the best way to keep her safe, but she deserved the truth.

"If I'd been sticking to the line-of-duty stuff, I never should have touched you."

For a moment, there was silence in the room, but Cat's voice was still cool when she demanded, "So why did my father really hire you—and I want it all. No more lies."

"You'd better sit down." Dino moved to the cabinet where she kept brandy and poured some into a snifter.

"How did you know I keep brandy there?"

"I searched this office while I was making the dollhouse."

"Of course you did."

When she took the snifter from his outstretched hand, Dino thought for a moment that he might end up wearing it. But she finally set it next to her on the desk and crossed her arms in front of her. "Tell me everything."

"As I said before, someone is using your shop to smuggle very high-quality cocaine from Mexico into Manhattan for an elite clientele."

When she didn't flinch, didn't argue, Dino knew with some relief that she'd already accepted the possibility.

"There's proof?"

"Enough to involve the FBI, the CIA, and Homeland Security."

Her brows snapped together. "Why Homeland Security?"

"They suspect that the profits from the smuggling are being funneled to terrorist cells in this country."

She reached for the brandy then and took a careful sip. Her hand only trembled a little, but her voice was perfectly steady. "Smuggling *and* terrorists. It just keeps getting better and better."

She began to pace. Was it only hours ago that he'd watched her do the same thing while she was trying to figure out what to do about the attraction they were feeling for each other? When she'd admitted to him that he was the only toy she wanted for Christmas.

"There have to be people involved at both ends. Do they know who?"

"They have their suspicions. According to your father, the CIA is handling the surveillance in Mexico. The feds and Homeland Security are trying not to trip over each other up here. They haven't moved yet because they don't just want to catch the people who are supplying and receiving the drugs. They want the kingpin behind the whole operation."

She stopped and turned to face him. "And they suspect someone in the Cheshire Cat is passing the drug-stuffed toys on to this kingpin?"

"Yes."

"Well, they're wrong. Adelaide and Matt love this store almost as much as I do."

Dino said nothing.

"As for Josie, well, to think that she's part of some kind of smuggling ring is ridiculous."

"People will do a lot for money. Or ideology."

Cat snorted. "Next, you'll tell me that they suspect me."

When he didn't immediately answer, she read it in his eyes. "They suspect me!"

"You're the prime suspect. But they also have their eyes on the others. Any one of your employees could be passing the drugs on. I've only spent a matter of hours here, but Josie and Adelaide know where everything is. I'll bet they both know the security code to the store. Matt, too, I'm betting. You trust them implicitly."

Her chin lifted. "Yes, I do. They're not involved in this. I'd stake my life on it."

Dino let his voice chill. "No matter how much you trust them, if you let any one of them know about this, you *are* staking your life on it."

"It's ridiculous to think that one of them would harm me."

But there was a frown in her eyes as she took another sip of the brandy. "So according to the FBI, the CIA and Homeland Security, I'm either a stupid patsy or I've decided to get a little extra excitement in my life by smuggling drugs. Who knows? Maybe I got into it to feed my own habit?"

Dino said nothing.

She glanced around the room once before meeting his eyes again. "What do you believe, Captain Angelis?"

He met her gaze steadily. "I won't lie to you. Your father believes you to be as innocent as the kind of child you cater to in this store. But originally, I had my doubts."

Her chin lifted. "And was seducing me part of your plan to clear up those doubts?"

He moved quickly then and grabbed her by the shoulders. "As I recall, the seduction was mutual. If I'd had any idea that we were going to become lovers, I never would have taken this assignment."

But hadn't he known on some level from the first time he'd looked at her photo that they were going to end up as lovers?

Dropping his hands, he took a careful step back. "If it makes any difference, I only had to be in this shop with you for half a day to know that you weren't involved."

Her eyes searched his face. "How could you be so sure?"

"You love this place. And you would never have used a doll your mother designed to smuggle drugs."

She stepped toward him then and wrapped her arms around him. Her cheek nuzzled into his neck in a gesture that he found incredibly endearing. In spite of his resolve, his arms went around her and held tight.

She should hate him for deceiving her. That might have made it easier for him to keep his hands off of her—to do his job. But each time he thought he could anticipate what she would do, she surprised him.

Dino found himself trapped again, this time not by her passion and fire, but by her vulnerability.

Finally, she lifted her head and said, "So, what are we going to do?"

He snapped his mind back to reality. "*We're* not going to do anything. I'm going to take you back to your apartment and you're going to sleep. And you're going to let Jase and me do our job."

Her eyes gleamed with determination. "The two of you haven't located the drugs yet, have you?"

"No."

"I think I know where they are." She tapped a finger against his chest. "They're in the damaged doll. All of the other dolls are the same. And anyone who knows me, would be certain that I wouldn't sell that doll to anyone."

Dino suppressed an inward sigh. That was his suspicion, too.

"This is my shop and I intend to find out who is using it to finance terrorists. You have two choices. You can work with me, or I'll work on my own."

As she took his hand and led him down the spiral staircase, he said goodbye to any hope he had of making her take a back seat while he figured out how to keep her out of trouble.

SOMETHING WAS WRONG. Dino sensed it the moment they reached Cat's apartment. For starters, there was a thin band of light seeping out beneath the door. Jase had checked out the apartment earlier, and he would have turned off all the lights. His friend had left once he'd seen them inside the front door of the building. Signaling Cat to be quiet, Dino positioned her on one side of the door and moved to the other. Then he listened for any sound.

Nothing.

"Didn't Jase check out the apartment?" Cat whispered.

Dino nodded and held out his hand for the key. Inserting it in the lock, he whispered, "You stay there until I say it's safe."

He pushed open the door and went in low. But there was no need to fan the room with his gun. A man was sitting on Cat's sofa with his feet propped on her coffee table. The Tiffany-style lamp on the table backlit him in a soft glow. He had stripped down to a bloodstained T-shirt. With one hand he was holding a pressure bandage to his right shoulder. His other hand held a lit cigar.

"Uncle Jack!"

Before Dino could stop her, Cat shot past him, but she stopped short of the coffee table. "You're hurt."

"It's just a scratch."

"I saw the blood in the snow."

"Most of that was from the other guy. He pulled a knife and sliced me, but I wrestled it away and managed to give him a taste of his own medicine."

"I'm going to get the first-aid kit." She dashed toward the bedroom, but in the doorway, she turned back. "Uncle Jack, this is my fiancé Captain Dino Angelis." Then she whirled again and was gone.

"I'd rather have a beer," Jack muttered.

Dino closed the door and leaned against it. In person, Jack Phillips looked younger than his years. He recalled Cat's description of him as a real life Peter Pan. It fit. "She doesn't have any."

"I know."

"I can offer you wine or bottled water. She may have some brandy."

"I'll pass for now." Jack met his eyes. "Why don't you put that gun away? We're on the same side."

"Are we?" Dino slipped his weapon into his jacket pocket. "Why don't you tell me what you're really doing here?"

Lowering his voice, Jack said, "I'm trying to keep my niece from getting her pretty throat slit."

"And breaking into her store is how you do that?"

Jack was saved from answering when Cat reentered the room. For the next few minutes, Dino watched Cat minister to her uncle's wound—which really was only a scratch. Evidently, the man could handle himself in a fight. A grudging admiration warred with something else as he observed the easy rapport between the two. Jealousy?

That was ridiculous. Jack Phillips was her uncle.

He had to get a grip. Whatever emotions she was pulling out of him, they were distracting him from concentrating on the job. One thing was clear. Phillips hadn't come to Cat's apartment to take advantage of her nursing skills. Dino let his gaze shift slowly around the room.

The signs were subtle, a drawer in the desk left slightly open, the shade on the window that overlooked the courtyard raised higher than when he'd seen the two men locked in that desperate struggle earlier.

Had Jack Phillips been alternately checking the courtyard while he'd been searching his niece's apartment? That's exactly what Dino would have done.

What was Jack Phillips' game? There wasn't a doubt in Dino's mind that Phillips was James McGuire's CIA informant. The question was how deeply was Cat's uncle involved in what was going on in Paxco?

"There." Cat laid a final piece of tape over her uncle's "scratch."

Then she rose and said, "Now, I want you to explain the remark you made to Dino about keeping me from getting my throat slit."

When Jack shot him a look, Dino smiled. "You might as well come clean. She knows just about everything."

"You came here to search my apartment," Cat said.

Dino shrugged. "See?"

Jack turned to Cat, a woeful expression on his face. "How can you accuse me of something like that?"

Cat crossed her arms across her chest and began to tap her foot. "I'm not a kid anymore, Uncle Jack. I saw you in that alley. The door to my shop was open, and Dino's friend Jase was taken out with a hypodermic syringe."

Jack tapped his chest with his free hand. "And you suspect *moi?*"

Cat fisted her hands on her hips. "It's more than a suspicion. Don't you remember bragging to me when I was *much* younger about special drugs that the CIA had that once injected into the victim would put him out for hours?"

Dino began to enjoy himself. He figured the score was Cat one; Jack zero.

"You might as well admit it. You were already there searching the dolls when Jase arrived—so you took him out with a hypodermic, didn't you?"

Jack shifted uncomfortably. "I'm taking the Fifth."

With a sound very much like a snort, Cat waved a hand in the direction of her tote bag. "And then there's the small matter that you moved my tote bag. Probably after you searched it. I'd already come to the conclusion that the doll with the ripped lace contained the drugs. Ask Dino."

"Shit," Jack muttered. He glanced at Dino. "They marked the doll by ripping the lace?"

"That's our current theory," Dino said. "We were about to check it out."

"I could use a drink. Maybe you could look for that brandy?"

Cat sent Dino a warning glance. "Not a chance. Don't give him a thing until he comes clean. To borrow a phrase, he's in this up to his 'pretty throat.'"

Ruffled, Jack rose to his feet. "I never thought I'd see the day when my own niece would turn against me."

"Hah!" Cat stepped toward him. "Who's turned against whom? You didn't express one iota of surprise when I introduced Dino as my fiancé." She pointed an accusing finger at her uncle. "You've been in contact with my father."

When Jack opened his mouth to protest, Cat raised one hand to cut him off.

"Don't bother to deny it. That's one of his cigars you're smoking. He's filled you in on everything, hasn't he?"

"I think it's the other way around," Dino said softly, his gaze on Jack Phillips.

Jack and Cat both turned to look at him.

"When he hired me, McGuire kept referring to his CIA informant. Since the CIA doesn't usually have the reputation of being loose-lipped, I had Jase Campbell check you out. When Cat told me that the last time you'd contacted her, you were in Mexico, it wasn't hard to put two and two together. You're running the CIA surveillance on the Paxco end of this operation, aren't you?"

Cat shifted her gaze from Dino to her uncle. "You knew my shop was being used to funnel drugs into this country and you didn't think you should tell me?"

Jack sighed. "I figured the less you knew the safer you'd be. And if the original plan had gone smoothly, it would be over. You'd be free and clear of it by now."

"I want to know everything you know, Uncle Jack." She rounded on Dino. "You, too. I won't be left in the dark about this anymore."

When Jack still hesitated, Dino said, "I'd advise you to tell her everything. Otherwise, she'll just poke around until she figures it out."

Noting that Cat's face had turned very pale, Dino moved into the kitchen, located a bottle of brandy and poured three glasses. When he'd told her about the smuggling earlier, she'd probably still entertained some hope that there was a mistake. Now it was beginning to really sink in.

"You and your father are so much alike," Jack said. "Stubborn, demanding. Why couldn't you be more like your mother?"

"Quit stalling. First, tell me everything you know about the drugs."

Dino distributed the brandy. "He knows a lot about them.

And when he found out your shop was involved, he contacted your father."

Jack glared at Dino. "Talk about loose lips."

"You and my father are actually working together on this?"

"You could say that." Jack took a good slug of the brandy.

"Then it must be serious." She shifted her gaze to Dino. "Uncle Jack and my father mix about as well as oil and water."

"It's deadly serious. That man I was fighting with in the alley was a pro." Jack glanced at Dino. "He came in just after I took out your man. I barely had time to duck back behind the cabinet. Seeing the body on the floor made him a bit wary, and his examination of the dolls was cursory. He must have known to look for the ripped lace. I didn't have a second hypodermic so I followed him out. But he must have sensed me. He jumped me the moment I stepped into the alley. He probably thought I had the doll."

"So whoever is behind this is desperate enough to hire a pro to do his or her dirty work," Dino said.

"The bastard has kept his distance right from the get-go. No one has a clue about who's running this thing. And it's not going to take a genius to figure out that if the doll containing the drugs isn't in the store, there's a good chance that Cat has it."

Jack met his niece's eyes. "You're in a pile of trouble, Cat."

10

CAT BADLY WANTED to sit down, but she kept her spine straight, her gaze steady on her uncle's. "Let's back up a bit. You mentioned an original plan. What exactly went wrong with it?"

Jack began to pace. "The whole thing was supposed to be over by now. We'd laid the perfect trap."

"We?" Cat asked.

"I have an informant who works in the place where your toys are crafted. We suspected the toys the drugs were being shipped in were one of a kind and, therefore, easily identifiable by whomever is on the receiving end up here."

"Do you know who that is?" Cat asked.

Jack shook his head. "My favorite candidate is Matt Winslow. He travels back and forth and so he's in a position to know what's going on at both ends. But my informant has never been able to definitively finger him. Which means Winslow is either innocent or very good."

"Are you usually in the store when a shipment is due to arrive?" Dino asked.

Cat nodded. "Always."

"Who else was on hand when the last shipment from Paxco arrived?" Dino asked.

Cat sipped her brandy, trying hard to bring the scene to mind. "The box arrived two weeks ago, right on schedule, shortly before noon. There were a variety of toys in the order—tin soldiers, each holding their weapon in a different position. Matt unpacked those and found a space for them on the shelves. Adelaide was excited about the drummer boy. He was two and a half feet tall. She put him on display in the window, I think." Cat sank onto the sofa.

"You're doing great," Dino said. "What else do you remember?"

"Josie oohed and aahed over the matadors. Each one had a different colored cape. And there were two dolls—Spanish dancers, one with her hair up and one with her hair down. I think she paired them up with two of the matadors and put them in the other window."

"So each toy was distinctive in some way?"

Cat nodded. "That's part of the charm."

"Do you remember which ones sold on the same day they arrived?" Dino asked.

"Right," Jack added. "The toy with the drugs is probably passed on right away."

"Or they put it aside so that it isn't sold until that person walks into the store," Dino pointed out.

"More than one sold that day. I remember wishing I'd ordered more. And there are some regular customers who stop by when they know a shipment is due. Could the person behind this be one of my regulars?"

"Possible but unlikely," Dino mused. "It would be very risky to show up in your shop regularly. And so far the person running this show has been very careful to keep his or her distance."

"So that means we're back to square one." Setting her brandy glass on the coffee table, Cat pressed her hands against her temples. "So tell me about the original trap you set, Uncle Jack."

"My informant told me that there was another order due to ship out to the Cheshire Cat the week before Christmas. We were pretty sure the man who was packing the drugs into the toy was the man who supervised the workshop."

"Juan Rivero," Cat murmured.

"Yeah. We knew exactly when the dolls were going to be shipped and we knew when they'd arrive. This time we were going to have our person in the store watching to see exactly what happened to each toy—especially the ones that were unique. That's when everything began to unravel."

"You discovered that the order was for twenty-five identical dolls," Dino said.

Jack nodded. "That was problem number one, and I didn't anticipate it. Then the drugs were late arriving in Paxco. By the time that problem was solved, the weather in the northeast was going south."

Cat rose from the sofa. "Every single one of my customers knew that they were ordering the same doll. So if the mastermind behind this is one of them, he or she was aware there would be a potential problem about identifying the doll at this end. Why run that risk? Why not wait for another shipment?"

"Never underestimate the power of greed," Jack said.

Cat recalled that Dino had used almost the same words earlier. But it was still hard for her to picture Matt or Adelaide or Josie being that hungry for money.

"They may not have had a choice. There may have been pressure from whomever is funneling the money to the terrorist cell," Dino pointed out. "Fanatics are not known for their understanding and patience."

"So they ripped the lace on the dress of one of the dolls to identify the one carrying the drugs," Cat said.

"That seems to be a likely possibility," Jack agreed. "That

way the person working on this end could easily identify it, and perhaps even offer to repair it."

"Removing the drugs in the process," Cat finished.

"Or perhaps just stretching out the repair process until the right customer walked in," Jack pointed out.

"There are a lot of ways the scenario could have played out," Dino commented.

"You got that right," Jack said. "It was a nightmare. I had five operatives set to masquerade as customers so they could try to identify the doll. It might have worked if it hadn't been for the blasted storm." Jack's tone held a wealth of bitterness.

As Jack continued to lament the string of things that had messed up his plan, Cat realized that the two men were actually enjoying their discussion—as if it were some kind of theoretical strategy game. But it wasn't. They were talking about drugs being shipped through her store.

"For starters, the shipment arrived when only Cat was in the store," Jack was complaining. "I had a man across the street ready to come into the shop the moment the delivery was made, but the prime suspects were all gone by that time. And then she closed up."

Cat had heard just about enough. "Sorry to have messed up your master plan, Uncle Jack, but Matt was stuck in Chicago, and I'd sent Adelaide and Josie home because of the weather. I hardly needed them in the store when there were no customers. So I'm the one who set aside the damaged doll. And we all know exactly where it is."

She moved behind the sofa to where she'd dropped the tote and leaned down. As she did so, she heard the sound of glass shattering behind her and in her peripheral vision, she saw the wood on the edge of her coffee table splinter. Then the breath was knocked out of her as Dino shoved her to the floor beneath the window.

"Get the lights, Phillips."

"Working on it."

Before Cat could fill her lungs with air, the room was pitched into darkness. She felt Dino pull out his gun. Then he began to ease himself off of her.

She grabbed his jacket. "Was that what I think it was?"

He pried her fingers loose. "That was a bullet aimed at you." His voice was hard, cold, and there was just enough light for her to see the flatness in his eyes. "So stay put."

Dino rose and pressed himself against the wall to the left of the window.

Cat wasn't sure she could have moved even if she wanted to. She kept hearing the glass shatter, seeing the coffee table splinter. The images played over and over like a video loop in her mind. If she hadn't bent over to pick up the tote at that particular instant…

Fisting her hands, Cat pushed the picture firmly out of her mind and focused instead on what her uncle and Dino were saying in hushed voices.

"Any idea where the shot came from?"

"Not from the ground," Dino said. "The angle's wrong. I'm betting from one of the offices above the Cheshire Cat."

"Makes sense," Jack said. "This rear window thing can work two ways."

And he should have thought of that sooner, Dino berated himself as he inched his way along the wall to the door. "I'm going to check it out. You make sure Cat stays put."

Dino punched in Jase's number even as he stepped into the hallway, then breathed a sigh of relief when his friend immediately picked up. "Tell me you're close."

"I'm still in front of Cat's building. I decided to hang around for a bit, just in case things hadn't settled down for the night."

"Someone just tried to shoot Cat through the window of her apartment."

"Is she all right?"

"Only because she chose that particular moment to stoop over and pick up her bag." He entered the stairwell and willed the image out of his mind of Cat framed in that window—the perfect target. He plunged down the steps, three at a time. He should have anticipated the danger. Should have—

Ruthlessly, Dino reined his thoughts in. He needed to think coolly. Objectively. "I'm betting the sniper took aim from one of the offices on the fourth floor over the Cheshire Cat." Pausing at the door leading to the courtyard, he scanned the windows he was referring to. Yeah, that's what he would have done. But they were all dark, all closed.

"Meet you there."

Pocketing his phone, Dino pushed through the doors and raced across the courtyard. When he stepped out of the alley, he spotted Jase standing in the doorway next to the Cheshire Cat's entrance.

"He's gone," Jase said. "I reached the corner just in time to see him dash out of here into a waiting car. By the time I got my gun out, they were more than a block away. In a hurry, though." Jase opened the door into a small foyer that offered both an elevator and access to a staircase. "He forgot to lock up."

Fear, anger and frustration roiled through him. Dino gave them a moment before he shoved them down. Then he turned to Jase. "I should have anticipated they'd try something like this."

"Why?"

Dino filled Jase in on what they'd learned from Jack

Phillips. "Whoever's behind this is getting desperate. Not only did they hire someone to break into Cat's store to get the doll, but I'm betting they also hired the thugs who tried to steal the shipment of dolls off the FedEx truck. Nothing about the operation is running the way it's supposed to. And I'm convinced that the person pulling the strings is beginning to fear exposure. At this point, they can no longer count on Cat being ignorant of what's going on in her store. And they may fear that she'll start putting two and two together and figure out which one of her employees is betraying her. I should have taken more precautions."

"Playing the blame game is never productive," Jase commented quietly.

"Right." Dino knew that. But the image was still there—of Cat framed in that window. He had to shake it loose.

"Why don't you get back to her? I'll check out the offices and let you know if I find anything."

Dino nodded and turned away. He wanted to get Cat away from this.

His need to protect her had gone far beyond the professional.

CAT AND HER UNCLE were in the kitchen when Dino returned. They'd pulled all the shades down and the only illumination in the apartment came from one of the red pillar candles they'd set on the counter. The doll lay in the space between them, its dress pulled over its head.

Jack turned to Dino immediately. "Did you get him?"

Dino shook his head. "He had a driver waiting. Jase is checking out the offices above the toy store. He's not going to find anything."

"We found something," Cat said. "This doll is definitely the one stuffed with cocaine."

She'd had to do something while she'd been waiting for Dino's return, something besides worry that he wouldn't. Her uncle had tried to soothe her by pointing out that the pro had been hired to get her, not Dino.

Small comfort that was. Just as it was small comfort to know that the doll in front of her actually contained smuggled cocaine. Her stomach did a quiet, long flip. She was beginning to realize that theory was one thing and reality was quite another.

When Dino placed his hand on her shoulder, she glanced at him. The understanding she saw in his eyes helped her to gather her strength. She finally asked the question that had been on her mind since he'd left. "Why does someone want to kill me? That wouldn't necessarily get them the doll and the drugs."

"They may be afraid that you're going to start putting two and two together and get four," Dino said. "So far you've been the innocent dupe, but this time things are going wrong on both ends of the operation. If there's even a chance that you know about the drugs, they might figure it's not going to take you long to figure out who's betraying you, and that person could bring our kingpin down."

"Plus, they may have felt that in the confusion of dealing with your untimely demise, they might have a chance to snatch the doll," Jack said.

Cat glanced down at the doll. "So the question is what do we do next?"

"*We're* not going to do anything," Jack said. "You're going to leave this up to your fiancé and me."

"When hell freezes over," Cat said. But whatever else she would have said was interrupted when her cell phone rang. Setting the doll aside, she dug the phone out of her purse and checked the caller ID. Her father.

"Dad? Is something wrong?"

"What's wrong is that you're not answering your cell. I've been trying to reach you for almost an hour."

Cat glanced at the two men who'd moved into the living room. No doubt to develop new strategies. Well, she had an idea or two of her own. "Things have been busy here."

"Busy? You close your store at 8:00."

"Thanks to you, I have a fiancé to deal with now."

There was a beat of silence on the other end of the line. "How is that going?"

"Fine." Cat briefly considered letting her father know that she was fully aware of what was going on in her store. What would he say if she told him that she had a doll stuffed with cocaine sitting on her kitchen counter and that someone had just taken a shot at her?

A glance into the dim living room told her that Dino and Jack had their heads close together, talking in low tones. The last thing she needed was another person strategizing how to keep her safely on the sidelines while the big strong men brought down the drug ring.

"Dad, what was so urgent that you needed to get in touch with me?"

McGuire cleared his throat. "I know it's late, but I had to make sure you knew. Lucia's plane made it into LaGuardia before it closed down, and she announced at dinner tonight that she intends to visit your store tomorrow."

Cat's stomach knotted. "Tomorrow? Absolutely not. Now that the weather's cleared up, do you have any idea how busy we'll be?"

Images of chaos flooded Cat's mind. Twenty-two customers were going to be picking up their dolls. The mastermind behind the drug ring or one of his hired minions was going to be looking for the doll with the torn lace. Uncle Jack's men were going to be in and out of the store hoping to make an arrest.

And in the midst of all that, she pictured Lucia Merceri, cane in hand, thumping her way through the store with the single-minded intention of grilling Dino.

Out of the corner of her eye, Cat could see that Dino was also on his cell—probably checking in with Jase. More plans were being made, she thought. Without consulting her. The little flame of anger that had been burning inside of her ever since that sniper had shot at her flared hotly.

"We won't stay long," her father promised.

Liar, Cat thought. How long they stayed would depend entirely on Lucia. "Just tell the Queen of Hearts she'll have plenty of time to get to know Dino at the ball tomorrow night."

"Don't you think I tried? Lucia claims there will be too much going on at a big charity event like that. And there'll be others demanding her attention. Your stepsister Lucy and her husband weren't able to make it for dinner tonight because of the storm. Besides, Lucia's heard so much about Dino that she can't wait to meet him. If it hadn't been for the weather, she would have visited your shop today."

Cat badly wanted to scream, but there were better ways of handling her father. "Daddy, you can talk her out of it, I know you can. Tell her we'll stop by the house before the ball. She can have some private time with Dino. Believe me, there won't be an inch of space in my shop tomorrow."

"I have no control over the situation. Plus, Gianna is bringing a dress she wants you to wear to the ball. She knows you haven't had any time to shop. It's two against one, little girl."

Right. Cat bit down hard on her tongue. "What time?"

Her father sighed. "About ten. I knew you'd understand."

"Oh, I do." What she understood was her father wanted to

poke his nose into the Cheshire Cat, too. He was probably tired of getting secondhand reports from Jack and Dino. Grimly, Cat accepted the fact that if she didn't fill her father in on what was going on, Dino or her Uncle Jack would.

"Would you like to talk to Uncle Jack?"

"I thought Jack was in Mexico."

"When I walked into my apartment tonight, he was sitting on my sofa smoking one of your cigars. I know that the two of you have been plotting together."

"I don't know what—"

"Give it up, Dad. My store was broken into tonight, and Uncle Jack fought with the burglar. And by the way, I know why you really hired Dino Angelis."

"Cat—"

"I don't appreciate being lied to. See you in the morning."

"Now wait—"

Cat dropped her cell back into her tote, then turned to study the two men in the dim shadows of her living room. So far everyone had been operating around her, keeping her in the dark. Her father, hiring a bodyguard in the guise of a fake fiancé, her uncle, joining forces with her father to catch a drug smuggler who was using her shop and her mother's dolls to finance terrorists.

And no one had thought she'd had a right to know?

Right now, she could tell that Dino and her uncle were hatching some plot to sideline her again.

In a pig's eye.

As Cat strode forward to join them, Dino turned. Since it was Jack's plan, he was going to let Cat's uncle break the news. And take the grief.

"You've come up with a plan."

Dino noted that it wasn't a question.

"Here's how it's going to go down," Jack said.

Cat's chin lifted, but she held her tongue.

"You're not going into the store tomorrow. Dino will tell your employees you spent the night in the emergency room— some kind of twenty-four-hour bug—and that he didn't have the heart to wake you up. That's the story your customers will hear. In the meantime, you'll be in the apartment next door with Jase Campbell, and one of my men will be here. When someone breaks in this place to find the doll, we'll have them."

"That's it?" Cat asked in a mild voice.

"Yes."

She moved until she was standing toe to toe with her uncle. Then she poked a slim finger into his chest. "That's a very interesting scenario, but we're not using it."

"Cat—"

She cut Jack off by poking him again. "For starters, Lucia Merceri, accompanied by my father and Gianna, are coming to the Cheshire Cat tomorrow morning at ten. Daddy claims he's outnumbered by the women, and has no control over the situation, and Lucia can't wait another minute to meet and cross-examine my fiancé."

"I'll call your father and talk to him," Jack said.

"Won't do you a bit of good. Wild horses wouldn't keep him away from my store tomorrow. I filled him in on what happened tonight. The part about the store being broken into. I didn't tell him someone tried to shoot me." She shot a look at Dino. "But I told him that I know my fake fiancé is really my bodyguard."

"Shit," Jack muttered.

"Even if you did talk Dad out of coming to the store, Lucia Merceri is a force of nature. The only thing that stopped her from coming today was the blizzard. I'm not leaving Dino alone to deal with her. And even if you did talk me into playing sick, the wicked witch would be over here in a flash. Dino isn't the only one she'll have questions for. If we go with your plan, my apartment stands a good chance of becoming Grand Central Station."

"I don't want you in the shop." Jack turned to Dino. "Tell her how much danger she's in."

"She already knows." Dino kept his eyes on Cat as she turned away from her uncle and began to pace in and out of the shadows. He knew her well enough now to recognize that she was thinking something through—in much the same way she'd thought her little proposition through just before she'd sprung it on him. Resting his hip against the small desk, he waited.

"The other problem with your plan, Uncle Jack, is that it has 'trap' written all over it. Dino's right—whoever's been running this operation is smart. The man you tangled with in the alley has probably already reported in. I think it's safe to say that the kingpin knows the store and my apartment are both under surveillance."

She was right about that, Dino thought. The alleyway and courtyard that connected the two buildings had been a very busy place tonight.

"Plus, my employees and my regular customers know that I'm always in the shop. Now, one of them knows or strongly suspects I have the doll with the drugs and suddenly I'm sick? No. Your plan isn't going to work."

Jack ran a hand through his hair, then glanced at Dino. "Can't you talk some sense into her?"

Cat whirled to face her uncle. "No, he can't. Someone has been using my store and one of the dolls my mother designed to smuggle filthy drugs into the country. And so far they've been able to do it very easily and with impunity. I want to catch the bastard. And I think I have a better plan than yours."

Jack sent Dino a pleading look. "C'mon, I need some backup here."

"I want to hear what she has to say," Dino said.

Cat smiled then. "I'm going to tempt whoever's behind this. When I open the Cheshire Cat tomorrow, I'll put this doll in one of the windows. She'll have a Sold tag on her arm, and I'll make sure that the torn lace is just visible. She'll be right there in plain sight."

Jack frowned. "You think someone may make a grab for it."

"No. That would be too dangerous. And just plain dumb. No one involved in this has been stupid so far." She began to pace. "I think one of my employees has to be involved. If they don't already know that the shipment has arrived, they will the moment they get to the store. I'll fill them in, tell them that Mr. Miller and Mrs. Lassiter have already picked up their dolls and that I've notified everyone else. I'll also tell them that I've put the damaged doll in the window so that we can take new orders. All day long it will be there right within reach. I want to toy with their minds. Someone may be tempted into revealing himself or herself. But I think they'll bide their time."

Dino began to wonder if Cat remembered they were there as she continued, "That's what I'd do. We're closing early tomorrow. Matt, Adelaide and Josie will all be attending the ball. I'm leaving at 5:00 because Gianna insists that I stand in the reception line. Adelaide and Josie will close the store an hour later. I'll make sure that they know that I'm taking the doll with me when I leave, that I intend to surprise my father with it at the ball."

For a moment, the two men regarded her in silence.

Then Jack scowled at her. "If you take the doll, someone will make a move on you at the ball."

Cat smiled. "Exactly. They'll think they'll have a better chance there."

"And they will," Jack said. "You're using yourself as bait, and I don't like it."

"If they don't think they have a good enough chance, they won't go for it," Cat insisted. "And if they don't feel they can make a move—a successful one—soon, whoever is behind this will probably cut his or her losses and walk away. We'll have lost our chance to catch them."

Dino waited three beats before he said, "She's right. Someone is going to believe that the ball is his or her best chance." He didn't like it—but the trap she was baiting had a better chance of succeeding than the one Jack had described. What he didn't say, what he didn't even want to think about was that catching the people behind the operation might be the only way to protect Cat's life.

He met her eyes. "I don't think your father could have come up with a better plan."

Jack turned to Dino. "You're not going to go along with this?"

"I'm not saying I like it," Dino said. "But I think she's right. No one will try and grab the doll in the store—at least not as soon as she lets everyone know she'll be taking it to the charity event. The ball opens up a lot of seemingly safer possibilities."

"Too many," Jack said.

"Enough to tempt someone to come out in the open," Cat said. "They won't be able to resist. It's the best chance we've got."

"She's right." Dino turned to Jack. "Between us, we ought to be able to come up with enough people to keep her covered. I'll be with her in the store all day—and at the ball. Jase can rotate some of his men through the store. What about you?"

"I've got the ones I was going to use for the original plan."

"Use them now for the ball."

Dino turned to Cat. "You're exhausted and you have a long day tomorrow. Get some sleep while your uncle and I hammer out the details."

"I'll need to know about them."

Dino moved toward her then and ran a hand down her arm. "We'll brief you in the morning. If this is going to work, you're going to have to put on the performance of your life tomorrow. Not only in the store, but also at the ball. That means you're going to have to be on your toes every moment. Get some rest."

IT WAS AFTER MIDNIGHT when the phone rang. The damp hand that picked the receiver up nearly dropped it.

"Do you have the doll?"

"Not yet. I called the number you gave me and made the arrangements, but the doll with the torn lace wasn't in the shop."

"Where is it?"

There was steeliness in the tone that chilled the blood.

"She must have it. It makes sense that she wouldn't sell a damaged product to anyone. She's probably repairing it."

There were three beats of silence on the other end of the line.

"You've delayed me again. The man who caused the drugs to be delayed in reaching Paxco no longer works for me. He met with an accident."

Fear surged up. "I can still get it for you. She'll be in the store all day tomorrow. I'll be able to pin down the doll's location. Give me until tomorrow night."

"We'll see. I have others who are more efficient than you."

"No! No—I'll get it."

The line went dead.

RAGE BUBBLED UP. There'd been too many failures. The robbery hadn't been successful, colleagues were beginning to panic, and Cat McGuire was still alive. The worst news was that there'd been two men in her apartment when the sniper had taken his unsuccessful shot. If Cat McGuire was being protected, there was a good chance she'd become suspicious. That meant time was running out.

Why was everyone so incompetent?

Think. There's still time.

The increasing risk of exposure would have to be dealt with. Quickly. Perhaps depending so much on others had been a mistake....

11

IT WAS JUST AFTER THREE when Jack finally left to return to his hotel. After locking the door of Cat's apartment, Dino glanced at the sofa where he was going to spend the rest of the night. Cat needed her sleep, and he knew if he joined her in bed, neither of them would get much.

The plan that he and Jack had come up with to keep Cat safe at the ball was a good one. Still, Dino had a feeling—the same kind of feeling that had plagued him on his last special ops mission. Something was going to go wrong. He pressed his hands against his eyes, then dropped them.

The trick was to keep Cat safe, but at the same time offer someone the opportunity to snatch the doll. Once he'd accepted the fact that his niece wasn't going to be sidelined, Jack had proven himself to be a good strategist. Since Matt, Josie and Adelaide were all still under suspicion, they'd come up with two plans. Each left Cat vulnerable for a time.

If Matt was the one who was receiving and passing on the drugs, he'd try to get Cat alone at some point during the charity ball. They'd have to let him succeed—at least until he incriminated himself.

The most obvious place for one of the women to isolate Cat was in the ladies' room, so Jase would station a woman operative there for the entire evening.

Jack had volunteered to bring Cat's father up to date first thing in the morning.

Dino surveyed Cat's living room. There was very little likelihood that Cat was in danger from any more snipers—at least for tonight. He and Jack had patched the section of window that the bullet had shattered. The shades were drawn, and the only light came from the red candle now burning on the coffee table.

He glanced at it, thought of the picnic they'd shared earlier and of how they'd made love right there on the floor. Had it only been nine hours ago? So much had happened since then. He picked up the candle and was on his way to the bedroom to check on Cat when his cell vibrated in his pocket. Alarm moved through him. If Jase was calling him at this hour…

Setting the candle back down, he pulled his phone out and smiled the moment he saw the caller ID. It was his cousin Kit. "Do you know what time it is?"

"It's just after midnight—the witching hour here in San Francisco. I'm up in the tower room with your mom."

Worry snaked its way up Dino's spine. He could picture them both quite clearly. Kit would be lounging on one of the comfortable sofas and his mother would probably be at her desk with her crystals spread out in front of her. After his father and aunt had died, everyone had moved into his grandfather's huge mansion. Its tower room was one of those special places on the estate where his mother's visions were strongest. The room itself was large and airy with long, narrow stained glass windows. On a clear night, she'd crank them open and let the moonlight pour into the room.

"Something wrong?" Dino asked. Of all his cousins, Kit, the novelist and PI, was the one closest to his mom.

"You tell us. Your mom is a bit worried, but she didn't want to make you worry even more. I'm thinking if you're in some kind of trouble, I could fly out there and act as backup. Theo is in court this week. But he wouldn't be much use to you anyway what with his wedding in five days. And Nik's too busy honeymooning in Greece. You'll have to make do with me."

Dino sank onto the arm of the sofa and stretched out his legs. "Has Mom seen something?"

"I'll let you talk to her."

"Dino?" His mother sounded tense.

"I'm fine, Mom."

"Yes. I've seen danger, but not for you. It's for the woman you're guarding. Someone is trying to kill her."

"Tried and failed."

"They'll try again."

Fear knotted in Dino's stomach. Hadn't his own feelings told him that? "Yes. But I won't let it happen."

"You're going to have to trust her. She's smart. She'll figure out a way when the time comes."

Some of his own tension eased at her words. "This may all be over sooner than I expected. I may be home if not for Christmas at least for Theo's wedding."

"Yes, I think you will. Bring her with you."

"I will." It wasn't until that moment that he acknowledged to himself that taking Cat to San Francisco to meet his family was something he very much wanted to do. "Tell Kit I appreciate his offer to fly out here, but I have some very good backup already—Jase Campbell, a man I worked special ops with in the navy."

"Kit will be disappointed," Cass said with a smile in her voice. "But I told him he wasn't going to escape that easily from the wedding preparations. Take care, Dino."

"I will."

Even after he pocketed his cell, Dino continued to sit on the arm of the sofa. For the first time since the bullet had shattered the window and missed Cat by inches, he felt that he was going to be able to protect her. He had to. Jase had been right that playing the blame game was only going to interfere with his instincts. And he was going to need every bit of the power that ran in his family during the next twenty-four hours.

Had his mother somehow sensed that? Of course. A sudden wave of longing moved through him. He wanted to see her and just be with his family. He glanced toward the bedroom door. But he also wanted to be with Cat. Just how he was going to resolve that he hadn't quite worked out yet.

Lifting the candle, he strode to the bedroom door and eased it open. She slept on her side with one hand tucked under her chin. She'd kicked off most of the covers and the oversized white T-shirt she wore just skimmed her thighs. One of those incredibly long legs was under the sheet, the other on top. It occurred to him that he hadn't seen her sleep before. It was hard to believe, but they hadn't known each other long enough for that. Though he might have imagined it, he'd never seen that glorious hair spread across a pillow. In the candlelight, the hint of flames that always seemed to flicker in the strands looked real.

She seemed to throw herself into sleep with the same single-minded determination that she threw herself into her work. Into lovemaking.

Because he simply couldn't help himself, Dino moved closer. From the first, she'd had the power to draw him like a magnet. He'd made a decision to keep his distance until this was over. He needed his objectivity, to keep his mind on the job. And if his mother was right, Cat needed to focus on keeping herself safe, too.

But his desire for her, the consuming need he had no control over wouldn't let him stop until he was at the side of the bed. This close, for the first time he noticed how delicate her features were, how slender her wrists. In sleep, there was a fragility to her that he hadn't noted before. Perhaps because the intense energy that seemed to emanate from her during every waking moment was absent now. She was so smart, so strong, with a mind every bit as agile as her body. She'd handled her uncle Jack just as easily as she'd handled him. She'd come up with her own plan for tomorrow and had neatly shoehorned them into it.

For the first time as he looked at her, it wasn't the hot stir of passion that he felt, but something quieter, warmer. Admiration, certainly, but also affection. It was then that he felt his heart go into freefall, and something bordering on fear moved through him.

When had it happened? When had he fallen in love with her? That first morning when he'd stood outside her store and witnessed her race down those stairs? Or had it been when he'd first seen her picture on his admiral's desk?

Setting the candle on her nightstand, he brushed a strand of hair behind her ear, felt that warm skin. It was only as she stirred that he realized he'd wanted her to wake up. Needed her to.

Her eyes opened and he watched them clear. She smiled at him and held out her hand. "Come to bed."

"It wouldn't be smart."

She levered herself up. "Here's the deal. Tomorrow we'll be smart. Tonight there's just you and me."

He stripped off his clothes, then joined her in the bed and helped her rid herself of hers.

She slipped her arms around him then and found his mouth. He kept the pressure light, remembering the tenderness he'd felt as he'd watched her sleep. He'd never been a particularly gentle lover, but she'd unlocked something inside of him.

Her lips were warm and soft as they moved over his. Her taste, her scent were so familiar now, as if they'd become a part of him. As they lingered, tasted, teased and took from each other, an ache, sweet and edgy, streamed through him. He was hers.

"Make love with me," she whispered against his lips.

"I am." With his mouth still nibbling hers, he threaded his fingers through her hair. Cat felt as if her body were melting molecule by molecule. Though she wanted to touch him, her limbs seemed weighted. A riot of sensations, sweet and bubbly as champagne moved through her. She wanted to indulge in each one—the flavor of his lips, the texture of his skin as his cheek brushed against hers. That dark penetrating gaze as he drew back to comb his hands through her hair again and again.

Then at last he touched her, fingertips only, tracing her face, rubbing her lower lip with his thumb, and circling her breasts. What was he doing to her? She'd felt his strength before, but this was different. His fingers didn't grip, his hands didn't press. Instead, they skimmed and lingered. So different. So intense. It wasn't fire he stirred in her this time, but a flood of emotions.

She watched the flicker of candlelight on his features. Those strong warrior cheekbones, the firm chin. And those eyes. She could read his desire in them, feel it in her bones. She ran her fingers over his face, absorbing, memorizing. Drawing his mouth to hers, she traced his lips with her tongue. Then she eased back and just looked and looked. This might be the last time, the very last time, they held each other like this.

His heart began to beat faster, the pulse of it matching her own. They both moved this time until their mouths met again and fused. Mists of pleasure swamped her as the ache in her throat built and built. She was vaguely aware that he took care of the condom, then linked his fingers with hers.

He said her name—only that—as he slipped into her. What she was feeling erupted and poured out and into him as they began to move. She was his.

Need turned suddenly sharper. Hands gripped, fingers dug in and they clung to one another. Greed replaced tenderness with a speed that devastated them both. Wrapped tight, they rolled across the bed, fighting to take each other further than they'd ever gone before.

Finally, he rose over her so that he was all she saw, all she knew. He drove into her almost violently and she met him thrust for thrust. His chest was heaving, as was hers. And still he held back, as if he wanted to keep them balanced, trembling on that edge—forever. Then his mouth crushed hers, and she heard only the sounds of their mingled moans as they poured themselves into each other.

IN THE MORNING, one of Jase's men drove them from the underground garage of her building into the alley by the side of the shop. Dino got out first, opened the door to the storeroom, turned on the lights and then came back to hustle Cat inside.

He took her hands in his. "Nervous?"

"A bit." It was the first time that morning that he'd touched her.

When she'd awakened, she'd been alone in her bed, the sheets next to her cold. Through the open bedroom door she'd caught a glimpse of Dino in the kitchen talking to her uncle. He was definitely back in bodyguard mode.

Trying not to feel hurt, she'd dressed comfortably for the long day ahead of her. The red sweater was for the season and the black pants and boots were to allow her maximum ease of movement. When she'd joined Dino and her uncle in the kitchen, the two men had been all business, briefing her carefully on the game plan for the day. Their eyes had been hard, their tone of voice flat and clipped. It had been the first time she'd noticed any similarities in the two men.

The plan had been simple and straightforward. And as it sunk in, nerves had knotted in her stomach. With no advance notice to her coworkers, she was going to leave the store two hours before closing at 4:00 p.m. And she was not going to return to her apartment.

"No sense in giving some sniper a second chance," Jack had said grimly. "I've reserved a suite at the Alsatian Towers where your stepmother's ball is taking place. Both of you will have to pack and take your ball clothes to the Cheshire Cat. Then you can dress in the hotel suite."

"Jase has arranged for a limo to pick us up in front of the store," Dino had added. "We'll go directly to the hotel. This is the weakest part of the plan. We're assuming that whoever is behind this will have been informed by then that you're taking the damaged doll to the ball. So once we get into the limo, they'll know our destination. To keep them from trying something then, Jase's man will drop us off at the delivery entrance and we'll use service elevators to get to the suite."

"Once you arrive at the ball, we'll have someone within three feet of you at all times. Jase's female op will be on duty in the ladies' room when you need a bathroom break," Jack had explained. "If someone makes a move on you, we'll have him."

Hopefully, she'd thought. But she hadn't said a word out loud. Odd that listening to the meticulousness of their plan hadn't eased her nerves. But now just the pressure of Dino's hands on hers had most of her anxiety draining away.

"Want a piece of advice?" Dino asked.

"Sure."

"For every move you make today, everything you say, you're going to have an audience. So think of yourself as an actress with a part to play. It's a technique I often use when I'm working a mission. It helps me focus and allows me to keep personal emotions under control and to stay objective."

Cat couldn't prevent the thought from slipping into her mind again. Was that what he'd been doing the whole time he'd been with her—playing a role? Was that what he was doing now? Quickly, she pushed the idea aside. The part she had to play didn't allow for that kind of speculation. Tilting her head slightly, she managed a smile. "I think I'll imagine myself to be a young Kate Hepburn."

He studied her for a moment. "Good choice."

He would have released her then, but she tightened her grip on his hands. "What if our plan doesn't work?"

He met her eyes. "It will. And when this is over, we'll talk."

Something moved through her—a mix of anticipation and fear…and something else she couldn't put a name to. Whatever it was, it had her heart making a good, hard thump.

"Ready?" Dino asked.

"Yes."

He pulled her close for a quick, possessive kiss. And there was no audience. Only the two of them.

"Break a leg," he murmured.

Turning, Cat moved onto her stage, crossed to one of the windows and baited her trap with the doll.

"JUST A SEC." The phone call from Matt came at nine-forty-five and had Cat scurrying to the second step of the spiral staircase to get the best signal. After pressing her cell to one ear, she cupped her palm over the other to block out the cacophony of noise that filled the store. Not even the rock version of "Jingle Bells" pouring through the speakers could completely drown out the sound of children's laughter and the din of conversation. "Matt?"

"I'm here."

"Go ahead. I can hear you now. Where are you?"

"I'm on my way in from LaGuardia." A wealth of disgust and exhaustion laced his tone. "They didn't open up the New York area airports until six this morning. I would have called earlier except we were circling, waiting for clearance to land for two hours. I should be at the Cheshire Cat within fifteen minutes. How's business?"

"Booming. We can definitely use your help." Cat kept her voice cheerful and excited as she glanced around the packed store. The bell over the door jangled and two more customers began to push their way through the crowd. She recognized them immediately. They were here to pick up their special dolls from Paxco. Earlier she'd brought them down from the office, and they were lined up next to gift bags on a shelf. Josie had taken over the distribution.

The door jangled again to let in three more people. It was as if shoppers were determined to make up for the time the blizzard had stolen from them the day before.

"Just wanted to let you know I'm on my way. I won't keep you. See you soon."

Cat stared down at her cell after Matt disconnected the call. He hadn't even asked about the shipment of dolls. Did that mean that he already knew they'd arrived? How? He hadn't been in touch with her since yesterday. But he had been tracking them on his Palm Pilot she remembered.

Then she shifted her gaze to Adelaide and Josie. She'd explained about the doll in the window display the moment they'd arrived in the shop, and they'd taken it in stride. No questions. Josie had offered to mend the ripped lace. Cat had declined her offer, explaining that she would take care of it later. For the life of her, she hadn't read anything in her eyes other than a desire to be helpful. Adelaide had merely stepped behind the counter to ring up a waiting customer. Cat wondered which behavior she should view as more suspicious. It was fortunate she'd gone into the toy business. She surely wouldn't make a very good detective.

And it made her both sad and angry to know that in less than twenty-four hours she'd gone from defending her employees to firmly believing that one of them had betrayed her.

But this wasn't the time to be reflecting on that. She had a role to play.

Pushing herself to her feet, she let her gaze sweep the store again. A few yards away to her right, Dino was crouched down next to a boy of about five, their dark heads close as they watched a train chug slowly up a steep hill. The thought slipped into her mind that he looked just right sitting on the floor of her store playing with a child. Something tightened around her heart. Unable to resist, Cat joined the man and the boy and murmured in a voice only Dino could hear, "Working hard, I see."

Dino sent her a bland look. "I'm providing a distraction while Mom shops."

Together they watched the train crest the hill. The little boy squealed and clapped his hands as it shot down the other side. Then Dino said, "There's something you should know. I asked Jase to run a check on Mrs. Lassiter and your Santa Claus man, Mr. Miller."

"Because they were so prompt picking up their dolls?"

"And because both of them had access to the tracking number and could have been involved in the attempted robbery of the FedEx truck. Mrs. Lassiter seems okay. Her husband is a very successful plastic surgeon with offices on Park Avenue. They don't seem to want for money. But the address Miller gave on his order form is the same as the Frick Museum on East 70th Street."

Cat put a hand on his arm. "He's our man?"

"Could be."

Something tugged at the edges of Cat's mind. "You know, from the moment he walked into the store, there was something familiar about him. At the time, I chalked it up to the fact that he looked a bit like Santa Claus." She met Dino's eyes. "But maybe it was more than that. I'm going to have to think about it."

"You do that." He squeezed her hand. "How's it going so far?"

"I've decided that good actresses don't get paid nearly enough."

Dino's laughter blended with the jangle of the bell over the door. Cat turned in time to see her father, Gianna, and Lucia Merceri enter. "Uh-oh, here they come."

Lucia was in the lead. The woman might be short, but she emanated a power and authority that had other customers stepping aside as she arrowed her way like a heat-seeking missile toward Cat.

Behind the parade, Cat saw Mrs. Lassiter and Matt Winslow both enter the store. Matt stepped to the window where the doll was displayed while Mrs. Lassiter pushed her way straight toward Adelaide at the counter. Cat knew a moment of panic as Matt leaned closer to the doll. Was he just going to snatch it, stuff it under his coat and run?

Keeping her hand in his, Dino rose with Cat. "Relax. Jase has it covered."

Cat had time to register that Jase had entered the shop seconds before Lucia reached them.

"Act Two begins," Dino murmured.

12

"SO THIS IS the fiancé?" Lucia demanded.

"Now, Mama Merceri, you know it is," Colonel McGuire said. "I showed you his picture."

Lucia glared at the colonel as she thumped her cane on the floor. "Does that mean I don't rate a formal introduction?"

"Of course not." Dino took Lucia's free hand and raised it to his lips. "I'm Dino Angelis, Signora Merceri. It's my pleasure to meet you. You also, Mrs. McGuire. Cat has spoken of you both."

"Humph," Lucia said, then pinned Cat with a look. "At least *he* has some manners. You're looking tired, young lady. Gianna says they never see you. High time you stopped working so hard."

She shifted her gaze back to Dino. "Checked you out. You're an old-fashioned Greek man. Maybe you can persuade her to get off this retail treadmill."

"Cat has a mind of her own. I don't believe I'll have much luck with talking her out of doing something she loves, something she's obviously so good at."

"My son-in-law says you're retiring from the navy."

"Because I want to. Not because someone pressured me into it."

"Humph." Lucia studied him for a moment. "Taking her side, are you?"

"Yes, ma'am."

Out of the corner of her eye, Cat saw that Mrs. Lassiter was first in line at Adelaide's counter and she was gesturing towards the display window. Matt hadn't touched the doll.

"The Cheshire Cat is very busy today, Signora Merceri," Dino said. "Why don't I give you and the colonel and Mrs. McGuire a tour while Cat deals with her customers?"

"That would be lovely." Gianna sent him a grateful smile.

"A little maneuver to take us off her hands," Lucia said.

Dino smiled at her as he tucked her hand into the crook of his arm. "Cat was right. She said that you'd see right through it. But since you've come all this way, you really ought to get the grand tour. First, I'd like you to meet my friend Tommy."

Cat stared for a moment as Lucia Merceri, the wicked witch, took time to acknowledge the introduction to the little boy Dino had been playing with. Then she remembered her role and hurried over to Adelaide.

Matt stepped into her path when she was halfway there. "I was wondering how you would handle the doll that didn't meet our quality control standards. I hoped to be here when the shipment arrived so that I could explain why I told Juan he could put it in. It was either that or the shipment would have been short a doll."

Cat studied her assistant buyer as he spoke. She'd never seen him look so disheveled before. And there was something in his eyes that went beyond fatigue. Was it fear?

Or was she just being paranoid about everyone who worked for her?

Guilt moved through her as she put a hand on Matt's arm. "I would have made the same decision. And it isn't a problem. I never mentioned it to you, but I ordered one of the dolls myself as a surprise Christmas gift for my father."

Matt's gaze shifted to her family. "I wondered why your family was here."

Dino had steered Lucia around the shop and was now escorting her into the storeroom. Gianna and her father were bringing up the end of the little parade.

"Do you want me to clean the doll up so that it's all set to go when they leave?" Matt asked.

"No. I'm planning on giving it to my dad tonight at Gianna's big charity ball. I figure she'll take care of the repairs."

It suddenly occurred to her that Matt didn't know about her engagement yet. Panic fluttered in her stomach, and her admiration for professional actresses and undercover agents shot up another notch.

Shoving her nerves aside, Cat beamed a smile at Matt. "They're here because Gianna's mother has made a trip over from Italy to meet my fiancé, Dino Angelis. He's giving them a tour of the shop to keep them out of my hair."

Matt stared at her. "You're engaged? Since when?"

Cat showed him her ring. "Dino proposed a week ago when we were skating at Rockefeller Center. We've been seeing each other secretly for a couple of months now. I didn't tell anyone because I figured if word leaked out to my family that I was dating someone seriously, Gianna would have been all over me. You know how much she wants me to marry and spend more of my time serving on boards and following in her footsteps. And Lucia is right with her on that."

Matt gave his head a little shake as if to clear it. "Who is this Dino Angelis?"

"Long story." And she was saved from telling it when Adelaide waved frantically for her to come over to the counter where Mrs. Lassiter's voice was on the rise. "Tell you later."

She took two steps before she turned back. "Would you mind helping Josie out until things slack off a bit?"

Relief streamed through her as Matt headed toward Josie, but it drained away when she reached Adelaide and saw the worry in her eyes.

"Mrs. Lassiter insists on buying the doll in the window," Adelaide said. "I've explained to her that it's only there for display purposes, so that we can take more orders."

"I'll give you twice what I paid for the other doll." Mrs. Lassiter's voice carried enough to have several customers joining the small crowd already gathered in front of Adelaide's work station.

Cat read both distress and determination in Mrs. Lassiter's eyes. Did the older woman know about the drugs? Was that why she wanted the doll? "I'm sorry, I can't sell you that doll. I ordered it as a gift for my father because it was created from a design my mother made. Besides, it's slightly damaged. We can certainly take your order for another doll."

Mrs. Lassiter waved a hand. "What about one of those on the shelves over there?"

There were three left, Cat saw. "They're already sold. There are children who are expecting them under the tree."

"You don't understand. I need another doll." Tears flooded Mrs. Lassiter's eyes.

She wasn't after the drugs, Cat decided. Any of the dolls would do.

Over Mrs. Lassiter's shoulder, Cat saw Josie slip one of the remaining dolls into a gift bag and the woman she passed it to clutched it to her body and headed straight for the door.

"Mrs. Lassiter, why don't you come with me?" Cat led the way to a less crowded space near the storeroom.

"Why do you need two dolls?"

The older woman took a deep breath. "My daughter-in-law just informed me that I have to give the exact same present to both Giselle and Charlene. They're only a year apart and they're beginning to fight over everything. She won't let me give Giselle the doll from Paxco unless I have one for Charlene. And I promised Giselle that doll."

Cat thought hard. She didn't have to be an ace detective to handle a panicked grandmother. "Didn't you buy the bride doll with the fashion trunk and accessories for Charlene?"

"Yes."

"I have another one of those over here." She led the way to a display table and squatted down to find the box. Thank heavens, they'd been too busy lately to keep up with unpacking everything. "Why don't you give the bride dolls to Giselle and Charlene for Christmas and wait for their birthdays to give them the dolls from Paxco? I should be able to get another shipment in by the end of January."

"I suppose I could do that," Mrs. Lassiter said. "Giselle's birthday is in early February."

"That isn't a very long time to wait."

Taking the bride doll box, Mrs. Lassiter met her eyes just before she turned away. "Thank you, Ms. McGuire. I think you've saved the day."

"Nice work."

Cat whirled to find Dino standing just behind her. She sent a panicked look over his shoulder. "My family? Is everything all right?"

He grinned at her. "Everything's fine. I made coffee for each of them and Lucia is presently on the phone talking to my mother."

Cat stared at him. "She's talking to your mother?"

"Claimed she was interested in meeting the whole family.

She even mentioned a trip to San Francisco. But from what I could tell the conversation is turning into a consultation. When Lucia ran a background check on me, she discovered my mother's reputation as a psychic. And Lucia is curious about her future."

Cat put a hand on his arm. "But your mother doesn't even know about the engagement."

Dino linked his fingers with hers. "Relax. I spoke with her earlier, but she probably knew we were going to meet and become involved before we did. I want you to meet her." Dino hadn't known he was going to say that, hadn't known the words were true until they were spoken.

He saw the immediate flash of nerves in Cat's eyes, felt her fingers slip from his as she glanced back at the storeroom. "And what are my father and Gianna doing?"

"Your father is holding down the fort, and Gianna sent me out to ask if you'll talk with her privately."

Cat frowned. "Of course, I will. Why would she have to ask?"

"I think she's embarrassed that she caused this whole situation by trying to placate her mother with the story that you were seeing someone. She's afraid you'll hate her now."

"Of course, I don't hate her. I'd actually forgotten that it was her storytelling that started this whole fake engagement thing."

He suppressed the urge to reach for her hand again. But he couldn't prevent himself from saying, "When this is over, we'll talk."

This time when the nerves flashed into her eyes, he felt some satisfaction since they echoed the ones jittering in his stomach. Around them chaos reigned as people jostled their way to displays or to the checkout counter. A child laughed, an adult scolded, and above it all, "I'll be Home for Christmas" filled the air. There was a part of him that wanted to settle things between them, but it was the wrong time, and certainly the wrong place.

Instead, he drew her into his arms, and after a second's hesitation, she laid her head on his shoulder. Just for a moment. "You're doing fine. Your uncle Jack has updated your father on everything that's happened."

"Shit," breathed Cat into his shirt.

"I figure that at the ball the colonel will provide one more set of eyes watching you."

She drew back then and met his eyes. "You're worried."

"No," he lied. All morning long, he'd been telling himself that there was no reason to be worried. But it was there, a steady thrum in the blood.

"I had Jase check out your office earlier, and he's up there now making sure it's empty. Once he comes down, it will be safe for you and Gianna to talk there. Jase will make sure no one disturbs you."

Drawing back, Cat nodded and made herself step away. As Dino headed toward the storeroom, his words drifted into her mind again. *When this is over, we'll talk.*

Why did that make her more nervous than the charade she was going to act out at the ball tonight?

The jangling of the bell over the shop door had Cat whirling toward it. This time it was Orlando, the Merceri family chauffeur who entered. Cat saw an instant of hesitation as he glanced around the crowded store. But he recovered smoothly once he spotted her and headed in her direction.

"Signora McGuire called me on my cell and asked me to bring this in for you." Orlando offered her the dress bag he was carrying.

Cat recognized the designer name discreetly printed on the top and took it from Orlando just as Gianna reached her.

"It's a peace offering," her stepmother said. "I want to talk to you."

Cat led the way up the spiral staircase, noting when she reached the top that Jase sat down on the first step as soon as Gianna moved past him, effectively blocking anyone from following them. To anyone who glanced his way, Dino's friend appeared to be playing with a puzzle game.

Gianna wasted no time once they were in Cat's office. "I'm so sorry."

"For what?" Cat hung the dress bag carefully on a hook.

"For getting you into this." Gianna threw her hands up and began to pace. "I don't expect you to understand. From what Jimmy says your mother was perfect."

"She was a special woman." Cat studied her stepmother. Gianna Merceri McGuire was the most pulled-together and composed woman she'd ever met. Cat hardly recognized the woman who was nervously pacing in front of her.

"I've lived all my life trying to measure up to my mother's expectations. She chose my first husband, and I went along with it." Gianna waved a hand. "Don't get me wrong. Donatello was a nice man, and he was very good at running the New York branch of Merceri Bank. I wasn't unhappy with him, and he gave me my daughter, Lucy. And I became exactly what my mother wanted me to become—a New York society matron."

She glanced at Cat, lifted her chin. "And I'm not unhappy with that, either." Gianna ran her fingers through her hair. "I'm rambling."

"What do you want to tell me, Gianna?" Cat asked softly.

"I was wrong to tell my mother you were seeing someone, and that I was pretty certain you'd be announcing your engagement in the near future. I've spent my whole life doing what my mother wanted. She told me she wanted great-grand-children, and I nudged Lucy to produce one. But you were… different. I couldn't nudge you in the direction my mother wanted. So I took the coward's way out and lied. Each time I told the story, I embroidered it a bit more. That was wrong. I should have stood up to her and defended you."

Gianna threw up her hands again. "Why should you have become the perfect model of a Merceri woman just because I married your father?"

When she paused as if waiting for an answer, Cat moved forward and took her hands. "I guess we can agree on that one."

Gianna squeezed her fingers. "I'm so angry with myself."

"Don't be."

"This whole mess started me thinking. What if my mother had objected to my marrying your father? I can't help wondering if I would have just gone meekly along with her decision." Keeping her gaze steady on Cat's, Gianna said, "That would have been a huge mistake because I love your father so much. I can't bear to think that I might have lost him."

Seeing the tears swim in Gianna's eyes, Cat threw her arms around her stepmother. "My father wouldn't have given up. He wouldn't have let you walk away."

Gianna drew back. "You think not?"

"I know not. He has a way of getting what he wants. And he's just as involved in this fake engagement charade as you are."

Gianna shrugged. "He just did it to save my neck."

"No. I mean it probably started out as a plan to save your neck, but then I think the plot expanded. He didn't just hire anyone off the street to play the role."

As she thought more about it, Cat began to pace. "He consulted with my godfather, Admiral Maxwell, and they hand-picked Navy Captain Dino Angelis."

Whirling, she fisted her hands on her hips and faced

Gianna. "I think he and Uncle Bobby decided to do a little matchmaking of their own."

Something flared in Gianna's eyes. "So Jimmy's not just trying to rescue me?"

"Not by a long shot." She couldn't tell Gianna about the more complex part of the masquerade. The fewer people who knew about the drug smuggling, the better. But she could certainly share the part she was just figuring out herself.

"I think he wants to see me married off as much as you and your mother do." Cat's eyes narrowed. "I wouldn't put it past him to have called your mother and planted the whole surprise Christmas visit in her head."

"Really." Gianna began to tap her foot. Then she threw her hands up in the air again. "The thing is, I think he's right."

"About what?"

"About you and Dino Angelis. I like your navy captain. Did you hear the way he defended you to my mother? No one stands up to her that way. And she liked it. She likes him, too. That was the other thing I wanted to talk to you about. Even if you're right about your father, I think you ought to grab the guy."

Knots twisted in Cat's stomach. "It's not that simple. He's from San Francisco, and his family is important to him. I run a store in New York."

Gianna smiled slowly. "So you have thought about it."

Cat was pretty sure she'd been thinking about it from the first time he'd strolled into the store and kissed her. "I think I love him."

Once the words were out, the knots in her stomach grew even tighter. "But I don't think he feels the same way. Once the ball is over, he says we're going to talk. I'm pretty sure he's going to tell me why he has to leave." Cat paused, took a deep breath. "I don't know why I'm unloading all this on you."

"You're talking to me because I'm another woman. If I hadn't been so influenced by my mother's agenda, we might have grown closer before this. I'm sorry about that, too. But the most important thing is what you're going to do when you and Dino Angelis talk."

This time Cat felt her stomach take a tumble. "He's a very kind man. He's going to let me down easily."

"And then you'll tell him what you want. And you're going to go after it." Gianna smiled at her. Cat realized that it was the first genuine smile Gianna had ever given her. "Didn't you just tell me that your father never would have let me walk away?"

Cat nodded.

"Well, you're your father's daughter. And you'll get your captain." She motioned to the dress bag. "I brought this as a peace offering, but I think it will work nicely on your Dino."

13

WITH DINO'S HAND at the small of her back, Cat dashed to the open door of the limo, ducked in and slid to the far end of the cushy leather seat. Outside, Dino paused to pass their duffels and her dress bag to the uniformed driver. She took the opportunity to close her eyes and summon up a kaleidoscope of images—the faces of her employees when she'd announced she was leaving early for the charity ball and that she was taking the doll with her.

She felt Dino slide in beside her, heard the door slam shut while in her mind's eye, she recalled expressions of surprise on Matt's and Josie's faces. But she was almost sure it was delight and approval she'd seen on Adelaide's. On her way to the door, her assistant manager had placed a hand on her arm and murmured in a voice only Cat could hear, "Good for you. If I had a hot-looking fiancé, I'd have knocked off at noon."

She'd smiled at Adelaide, but she wondered now if the woman she'd thought of as a close friend was only playing a role—and a deadly one at that. As the limo eased away from the curb, Cat let out a frustrated sigh and began to run the day's events through her mind again. But there was nothing there—nothing in anything her employees had said or done that was definitively suspicious.

She fisted her hands on the leather seat. "I'm absolutely

no good at playing detective. I've been watching them like a hawk all day. But I'm still clueless about whether it's Matt, Josie or Adelaide who's unloading the drugs on this end."

"We need a break," Dino said.

"But what if we don't get one? What if this whole trap we're setting turns out to be a bust?"

"I'm not talking about a break in the case."

The sound of a cork popping had her opening her eyes. Dino tipped wine into two flutes and Cat watched bubbles fizz to the rim. Then he handed her a glass and raised his in a toast.

"To breaks."

There was something in his eyes that had her blood heating, her heart pumping. She sipped her champagne. "What kind of break are you thinking of—exactly?"

Dino took the glass from her and set it with his on a small tray. "I suggested to the driver that he take a circuitous route to the Alsatian Towers—to make sure we weren't being followed."

Cat glanced back over her shoulder through the smoky glass. Though it was only four, cars had their headlights on. And traffic was heavy. "Do you think someone is on our tail?"

"No. There's no need. Everyone knows where we're going."

"Then why—" When she turned back, he'd moved close enough to trace a finger down her throat to where her sweater formed a V. The tremor skittered through her all the way to the pit of her stomach.

"Twelve hours," he murmured. "Twelve endless hours. That's how long I've been wanting to touch you and couldn't."

He framed her face with his hands and Cat felt the pressure of each one of his fingers. But it was the heat in his eyes that transfixed her.

"I shouldn't be touching you. I told myself I wouldn't until this is over. But I couldn't stop myself from making love to you last night. And I can't help myself right now."

The thread of frustration she heard in his voice had a feeling of power moving through her. "Go ahead. Touch me. I want you to."

He drew her closer, brushed his mouth over hers. His tongue slipped between her lips and slid over hers. Then he traced a line of featherlight kisses to her ear and whispered, "Have you ever made love in a limo before?"

Heat arrowed through her. "No."

"We'll have to be fast and quiet."

He was already moving quickly, shifting to the floor so that he was between her knees and pulling her slacks off. She heard his breath catch and then his fingers began to toy with the lace at the top of her thigh-high stockings. Pleasure spiked through her as he traced a lazy pattern higher and higher on her legs.

"Fast," she reminded him.

"Oh, I think we have a little time." Pushing aside the thin lace of her panties, he slipped two fingers into her.

She arched. *"Dino."*

"Shh." He crushed her mouth with his.

It was her turn to move quickly then as she dragged off his belt and ripped open the snap on his jeans. It took both of them to get the jeans down his hips. Then he made quick work of the condom, tearing off the foil and slipping it on. She helped him by pulling aside her panties.

And then she bit down hard on her lip as she watched him push slowly into her body. Pressure and heat shot through her. Dizzy with the sensation of his penetration, Cat met his eyes and what she saw in them—the desperation, the longing—was enough to trigger the first convulsion. As it rippled through her in an ever-widening wave of pleasure, she wrapped arms and legs around him.

Dino waited, keeping his own needs reined in. Her eyes were open and on his, and he knew as her climax peaked that she thought only of him.

Then he began to move, one stroke and then another. On his third thrust, she began to move with him, settling into his rhythm. He'd planned to keep his movements slow, to draw out the pleasure for both of them, but as she tightened around him again, he felt his control begin to shred. In the dim, intermittent flash of streetlights, all he could see was her. First in shadow, then in light. The effect was incredibly erotic.

As his need built, all he could think of was Cat. All he wanted was Cat. Grasping her hips, he pushed into her faster and harder until all he knew was Cat. She filled him until there was nothing else, no one else but the long explosion of pleasure that they brought each other.

Afterward, he held her tightly against him, for his own sake as much as hers. He didn't want to let her go. Couldn't let her go. And he was going to have to tell her. Soon.

DINO HAD TO HAND IT TO Gianna Merceri McGuire. She'd transformed the Grand Ballroom of the Alsatian Towers into a Christmas fantasy. Twinkling white lights cascaded from the ceiling, competing with the glow of the crystal chandeliers. White poinsettia plants lined three mirrored walls and were clustered at intervals along the dance floor. The scent of candles blended with expensive perfume. Silver gleamed on snow-white tablecloths, and a wall of French doors opened onto a glassed-in terrace offering a view of the Manhattan skyline.

For over an hour, Cat had stood next to her very pregnant stepsister at the end of the reception line, greeting guests as they'd filed in to fill their assigned tables. No one could tell by looking at her animated expression the kind of day she'd put in.

Nor what she still had to do.

The woman was amazing. Before they'd left the shop, she'd plucked the damaged doll out of the display window and everyone had seen her tuck it into a Cheshire Cat gift bag.

Right now that gift bag was in plain sight at the McGuires' reserved table, and the hair of the doll was just visible. Jack Phillips, who had gone through the reception line early on, was now seated within arm's reach of the "bait," entertaining Lucia Merceri until her family joined her. Across from him sat Admiral Robert Maxwell and his wife who'd also been among the first to arrive.

His admiral's presence had come as a surprise to Dino. And it worried him a bit. He didn't doubt for a moment that Cat's father had filled his best friend in on exactly the kind of trap they were setting tonight.

The problem was the ballroom now contained a lot of people who were concerned for Cat's safety and who wanted to nail the bastard who was behind the drug smuggling. Hopefully when something went down, they wouldn't all trip over each other. An even bigger problem was that even though he'd watched every person who'd made their way through the line, he hadn't gotten any "feelings" about any of them. In fact, the only thing his gut instinct had been telling him since he'd entered the ballroom was that Cat was in danger.

Dino shifted his gaze back to Jack. From the look on Phillips' face, he wasn't having an easy time of it with Lucia. But in Dino's opinion, the woman wasn't nearly the ogre that everyone made her out to be. His mother had enjoyed her conversation with Lucia immensely.

Dino let his gaze sweep the room which was nearly full

now. When they'd arrived, Matt Winslow, Josie Sullivan and Adelaide Creed had been escorted to a table near the back of the ballroom. He'd noted Dr. and Mrs. Lassiter's entrance with interest. They'd been seated closer to the dance floor in what looked to be an area reserved for VIPs. Dino recognized some of the other people at the Lassiters' table—the governor, a state senator, a film star. But it was the woman seated between the governor and Mrs. Lassiter who drew his gaze. She was striking in a long-sleeved black sequined dress. Bangs fringed her forehead and the rest of her dark hair fell in a smooth line to her shoulders.

When Dino sensed Jase at his side, he said, "Who's the woman in the black dress sitting next to the governor?"

"Jessica Atwell, our famous 'get kids off drugs' attorney general. If you were a New Yorker, you'd recognize her from the TV campaign she's been running. She's even got her face on a billboard over Times Square."

Dino was about to look away when Jessica Atwell took out a pair of reading glasses and put them on. A tingle of awareness moved through him—the first he'd had all evening. "What else do you know about her?"

"Just what everyone knows. She started out forty years ago in Hollywood and made several movies. Then she became an activist and later a congresswoman. Word is she's trying to raise money for a Senate run."

Dino glanced back to the McGuires' table. Jack was standing.

"You'd better get back in position," Dino said. "It looks like Jack Phillips is headed toward the bar."

Jase was seated at the table next to the McGuires'. If anyone made a grab for the doll, he and Jack were in charge of grabbing the person. But Dino's gut feeling was that it wasn't going to go down that easily. What he didn't like, didn't like at all was his lingering feeling that in spite of the precautions he and Jack and Colonel McGuire had taken, Cat was in mortal danger.

It was the same feeling that had thrummed through his blood before he'd taken a bullet on his last op. Not good.

His gaze returned to Cat. Another problem all evening had been taking his eyes off of her. Ever since she'd changed into that dress her stepmother had brought as a peace offering, she'd simply stolen his breath away. The red silk clung to her like a second skin, and the view from the back was even more dangerous to his breathing than the view from the front. In his opinion, the dress perfectly captured the passion of the woman.

But even without the dress, she was beautiful. He'd known that from the first time he'd looked at her photo. But now he knew the depth of that beauty. She was smart and strong and passionate. And she'd done a hell of a job that day at the store.

While she'd been watching her employees, he'd been watching her, and she'd done nothing, said nothing to indicate to any one of them that she knew anything about the drugs that had been smuggled into the country through her store. If he'd still been in the business of undercover ops, he'd want her on his team.

"She's a beautiful woman."

"Yes." Dino swore silently as he turned to face Matt Winslow. He hadn't sensed the man's approach. His mind had been too filled with Cat.

Matt carried two glasses of champagne and he sipped one of them as he studied Dino. Winslow had been animated and smiling in the reception line, but now his eyes were assessing, his expression cool.

"How did you and Cat meet?"

The blunt question had Dino wondering if the man was a

suspicious drug mule—or just jealous. As far as he knew, Cat looked on Matt Winslow as a brother. Had Matt wanted a deeper relationship? Or was he merely being protective of a friend? "Cat didn't tell you?"

"She's never even mentioned you," Matt said. "I was under the impression that since she opened the store, she wasn't dating, didn't have the time. And we hardly had the chance to chat today in the store."

He *had* wanted more, Dino decided. And he'd thought he'd have plenty of time to make his move. Dino might have worked up some sympathy for Winslow, if he hadn't wondered exactly how a man found the control to bide his time with a woman like Cat McGuire. He hadn't even been able to wait until his bodyguarding job was over.

And just why had Winslow been so willing to wait? He recalled what Cat had told him—that Matt saw the Cheshire Cat as a stepping-stone and that his goal was to become a millionaire. Was smuggling drugs another stepping-stone?

"Well?" Impatience shimmered in Matt's tone.

"We ran into each other a couple of months ago on the skating rink at Rockefeller Center. Literally. A week ago, I proposed to her there."

Matt frowned. "She never told me she'd started skating again. I would have gone with her."

Dino met his eyes levelly. "Evidently, there are lots of things she doesn't tell you." Beyond Matt's shoulder, Dino spotted Jack at a nearby drink station.

"Excuse me." He moved past Matt to join Jack at the bar.

"You're supposed to be guarding Cat's bag."

"I'm on a mission to get her royal highness a martini, straight up with an olive. An Italian olive. Working undercover for the CIA is a lot easier than this."

Dino grinned.

"If anyone goes for the doll while I'm gone, Signora Merceri will take them out with her cane."

Dino didn't doubt it for a moment. "You should know that I'm beginning to get a bad feeling about this."

Frowning, Jack took the martini from the waiter behind the bar. "We've got everything covered."

"Just wanted to let you know."

Jack had no sooner drifted away in the direction of the McGuires' table when the reception line broke up, and Cat turned to join him. Together they fell in line behind Gianna and her father. As they moved to their table, waiters flowed into the room and began to serve the first course.

"The ball has officially begun," Cat murmured.

Dino let his gaze sweep the room, tracking the usual suspects. This time, for a long moment, his gaze locked with someone else's. A heightening of awareness, a surge of adrenaline, mixed with surprise. He strongly suspected he was looking into the eyes of the person who was running the drug smuggling operation. It was only a premonition, a "hunch." But if he was right, it more than explained the attempt on Cat's life.

He had no way of proving it. Not yet. But his mind raced as he pulled out Cat's chair and settled himself in the one next to hers. Others had to be involved, and one of them would provide the link.

The question was who would make the move on Cat to get that doll?

IT WAS NEARLY AN HOUR before the dancing began. Gianna and her father were the first to rise from their table. Her stepsister Lucy and her husband followed, then Dino offered his hand. Cat put hers into it, rose and moved with him to the dance floor.

The moment she stepped into his arms, she felt his tension. "You're worried."

"Just watchful."

"Nothing's happening." Impatience rolled through her. "Maybe we were wrong to think that someone would make a move tonight. Maybe they're not even here."

"They're here all right. I think I know who's behind the drug operation."

She met his eyes and saw the truth of his statement. "Who?"

Instead of answering immediately, he danced her across the floor. "Look at the people seated at the table directly to your right."

Cat glanced at the table. "Mrs. Lassiter?"

"No. Look again."

This time she let her gaze sweep the table more slowly. She recognized a state senator, the governor, the attorney general, and a film star whose name she couldn't quite pull up. Then as if they could feel her gaze, one of them looked up and met her eyes. And suddenly the memory that had been tugging at the edge of her mind for a day and a half clicked. "It's George Miller."

"I think so, too," Dino murmured as he swung her to the center of the dance floor. "But there's no evidence we can take to anyone yet."

"What are we going to do?"

"There has to be an accomplice—one of your employees. So we'll go ahead with our plan and hope that they can provide the proof we need."

Her uncle Bobby tapped Dino on the shoulder. "My turn."

Her godfather smiled down at her when Cat stepped into his arms, but his eyes were serious. "Are you all right?"

"Don't I look all right?"

"A little tense, that's all. But you still manage to look beautiful."

"You're biased."

Her godfather laughed then, and for a moment Cat felt almost normal—as if she were just a woman dancing with her father's best friend at a Christmas ball. As he swirled her toward the center of the dance floor, she relaxed in his arms.

"So what do you think of Dino Angelis?"

Cat's eyes shifted to where Dino was standing at the edge of the dance floor. He was wearing his navy dress uniform and just the sight of him had her pulse leaping. Then Cat narrowed her gaze on her godfather. The innocent look in his eyes had her recalling her earlier conversation with Gianna and it confirmed her suspicions.

"What do I think of him? What I think is that when you and my dad selected Captain Dino Angelis to be my bodyguard, a certain amount of meddling matchmaking was involved."

"Meddling?" Maxwell frowned. "I don't know what you're talking about. Your father called me, told me what he suspected was going on at your store, and I sent my best man."

Cat stepped back out of his arms and tapped a finger on his chest. "You can just cut the innocent act. I've already told Gianna what I think went down. I'll bet you and my father even have a little wager riding on the outcome."

Maxwell's face remained blank. "I'm taking the Fifth."

She snorted. "How much did you bet?"

"You're too smart for your own good."

Cat fisted her hands on her hips. "How much?"

The admiral sighed. "All right. I bet him fifty bucks that you and Angelis would hit it off and that the engagement would become real."

A little band tightened around Cat's heart. "Well, it's not

going to become real." She might want it to—in spite of the fact that she'd been set up—but...

"Dino's family lives in San Francisco. One of his cousins is getting married two days after Christmas. Once he's finished his job with me, he's going to be on the first plane out of here."

Unless she followed her stepmother's advice and persuaded him differently. Or went with him?

FROM THE SIDE of the dance floor, Dino watched as Cat and his admiral danced. The ballroom was growing warmer, and behind him, wait staff were opening the French doors to the terrace.

Suddenly, Cat and the admiral stopped dancing. She poked a finger into his chest.

Dino took one step forward, intending to cut in for another dance and rescue his boss when a vision slammed into him, filling his mind. Someone pointing a gun at Cat.

Fear froze him to the spot.

On the rare occasions when he experienced them, his visions were only a blurry flash—a quickly fading image in black and white. Cat was in a confined space—an elevator? A closet? The details weren't clear. And it was too dark to make out the face of the person holding the gun on her. He couldn't even be sure if it was a man or a woman.

Then all he saw was a flash of fire as the bullet exploded from the gun.

For a moment, his heart simply stopped. Someone was going to get to Cat and he couldn't tell who it was.

Or how to stop it.

14

"YOU OKAY?"

The voice was barely audible, but Dino recognized that it belonged to Jase who was standing to his right. He pulled himself together. Dancers swirled past them, and Dino finally spotted Cat now dancing with her father.

Without looking at Jase or acknowledging his presence in any way, Dino spoke in a voice that didn't carry. "Someone's going to get to her and they have a gun." Fear had formed a tight knot in his stomach.

"Got any details?"

Keeping his gaze locked on Cat, Dino filled Jase in on what he'd seen and what he knew.

"Have you told her?" Jase asked.

"About the person I suspect is running the operation— yes. She agrees. Something about Mr. George Miller struck her as familiar the moment he stepped into her shop. But I haven't told her that someone is going to hold her at gun-point."

"I'd do it now," Jase said.

Moving to the dance floor, Dino tapped Colonel McGuire on the shoulder and once more took Cat into his arms. Then he skillfully steered her through the open French doors to the terrace.

THE DIMLY LIT SERVICE HALLWAY that led from the ballroom to the kitchen was deserted except for the two figures. Scents from the recently served dinner mingled with the smell of cleanser. The sound of the orchestra and the chatter of the guests were muted here.

One of the figures was partially hidden behind an open door. "You've studied the blueprint I gave you?"

"Yes."

"Here's the syringe, the key and the gun."

All three were slipped into a pocket. "She's being very well guarded. Her uncle is here—he's CIA. And her fiancé never lets her get more than a few feet away."

"Do I have to spell out everything? There's one place she can go where the men can't follow her."

There was silence as a waiter hurried by carrying a tray of dirty china and silver to the kitchen.

"Remember that when you've got the doll, Ms. McGuire must be eliminated."

Fear turned icy, and the words gushed out. "I didn't sign on for murder. I don't know if I—"

"You can and you will." The voice was calm, cold. "If she hasn't already figured out that you betrayed her, she will soon. Think of it this way. It's Ms. McGuire or you. If I have to take steps, I'll eliminate you, too."

The figure half hidden behind the door stepped out and walked back into the ballroom.

"THIS IS BETTER," Dino murmured as he guided her toward the railing that lined the glass-walled terrace. Beyond it, the skyline of Manhattan shone as brightly as any Christmas tree. "I need to talk to you for a moment."

Cat turned to him. "I need to talk to you, too. I found out that this whole fake fiancé thing is a setup."

Dino studied her. "We both knew that it was a cover so that I could protect you."

Cat waved a hand. "I'm not talking about that. I'm talking about the fact that my father and Uncle Bobby have a second hidden agenda here. They're playing matchmakers and hoping that the engagement will take, that it will become real."

She whirled to pace a few feet away. "In fact, your boss has even bet fifty bucks on a successful outcome."

She paused, waiting for a reaction. When Dino said nothing, she strode toward him. "You're not surprised? Were you in on it?"

Dino raised both hands, palms out. "No way."

Cat put her hands on her hips. "How did you figure it out?" She narrowed her eyes. "Was it some kind of precognition? Because if it was, you should have—"

"It wasn't."

"When did you know?"

"I'm not sure, but I got an inkling that the setup was a bit more complicated than your father was letting on when I first met him in his office."

Cat began to tap her foot. "What did he say? He and I are going to have a little talk about this."

Dino moved toward her and placed his hands on her shoulders. "It wasn't anything definitive. Just as I was leaving the office, he mentioned that while I was pulling off the charade and bodyguarding you without your catching on, he'd appreciate it if I saw to it that you had some fun. And usually fathers don't ask soldiers to show their daughters a good time."

"I'm going to kill him," Cat said. "Better still, I'm going

to steal his secret cache of cigars and destroy them." She met his eyes. "I'm sorry."

He kissed her forehead. "I'm the one who should apologize. I really haven't gotten around to making sure you're having fun."

She smiled then. "Not true. I'd say that what we did in the limo was the most fun I've had in a long time—unless you count the fun we had in my office—or on the floor of my apartment—or—"

Dino silenced her then by pulling her close for a kiss. It had temper, nerves and fear streaming away. When he finally released her, she was breathless and tingling.

"I needed that," Dino said.

"Me, too."

"We'll have more fun, I promise, but I brought you out here to tell you something."

"What?"

He told her about the vision.

She met his eyes steadily. "I think it's a sign."

"It's a sign all right, and I don't like it. I didn't see enough."

"I think you did. If we want this person to make his or her move, we have to give them the opportunity. And we discussed the best scenario for that. You ask Gianna to dance and I take the doll and head to the washroom. If Matt's involved, he'll make his move then. If it's Josie or Adelaide, they'll follow me into the ladies' room."

"Jase's operative is stationed there. She's dressed as a washroom attendant, and she's supposed to make a move if someone follows you. But it's not going to go down the way we want it to."

"Because of your vision, we know that. So we've been forewarned."

Dino grasped her shoulders again. "I still don't like it."

"Neither do I. But it's a chance we have to take if we're going to catch the people behind this and put them away."

Dino pulled her close, held her tight. "Just remember that Jase and I won't be far behind."

"Don't worry. I'm not about to forget that." Cat allowed herself to stay in his arms for just another moment before she led the way back into the ballroom.

THE MOMENT CAT STEPPED into the hall outside the ballroom, she saw Matt standing across the way, as if he'd been waiting. She ruthlessly pushed away fear, disappointment and anger as he strode toward her, and summoned up a smile. Matt didn't return it. All she read was anger and something else in his eyes. Hurt?

"Can we talk for a moment? In private?" Without waiting for her assent, he took her arm in a firm grip and steered her to the end of the corridor. When they reached it, Cat saw that hallways branched off to the left and to the right. If Matt pulled her into one of them…

She didn't dare look behind her to see if either Jase or Dino had stepped out of the ballroom yet. Instead, she dug in her heels. "This is private enough. What is it, Matt?"

"Your engagement. Why didn't you tell me about it?"

She studied him, trying to read his expression. He hadn't released his grip on her arm. "I didn't tell anyone."

"Well, you should have. You told me you weren't dating. You didn't have time for relationships. I respected that. And I waited. I was trying to give you the time and the space you needed before I told you how I felt. And now…"

He wasn't the one who'd betrayed her, Cat thought as twin waves of relief and sympathy moved through her. "I never lied to you. I wasn't dating until I met Dino. And I wasn't looking for a relationship until him."

Matt turned, paced away, then turned back to face her. "I should have spoken sooner. Would it have made a difference if I had?"

Cat shook her head. "What I feel for you, what I've always felt for you is friendship."

Though he didn't move a muscle, Cat could see that her words struck him hard.

"Friendship." There was bitterness in his tone. "There's no way I can change your mind?"

Cat thought of Dino, and if she hadn't known it before, she did then—he was the only man in the world for her. "No. But I hope we can continue being friends, Matt."

He didn't say anything. Cat watched in sadness as he turned and made his way back into the ballroom. She saw no sign of either Jase or Dino. But then she wasn't supposed to. The whole idea was that she was to appear alone, vulnerable. Taking a deep breath, she walked back down the hallway toward the ladies' room.

She'd told everyone at the table that she was going to the restroom. Whoever was watching had to have seen her pick up the gift bag and leave.

Right now she could feel goose bumps on her arms and hairs on the back of her neck were standing up. Someone was watching her. She was sure of it. She suppressed the urge to whirl around and see who it was. Instead, she reached for the door handle and entered the ladies' room.

Lounge was a more appropriate word, Cat decided as she took in the French Impressionist prints, the leather cushioned seats and the mirrored wall. One woman in what Cat was sure was a Dior design was retouching her lipstick. There was no sign of a washroom attendant.

The woman met Cat's eyes in the mirror and said, "You're Gianna's stepdaughter, right?"

"Yes."

Rising, the woman extended her hand. "Lydia Hathaway. I worked on one of her committees for this extravaganza. She speaks highly of you."

Cat shook the hand. "Nice meeting you."

When the woman walked out, Cat moved into a second room lined on one side with closed stall doors and on the other side with marble sinks. Two of them were in use. One of the ladies was gray-haired with a queen's ransom of diamonds dangling from her ears. The other one was in her midtwenties and looked as if she was battling an eating disorder. The older woman left first, and two other women entered from the lounge area and stepped into stalls.

Where was Jase's operative? Cat's nerves tightened as she moved to a sink and turned on one of the faucets. Then her stomach sank as she glanced in the mirror and saw a very familiar figure step out of the first stall and move toward her. She managed a smile before she dropped her eyes and tried to gather her thoughts.

Play dumb. Stall her.

"Cat, I was hoping for an opportunity to talk with you. Your stepmother has outdone herself this year."

"Gianna excels at this sort of thing."

As another woman stepped out of the stall and moved to a sink, Cat felt something hard press into her side. The voice in her ear was barely a whisper. "The washroom attendant is unconscious in the stall I just left. If you don't want someone else to get hurt, you're going to lead the way to that door over there."

"I don't understand." Cat spoke softly as she moved to a door marked Storage. "What's going on?"

"We're taking a little walk," Reaching around Cat she shoved a key in the door and opened it.

Disbelief, disappointment, fear. Cat struggled to suppress the emotions flooding through her as she led the way into a small room. She had time to note the large cart filled with cleaning supplies before the door swung shut, cutting off all the light.

Was this what Dino had seen in his vision?

Panic rose, but Cat fought it back. She needed a clear head. A shot would be too risky here. Still, Cat jumped when the gun poked into her back.

"Move. The exit door is just ahead of you."

Stretching her hands out in front of her, Cat groped for the handle, turned it, and stepped into an empty corridor. Doors on either side led to hotel staff offices, all closed for the night. The music from the ballroom was faint. Cat realized that the chance of party guests wandering this far was slim to none. How was Dino going to find her?

At gunpoint, Cat led the way across the hall, through a door, and into a stairwell. A lightbulb overhead barely illuminated the steep flight of stairs and the narrow landing below.

A sinking feeling in her stomach told her this was the place Dino had seen in his vision. Panic surged again, and Cat forced herself to take deep calming breaths.

"We're going down. We're still too close to the ballroom. I don't want to make it easy for your protectors to find you."

"My protectors?"

"Don't play dumb. Your fiancé, your uncle, your father— and I'm sure there are more. It wasn't hard to spot the woman they had staked out in the ladies' room." The gun poked her again. "Move. I won't hesitate to use this."

Stall. Stall. As she reached the landing at the bottom of the first flight of stairs, Cat made herself stumble and fall to her knees.

"No, you don't. Get up or I'll shoot you here."

Cat got to her feet and they descended two more flights.

"Far enough. Put the bag on the floor and then back up a couple of steps."

Facing the barrel of the gun, Cat's mind raced as fast as her heart. She thought of the woman she'd known for a year and a half. The woman she'd worked with, laughed with. It couldn't have all been an act.

"You don't want to do this. Even if you get away with the doll, you're going to be discovered and arrested. The FBI, the CIA—they're all looking at the store. They're closing in."

"You're lying. Put down the doll." Her voice was firm, but the hand holding the gun trembled until she brought her other hand up to steady it.

Cat drew the bag around in front of her, using it as a shield. If she pulled the trigger, she'd have to risk putting a bullet through the drugs. "Why, Adelaide? Don't I at least deserve an answer to that?"

SOMETHING WAS WRONG. The bad feeling he'd had all day solidified in Dino's gut. Three full minutes had dragged by, and there'd been a steady stream of women entering and leaving the ladies' room. Not one of them had carried anything large enough to hold the doll.

And Cat hadn't returned.

As he strode to the door, Jase joined him. "Winslow's at the bar. Josie's still at the table, but Adelaide and our prime suspect are missing."

"Adelaide didn't follow Cat into the washroom."

"Maybe she was already in there."

Dino's hand was on the knob when a vision flashed into his mind. He could only see their backs, but he recognized Cat and the woman holding a gun on her—Adelaide. Cat led the way though a door with an Exit sign over it. The image was fading to gray, but before it vanished, Dino made out the letters on the door—*Stairs*.

The vision had barely faded before another filled his mind. The same one he'd seen before—Cat and a person holding a gun in a dimly lit space. Once again he saw the flash of fire and heard the deafening sound of a gunshot.

Pushing down his fear, Dino whirled away from the ladies' room and strode back to where one of the hotel employees was standing at the entrance to the ballroom. To forestall questions, he said, "This may be an emergency. Where are the staircases on this floor?"

"There are two—"

"Which one is closer?"

The young man pointed to the end of the corridor. "Take a left. Should I notify someone?" he asked.

Dino was already running. "We'll let you know."

With Jase at his side, Dino went left and prayed that he'd made the right choice. When they reached the stairs, he gripped the handle, turned the knob carefully and pushed the door open just a crack. He heard voices. Signaling Jase to stay where he was and hold the door ajar, Dino slipped through a narrow opening and moved quietly to the railing. On a landing, three flights down, he saw Cat clutching the gift bag to her chest. He couldn't see Adelaide's face, but he saw the hands holding the gun. They were shaking.

Then he caught it. Just the barest hint of a shadow on a lower level, slowly climbing toward Cat and Adelaide.

Fear pounded through him. Backing up, he whispered to Jase what to do and quietly closed the stairwell door. Then he slipped out of his shoes and silently started down the stairs.

15

"WHY DID I DO IT?" Adelaide's mouth twisted slightly. "Money, of course."

Cat's eyes widened. "You can't need it. I know that you're not earning a lot in my shop, but you have your retirement money."

"*Had* my retirement money. A year ago, I got greedy and took some risks with my investments. When they didn't pay off, I took more risks. I came to work for you because I needed the money. And that's when she approached me."

"Who?" In spite of the dim lighting, Cat could read fear in the other woman's eyes. "You're talking about Jessica Atwell, aren't you?"

Adelaide's face drained of color and her voice dropped to a whisper. "How do you know?"

"She's on TV all the time. The moment that George Miller walked into the shop, I knew there was something familiar about him. At first I thought he reminded me of Santa Claus. But he has Jessica Atwell's eyes. What exactly did she ask you to do?"

"She'd done her research—on both of us. She knew your family connections and that your reputation was stellar. She also knew I was desperate for money. And she offered me a lot. All I had to do was to make sure certain toys that you imported from Paxco got to her. It was so easy."

Above the sound of Adelaide's voice, Cat thought she heard the sound of a door opening somewhere below them. Was it wishful thinking? Or was it Dino? She badly wanted to shift her gaze to the railing and glance down, but she kept her eyes on Adelaide.

"Who handled the Paxco end?" Cat asked. "Was it Matt?"

"No. I don't know what went on in Mexico. Just before a shipment, I would get a phone call describing the toy the drugs were in."

AT THE NEXT LANDING, Dino edged as close as he dared to the railing and glanced down. The shadow he'd seen earlier was clearer now. Light glinted off the sequins on the dress the woman was wearing. There wasn't a doubt in his mind that it was Jessica Atwell and she was closer to Cat and Adelaide than he was.

No sign of Jase. But there wouldn't be. Fading back to the wall, Dino increased his pace. He heard women's voices more clearly, but he still couldn't make out what they were saying.

Keep her talking, Cat. I'm almost there.

Two landings above Cat and Adelaide, he paused. Once he started down the next flight of stairs, Adelaide would be able to see him if she glanced up, and she still had her gun aimed at Cat. Dino waited, biding his time.

"ONCE I KNEW which one carried the drugs, I'd write up the order in a fake name, pay for it with cash, and that night, a limousine would be waiting a few blocks away. I'd deliver the package on my way to the subway. Six months, she promised, and I'd make back twice what I'd lost. I did. Then she kept saying one more shipment. She had customers she couldn't disappoint. It's been a year. But this is the end of it. Once you're gone, the operation will be over. I'll be free. Give me the damn doll."

Cat backed up a step and clutched the bag more closely. "Giving her the doll won't end this for you. She's going to have to kill you."

"No." Adelaide nearly shouted the word. "She told me it was you or me. It's going to be you. Give me the bag."

"She can't afford to let you live." In her peripheral vision, Cat could see a shadow on the stairs below them. Praying that it was Dino or Jase, she kept her gaze steady on Adelaide. She had to keep the woman's attention focused on her so she backed up onto the first step of the stairs they'd just descended.

"She has two sets of customers. Did you know that?"

Adelaide took a step toward her. "What are you talking about?"

"There's the people she supplies with the drugs, and then there's the terrorist cell she funds with the profits."

Adelaide's eyes widened. "You're lying."

"You didn't know?"

"No. I would never— No."

"That will work in your favor. If you name her, you'll be able to make a deal. Adelaide, you haven't killed anyone yet."

"No, she hasn't. And that's a problem."

Cat's heart sank as she saw Jessica Atwell step into view on the landing below them.

"Jessica," Adelaide breathed.

"Put the gun down Adelaide and move over next to Ms. McGuire." As Adelaide jerkily followed her instructions, Jessica moved quickly up the stairs. Her cold and clipped tones were a sharp right turn from the voice she used on TV. "I can't trust you to do anything. You don't even have the doll yet."

When Jessica reached the landing, Cat finally saw her gun with its businesslike silencer on the end. Jessica pointed it in Cat's direction. "I'm pressed for time, Ms. McGuire, and unlike Adelaide, I'm not in the mood for a chat. Put the bag on the floor and shove it toward me."

Cat held on to the doll. Then she heard a noise behind her.

"Drop the gun, Ms. Atwell."

Dino. Then as if she were viewing a film in slow motion, Cat saw Jessica look beyond her and shift the barrel of the gun.

"No." Cat acted out of blind instinct, hurling the bag, then leaping after it to push Jessica off balance. Cat saw the flash of fire, heard the deafening sound of the gunshot. Then she and Jessica tumbled head over heels down the flight of stairs. Pain sang up her elbow, then her shoulder. But it was her head that took the worst hit. She saw swirling stars before Jase pulled the woman off of her and Dino sank to his knees beside her.

"You all right?" Dino asked.

"What took you so long?"

He pulled her into his arms and she held on for a long time.

DINO LEANED AGAINST THE WALL in one of the Alsation Towers' executive offices. Jack Phillips stood to his left and Jase flanked him on the right while Cat sat on a carved oak desk and fielded a barrage of questions from her family.

She looked only a little worse for wear, Dino thought. The hotel doctor, a young Asian woman, had checked Cat out, bandaged her elbow, and pronounced that her patient was going to have a stiff leg, a sore shoulder and a goose egg on her head that wouldn't fade for four or five days.

"Smuggled drugs, terrorists, and the Cheshire Cat is right in the middle of it. It's better than a movie. No wonder you don't want to give up your business and settle down." Lucia Merceri thumped her cane on the floor as she shot an approving look at Dino. "And he's on your side. Seems to me you've got yourself a keeper there."

Then Lucia turned her attention to her son-in-law. "With all this excitement and adventure, I may have to visit New York City more often."

Later, Dino might find time to be amused by the expression on Colonel James McGuire's face. But right now, he couldn't quite summon up a grin. However, Cat's burst of laughter did more than the doctor's diagnosis to begin to untangle the knot of fear in his stomach. She was all right.

It had been a close call. He would never forget the fact that he'd nearly been too late. While he'd silently descended three endless flights of stairs, he'd realized what Cat was trying to do—keep Adelaide focused on her. But he'd also sensed the escalating fear and panic in the older woman. And she'd had that gun aimed directly at Cat. It was a high-risk situation and he'd purposely spoken to attract Jessica Atwell's attention, never expecting that Cat would launch herself at the woman.

Once again the image of Cat hurtling down the stairs replayed itself in his mind. She could have broken her neck. He could have lost her forever.

"Stop beating up on yourself," Jase said. "Your visions are what saved her. She was forewarned, so she had an advantage. And you knew just where to find her."

"Visions?" Jack Phillips asked. "You have visions?"

Dino winced inwardly, but luckily, Jack's cell phone rang.

"Yeah," Jack said. After a moment, a smile lit his face. He pocketed the cell and turned to Jase and Dino. "Good news. Adelaide is singing her heart out and her song is all about Jessica Atwell. She's confessed to hiring the man who knifed me, but denies any responsibility for the attempt on Cat's life. Of course, she's cooperating fully in the hopes of making a deal that will lessen her sentence. Down in Paxco, my team has taken Juan Rivero into custody. So far, Atwell is only talking to her lawyers, but now that we've identified her, we'll find a paper trail, and Creed is a credible witness."

"What about Atwell's connection to terrorists?" Dino asked.

"The CIA is checking into it. I'm figuring it must date back to her days as an activist. There was a time when she was very anti-American and she spent time in Central and South America. And a Senate run takes money. We'll find the connection." Jack's grin widened. "And with Homeland Security involved—well, they have a lot more freedom than we do in questioning a suspect."

Dino's attention was suddenly drawn back to Cat as her father said, "Little girl, why don't you come home with Gianna and me tonight? You're not going to want to go back to your apartment."

"No." Dino strode over to Cat and took her hand. "Cat and I have plans for the rest of the evening."

James McGuire frowned at him. "She's injured and exhausted. And safe. Your job is over."

"What do you mean 'his job'?" Lucia Merceri asked.

"Yes. What do you mean?" Admiral Maxwell chimed in.

With Cat's hand in his, Dino met each one of their eyes—McGuire's, his boss's, and Lucia Merceri's. "Colonel McGuire is talking about the fact that he originally hired me to protect Cat, to keep her safe until this drug smuggling operation was wrapped up. And he's right, my job is over. But Cat and I have some unfinished business to take care of. We'll see you tomorrow."

EVERY BONE IN HER BODY ACHED, and the pretty little Asian doctor had predicted that it was only going to get worse. So Cat wasn't particularly thrilled when Dino escorted her out of the hotel and into the same limo that had brought them to the Alsatian Towers. She'd been hoping they were headed for the suite they'd dressed in earlier. Leaning back against the leather seat, she watched as he handed the driver money.

When he joined her and the limo pulled out into traffic, she slipped her hand into his. "If you want to have sex with me, I'm game, but you're going to have to do most of the work."

"I don't want to have sex with you." His voice was just as clipped and neutral as it had been when he'd talked to her father in the executive offices.

"Lean back and relax."

Cat tried, but she couldn't. She turned to study him, but he didn't return her gaze. As the limo passed in and out of streetlights, his profile looked very grim. And focused.

I don't want to have sex with you? My job is over. Cat and I have some unfinished business to take care of.

The words replayed themselves in a continuous loop in her mind. The adrenaline that had been fueling her ever since Adelaide Creed had stepped out of that washroom stall was fading fast, but the fear blossoming in its place was more fierce than what she had felt when she'd been looking into the barrel of that gun.

Cat and I have some unfinished business to take care of.

He was going to say goodbye. The realization struck her like a blow to the stomach. His job was over, and he would want to join his family in San Francisco for Christmas.

Turning away from Dino, she stared through the smoky glass of the limo, trying to focus, but all she could see were blurred lights. Was she crying?

Cat swiped at her cheeks and found them damp.

The limo suddenly stopped, and Dino didn't wait for the driver. He pushed the door open, and sprang out. Then he turned back and extended his hand. "We're here."

Cat stepped out into the cold and glanced around quickly at her surroundings. She'd wiped away her tears, but her eyes had evidently filled again because she had to blink fast to bring the lights on the huge Christmas tree into focus. Her heart skipped a beat when she realized the limo had dropped them off at Rockefeller Center.

The wind sweeping between the tall buildings surrounding them was icy, and she couldn't prevent a shiver.

Dino swore softly. "I forgot to stop and get your coat. Here." Slipping out of his dress uniform jacket, he dropped it over her shoulders. Then he dragged her forward through the crowd of milling people.

They were at the railing above the skating rink when he stopped short and turned to face her. "This isn't what I planned. I was going to bring you here tomorrow afternoon— after you'd rested."

Blinking the last of the moisture out of her eyes, Cat took a good look at the man standing in front of her. Gone was the laid-back control that Dino usually projected. In its place was a fury that practically crackled in the air around him.

"But you're not going to be in any shape to come here tomorrow. You're not in any shape to be here tonight. C'mon." He grabbed her arm. "We'll do this in the limo."

Cat dug in her heels as her temper sliced through the little pity party she had been indulging in back in the limo. If he'd brought her here to say goodbye… Well, she'd have something to say about that.

She jerked her arm free of his grip. "I don't care to go back to the limo yet. You told my father we had unfinished business to settle. Let's do it. You're going to tell me that you're going back to San Francisco."

He stared at her then. "No."

She fisted her hands on her hips. "You're not going back to see your family for Christmas or to attend your cousin Theo's wedding?"

"Yes, but that's not—"

"Well, I'm coming with you. Get used to the idea."

FOR THE LIFE OF HIM, Dino couldn't find his voice. He was vaguely aware that the people walking past them were sending them curious glances, but he couldn't take his eyes off of Cat.

She poked a finger into his chest. "I know that our original deal was just sex—"

"And it was a very good deal," he said, capturing one of her hands, then the other.

She raised her chin. "Not good enough, evidently. You said in the limo that you didn't want to have sex with me."

For the first time he looked deep into her eyes, and what he saw there—the same mix of fear and hope that he was feeling—finally made the image of her hurtling down the stairs fade away. "I want more than sex."

"You do?"

He brought one hand to his lips. "A lot more."

She swallowed hard. "Me, too."

"I'd planned on bringing you here tomorrow and taking you skating. I wanted to start over where the fictional story began and make it all real." He lifted her left hand and wiggled the engagement ring off. "You'll have to settle for this."

As Cat stared, he dropped to one knee and held the ring out to her. "Marry me, Cat."

She dropped to her good knee, held out her hand and let him slip the ring back on her finger. "Marry me, Dino." Then she threw her arms around him and held on tight.

Around them the crowd broke into applause. Cat found she

was blinking back tears again, but she managed to whisper, "I can always open a toy store in San Francisco."

"Jase has offered me a job here in Manhattan. He thinks we make a good team."

"We can talk about it later. For now, can we please go back to the limo and make love? Come toy with me, Dino."

"I thought you'd never ask." Laughing, he drew her to her feet, scooped her into his arms, and carried her to the waiting limo. The crowd cheered them as they went.

Epilogue

DINO HANDED CAT A frothy glass of champagne, then leaned close to her ear, pitching his voice so that he could be heard above the music and the din of the conversations going on around them. "What do you think of my family's restaurant?"

"It's amazing."

"I've always thought so." Dino let his gaze sweep the room. The Poseidon was aglow with Christmas lights and filled with flowers for Theo's and Sadie's wedding reception. The tables in the main dining room on the lower level had been shoved to the back wall and were now laden with a wide array of Greek and Italian food. His uncle Spiro and Helena were inspecting the spread and giving last-minute instructions to the wait staff. Chairs had been clustered in corners and along the other walls. Some of the guests were crowded around the bar area, others were dancing, and still more had spilled out onto the terrace. Waiters moved among them with trays of champagne and hors d'oeuvres.

Dino turned his gaze back to Cat. "I wanted to see you here."

Cat met his eyes and smiled. "And now that you have?"

He took her free hand and raised it to his lips. "You fit. Perfectly. Now, tell me what you think of my family?"

"They're amazing, too. But I'm still a bit nervous." Cat touched her glass to his, then sipped the icy liquid. "There are a lot of people to keep straight."

Their trip to San Francisco had been delayed, first because the FBI and the CIA had both wanted to question her, and then because of the Christmas day arrival of Lucy's baby, little Merry. They'd both wanted to visit the hospital to greet the new arrival to the family before they left. When they'd finally arrived late last night, the wedding preparations had been in full swing, and she'd only had the briefest of introductions to his family.

"I'm in total sympathy with you on that. My family has doubled in size since the last time I was here. I'm still trying to sort them out myself."

Cat met his eyes and voiced the worry that had been plaguing her ever since she'd stood between Cass and Dino in the church and witnessed the brief but lovely wedding ceremony. "Are you regretting your decision to work with Jase and stay in New York? Because if you are—"

Dino cut her off by placing his fingers on her lips. "I'm not regretting my decision to settle in New York at all. We'll visit my family often. I don't ever intend to be as disconnected from them as I was during my two years working special ops. And who knows, you may eventually decide to expand your business and open a Cheshire Cat in San Francisco." Then removing his fingers, he leaned down and brushed his lips over hers.

Cat felt a little knot of tension unravel. She was considering the feasibility of opening a store in San Francisco. Then she narrowed her eyes, studying him more closely. "Have you had one of your feelings about that?"

He laughed. "No. But my mother mentioned the possibility. And she's the one with the real powers in the family."

He gestured with his glass to the upper level of the restaurant where the bridal party was having pictures taken. "I'll help you out with my cousins' names if you'll refresh my mind about the women."

"You're on." Cat studied the line of people the photographer was working with. The bridesmaids wore dresses in pastel hues of blue, pink, lilac and sea-foam green. Each one of the men was so tall, dark and handsome that it almost hurt her eyes to look at them.

"Theo's the one with the bride on his arm," Dino began.

"Thanks." As Cat smiled, the rest of her tension eased. "And the bride's name is Sadie. Those two I'm pretty sure of. And I think I have Nik and Kit figured out. Kit's taller and he's almost always smiling. Nik usually has a serious expression on his face and he's quieter."

"Probably because he's a cop. I like his new wife, J.C. She seems to complement him quite nicely."

Cat shifted her gaze to the short redhead in the green dress. J.C. was easy to remember because she had a very outgoing personality and hardly ever stopped talking. "I like her, too. Now, using the process of elimination, I think the tall blonde is Drew. She designed Sadie's wedding dress and the bridesmaids' dresses, and she goes with Kit."

"She goes very well with Kit indeed," Dino agreed.

"And the very pretty woman with the short dark hair is your cousin Philly. But then I'm stumped," Cat said. "I know that the other tall, dark and handsome man is Philly's new fiancé, but his name escapes me."

"He's Roman Oliver."

Cat turned to find that Dino's mother and a tall man she recalled talking to Cass in the vestibule of the church had joined them.

"And the other couple in the wedding party are Sadie's sister Juliana and her fiancé, Paulo Carlucci," the man continued.

Cass cleared her throat. "Cat and Dino, I'd like you to meet Mason Leone. He's worked security for the Oliver family for years."

Mason Leone shook Cat's hand first. She found his grip firm, and she sensed a quiet intensity about him that was not unlike Dino's.

When he gripped Dino's hand, Mason said, "I'd like to have a word with you in private."

Dino said nothing as he led the way to a hallway that ran off the dining room.

"Wish me luck," Cass murmured to Cat in a low voice.

As she turned to face Dino's mother, she noted that the color had risen in Cass's cheeks. "Is something wrong?"

Cass shifted her gaze to meet Cat's for a moment before she looked back at the two men. "I hope not. I'm just a bit nervous. I've been seeing Mason for several months now. He's very old-fashioned in many ways and I think he's going to ask Dino's blessing to ask me to marry him."

Cat glanced back at the two men. They were both standing rather stiffly as if they were taking each other's measure. She slipped her hand into Cass's. "Don't you know what Dino's answer will be?"

Cass shook her head. "My powers don't seem to work where Mason is concerned. I didn't even know I was in love with him for a while. With Dino's father, I knew the moment I saw him."

"That's exactly the way I felt with Dino." Then curious, Cat asked, "What will you do if Dino doesn't give his blessing?"

Cass glanced at her with a smile. "I suppose I'll just have to take matters into my own hands and propose to Mason."

"Good. That was my plan with Dino, but he beat me to it."

Cass raised their joined hands and looked at Cat's engagement ring. "It looks right on you."

"It feels right." The two women looked back at their men in time to see them move to the bar. A moment later, a bartender put two beers in front of them. Lifting his bottle, Dino tapped it against Mason's before they drank.

"I think it's going well," Cat said.

Still, she noted that Cass didn't completely relax until Dino and Mason returned. Then her throat tightened as she watched Dino hug his mother and place her hand in Mason Leone's.

LATER, CASS STOOD on the entrance level of the restaurant with Mason at her side and watched her family on the dance floor below. The band was playing a waltz. It had been nearly a year since the weekend when everything had started. Now her sister's children and her son were each dancing with the person the Fates had meant them to be with. Because each of them had said yes to what the Fates had offered them.

Just as she had said yes. She glanced down at the bright new engagement ring that Mason had just put on her hand.

"Dino has invited us to visit him in New York," Mason said. "He wants me to meet his friend Jase. He claims that his old navy buddy has top-of-the-line security gadgets that he thinks I might be interested in."

Cass glanced up at him. "You're trying to make me feel better because Dino won't be returning to live in San Francisco."

He smiled at her. "It's going to be hard being married to a woman who sees right through me."

Downstairs, the music changed to something that reminded Cass of Greece. Spiro led Helena to the center of the floor. Two by two, the rest of her family followed until they formed a large circle. For a moment, she and Mason watched as Spiro led them into a traditional Greek dance. Roman, Sadie and Cat were a little hesitant, but their partners guided them.

"Shall we join them, Cassandra?" Mason asked.

Cass looked up into her new fiancé's eyes and in that moment, she knew. Along with her children, she had been right to choose what the Fates had offered.

* * * * *

*Vampire Viviana Darland is in Skull Creek, Texas,
looking for one thing – red-hot sex! And she knows
just the man to give it to her – vampire Garret Sawyer.
She knows her end is near and wants one good climax
before she goes. And she intends to get it before
Garret delivers on his promise to kill her...*

Turn the page for a sneak preview of

A Body to Die For
by Kimberly Raye,

*available from Mills & Boon® Blaze®
in December 2009*

A Body to Die For
by
Kimberly Raye

HE SMELLED LIKE SEX.

Rich. Potent. Mesmerizing. Like a creamy dark truffle mousse with a drizzle of imported white chocolate, a dollop of whipped raspberry cream and a sprinkle of cinnamon-crusted pecans.

The crazy thought struck as she stood in the middle of The Iron Horseshoe—a rough and rowdy bar just off the interstate—and stared at the man who sat at a nearby table.

Crazy because Viviana Darland didn't normally think in terms of food.

She didn't do chocolate or whipped cream or pecans. She didn't do anything edible, period. She was a vampire who thrived on sex and blood, and so her thoughts rarely read like a transcript of the latest Rachael Ray episode.

But sheer desperation—coupled with the past two days spent holed up at the Skull Creek Inn, watching the Food Network and trying to work up her courage to approach Mr. Luscious and Edible—was new to her and so it only made sense that she would act out of character.

After all, her days were numbered.

A wild, rebellious southern rock song poured from the speakers and vibrated the air around her. Her heart beat faster, keeping tempo with the steady ba-bom ba-bom ba-bom of the drums. A neon Harley Davidson sign glowed above the bar and various motorcycle memorabilia—from studded leather chaps to an *Easy Rider* poster—decorated the walls.

Several truck drivers, their big rigs parked out back, sucked down a round of beers at a nearby table. A group of leather-clad bikers clustered around a dartboard in the far corner. A handful of men sporting long hair, beards and Golden Chopper Motorcycle Club jackets chugged Coronas at the massive bar that spanned the length of one wall.

The loud clack of pool balls echoed above the music. Cigarette smoke thickened the air. The sharp smell of Jack Daniels hovered around her.

It was a far cry from the latest "it" bar down in West Hollywood. She swallowed against a sudden lump in her throat.

So?

You're a vampire. You adapt to any place, any time, any situation. Stop making excuses, walk over and just tell him what you want.

The command echoed in her head and urged her forward. Unfortunately, her body didn't obey any more now than when she'd first spotted him a few days ago.

The memory rolled through her as she turned left and headed for the bar. She angled herself between two big bruisers and ordered a house beer.

She'd been on her way into the desperately small Texas town when she'd seen the hunky guy parked outside the city limits on the side of the highway. Wishful thinking, or so she'd thought.

But Garret Sawyer had been more than a figment of her imagination.

He'd been flesh and blood and oh, so real.

As real as the day she'd first met him. Touched him. Kissed him. Loved him.

Talk about opportunity. Forget tracking him down and arranging a chance meeting. She could dispense with formality and cut right to the chase.

At least that's what she'd told herself when she'd climbed out of her car and approached him.

But then she'd glimpsed the surprise in his gaze, the anger, the hurt and her resolve had crumbled. She'd barely managed a "Long time no see" before she'd hightailed it back to her car.

She hadn't seen him since.

But she'd asked around.

With Skull Creek being the quintessential small town, she'd gotten an earful from everyone—from the clerk at the Piggly Wiggly, to the fry guy at the Dairy Freeze.

She'd learned that Garret was the skill and expertise behind Skull Creek Choppers, the town's one and only custom motorcycle shop. He'd opened his doors a few months ago and bought a small ranch just outside the city limits. He had two business partners—Jake McCann handled the design and Dillon Cash monitored the software and computer system.

Garret bought coffee at the local diner every evening and subscribed to the *Skull Creek Gazette*. He also sponsored a local little league team, donated to the senior's center and served on the board of the Skull Creek Chamber of Commerce.

Exactly what she would have expected from a thirty-something businessman trying to establish himself in a new location.

Exactly what she wouldn't have expected from a two hundred-year-old vampire who'd always avoided hanging around too long in any one place.

"It's on me," the bruiser to the right said when she slid a five across the bar to pay for her drink.

Her head snapped up, and she found herself staring into a pair of interested brown eyes.

The man had long, black, greasy hair and a thick beard. He reeked of beer and cigarettes and sexual frustration. He missed his wife. But not because she'd been a fine upstanding woman who'd taken her vows seriously. No, she'd been the opposite. A slut who'd slept around on him every time he'd pulled out of town.

What he missed was having a warm body to turn to in the dead of night. He'd never been much of a player, and so he hadn't actually dated much before he'd met his missus. He wasn't even the type of man who offered to buy a woman a drink.

Until tonight.

Viv read the truth in his eyes and felt his desperation. And suddenly it didn't matter that he wasn't the most attractive man she'd ever met. All that mattered was the sexual energy bubbling inside of him.

The desire.

The need.

Her own hunger stirred, reminding her just how long it had been since she'd fed. Her chest tightened, and her stomach hollowed out. Her hands trembled, and it took all of her strength not to reach out and take the man up on his blatant offer.

But this wasn't about getting a quick fix and fulfilling some stranger's fantasies.

This was about fulfilling her own.

2 FREE BOOKS
AND A SURPRISE GIFT

We would like to take this opportunity to thank you for reading this Mills & Boon® book by offering you the chance to take TWO more specially selected titles from the Blaze® series absolutely FREE! We're also making this offer to introduce you to the benefits of the Mills & Boon® Book Club™—

- **FREE home delivery**
- **FREE gifts and competitions**
- **FREE monthly Newsletter**
- **Exclusive Mills & Boon Book Club offers**
- **Books available before they're in the shops**

Accepting these FREE books and gift places you under no obligation to buy, you may cancel at any time, even after receiving your free books. Simply complete your details below and return the entire page to the address below. You don't even need a stamp!

YES Please send me 2 free Blaze books and a surprise gift. I understand that unless you hear from me, I will receive 3 superb new books every month, including a 2-in-1 book priced at £4.99 and two single books priced at £3.19 each, postage and packing free. I am under no obligation to purchase any books and may cancel my subscription at any time. The free books and gift will be mine to keep in any case.

Ms/Mrs/Miss/Mr _____ Initials _____

Surname _____

Address _____

_____

_____ Postcode _____

Send this whole page to: Mills & Boon Book Club, Free Book Offer, FREEPOST NAT 10298, Richmond, TW9 1BR